DEFCON 1

Gilly Simpson

ISBN: 9798413030639

ACKNOWLEDGMENTS

Before anything or anyone else, I want to thank my wife, Cindy Simpson, for your ability to look at this page right now. Sure, I wrote the book. After that, it was all Cindy. She was the driving force that got me past every obstacle, from the completion of the writing to the editing, formatting, and publishing. She was also one of my proofreaders. Mike Simpson (my father), Rob Nelson, and Robin Thompson were my other proofreaders, and I would like to thank them as well.

If Cindy was the person who executed the plan and brought it to fruition, Belinda Buchanan was the person who gave us the information needed to put the plan in motion. Belinda is a self-published author with five novels that I highly recommend, if you are interested in mystery novels and/or women's fiction. To date, I have not met Belinda in person, but she was referred to me as a resource by a family member. I emailed her numerous times throughout this process, and she spent an inordinate amount of time helping someone she did not know. Thank you, Belinda.

I would also like to thank my cousin, Cassie Simpson, for designing the cover. She was very patient as I walked her through the plot of the book. I leaned on Cassie heavily with any number of ideas and styles as she patiently developed different looks, while I rejected or changed numerous ideas. But in the end, she nailed it. What a talent!

Lastly, although this might sound strange, I want to thank the Barnes & Noble bookstore on Hurstbourne Lane in Louisville. When I had free time, I sat in the coffee shop inside the bookstore and researched, wrote, and edited. Being surrounded by books and the atmosphere that a bookstore provides always generated a creative spark that I had trouble finding at home.

AUTHOR'S NOTE

In December of 2015, I read a nonfiction book by former *Nightline* anchor Ted Koppel. It was titled *Lights Out*. It was a hypothetical example of what could happen if there was an attack on the American power grid. Much of my research about a potential attack and the possible aftermath came from that book.

Soon after that, I began developing details for this novel. Due to life obligations, I was never able to commit to writing full time, so it took me more than three years to complete it. At the beginning of 2019, my wife gave me a deadline of July 4 to finish the book. She also gave me the flexibility to spend the time needed to do it. I finished on July 2. After researching the process to get a literary agent and reading repeatedly that I should prepare myself for dozens upon dozens of rejection letters, I found a site that listed the top 20 agents for the type of novel I had written.

Two months to the day after completing the manuscript, on September 2, 2019, via email, I started sending query letters and a summary of the manuscript to the agents on the list. Bob DiForio was number four. I emailed him the information at 6:18 PM on September 2. He replied 37 minutes later, at 6:55, stating that he had read enough to know that he wanted to represent me, and he sent me a contract. Suddenly, I had a literary agent! Bob has worked with the likes of Stephen King and Ken Follett, so I could not have been more excited.

Unfortunately, he could not get any of the big publishers to purchase the manuscript. After two years, and because this is a current events type of novel, I decided to self-publish once Bob graciously agreed to release me from our contract. It was Bob's unbelievably quick response and representation that gave me confidence that I had put together a quality story. I hope you enjoy it.

PROLOGUE

November 3
Washington, D.C.
5:45 AM

There was a slight breeze as Sam Clark began his morning walk. It was still dark, and although most people would consider 47 degrees and breezy to be terrible walking weather, Sam loved the crisp morning air. He thrived on it. Walking beside him was Patrick Henry. This Patrick Henry was not, of course, the founding father who famously said, "Give me liberty or give me death," but he was named after him. This Patrick Henry was an eight-year-old beagle. He was the latest in a series of dogs owned by Sam to be named after founding fathers. He had owned a Benjamin Franklin, a George Washington, a Thomas Jefferson, and a Samuel Adams. Holding true to this patriotic tradition, Sam also preferred the beer version of Samuel Adams.

Much like Sam, Patrick had a little bit of gray around the edges, but also like Sam, he had a lot of living left to do. It was obvious that he enjoyed these early morning walks even more than Sam, as evidenced by the vibrant wagging of his tail and his active nose scoping the ground for an enticing scent as they strode along their mile and a half route.

Sam missed the old days when it was just the two of them. They could walk wherever and whenever they wanted, and Sam could get lost in the one-sided discussions he had with Patrick about the events of the day or whatever problems were weighing him down. Patrick was a great listener. However, Sam felt awkward talking to a dog when he was trailed, by just a few feet, by two not-so-discreet walking partners. Those walking partners were mandatory now, since it was only six hours ago that Sam Clark had been elected President of the United States.

ONE YEAR LATER
Monday, December 19
The Truman Building
Washington, D.C.

Secretary of State Vance Harrison was in the middle of a mundane discussion with the ambassador of Chad, about the effects of climate change on a specific species of lion in Northeastern Africa, when his chief of staff Ron Barbour came into the room. From the look on Barbour's face, nobody else in the room would have been able to tell that anything was wrong. However, Harrison knew something serious was going on for two reasons - first, he knew that poker face better than anyone. Second, if it wasn't something urgent, Barbour would have sent someone else.

"Pardon me, Mr. Secretary," Barbour said. "I am so sorry to interrupt but there is a matter that I need to speak to you about that is quite time sensitive."

"Sure, Ron. My apologies, Mr. Ambassador. I will be back momentarily."

The two men walked out into the hall. "What is it, Ron?"

"Mr. Secretary, we have the Chinese ambassador on video feed from his embassy, and he is demanding to talk to you immediately."

"Video feed? Why can't he schedule an appointment or just come down here?"

"I have no idea, but I'm guessing that the answer to that question cannot be good."

"Come in with me Ron," Harrison said as they approached his office.

Harrison sat down in front of the video monitor, where the Chinese ambassador was indeed on the other end of the video feed. "Mr. Zhang, what can I do for you? I hope nothing is wrong."

The Chinese ambassador wasted no time. "Mr. Harrison. As we both know, we carry a great deal of your country's debt. I think we can agree that we have been there to purchase some of this debt during America's darkest times. However, it is now my country that is facing some economic challenges, and we are calling some of that debt. We will need payment on this within the next 72 hours."

Vance Harrison was a professional statesman. He negotiated for a living, and one of the primary requirements of his job was to be diplomatic. This, however, tested his skill in those areas. "What are you talking about? I am aware of the recent economic hardships in your country, but this is a highly unusual way to make such a request. Beyond all of that, I have never heard of a request like this. Or should I say a *demand* like this. It is a breach of protocol. There are proper channels through which such a request is supposed to travel. Although I admit that in such a case, I have no idea what those proper channels are, I feel pretty sure that a video feed from your embassy to the Secretary of State is *not* how this should be handled."

"I understand your position Mr. Secretary, and this is not our formal request. The formal request will be sent directly to President Clark in a matter of hours. But because I know it won't be easy to execute this transaction, I wanted to give you as much notice as possible."

Harrison's head was spinning, but he remained poised. "Let's say, just hypothetically, that this demand is not completely out of bounds from a protocol perspective. What kind of dollar figure are you talking about and when do you need it?" Harrison knew that using the word 'demand' instead of 'request' in his question would express his dissatisfaction in the most diplomatic way possible.

"One trillion dollars by the end of the week." The words themselves, as absurd as they seemed, were spoken as nonchalantly as could be imagined. Harrison would have used a similar tone and delivery at the drive-thru window of a fast-food restaurant.

Harrison laughed out loud. "You can't be serious."

"Unfortunately, I am quite serious. I assume you will be there for our country in our time of need, just as we have been there for you. Good day, Mr. Secretary."

Before Harrison could reply, the video feed was cut. He looked at Ron Barbour. "Let the President know that I'm on my way, and that he will need to get the team together ASAP."

By the time Harrison reached the Oval Office, the President had somehow already gathered several people together. In the room were the Vice-President, the Treasury Secretary, the National Security Advisor, and the President's chief of staff. The Defense Secretary and the Chairman of the Joint Chiefs of Staff were present via video.

"What in the hell did he say?" Clark asked before Harrison could even sit down.

"Well," Harrison said, "I'm not sure where to begin. He said the Chinese government has fallen on hard economic times and that they have to call one trillion dollars of our debt." Harrison chuckled in a tone that was more bewildered than comical. "And they want it by the end of the week."

The room fell silent for a few moments, then Clark spoke. "This is out of line in so many ways. Aside from the odd way they made such a huge request, the more fundamental problem is that the country's debt is on a structured repayment. Is the calling of these loans even legal?" He looked at Treasury Secretary Helen Donovan without asking her directly.

"I'm not sure who the proper person is to answer that question," she replied. "Attorney General McMillan would be my starting point, and he will need to be brought up to speed as soon as his plane lands. In the meantime, three things worry me. The first is that they absolutely know they are breaking the terms of the debt issue by making such a ridiculous demand. So why do it? Second, they are *not* in the kind of financial bind where they would need a trillion dollars by the end of the week. And again, they know that we know that, so what are they doing? The third and most concerning thing to me is this. This demand must have been planned for some time. They know we don't just have trillions of dollars lying around in some bank account. What is their goal here? When we say no to their demand, then what? I feel sure that they have an answer to that question, and I feel like we are *not* going to like what it is."

Once again, the room momentarily fell silent. "I guess we will find out soon enough," Clark said. "I am scheduled for a call with President Ming in 10 minutes." Clark looked at the video monitor.

"Harold and Tom, you guys need to be prepared for another video conference as soon as this call is over. You should also begin making plans to be back in Washington ASAP."

"Yes sir, Mr. President," came the answer, nearly in unison, from the Defense Secretary and the Chairman of the Joint Chiefs.

The rest of the room cleared out, except for Helen Donovan. "Helen, I need you here to answer questions about Treasury policy, if and when they come up. I'm not sure exactly how this discussion is going to go, but I damn sure want my Treasury Secretary in the room when people start asking us to gather up a trillion dollars by the end of the week."

"Yes, sir." Donovan smiled, unsure if the comment was a moment of levity or frustration.

Moments later, President Ming came on the video screen. "Good morning, President Clark," Ming said cordially.

Clark was in no mood for small talk. "My morning isn't so good to this point," he replied, "mostly because of your ambassador's conversation with my Secretary of State. I find myself quite curious as to which part or parts of this conversation got lost in translation. Or perhaps I simply misunderstood."

Ming replied with the same demands that his ambassador had made, almost verbatim. "...and we need the trillion dollars by the end of the week. We're not requesting the entire amount of the debt, just enough to get my country stabilized."

Clark stared at the screen long enough to make some of the people in the room uncomfortable. "I am going to assume that you already know your demand cannot be met. I am also going to assume you know that your demand would not be met even if it was feasible for us to gather that amount of cash together that quickly. Third, you know that the terms of the debt you are carrying are set on a structured repayment and that the debt cannot be called all at once like this. On top of all of that, I love the fact that you're claiming not to be demanding the entire amount of the debt. We owe you 1.2 trillion dollars. Thanks for sparing us the 'point two.' What exactly is this *really* about, Mr. President?"

"My country finds itself in financial peril..." Ming did not get to finish his sentence.

"Mr. President. Please. My inner circle probably knows as much about your current economic situation as you do, and we know you are not in any kind of financial peril that would justify a demand like this, or anything close to it."

Now Ming stared at the screen. "Since we're being blunt, Mr. President, let me just cut to the chase. We will take cash payment. If that much cash is not available, we will accept a like amount in gold. A third option is some of your military technology. I feel sure we could agree to a fair market value on some of your advanced systems."

Clark's patience was wearing thin. "Under no circumstances will we even entertain these outrageous demands. I will be placing a call to the United Nations as soon as this conversation is over, and they can work out the details."

"I was hoping it would not come to this," Ming said. "But you will either meet our terms by the end of the week or we will consider you in default on your debt and we will have to find other ways to get our hands on the assets needed to stabilize our country."

"What do you mean by 'other ways?'" Clark asked. But the sentence had not quite been completed before the screen went dark. Ming had terminated the call.

PART I

CHAPTER 1

December 23, 2004
Fallujah, Iraq

Although the heaviest fighting in Fallujah and the surrounding area in the Al Anbar province had taken place from early-to-mid-November, it would have been hard to convince the Marines hunkered down in an abandoned warehouse that they were not currently involved in the most dramatic action of the entire combat operation. Urban warfare had become a way of life in Fallujah. To a man, everyone woke up each day knowing this could be the last sunrise he ever witnessed.

Sam Clark did not think that way. He *could* not think that way. Any time spent with thoughts like that was entirely impractical. It served as a distraction from the mission, and it actually made him *more* likely to be injured or killed. So, Sam used one of his strongest traits - a laser-like focus - to lead his men through Fallujah day after day.

Sam Clark was raised in Pine Bluff, Kentucky, a single stoplight town of less than 1,000 people. He always told people it was just like the town of Mayberry in *The Andy Griffith Show.* Everyone literally knew everyone, and strangers in town were noticed (and scrutinized) immediately. Sam grew up in a devoutly Catholic family as a descendant of pioneers who had left the area in and around Baltimore to travel west during the last decade of the 18th century.

Like so many others, Sam answered the call to a military career following the terrorist attacks on 9/11. Unlike most, however, Sam had already established himself in the world. An entrepreneur by nature, Sam had completed his Business degree at Loyola University and was soon running a small printing company in nearby Hartsfield. By the time he was 24, Sam was on the Pine Bluff City Council, and he was elected as the town's mayor at the ripe old age of 28. That election had taken place in November of 2000. By November of 2001, Sam had resigned his post and was in Marine boot camp at Camp Pendleton in San Diego.

Admittedly, his decision was made substantially easier by the fact that he was single and had no children. Sam's father, John, had always been a thoughtful and discerning man, and he had talked to Sam at length to make sure he wasn't making a rash decision. By this point in his life, Sam had figured out that his father wasn't dull; he wasn't boring; he was wise. Sam always listened to him and frequently sought his counsel. By the time they had discussed the matter fully, both men knew that Sam was making the right decision. Sam knew in his heart that this was not only what he needed to do; it was also what he wanted to do.

John had run a successful business for more than four decades, and he had turned over the day-to-day operations years ago. He was enjoying retirement, but he kept himself busy with a substantial amount of volunteer work. He gladly agreed to step in and run Sam's printing business while he was gone.

Sam's leadership skills were evident from the time he set foot on the grounds at Camp Pendleton for basic training. He had managed to get his degree in four years while also playing football at the collegiate level. Then he had started a business within two years of his graduation. Upon completion of basic training, Sam was given the rank of First Sergeant with the 3rd Battalion, First Marines.

The mission in which Sam and his fellow Marines were currently involved was officially called Operation Phantom Fury. It would later be called the Second Battle of Fallujah. The coalition force consisted of just over 10,000 American troops, 2,000 members of the Iraqi security force, and about 900 British troops.

The operation was retaliatory in nature. In February of 2004, the 82nd Airborne handed over control of the area in and around Fallujah to the First Marine Division. Approximately six weeks later, on March 31, insurgents ambushed and killed four American private military contractors who worked for Blackwater. Graphic images of their bodies were shown worldwide on different media outlets.

Four days after that, the Marines launched Operation Vigilant Resolve, and by the end of the month, the insurgents had been driven out and control of the city was turned over to the local security forces. Unfortunately, that control did not last long. By September, the U.S.-led forces had to be called back in. By that time, over 4,000 insurgents were hunkered down in Fallujah.

Sam had his back against the outer wall of the warehouse, approximately twenty feet from the exit. Members of his unit were currently attempting to flank the insurgents, but Sam was unsure how much longer they could hold their position. With a nod of the head, he signaled Gunnery Sergeant Clint McGuffey to break the window beside him and open fire. Sam sprinted to a position behind some furniture amid heavy gunfire. He fired back through the open door. He killed two men immediately and saw nothing else happening.

McGuffey and another soldier both fired a couple of dozen rounds before they stopped hearing shots from outside the building. They heard familiar voices sound an all-clear. The flanking maneuver had been successful, and the area had been cleared of another pocket of insurgents. It was only then that Sam's adrenaline gave way to his senses, and he finally acknowledged the pain in his right leg. He looked down to see pieces of his femur protruding through the skin, and blood squirting from the open wound. That was the last thing Sam remembered as everything around him first became fuzzy, and finally dark.

CHAPTER 2

When Sam attempted to rise from his bunk the next day, he realized he was in a hospital bed. As some flashes of memory came back to him, he slowly began to recall what had happened. What he did not know was where he was at the moment. It appeared to be a hospital room. A woman entered the room and approached his bed. She looked nurse-like, and Sam was now officially dreading the fact that he was separated from his unit.

"Good morning, sunshine!" Sam rolled his eyes at the woman's cheerfulness. He had no time for small talk.

"How bad is it?" he asked.

"You're alive, so it's pretty good. A lot of soldiers don't wake up the next day." Her tone was somehow still pleasant despite the obvious rebuke. "The doctor will be in momentarily. Oh, and Merry Christmas!"

Merry Christmas? How long had he been unconscious? The firefight was on the morning of the 23rd, so his last memory was from at least 48 hours ago. That could not be good. So many thoughts were racing through Sam's mind. What was going on with his unit? When could he get back and join them? How bad were his injuries? As the doctor entered the room, Sam immediately asked the most pressing question. "Where the hell am I?"

The doctor chuckled. "That's a fair question. You are in a Landstuhl military hospital in Kaiserslautern, Germany."

"Germany?" Sam was incredulous. "I need to get back to my unit. When can I get out of here?"

"You can get out in a couple of more days, but you won't be going back to Iraq, son. We will be transporting you back home to Walter Reed hospital. Your fighting days are over."

"Okay, Doc, here are your choices. You either release me from this hospital and get me on the first flight back to Fallujah, or I walk out of here and do it myself." I am *not* going back to the States until the job is finished."

The doctor sat down on the edge of Sam's bed. "I have some good news for you. The 'job' you were in is finished. Fallujah is back under coalition control. The fight your unit was in was actually the last skirmish. Congratulations."

Sam was trying to take it all in. He was pleased with this news, and proud of his unit for their role in removing the insurgents from Fallujah. His thoughts were soon interrupted.

"But there is also some bad news," the doctor said. He looked Sam right in the eye. "You were shot twice in the leg. Both bullets hit within a half inch of each other. Your femur was shattered, and it severed your femoral artery. You were hit shortly before the fight was over, and a medic was working on you almost immediately. That young woman saved your life. You would have bled out quickly had she not been there."

Sam braced himself for the worst. "How bad is it?"

The doctor never broke eye contact. "I'm sorry, son. We couldn't save your leg."

CHAPTER 3

December 26, 2004
Landstuhl Military Hospital
Kaiserslautern, Germany

The nurse came in the next morning, and again greeted Sam cheerfully, which was irritating him greatly.

"Can I get you anything?" she asked.

"You can get me out of here," he replied without looking at her.

"Sorry, I can't do that," she said with a smile. "But I can get you something to eat if you would like."

"No, thank you."

The nurse tried something different. "I see that you're wearing a crucifix. Are you Catholic?"

"Can you just leave me alone, please?" Sam replied in a monotone voice.

"Yes, I can," she said. She followed that with a change in her tone. "Let me tell you what else I can do. We haven't met officially, but my name is Monica. If you are Catholic, you should know the story of St. Monica. I am trying my best to follow in her footsteps. I am keeping a list of the first names of every soldier I have treated over here, and I am praying for them every day. You are now on my list, Sam, along with Frank, Miguel, Wanda, Alex, and James. I haven't been here long, and I know my list will get much longer, but I promise to pray for you every day. Is that okay with you?"

Sam turned to look at her. "If I say yes, will you leave me alone?"

She smiled and reverted to her prior cheerfulness. "You got it!"

Sam knew the story of St. Monica very well. She spent years and years praying for her wayward son to find the path to God. Eventually, her prayers were answered, in a big way. Monica's son was St. Augustine, one of the most prominent religious leaders in the history of Christianity. Monica was insisting to Sam that she would never cease praying for his recovery. Prior to December 23, such an act of kindness and faith would have been extremely moving to Sam. Today, however, it was no more than a passing thought.

Sam reflected on everything he had lost in the last three days - his leg, his military career, his future. What would he be able to do with one leg? What would he *want* to do? He thought about how much he was letting his unit down by allowing himself to be sent home, although it wasn't as if he could break out of the hospital and run away. What would they think about him?

Somewhere in the back of his mind, Sam was hearing a voice telling him to knock it off and move forward, to stop acting so childish. But he could not tell if that was an inner voice or the pain medication. He wasn't sure what was what, other than he wanted to get out of this place as quickly as possible. That was his last thought as the medication took over and he faded back into a restless slumber.

CHAPTER 4

February 7, 2005
Walter Reed Military Hospital
Washington, D.C.

Sam was lying in his bed, staring at the sunrise. It was a typical winter day in Washington - cold, gray, and dreary. It greatly resembled Sam's mood. He had gone through a complete life transformation in the past six weeks. He had lost his leg, and he no longer had a military career. He was sent back to the United States, and although he was greeted warmly by family and friends as a returning hero, he felt guilty and useless.

Sam had learned more about the events of December 23. Three of his men had been killed in the firefight. Meanwhile, they had killed 24 insurgents. Sam also cursed the bad luck of losing his leg in what was literally the last few minutes of a six-week operation. He was unable to find solace in the success of the mission, because he was now on the outside looking in.

Sam had been fitted for a prosthetic and educated about residual limb care. He was currently in physical therapy. His emotions were all over the place. He had been through phases of anger, sorrow, depression, and self-pity. He had days when he was motivated to meet the challenge head on, but they were few and far between. The shots that Sam fired out the door of the warehouse, killing two men who had declared war on him and all that he believed in, would be the last ones he would fire as an active-duty soldier. That was the hardest part of all.

Operation Phantom Fury had been the bloodiest battle of the entire Iraq war. One hundred seven coalition forces were killed, while another 613 were wounded. Of the estimated 4,000 insurgents in Fallujah, approximately 3,000 of them were either killed or captured. The Marines had done what they came there to do, but it was done at a significant cost.

CHAPTER 5

February 13, 2005
Walter Reed Military Hospital

"Good afternoon, sir. How may I help you?" The receptionist was polite but clearly bored with her job. The man across the desk from her would not stand out in a crowd. He was six feet tall, fit but not muscular. He was only five pounds over his college weight of 180 pounds. He wore a military-style haircut and spoke to the receptionist in an even-keel tone.

"I'm here to see Sam Clark."

The receptionist looked down at her patient list and then handed the man a clipboard on which to sign in as a visitor. "He is in room 509."

Doug Mitchell signed his name and looked up with a smile. "Thanks for your help." Mitchell walked up to the door at room 509 and took a deep breath. Then he entered the room.

Sam was lying in bed, staring out the window. "Up and at 'em, Clark!"

Sam turned his head and saw his college roommate. Without speaking, he turned his head back to the window. This was even worse than Mitchell had expected.

"What the hell kind of way is that to greet the guy who spent so much time getting you through Art History?"

"What are you doing here, Doug?" Sam said to the window.

"Well, I heard there was a pity party in room 509 and I thought I would come in for some cake and ice cream."

Sam turned his head and stared at his best friend intently. "Get out of here."

"Jesus Christ, Sam. You're alive. Why are you..."

"Get the hell out of here!" Sam shouted at the top of his voice. His eyes were moist, but Doug recognized the resolve behind the tears as well as the set of his jaw that he got when he was at his most determined.

"Fine," Doug answered quietly. "But I'll be back. You and I have work to do, and we don't have time to waste."

CHAPTER 6

February 15, 2005
Walter Reed Military Hospital

Sam was on his way back from another unproductive round of physical therapy. As he entered the room, a familiar face was sitting in the chair beside his bed. Before Sam could speak, Doug Mitchell stood up and said, "Shut the hell up and listen, Sam. You and I have been through too much together for me to bullshit you. You have *got* to get off your ass and stop rotting away in this God-awful hospital. This place is depressing. You've got too much to offer to let this control the rest of your life. Capiche?"

Sam looked at his friend. "Don't you have a job that you need to go back to?"

"Damn straight," Doug replied. "So, I don't have time to waste. I've got an opportunity for you, but this job requires a real go-getter, not some panty-waist quitter. Do you want me to continue?"

Doug was the police chief in Hartsfield, Kentucky. He had regrouped after his unsuccessful visit two days earlier and realized he needed to talk to Sam the way they did when they played football together at Loyola, and a bit like he did when he was interrogating a suspect.

Sam recognized the same thing in his friend. He also knew Doug would keep coming back until Sam talked to him about this "opportunity." Now was as good a time as any. "Okay, let's hear it."

Doug saw a glint in his friend's eye. Sam was curious. The one thing that Doug knew about this man in front of him was that he was not a quitter.

Everyone needed inspiration sometimes - something or someone to push them. Doug was determined that Sam would get his ass out of that bed and out of this hospital, even if he had to drag him kicking and screaming.

"Snider's seat is about to come open." Doug said no more.

"What are you talking about?" Sam replied.

Doug laughed out loud. "I see it! I see it in your eyes. You know damn well what I'm talking about, and I've got your attention."

Sam finally chuckled and realized that his friend knew him all too well. "Asshole."

They both burst into laughter. Sam had not laughed since before the last firefight. It felt good. It felt really good. "Okay, I'll bite. What's going on back home?"

"Snider has terminal cancer. He just found out. He is planning to resign to spend more time with his family. He ran unopposed in the last primary because nobody could touch him. Now the seat is wide open and there is total chaos."

"And what is it you want from me? Do you want me to campaign for someone as the one-legged wonder kid?"

Doug laughed again. Sam just poked fun at himself, which was positive. But he clearly had no idea what Doug wanted.

"No, dumbass. We want you to run for the seat."

Sam stared at him in total confusion. "Run for Congress?" Then the confusion gave way to another fit of laughter. Doug let him laugh until he stopped. Then he watched Sam ponder the idea. Then he saw that the magic word had registered with his friend. "Who is *we*?"

"Are you ready for this?" Doug was all business now.

"Ready for what? Stop talking in circles and spit it out!"

"Well, it was actually your dad's idea. He's the one who sent me here. When he came to visit, he realized this was going to be more difficult than he had originally thought. He was also smart enough to see that this wasn't a situation for a father/son type of pep talk. He needed someone who could be more forceful with you than he felt he could be. Here I am."

"So, you and Dad want me to run for a seat in the Senate. Pardon me for not being more impressed by your version of 'We.'"

"Sammy boy, brace yourself. Your Dad approached some significant people with the idea, and they ran with it. The Judge Executives of three of the counties in our Congressional district are already behind you, along with all of the VFW halls. And I was sent here by the FOP. Impressed yet?"

Sam's mind was now officially racing. "I don't have any experience. I mean, nothing against Pine Bluff, but two City Council elections and being elected mayor of a town of 800 people doesn't qualify me to run for Congress."

"We've got that covered." Doug's smile was ear-to-ear, and Sam knew he was about to hear the closing argument. "Sam…Senator Greenwell is on board." Rick Greenwell was the senior Senator from Kentucky. He had been in the Senate for more than 20 years and was the chair of the Armed Services Committee. "Greenwell says he can put a team together to run your campaign. He sees this as a golden opportunity. But he asked us the same question we have all been asking ourselves. Are you willing to get up off your ass and try?"

CHAPTER 7

May 4, 2005
Pine Bluff, KY

Sam rose from his bed at 6:15 AM. It was election day, for him at least. Roger Snider was fighting a brave battle against cancer, and his resignation was the cause of this special election. Sam and Barry Windsor were the only two people on the ballot. The winner would hold the seat until the next general election, which was a full eighteen months away.

Sam sat on the edge of his bed and thought about the whirlwind that his life had become. Less than six months ago, he was in Fallujah with the men and women in his unit, fighting the insurgents. Less than three months ago, he had been lying in a hospital bed at Walter Reed, depressed and completely unmotivated. He had no purpose, and seemingly no future. Then the people who cared about him most stepped in and saved him from himself. For that he would be eternally grateful.

Since returning to Kentucky, Sam had spent nearly every waking moment campaigning. His father, John, continued to run his print shop. Sam repeatedly tried to get him to turn it over to someone else, but once again Sam's friend Doug Mitchell had helped him see the light. Sam's mother had died three years earlier, and John had never seemed the same. However, going back to work had given him a routine and a sense of purpose, and Sam now realized that it was good for his father to continue to run the business.

Sam shook his head and smiled at the curve balls that life could deliver from time to time. He had come to the realization that everyone was going to get knocked down, sometimes more than once, and occasionally it was over and over again. But the winners did not stay down. The winners got up and continued to fight. That was the thought that was in Sam's mind as he reached for his prosthetic leg and attached it to his hip.

For the moment, Sam was still living in the house in which he grew up, and he was still sleeping in the bed he had slept in as a teenager. He had sold the home he owned before he left for boot camp. Win or lose, he was going to get a place of his own after the election. If he lost, a thought that he did not allow himself to consider very often, he would go back to the print shop, and he and John would run the business together.

John was eating breakfast when Sam arrived in the kitchen. "There's plenty. Have a seat," John said without looking up from the newspaper.

"Thanks," Sam replied. "Anything interesting in the paper today?" Sam grinned as his father lowered the paper a bit and peeked over the top.

"What do you think?" John did not waste words. If he could make a statement or ask a question in a few words, he would do so instead of turning it into a paragraph.

"It's anybody's guess," Sam replied. "I've been outspent three to one, but I do know that I've knocked on ten times more doors than he has. If retail politics plays a role, I like my chances."

"Agreed," John said as he got up from the table. "Good luck, son."

"Thanks, Pop."

Sam cast his vote at the Pine Bluff Middle School, and he did a couple of quick media interviews. He then drove to the cemetery to pay a visit to his mother. Sam felt his mother's presence in nearly every aspect of his life, and sometimes the presence was so strong that he felt as if he would see her if he turned around fast enough. But he never felt closer to her than he did right here on this gorgeous hillside, surrounded by farmland. Sam spoke to her like she was physically present, and he filled her in on the latest election news and everything else that was going on in his life. Then he listened. A few seconds later, he smiled. He placed his hand where her name was located on the tombstone and closed his eyes in prayer. Then he kissed his hand and rubbed it over her name. As he prepared to walk away, he said one last thing to her. "I agree, Mom. I think we've got this."

CHAPTER 8

May 4, 2005
Pine Bluff, KY

The only place in Pine Bluff that was big enough to host the election night party was the middle school gym. However, because the school was a polling place, electioneering laws prohibited Sam from having the party there. Instead, he rented the ballroom at one of the hotels in Hartsfield. Sam's campaign staff was present, as was his father, and Doug Mitchell. Rick Greenwell, Kentucky's senior Senator and part of the 'we' that Doug had referenced at Walter Reed when describing the people who were backing Sam's candidacy, was present also. He had flown in from Washington to campaign for Sam the last two days.

Almost a thousand people were in the ballroom, all of them hoping to celebrate a victory. Sam was in one of the hotel rooms trying to get some news on the early returns. The race was predicted to be tight. As expected, Sam carried his home county of Nelson by a significant margin. As more returns came in, Sam carried the areas in and around. This early lead was right on par with expectations. Barry Windsor was from a small town in the western part of the district. that area was in the central time zone, so those returns would come in an hour later.

As the evening passed, Sam had done worse than expected in Elizabethtown and some of the surrounding small towns. The entire election was going to come down to the areas in the central time zone. Sam realized that Windsor would carry those towns, but he had to keep it from being a landslide.

As more precincts reported, things began to look more positive for Sam, and he was a little bit ahead of his expectation with only five small precincts left to report. He would have to win 43% of those votes to clinch the victory.

Everyone in the room was staring at the TV. Sam looked around him and realized that he was surrounded by a fantastic group of people. Some of them were political acquaintances, but an overwhelming majority of them were people that Sam cared about deeply, and they felt the same way about him. It was a moment of peace that made him realize that the results of this election were not the be-all, end-all for him. It was a step in his life that would lead him in one of two directions. No matter how stark the difference was between those two directions, Sam was prepared for whichever road he was getting ready to take.

The last precincts reported, and as the vote tallies from those precincts came on the screen, people began doing the math and the room fell eerily silent. Sam's father was the first one to make a sound, and it was a shout of "Yes!" He proclaimed that Sam had received 46% of the vote in the remaining precincts, which should show Sam as the winner by an overall vote of 52%-48%. Doug Mitchell was the second person to comment, stating loudly, "That's what I've got, too!" He came over and put Sam in a bear hug.

"Wait, Doug! Wait!" Sam was laughing hysterically. "Let's wait for the announcement from someone official, which you clearly are not."

Moments later, local television and radio reports began to come across that the election had been called for Iraq War Veteran and political newcomer Sam Clark. The room erupted in shouts of celebration, and John Clark walked across the room and hugged his son. As they separated, Sam looked at his father. "Pop, I'm going to need you to hang on at the print shop for a while longer."

"You better believe it, Congressman," John replied with a smile.

CHAPTER 9

June 26
Washington, D.C.

Washington, D.C. was not really Sam Clark's style. He had never liked the city life. He was a country boy at heart. On the flip side, there was one thing happening in Washington that got Clark's juices flowing. This is where things got done. He wanted to do his part to make his country a better place to live, but he knew it would be a long and frustrating struggle. He knew the tentacles of Washington politics were far-reaching, and they did not like to let anything of significance leave town, whether in the form of money, power, or opportunity. Sam's goal was to help some of those things escape across the Potomac.

He was eating dinner with a colleague one night after a late vote, and Sam was reminded of the history behind the phrase "red tape," and its meaning of being bogged down by bureaucracy. He was trying to recall where he first heard it. Was it one of Paul Harvey's classics from "...now you know the *rest* of the story?" His colleague had never heard it, so Sam put on his useless trivia hat and began his Paul Harvey imitation.

"So, once the Civil War was over, there were tens of thousands of military veterans who were eligible to draw pensions. Because the government had been so focused on running the war, they were ill-prepared for the massive waves of paperwork and processing that would be required. As the payments were delayed by weeks, then months, then years, veterans made their way to the capitol in large numbers demanding what they were owed. After looking for the paperwork for the men, it was discovered that nobody knew where it was. Eventually, most of the applications were found in the basement of one of the buildings - stacks and stacks of pension applications just sitting there, collecting dust. In order to avoid them getting scattered everywhere, each stack had been wrapped in bundles...with red tape. And *now* you know the *rest* of the story."

As Sam was inclined to do, he leaned back in his chair and laughed heartily at his own joke.

"Is that even remotely true?" his colleague asked.

"Is any good story completely true? No. But there is truth in it. I have learned through the years that red tape dates back centuries before the Civil War in other countries, but the concept is the same. I think it just got Americanized."

Sam's election, his background, and his military story quickly made him a valuable asset in the eyes of the party bosses. Sam had no interest in politicizing any of that, but he understood that sometimes it would be necessary to play those cards to get him into a position to help the folks back home, as well as those in small towns across the country. And so, it happened. Sam was placed on the Armed Services Committee during his first term.

He quickly learned that the chastisement of the current President as being extremely weak on foreign policy was not just political. He *was* weak on foreign policy - dangerously weak in Sam's opinion. He was consistently on the losing end of diplomatic negotiations with powerful foreign leaders, and it seemed that the more brash the opponent, the more ground he yielded.

But, as Bill Clinton had said in the 1990s, "It's the economy, stupid." People behind the scenes knew that it was James Carville who had coined the phrase, but Clinton rode it to election in 1992 and re-election in 1996. The same thing had happened with the current President. Despite the Neville Chamberlain comparisons, the economy was strong, and there was still a great deal of Iraq/Afghanistan fatigue. Nobody wanted another war, so the weakness was explained away as diplomacy, and he had won re-election relatively easily.

CHAPTER 10

January 2
Clark Family Farm
Pine Bluff, KY

"There he goes!" The rabbit jumped out of the briars in front of Sam, and he fired. The rabbit never broke stride, and Sam lost sight of it as it entered a large brush pile. The dogs gave chase, their incessant "singing" informing the hunters that they were hot on the trail, but they stopped abruptly at the brush pile. The rabbit had not come out of there, and was not likely to do so.

"Nice shot, Congressman." Doug Mitchell's words could not have possibly been dripping with any more sarcasm. "I don't think you've hit a rabbit since you got elected. You need to spend more time in the woods."

"Don't I wish," Sam replied. "You wouldn't have hit that one either. I could barely see him. Plus, I just wanted to hear the dogs sing."

Doug rolled his eyes. He was just glad to see Sam in hunting gear again. It had been a long time and a lot of rehab before Sam could negotiate, in a prosthetic, the paths where rabbit hunters trod. However, like every other challenge, Sam had met it head on. Not only had he managed to get back in the field, he was right there with the dogs in the thickest brush.

The two men were hunting on a farm that Sam's family had owned for nearly a century. Sam was a sixth generation Clark family rabbit hunter on this property, and every November, friends and family would migrate to the Clark farm for opening weekend. Much had changed through the years, but nothing had changed rabbit hunting in Kentucky more than the effects of the winters of 1977 and 1978. During January of 1977, there were 28 days when the temperature was below zero, including one day when the air temperature (not the wind chill) was 25 degrees below zero. The Ohio River froze, and some reports had the ice on the Ohio twelve inches thick.

It was believed by many that coyotes first entered Kentucky from Indiana, thanks to the frozen river. Over the course of time, coyotes had greatly affected rabbit hunting. Because they were prey to the coyotes, rabbits tended to sit tighter in dense brush, and were rarely seen "sunning" in thin cover in an open field, as they had in the past. They also tended to go straight to the nearest hole now, rather than the old way of leading the dogs in a circuitous route that would eventually lead right back to where they started. Those "chases" still happened, just not as frequently.

Sam had been elected to the Senate fourteen months ago. Between the whirlwind of the first year, and the idea that he was already campaigning for re-election, Sam realized how easy it was for people to fall into the trap of losing touch with their previous lives and the day-to-day trials of ordinary people. He was one of them, so he had to focus on remaining committed to those people. Today marked the first time he had been able to go rabbit hunting since the election. Unacceptable. Entirely unacceptable. He would have to find a way to create more balance in his life. The country air was bringing his logic back.

Patrick Henry was still poring through the brush pile, but Sam knew that particular rabbit had probably gone deep into a hole, safe and warm.

"Come on, Patrick, let's find another one. I'll try to do better this time."

CHAPTER 11

Six Years Later
U.S. Capitol
Meeting of the Armed Services Committee

It had not taken Sam long to establish himself in Washington. He had quickly become a well-respected member of the House of Representatives. He had not been seriously threatened politically since he had come to Washington, and he had yet to face a challenge in a primary. Aside from that, he was a media darling - and not because he was always sticking his face in front of any camera that entered the building. In his case, it was just the opposite. He had well-informed and intriguing opinions, and his indifference toward the media made him even more appealing to them, much like the high school girl that keeps to herself and has all the boys chasing her.

Sam kept long hours in Washington. He could frequently be found in late night meetings at the Capitol, or out to dinner at a local restaurant in meetings that involved entirely too much work and not enough fun. Colleagues and advisors told him he needed to pace himself to avoid getting burned out. Sam always told them he would slow down, but he had never really meant it. He had a small apartment in Washington, but he frequently slept on the couch in his office. One magazine article had written a piece on the members of Congress who were wasting the most money on their living arrangements and travel accommodations. Sam winced as he read how much some of his colleagues were spending on what he could only call their 'lifestyle.' He winced again when he read the end of the article, where he was ranked the most frugal person in Congress in that regard.

Truth be told, Sam was garnering more media attention than he cared for. There was a large group of people, however, who greatly enjoyed the media attention that Sam was receiving - the leaders of his party. Sam had not yet been made aware of it, but those leaders had plans for him, and they were much bigger than the ones he had in mind for himself. The other tidbit he did not yet know was that the opposing party was also aware of his rising star, and they were already looking into his background for information they could use against him, if necessary.

The topic of today's hearing was China's recent history of trying to compete with the United States as one of the world's few superpowers. Sam had done a good deal of research in this regard, but he was interested to hear from these folks, who watched China closely for a living. The current testimony was regarding China trying to find unique ways to gain a competitive advantage. White House special envoy Jake Williams was in the seat in front of them.

"For the sake of today's hearing, I want to focus on the Cold War and post-Cold War years of this competition between the two countries," Williams began. "Beginning in the 1970s, there were Chinese agents who were working for defense contractors and in the university system that smuggled information out of the country about American cutting-edge technology. This included information about several of our aircrafts and many of our weapons systems. The Chinese government spent the 1980s trying to find a way to catch up with us. By then, they had come to the realization that we were light years ahead of them from both military and technological perspectives. Rather than try to catch up, they began delving into the realm of cyberspace. They spent a fortune training agents to become hackers. They spent another fortune on black market hackers when they realized how long that training process would take. By the end of the 1990s, they had made significant progress, and in the first decade of this century, they began exposing a lot of our weaknesses in cyberspace."

"How so?" Sam's colleague had spit out the two-word question before Sam could ask a more detailed and pertinent one. He hoped Williams would continue his in-depth analysis.

"The Chinese had figured out by that time that the internet offered free reign for anyone to explore, and that security features, even at the highest levels of the corporate world, and even the government, were greatly lacking. One Chinese expert wrote that 'a superior force that loses information dominance will be beaten, while an inferior one that seizes information dominance will be able to win.' One high ranking Chinese official wrote boldly about the concept of *zhixinxiquan,* or 'information dominance.'"

Williams paused momentarily. "*But,*" and he said the word with extra emphasis, "the most startling statement was made by Major General Dai Qingmin of the General Staff. He said that dominance in this area could only be achieved in one way - by preemptive cyber attack."

"Preemptive?" Sam gritted his teeth as the same colleague beat him to the punch again.

"Yes, sir," Williams replied.

"Mr. Williams," Sam blurted out to establish himself. "From what I have read, the Chinese have taken great advantage of us in the last few decades in this regard. Is this how they gained access to the technology on our F-35s?"

"Absolutely." Williams seemed pleased with the question. "A few years after 9/11, the U.S. had completed work on the F-35, also known as the Joint Strike Fighter. It was a next-generation aircraft, and it included the most updated and sophisticated designs and weapons systems. The price tag was huge, approximately $337 billion. Then, in 2006, it was discovered that China was privy to highly classified information about the jet. We had no idea how they had learned the information, so we immediately locked everything down and began intense interrogations of those who had access to the information. It was during this process that some of our agents in the area of cyberspace realized that we had just entered an entirely new world of espionage. Someone had gained access to every detail of the plane's engineering and technology, including things as detailed as how the plane evaded enemy radar systems. And they did this by hacking into our system. All signs pointed to China, but such things are seldom able to be proven with enough evidence to make a direct accusation."

Linda Duvall, a smart and discerning Congresswoman from Louisiana, followed up on that point. "Am I mistaken, or didn't something similar happen within CENTCOM?"

Williams nodded. "Yes, ma'am, it did. In 2008, an NSA employee noticed a program running on one of our dedicated military networks. It was sending out a beacon seeking instructions. That alone is not unusual. However, the beacon was originating inside of Central Command's classified network, which at that time was running the wars in Iraq and Afghanistan. The biggest concern was how this was even possible, because that particular network wasn't even connected to the internet. Although the source was never fully determined, it is now believed that a soldier innocently inserted a thumb drive that carried a virus into the system. This, of course, led to the banning of such USB drives on all military systems."

Duvall followed up. "It seems as if we are consistently finding ourselves in reactive positions rather than proactive ones. Am I misreading that?"

"No, you're not," Williams replied. "It is nearly impossible to stay in front of these matters. We continuously get better at defense while they get better at offense. In that regard, frankly, we are not much better off today than we were twenty years ago."

CHAPTER 12

April 3
Louisville, KY
The Omni Hotel

After nine years in the House of Representatives, and following a great deal of prodding from family, friends, and political advisors, Sam Clark decided to throw his hat in the ring as a nominee for the President of the United States. Despite being what political experts would call inexperienced, Sam felt he had a good understanding of how government functioned. The question was whether he had the ability to lead the way in *making* it function. Sam was confident that nobody who had ever been elected President had the ability to do that by himself. It would take a team, and that was the part that Sam thought he could do well. He felt strongly that he could form a strong and diverse team that could get things done in Washington, D.C.

The primary was 13 months away, and Sam found himself in front of a capacity crowd of over 1,100 people in the Omni's largest conference room, the Commonwealth. It was a joint event – Sam's formal announcement and a black-tie gala for the Fisher House Foundation. With a two-term president leaving office, and the sitting vice-President deciding not to run, the field was wide open. Sam knew his announcement would be the grandest of any of the nominees, and he also knew that he had more political heavyweights in the room than anyone else would have.

The ovation as Sam was introduced was nearly deafening. This was indeed an impressive announcement. Sam had a big part in writing his speech, despite advice from the old guard to let the professionals handle it. He was satisfied with the blend of the two approaches. He stepped up to the microphone. After some typical thank-yous and introductory remarks, Sam got into the substance of his speech.

"It's hard to believe that it has now been more than a decade since I woke up in a hospital in Germany, my active military career having ended in the blink of an eye. It was a dark, dark time in my life. Every one of us has those dark times. They are worse for some people than others. Some of that is due to the circumstances in a person's life, and some of it is because of the mental and emotional health care, or lack thereof, that is one of the biggest problems in our society today."

The speechwriters had written the words 'pause for applause' several times throughout the speech. This was one of those times. "They are *really* good at this," Sam thought to himself as the crowd cheered right on cue.

He continued. "That is why, after decades of either ignoring this problem or acknowledging it only on the periphery of an agenda, I am going to make improvements in our country's awareness and treatment of mental health one of the primary goals of our domestic platform."

Applause, again on cue.

Sam continued with his speech, and prepared for his conclusion, which would end on a personal note. The speech writers had recommended this, and Sam knew he wanted to tell a story right here in front of the world that he had never told anyone before.

"When I lost my leg, I really thought my life was over. I was so active, and the idea of not being whole just seemed like more than I could bear. But I had a nurse in Germany that never failed to try to lift my spirits, no matter how nasty I acted toward her. I did not make any progress from a mental or emotional perspective until long after I left that hospital. So, to all the nurses and doctors and others who help all of us in our time of need, when we are at our most vulnerable, thank you."

One last round of applause before the final lines.

"Once I came home and got my act together, I decided to be the best at everything, even with a prosthetic leg. Those who have lost their sight or hearing make up for it with their other senses, which become extremely keen. I decided to do that in a physical way. My other leg would be the strongest leg. My arms would be stronger than those of others. My mind would be stronger. I would not let this define me. In fact, I wanted it to make me better, stronger, than I had ever been before. And I decided it would never...*ever* limit me. That is why I stand before you today, announcing my candidacy for President of the United States."

The room erupted. Balloons floated down from the ceiling, streamers flew, confetti cannons covered the room in small pieces of paper. Sam waved to the crowd as his personal theme song played over the speakers. Sam was a huge country music fan, and he really liked a singer named Rodney Atkins. Although Atkins wasn't one of the mega-stars of country music, Sam liked his music a great deal, especially this song. It was called "If You're Going Through Hell," and Sam had listened to it ceaselessly as he rehabilitated himself physically, mentally, emotionally, and spiritually. Sam listened to the words as he continued to wave to the crowd.

Well I been deep down in that darkness
I been down to my last match
Felt a hundred different demons
Breathing fire down my back
And I knew that if I stumbled
I'd fall right into the trap that they were laying

If you're going through Hell
Keep on going, don't slow down
If you're scared, don't show it
You might get out
Before the devil even knows you're there

Sam was joined on stage by his friends and family. He hugged his dad, and he hugged Father Jerry Murphy. Sam had known Father Jerry since Sam was an altar server and Father Jerry was a young priest. This man had been in the darkest spiritual places with Sam, when his previously strong faith had wavered. He was the only living human who had heard about some of the things that Sam had experienced and done. He had been there throughout Sam's recovery, and this was the man that Sam wanted next to him on this day more than anyone else on the planet, except for his dad.

CHAPTER 13

Thirteen Months Later
May 26
Pine Bluff, KY

Sam exited the polling place and thought back to the first time he voted for himself in the special election for Roger Snider's Congressional seat. This time was considerably different. Every major media outlet had a spot outside of Pine Bluff Middle School, and Sam walked over briefly to discuss his plans for the rest of the day.

He would never say such a thing out loud, but the primary was basically locked up. What had started with six candidates had been quickly reduced to four, and eventually down to Sam and Cathy Filson, an up-and-coming African American Congresswoman from Georgia. Sam knew Filson was a future star, and their camps had talked behind the scenes about potential cabinet opportunities for the other, depending on the outcome of the election. Sam had left open the possibility, but Filson had said that if she did not win, she wanted to go back to Congress and represent her constituents. Sam admired that.

As expected, Sam won the primary relatively easily. He and Filson had been competitive but extremely professional toward each other. The first thing his advisors told him was that those days were over. The general election would be contentious at best. Sam had replied that he was well aware of that, but he asked if he could at least enjoy the night before they began preparing for the next campaign. They smiled collectively. Sam smiled back and said, "But after tonight, it's full steam ahead to November 2."

Sam drove himself from place to place as often as possible, although those times were quickly becoming more seldom. As he left the parking lot, he made a left turn onto the highway. One of the aides looked at Sam's father, John. "Where is he going? He lives the other way."

John smiled. "He's going to the cemetery to talk to his momma."

CHAPTER 14

September 9
Richmond, VA
First Presidential Debate

Sam had come out of the presidential primary season victorious and relatively unscathed. With their eyes on the general election, Sam and his team knew exactly what they faced. Sam's opponent was Martin Faulkner, the current Senate majority leader. The contrast between the two candidates could not have been starker. Faulkner was the classic presidential candidate - Harvard Law graduate, five terms in the house, three terms in the Senate. Faulkner had been in Congress for nearly 30 years, and he knew the world of Washington politics inside and out. He was a tough and seasoned politician.

Clark, on the other hand, was not Ivy League educated. He was not an attorney. He did not have a great deal of political experience. He was not diplomatic, and he knew little about the ins and outs of the world of Washington. And his team loved every aspect of the differences. They felt that the country was ready for a sea change in the type of people they elected to the highest offices. If they were correct, Clark had a good chance to become President of the United States. If they were wrong, however, they could be on the losing end of one of the biggest electoral landslides in the nation's history.

Faulkner's team had won the first debate, which was about how many debates there would be. Faulkner had a big edge in name recognition, and most people knew where he stood on the issues. He had led in every poll taken since the two men had won their primaries. Faulkner's team preferred to coast to the White House. Debates were a no-win situation. If he wiped the floor with the less experienced candidate, it would be no more than the expected outcome. If Sam even held his own, it would be considered a win for him and a loss for Faulkner. The Clark team had wanted as many debates as possible, and Faulkner countered with one. Two was the number that was eventually agreed to by the party leaders.

The latest polls had Faulkner ahead 52% to 37%. The polls in Iowa and New Hampshire showed similar numbers. Clark's team did not see that as a negative. Faulkner was well known and had nearly 80% name recognition. Much of the American electorate did not yet know anything at all about Sam Clark. They felt that Sam's personality and his background were strong positives that could boost his poll numbers once his story became known. Plus, 11% were admittedly undecided, and they felt strongly that an overwhelming majority of those people would either stay home on election day or be Clark supporters. It was their job to convince those people that Sam was worth their vote.

As the debate moved past an hour in length and the closing statements approached, Faulkner made his move. While answering a question about foreign policy, the Pennsylvania Senator played the inexperience card.

"I just don't know if Sam Clark has the experience needed to make tough decisions in difficult situations. Can we afford to gamble on someone so unproven?"

Clark was ready for the exchange, and he tried to speak calmly. They had practiced his tone ad nauseum. "In response to the Senator's comments about my lack of experience, I would put forward the idea that making split second decisions during three tours in Iraq and Afghanistan should count for something. My decisions impacted not only whether we won a particular skirmish, but also whether my team survived to fight another day. Granted, I can't compete with the Senator's experience in the political sphere, where he calls floor votes in the middle of the night to give himself a pay raise. In my line of work, that isn't exactly what we call valor."

Clark's words were filled with sarcasm, and although the statement was clearly enjoyed by those in attendance, he had played into the Senator's hands.

"This is exactly what I'm talking about," Faulkner said calmly. "I wasn't trying to insult Mr. Clark. I was just stating an opinion. His tone and his thin skin are *exactly* what I'm talking about when I say that he doesn't have the necessary experience for this job. If he takes that tone with a world leader at an important summit, the discussion is over. No leader of a country is going to be talked to in that manner. He or she will simply get up and walk away. Mr. Clark has no diplomatic skills."

The debate's moderator forced the candidates to move on at that point, and Clark's inner circle was split into two camps for the rest of the debate. The political team felt Faulkner was correct, and he had deftly taken advantage of Clark while exposing a weakness. Clark, indeed, *was* more hot-tempered than they would like. The other group, who jokingly referred to themselves as 'the ordinary folk,' thought the comment was a knockout punch and would win the debate for Clark unless something radical happened in the last fifteen minutes. It was their opinion that voters were sick and tired of politicians whose primary goal was not to offend anyone. They pointed to Congress' approval rating as proof that the electorate was ready to pull the lever for someone who was anything but part of the status quo.

The rest of the debate passed without either candidate stumbling or standing out. Most experts considered it a draw, which was a good result for Clark. He had to prove that his lack of political experience was not a detriment. Being able to stand toe-to-toe with Martin Faulkner was a good start.

CHAPTER 15

October 1
11:15 PM
Tallahassee, FL

Sam had just finished a whirlwind day of campaigning, with stops in four battleground states. He was flying all over the country in the closing weeks of the campaign, but today had been exceptionally long. His day had started with a breakfast Q&A in Madison, Wisconsin. He had followed that with stump speeches in Des Moines and St. Louis, before closing the night here in Tallahassee. Tomorrow was an off day, which meant that Sam could knock out some reading before calling it a night. That would allow him to sleep in the next day, maybe as late as 8:00.

Sam smiled at the thought. He had long ago learned to function without sleep. During his time in the Middle East, there were times he went two or three days with nothing more than a 10-minute cat nap. He was tired tonight, but not nearly as tired as he had been on many occasions in Iraq. Plus, in the comfort and security of a hotel room, once he did go to sleep, he could fully relax and sleep soundly.

Sam was consuming himself with learning as much as possible about the political and financial cultures of some of the world's other powerful nations. He was already well-versed with most of the countries that comprised the European Union, so he was focusing primarily on Russia, China, and North Korea. Tonight's stack was about China. Sam kicked off his shoes and changed out of his suit. He removed his prosthetic, put on a clean white t-shirt and some running shorts, and propped himself against the headboard.

He skimmed through some of the historical information about China. He was already aware of much of it, including the days when their political leaders literally considered China as the center of the world. Then came what was known in China as the 'century of humiliation.' Starting in the mid-19th century, China had suffered numerous defeats at the hands of Japan, as well as several Western countries. Then the country became poverty-stricken and fell into a civil war.

For the last half century, China had built its way back. While some of its leaders came around and began adjusting to the changes around them, primarily globalization, many of its leaders did not take kindly to the 'century of humiliation.' They were more adversarial. Sam remembered reading about those leaders and their goals for revenge. It was just about that time that his briefing material came to a famous quote by Chiang Kai-shek in the 1940s: "during the past 100 years, the citizens of the entire country, suffering under the yoke of the unequal treaties which gave foreigners special concessions and extra-territorial status in China, were unanimous that the national humiliation be avenged, and the state be made strong."

Since that time, China had become more and more powerful. Their influence was broad, and their economy was quickly approaching the size of that of the United States. Sam abhorred Communism, but he kept reading with an open mind in the hopes that he could gain a deeper understanding. The next section was about the last two decades of the 20th century, which started with the Reagan era and the struggles between the American way and the Soviet way.

Meanwhile, from China's perspective, the biggest event during this time was the crackdown in Tiananmen Square. The condemnation of China from most of the world was led by the Americans. When combined with the collapse of their fellow Communists in the Soviet Union, the Chinese leaders once again grew sensitive about outsiders trying to force their way of life on their proud and ancient culture.

The Chinese began to get more detailed into teaching an appreciation of and love for the Chinese way of life in their schools. This curriculum emphasized the century of humiliation and drew direct comparisons to current events. The solution to the potential problems in this regard was taught as a strong central government.

Within the last five years, a top Chinese leader had made a nationally broadcast speech in which he reminded the adults of those dark times, and he issued a call for national rejuvenation. Sam put the papers down and looked out the hotel window. He had not realized that nationalism was that strong in China, especially among its political leaders.

Sam thought to himself that China, although Communist, was more of a friend than an enemy. No recent presidents had said or done anything to make the country think any differently. China had not only accepted the idea of a market-based economy; they had taken it by the reins. This had led to negotiations and trade deals between China and many countries around the globe. Those deals were not always successful, but China was frequently seen as cooperative, and they had definitely become an equal player on the world stage, diplomatically as well as economically.

This embrace of capital markets had led to rising living standards in China, which in turn led to political stability. This had allowed China to create a new and improved reputation in the international community. Aside from that, although their economy was growing by leaps and bounds and their military spending was increasing dramatically, in most areas of the world they had not been considered a rising threat.

Sam's sight was getting blurry, and he was beginning to lose focus. He decided to call it a night. He noted in his mind, however, that he would begin looking a little more closely at China.

CHAPTER 16

October 11
Raleigh, North Carolina
Sullivan's Steakhouse

Sam had to admit it, he was sick and tired of the campaign. The same speeches over and over, day after day. Twenty-two more days, he kept telling himself. When he woke up in the morning, it would be twenty-one. He could do this.

One of the things Sam hated most about the campaign was how unhealthy the lifestyle was. Aside from zipping in and out of different time zones every day, there was little time for exercise and there was hardly any time to sit down and enjoy a good meal. This was a night that allowed for a bit of rejuvenation for him.

Sam could not remember the last time he had a good steak, and he was looking forward to eating one at Sullivan's. And instead of reading memos about current events, he was being briefed in a private room at Sullivan's by Jim Graham, one of the country's top minds on China, and an advisor in the current administration.

Graham sat down following introductions, as the two men had never met. "I won't take a great deal of your time, Mr. Clark, but I understand you have some questions about our relationship with China."

"Yes, I do," Clark replied. "I have read quite a bit about China recently, and I just want to get the most current information to make sure I am properly understanding the give and take between us."

"Yes, sir," Graham replied. "What questions do you have?"

Sam thought for a moment, making sure that his direct questions did nothing to make Graham think he was being judgmental about current policies. "I think I have a grasp on our relationship with China from a unilateral perspective. However, globally, how much traction is their model gaining - using the combination of the capitalist markets with an authoritarian political regime?"

Graham was impressed. "Great question," he replied. "China is indeed gaining traction with much of the developing world, as well as the third world. Many of these smaller countries have leaned on China for financial assistance, and they are asking more questions of China than they are of the United States regarding how the capitalist model functions. As strange as it sounds, China stands poised, during the next two decades, to challenge us as the global leader in developing capitalist markets around the world. Frankly, they are being much more proactive with these countries than we are."

Clark took a sip of tea and digested the information for a moment before saying, "Please continue."

"When China, along with India and the countries that made up the former Soviet bloc, entered the workforce in capitalist markets, it added more than three *billion* workers to the global labor pool, which obviously watered it down significantly. The United States and the other developed countries of the West had enjoyed decades of dominance with very little global competition. Those days are gone, and we haven't fully realized it yet. The rest of the world is catching up with us.

"Frankly, sir, we are witnessing the Chinese transitioning into an aggressive competitor, not by trying to change the playing field, but by trying to beat us on *our* field. Their Premier spoke in Russia recently about the need for a new international economic and financial order, so the world could protect itself from another 2008-type meltdown. It was a direct shot at our way of doing business. In other words, they were saying, 'Let's get together and make sure America doesn't lead us down this path to destruction again in the future.'"

Clark leaned forward in his chair. "Am I missing something, or should this be a more pressing matter? I read similar things in my briefing memos, but I am not hearing it from members of Congress, or even in the media."

Graham shrugged his shoulders. "We have a bad habit of letting international situations get pretty desperate before we address them. Just look back historically. How many times did Osama bin Laden attack our interests overseas without people caring a great deal, except within the deepest layers of government? Then 9/11 happened. Even an event as globally encompassing as World War II was virtually ignored by our country until Pearl Harbor. The war in Europe had been raging for more than two years by that time."

Clark was nodding. "So, I am not overreacting by thinking this situation needs some proactive attention, even if it is no more than closely monitoring matters."

"Not at all." Now Graham leaned forward. "In fact, let me add this. As China's economy has exploded with growth, so has the build-up and modernization of their military. They are spending a fortune on R&D, with average increases of 17% over the last seven years. The budget for the P.L.A. … (Graham paused and Clark nodded, acknowledging his understanding that Graham was referencing the

People's Liberation Army), was just under $30 billion in 2000. By 2008, it had increased to more than $60 billion. Today it is over $85 billion."

Clark was thoroughly enjoying the steak that was placed in front of him. It was pure perfection. But as he was two bites from finishing it, he had one more question for Jim Graham. "How much does the memory of the 'century of humiliation' factor into current thinking in China?"

"Substantially," Graham said forcefully and without hesitation. "Political and military leaders in China are quick to point out, without reservation, that China is not 'emerging' as a global power. They want the world to know that they are 're-emerging.' Until the century of humiliation, China was the dominant economy in the world, not for two centuries, but for two *millennia* – for two thousand years!"

Sam was shaking his head as he removed his napkin from his lap, wiped his mouth, and laid the napkin on the empty plate. "This reminds me a great deal of the Cold War. They are building and building, while we are a nation of fat and happy people, many of whom have become weak and soft. We need them to know that they cannot destroy us from within."

Graham nodded. "If you are elected, sir, I wish you the best of luck with that idea."

CHAPTER 17

October 16
Denver, CO
Final Presidential Debate

Throughout the summer and into the early part of the fall, Sam Clark had proven himself quite capable as a politician, although he hated the word. Another phrase that drove him crazy was 'public servant.' Part of his stump speech included the concept that in the early days of the country, when the citizens would leave their farms and blacksmith shops to serve time in Congress, it truly was public service. They were serving their country for a designated period of time, then going back to whatever trade it was that provided their livelihood. Clark railed against the modern 'lifers,' those who held elected positions nearly all their adult life while building a ridiculous net worth, based on speaking engagements and serving on the boards of directors for major corporations.

In speeches across Iowa, New Hampshire, and South Carolina, Martin Faulkner became the face of a 'lifer.' Clark, meanwhile, continued to speak of his small-town upbringing and his military career. At first, he did not want to speak of the dark times after losing his leg, but eventually he came to the realization that his story could help other veterans who had experienced similar (or worse) situations.

Clark's poll numbers had improved steadily since the first debate. He currently held a six-point lead in Iowa. He trailed by nine in New Hampshire, but he knew that if he did in fact win Iowa, those numbers could change quickly. He felt very good about South

Carolina. If he could win two of those three, his team felt they had a great chance to win the election. If they swept the three, the election was basically over.

The debate held to form. Faulkner spoke in extensive detail about his experience, while Clark described himself as an outsider. Those in attendance were a bit underwhelmed by the whole thing. Faulkner's closing statement was strong, and as all eyes turned to Clark for the final words of the debate season, he felt a surge of confidence. He would never say this, even to his closest advisors, but he felt presidential.

Clark began his closing statement by thanking the moderator and those in attendance. That was the only part of the statement that sounded anything like a typical debate moment. Clark hit on his main themes - a strong national defense and fiscal responsibility. Then he transitioned to what he called his 'common sense platform.'

"As I stand here, I want everyone to know that I am not Ivy League educated. My opponent seems to think that is a negative, but I would beg to differ. In my 'lesser' education, math is simple. Households, companies, and governments have these things called budgets. You find ways to generate income to pay for your expenses, and hopefully you have money left over at the end of the month, and eventually, at the end of the year.

"Evidently, the math they teach in the Ivy League schools is entirely different. Instead of debits and credits, they teach deficits and credit cards. If they are saying I'm not qualified to be President because I don't understand the 'intricacies' of government, they are 100% right about that from a financial perspective. But I think the 'Ivy League way' has run its course. Where has that gotten us? We are twenty-something TRILLION dollars in debt! And the reason for that isn't Republican or Democrat - both are to blame. However, the one common thread among the leaders in both the executive and legislative branches during the decades that we have run up this seemingly insurmountable debt is that an overwhelming majority of these geniuses from both parties are Ivy League graduates. Can you imagine if we ran our households the way the federal government is run? It's a long road back to fiscal sanity, but every journey has a first step, and I would like nothing more than for you and me to take that first step together on November 2. Thank you."

That sealed the deal. Clark was already ahead in most polls, and although the electoral map was also in his favor, some of the swing states were close enough that a bad debate or misstep on the campaign trail during the last few days could turn the election. The debate swung it the other way, and election day saw Clark win 41 states while garnering 56% of the popular vote. Both numbers were the biggest margins of victory since Ronald Reagan's landslide election in 1984.

CHAPTER 18

December 23
11:15 PM
Washington, D.C.

As Sam Clark sat on the edge of his bed and removed his prosthetic, he thought about what a long and mundane day he had just completed. "As mundane as a day as President-Elect of the United States can be," he thought to himself. The morning had started with a relatively uneventful PDB. The Presidential Daily Briefing was a concise summary of the things that the president needed to be made aware of - a checklist of priorities from around the world. Since his election, Clark had quickly learned that a day as President-Elect was just like a day as President, minus the ability to make any decisions.

Sam had then attended a cabinet meeting, followed by a working lunch with his incoming chief of staff and vice president. The afternoon consisted of two more staff meetings and a handful of meetings with members of the Congressional leadership, trying to find a way to work out the impasse they had come to with the current President regarding a defense appropriations bill that had stalled in committee.

Sam looked at the seventy pages of briefing memos sitting on his nightstand. He was an avid reader, and he was quite a civics nerd. He still remembered learning about the process of how a bill becomes law by watching the classic cartoon skit on the kids' TV show *Schoolhouse Rock*. The cartoon showed a walking scroll named Bill, discussing his process with a schoolboy. By putting it to music with a catchy tune, it was highly effective. People close to Sam's age still remembered the skit and many could still sing the song.

"I'm just a bill, yes I'm only a bill,
and if they vote for me on Capitol Hill,
well then I'm off to the White House where I wait in a line
with a lot of other bills for the president to sign.
And if he signs me then I'll be a law, how I hope and pray that he will,
but today I am still just a bill."

Sam loved the nuances of the way the government functioned, but he equally despised the politics involved when people did their best to keep it from functioning. He had seen it up close, and he realized that it had become a deeply flawed system that those in power had learned to manipulate for the sake of their own self-interest.

Sam laid back on his bed, stretched his arms above his head and let out a deep yawn. He was tired but not that sleepy. He had something to do before he began reading. He rolled over on his side and turned on the TV. Years ago, he had recorded a speech that had been delivered at the National Press Club. The speaker was Gary Sinise. Sinise was best known for his role as Lieutenant Dan in *Forrest Gump*, but Sam knew him better as a strong and willing advocate for veterans and their families.

Sam had met Sinise several times, and Sam loved his approach regarding how people could help veterans. Sinise always talked about how everyone wants to do something big, but that if people would simply focus on the veterans in their own communities, they would be much better served than by trying to do everything on a national level.

Sam listened to the speech, as he did every year on the anniversary of the firefight in which he lost his leg. Through the years, he had finally realized how fortunate he had been to survive that day. He felt less guilt about surviving, but it still lurked beneath the surface. Although he still struggled with it, Sam had learned to control it. However, he had decided long ago that he did not want to forget that feeling. Plus, in an odd way, it motivated him. Every year on this date, Sam found himself entirely enthralled while listening to Sinise talking about witnessing an Angel Flight ceremony. Unfortunately, Sam had been involved in several of them. Sinise's story hit home and brought back some vivid memories.

"During the Thanksgiving holiday of 2009, I was visiting Bagram Air Force Base in Afghanistan, and General Mike Scaparrotti, who was the Director of Operations for United States Central Command, providing oversight to all military operations throughout the CENTCOM area of responsibility, including Iraq and Afghanistan, he came to me and he informed me that there would be an Angel Flight early the following morning for a fallen Special Forces soldier who had been killed in action. The general invited me to the ramp ceremony, where the U.S. military would load the casket of our fallen American hero on a plane, to repatriate his remains back to America.

"What my eyes saw and what my heart felt that day has always stayed with me. I watched hundreds of American service men and women from all branches, most of them, including myself, never knew this soldier personally. They gathered in formation in his honor to pay their respects and offer a farewell salute to a brave American soldier. The

mood was somber. The casket, draped with an American flag, was carried by eight members of his unit moving slowly and somberly on to the plane as the formation was commanded to give their final salute to an American who gave his last full measure and devotion for his country. Indeed, a sight to behold.

Members of his unit, who the day before were fighting by his side, placed his casket on the bed of a C-17, knelt down around it and offered their final prayers and farewells to their brother. Then the rest of the formation followed suit, rank by rank, traveling up the ramp of the C-17, to pay their respects. It was my sobering honor to be by General Scaparrotti's side as we entered the plane and knelt down beside the casket. I was flooded with emotion for this young man and his family, a painful and sobering reminder of the cost of freedom."

Sam felt a lump in his throat as Sinise was forced to pause to collect himself. As Sinise went on to talk about the heavy burden that many of the survivors bring home with them, Sam had to turn it off. To this day, he still had dark times, and in those moments, he simply had to remove himself from the situation. He had battled himself for years about that process. Initially, he thought that by forcing himself to stop thinking about what he had experienced, he was betraying the memories of those who had fallen. As time moved on, however, and after talking with others who found themselves feeling the same emotions, he realized that he was doing the right thing. Wallowing in sorrow did nothing to honor them. Moving away from the things that brought back those memories did not mean he was forgetting the fallen, only that he had to get himself moving to find ways to honor them.

He had taken that line of thinking all the way to the Oval Office, where he was soon to become the Commander-in-Chief. Every morning when he got out of bed and attached his prosthetic, he said a quick prayer for those in active duty, and that the Lord would guide him to do his very best to honor and protect them. Sam smiled at that idea as he looked at his nightstand. Briefing memos might not seem like the best way to honor them, but they did educate him so that his decisions were well-informed ones. He grabbed the stack, his reading glasses, and his highlighter. He glanced at the clock before he began reading. It was 11:44. Sam smiled as he realized that even a 'mundane' day in this job ended well after most people had gone home and put their feet up for the night.

CHAPTER 19

January 20
12:00 PM
Washington, D.C.

"I, Samuel Henry Clark, do solemnly swear..." Sam continued to repeat the words spoken by Chief Justice Norman F. Thompson. Sam's left hand was placed firmly on his family Bible, and his right hand was raised. As the oath continued, Sam made a point to focus on the words.

"...and will, to the best of my ability, preserve, protect, and defend the Constitution of the United States, so help me God."

As soon as Sam finished the oath, the United States Marine Band played Hail to the Chief. Sam shook hands and accepted the congratulations of the Chief Justice, then turned to wave to the huge crowd. He felt a rush of emotion as a flood of memories passed through his mind. Some were recent, others more distant. Some were good, some were bad. They came in flashes, moments in time. Sam continued to wave as he brought himself back to the present. He had a speech to give.

CHAPTER 20

January 20
9:20 PM
The National Building Museum

Sam waved to the crowd as he walked into the museum, which was the site of the fourth and final inauguration ball on Sam's schedule. Aside from the fact that he was the first person with a prosthetic to be elected President, he was also the first one since 1886 to be a bachelor. He had not given that any thought at all during the campaign, or even during his time as President-elect. It was only as the inauguration balls were being planned that it became relevant, as there would be no dance with the first lady. Sam's response was typical Sam. "Don't we have more important things to worry about?"

This final stop of the night was a military ball, and Sam finally felt comfortable. His old friend Clint McGuffey approached, and the two men hugged. Sam had gone to dinner with Clint the night before, and that marked the first time they had seen each other since the firefight in which Sam was shot. Clint took no time at all to poke fun at his friend's new title. "Well, hello Mr. President."

Clint McGuffey was a unique person. He was tall and lanky, a true Irishman who had come to America and grown up in the south. He had a bit of an Irish accent that blended with his southern drawl.

"Am I going to get tackled by the Secret Service for hugging you like this?"

They both laughed, and Sam replied, "One thing I have learned already is that the cameras are always on. So, I'm not going to say what I want to say to that comment."

Clint laughed, but he wasn't finished. "Wanna know what the talking heads were saying before high noon?" Clint kept referencing 'high noon' during dinner the night before, in reference to the Presidential oath being administered at 12:00 sharp.

"No, I don't," Sam said, quite aware that he was going to hear it anyway.

"They were talking about how important your speech was, and they said the world would soon find out if the moment was too big for you."

"No, they didn't."

Clint laughed out loud, so loudly that it drew some attention from a few people standing around them. "Swear on my soul!"

Sam shook his head. Clint continued. "Since you can't speak your mind anymore, I'll say it. If they thought *that* moment was too big for you, I will gladly take a few of them to our old stomping grounds in Fallujah, and we'll see what they think afterward."

"Tell them to bring extra underwear," Sam replied.

Sam knew that moments like this, and like dinner last night, were soon going to be few and far between. He would miss such casual conversations as the one they were having the night before, about whether Sam would say "So help me God" at the end of the Presidential oath. Clint's wife, Mary, had asked why he wouldn't say it. Clint had been glad to explain.

"You see, Sam here is torn between his 'by the book' nature and his Catholic-ism." Clint always said Catholicism like it was two separate words – 'Catholic' and 'ism', mostly just to irritate Sam. "As

Sam knows, the only words in the entire Constitution of these United States of America that are inside quotation marks are the words of the Presidential oath. And the Constitution version does not include 'so help me God.'

"Really?" Mary replied with sincere interest.

"I don't really know," Clint said. "But that's what the trivia nerd here told me one time."

"That's right," Sam said. "There is an ongoing dispute as to when it was first said. Most historians think it dates all the way back to George Washington, but others think the first one to say it was Chester Arthur."

Clint jumped back in. "And you see, Mary, Sam here has to decide whether or not to follow what we know for a fact is written in the Constitution. But if he does, and fails to include 'so help me God,' he knows good and well that the Pope is gonna kick him right out of the church. Decisions, decisions."

Sam could not help but laugh at his goofy friend, who also happened to be the bravest person he had ever met. He had proven it repeatedly during their time in Iraq. It was too early to think about the next election, but in either four or eight years, Sam was looking forward to spending a lot of time with Clint McGuffey.

CHAPTER 21

February 14
Brussels, Belgium

"Happy Valentine's Day, Elaine." George Leonard kissed the woman as he handed her a heart-shaped box of chocolates.

"You better come stronger than this, Mister." Elaine looked at him and smiled playfully.

"Oh, the candy is just the introduction to the evening," George replied. "We have reservations at Comme Chez Soi and tickets to Cirque Royal. Is that strong enough?"

Elaine nodded her head. "Impressive, Mr. Leonard. Impressive indeed. French food and performing arts. And chocolate when I get home. What more could a girl ask for?" She took his arm and he led her out the front door. He opened the passenger door to his Bentley Continental and watched her closely as she maneuvered her body into the seat. As he walked around to the driver's side, George smiled at his good fortune.

George Leonard was in his 50s. He was the son of a Russian mother and a British father. His given name was Yuri, but when away from Russia on business, he preferred the Western version of his name. He was a consultant for an energy conglomerate, and he was in Belgium for three months implementing a recently negotiated deal with a Belgian energy conglomerate to use Russian oil.

George was heavy but not obese. He was attempting to cover his increasingly large bald spot with a poor comb-over. The only thing George really had to offer the ladies was his wallet, and that seemed to be enough for many of them.

He had known Elaine for three weeks. They met at a nightclub, and even though George had been there with another woman, he had spent most of the night trying to impress Elaine. She told him if he was really interested, he could come back the next night without a date. George had done just that, and the two had spent most of their free time together since that point.

Elaine was gorgeous. She had long brown hair that she straightened. She was petite but curvy in all the right places. She had big brown eyes that dominated every room that she walked into. What George liked most about her was Elaine's ability to look like the girl next door when she went out for a morning jog, and like a Hollywood star when she dressed up to go out at night.

George knew that Elaine was at least 15 years younger than him, although he wasn't stupid enough to ask her age. As big as his ego was, he realized it was likely that her only interest in him was his money. In that way, she was just like all the others. But in other ways, Elaine was different. For the first time since he met his third wife six years ago (they were divorced two years later), George was spending all his time with just one woman.

CHAPTER 22

February 22
8:35 AM
The Oval Office

"Bless me Father, for I have sinned. It has been three weeks since my last confession." Sam made the sign of the cross as he said those words. After a brief discussion, Sam confessed his sins. There was nothing earth shattering to disclose, but Sam had been raised on the importance of the sacrament, and he had been going to confession no less frequently than once a month since he was in college. He explained to people how good it made him feel - as if the weight of the world was being lifted off his shoulders. This was especially true since he had become the President of the United States.

Once Sam had discussed his sins with the priest and made his Act of Contrition, Sam bowed his head as the priest reached out and put the palm of his hand near Sam's head. "God, the Father of mercies, through the death and resurrection of His Son, has reconciled the world to himself and sent the Holy Spirit among us for the forgiveness of sins; through the ministry of the Church, may God give you pardon and peace, and I hereby absolve you of your sins in the name of the father, and of the Son, and of the Holy Spirit."

"Amen," Sam replied, as he made the sign of the cross. "Thank you, Father Jerry." Sam smiled sincerely. The old priest sitting in front of him, Father Jerry Murphy, had been Sam's parish priest from the time he was baptized until he left for college. Sam's Mass attendance was sporadic while he had been away at Loyola. He knew that Mass was about Jesus, not the priest, but Sam could never get as much out of Mass when Father Jerry wasn't presiding. Father Jerry, when hearing this story, scolded Sam. "Nonsense," he uttered. "Maybe Mass isn't about what you get out of it. Maybe it's about what you put into it."

It had always been this no-frills, common-sense approach that Sam had loved so much about his pastor. Despite the rebuke, Sam's Mass attendance was based on following Father Jerry to whatever parish he received as an assignment. This had been the case from the time he had graduated from college until he became President, with the only exception being the time he had spent in the military. And now, Father Jerry had been 'loaned' to the diocese of Washington, D.C. as the spiritual advisor to the President of the United States.

"So, how have the first thirty days been?" the priest asked.

"Unbelievable," Sam replied. "Literally."

"I can only imagine," Murphy said, shaking his head. "I will keep you in my prayers. Every day for eight years."

Sam smiled. "I'm just focusing on the first eight weeks right now."

Sam walked the priest to the door of the Oval Office. "Thanks for coming, Father Jerry. I know you are busy. I truly appreciate it."

Father Jerry placed his hand on Sam's arm and gave him a reassuring smile. Then he began to chuckle as he walked out the door. Without looking back, he said as he was walking away, "From what little I know about politics, you're going to need confession now more than ever."

Sam smiled broadly as he watched him walk away.

CHAPTER 23

March 3
Matveev Kurgan
Rostov Region, Russia

Russian President Nikolai Volkov was sitting on the balcony of his dacha, which was located within an isolated area near the Ukrainian border. He was smoking a fine Cuban cigar that he had received from Fidel Castro during a visit to Havana in 1998. Castro had given Volkov two boxes of Montecristos, and Volkov smoked them sparingly, nearly always in celebration.

In this case, Volkov was celebrating the death of a political opponent. Anton Sokolov had been Russia's Prime Minister since 2008, and he was in the Gorbachev mold, which was no compliment from an apparatchik like Volkov. Volkov had mistaken him for a hard-liner when he had appointed him, and Sokolov had frequently given him cause to regret the decision, especially in the last 18 months. Volkov had battled prostate cancer a decade earlier, and he found motivation in his goal of simply outliving Sokolov.

After the fall of the Soviet Union, the government was structured so that the president appointed the prime minister. The prime minister was the head of the executive branch of the government. The president, meanwhile, was the head of state as well as Commander-in-Chief. The prime minister ascends to the presidency if the current president dies, resigns, or becomes incapacitated. The thought of Sokolov as president of the Russian Federation made Volkov shudder.

Volkov had meetings planned over the next few days to begin the process of selecting the new prime minister. He would not make the same mistake twice. If Russia was going to reclaim its dominant position in the world, he would need to make sure this next appointment was a home run, to use a baseball analogy. Baseball was one of the few things that Volkov considered good that came from America. He thought about that as he put his feet up, took a long draw from the Montecristo, and followed it with a bend of the elbow to take a nice drink from his glass of Russo-Baltique vodka.

The container that the vodka came in (it could hardly be called a bottle), was shaped like the front end of a car, headlights included. It was patterned after an actual car that had been driven from Russia to Monaco in 1911. Volkov had heard that a bottle of this high-end vodka had recently sold in America for $1.4 million. Dumbass Americans.

The owner of Russo-Baltique made no secret about the idea that this vodka was not to be consumed. It was to be handed down unopened from generation to generation, and it should be considered part of a family's art collection. Volkov chuckled at that idea as he enjoyed the flavor of the vodka and stared at his glass. What good is an unopened bottle of vodka?

CHAPTER 24

March 20
9:15 AM
The Oval Office

It was a beautiful spring day in Washington, D.C. Due to the above average temperatures of the previous weeks, the cherry blossoms were in full bloom. They typically did not get to this stage until the end of March or even the first week or two of April. Sam Clark had been the President of the United States for a full 73 days, and it still seemed like he was drinking from a fire hose. Detailed information about dozens of topics was fed to him daily by every department of the government. He was soaking up as much of it as he could, but Sam realized how important it was to have a good team surrounding him. He had one, and he was glad now that he had spent so much time agonizing over some of those decisions.

Today's meeting was an intelligence briefing. The amount and scope of the potential threats that existed in the world day after day was something that had shocked Sam, despite his time in the middle of much of it. Most Americans were aware that there were threats from terrorist groups. They also knew of the potential dangers of North Korea, or China, or Russia. If they knew, however, that the most significant source of danger for the average American citizen was this close to them, it would cause a mass panic. America's biggest threat, Sam had learned very early in his presidency, originated not in the sands of the Middle East, nor in the Kremlin, nor in Beijing. The biggest threat was right in front of them every day. It was a place known as the Internet.

Cyber warfare was the topic of this particular meeting. Clark was present, as was his chief of staff Patrick Welch, assistant CIA director Richard Roberts, and his national security advisor Tammy Leeds. Leeds was the presenter today, and Clark's goal was to better understand potential threats while also receiving an update on some existing operations.

Leeds began. "I would like to start with a brief history of the concept of cyber warfare, just for the sake of understanding where we are today."

Clark nodded affirmatively.

"The United States was using computers long before the average American citizen had any idea what they were. Military experts and those in Silicon Valley had imagined the concept of cyber warfare as far back as when some of today's members of Congress were no more than a glint in their fathers' eyes. The Pentagon began developing concepts in the 1960s to gain military advantages over other countries by disabling computer networks of other countries."

"The nineteen *sixties*?"

"Absolutely. The concept was in its infancy then, but the greatest minds of our time are always a quarter century to a half century ahead of the rest of us. As the idea developed, it became more mainstream. A 1993 RAND article made a prophetic statement. It said, 'we anticipate that cyber war may be to the 21st century what blitzkrieg was to the 20th century.'"

She continued. "That same year, the Air Force was the first to take steps to prepare for this paradigm shift. It changed the name of what had been known as the Electronic Warfare Center into the Air Force Information Warfare Center. By 1995, they had established the 609 Information Warfare Squadron. This, Mr. President, was the world's first cyber combat unit."

Clark nodded, indicating that he was following her so far.

Leeds continued. "The unit quickly proved that the best defense is a good offense, and this led to our first 'uh-oh' moment in 1997."

"What happened?"

"The military decided that we needed to find out how our systems would hold up once the rest of the world caught up to our hacking capabilities, or if someone sold out as a traitor. We needed to see where we stood. They held a cyber war game that was known as 'Eligible Receiver.' A team of NSA hackers went up against the cyber security system of the US Pacific Command in Hawaii."

"And?"

"No contest. The NSA won the exercise in such a startlingly easy fashion that cyber defense became a new line item in the military budget. It was the first wake up call to how vulnerable our own technology was making us. But Pandora's box was open. At that point, we were stuck trying to figure out how to contain the water from a broken water pipe in a drinking glass."

Clark was leaning forward in his chair. "This isn't very reassuring so far."

Leeds continued, not surprised by the reaction. It was the same for everyone the first time they heard the backstory.

"All of that is extremely old news, sir, but important to know, nonetheless. Here is where we stand presently. As you have read several times in the last few weeks in your PDB, we are continuing to monitor dozens of threats from all directions against our security systems. There is nothing new to report in that regard. Today, however, I want to update you on a matter regarding some irregularities in a few of our security systems as they relate to infrastructure."

"Very well," Clark replied. "Proceed."

"Let me talk a bit about the areas that are deemed to be 'critical infrastructure.' Those areas are broadly labeled under sixteen categories, which include the following: agriculture and food, banking and finance, chemical, commercial facilities, critical manufacturing, dams, defense industrial base, drinking water and water treatment systems, emergency services, energy, government facilities, information technology, nuclear reactors and waste, public health and health care, telecommunications, and transportation.

"We have cyber security teams for each of these areas of our infrastructure system, as well as an overarching comprehensive system that manages all of our cyber security. In our world, Mr. President, we live with certain realities. Most of the major countries of the world know and understand that we have the capability to get into each other's systems. It's just a fact of life in our world. Offense will always be ahead of defense. That said, the security systems we have in place do allow us to recognize breaches in real time and to deem the threat level of each. That is the crux of our meeting this morning."

Clark interjected at this point. "Just so I understand, this sounds eerily familiar. It sounds much like the MAD doctrine of the 1980s - Mutually Assured Destruction. Is that a fair comparison?"

"Absolutely, Mr. President," Leeds replied. "Because we all realize the damage that can be done through a major cyber attack, and because we realize that if attacked, we would be able to turn right around and equally cripple the guilty party, there is a general understanding among all of us - it's a standoff basically. Aside from that, a cyber weapon doesn't hit the ground and explode. It can be used again. If a digital weapon is used against us, we can pick it up and fire it right back at them."

"Regardless, I hate situations like this," Clark said with obvious frustration. "It only takes one idiot to start a catastrophic chain of events."

"Agreed, sir." Roberts chimed in at this point. "That is why we are on the offensive all of the time. The amount and breadth of our offensive capability is staggering. We have a vast roadmap of technologies on our shelves. We also have the ability to anticipate future technologies and to develop attack capabilities. On top of that, we own a plethora of the world's best hacking tools - viruses, worms, exploits, logic bombs...the works.

"As Tammy mentioned, the best cyber defense systems in the world are here. We have them. Unfortunately, they simply are not enough. That's why we also still have a great number of physical assets on the ground around the world. Those assets, in some cases, are our best defense. We have people infiltrated in every major government that we deem to be a threat, as well as within some organizations that we regard as potentially dangerous."

"Organizations?" Clark asked. "Like terrorist groups?"

"In some cases, Roberts replied. "In other cases, it is more like the black market. There are groups who produce cyber weapons for sale to the highest bidder. We know who most of them are, and we have people either in or close to those organizations. This is the hardest work because these groups are small and extremely secretive. It's not like finding your way into the Russian bureaucracy.

"Aside from that, the advantages of cyber combat over standard warfare are pretty obvious. In an era when all aspects of war are televised, including images of body bags and caskets, cyber warfare quickly became an alternative that the public could more easily tolerate. There are other advantages, as well. Although it takes a lot of time, effort, and money to conduct a cyber war, it is still exponentially cheaper than traditional warfare. There is also the alleviation of concerns about things like bases of deployment and being 'in range of specific targets."

Clark nodded while formulating what was probably an obvious question. "Are there drills we are running in preparation for something like this? Are we prepared if something were to happen?"

Leeds answered. "Yes, sir. We have exercises that simulate digital attacks against the sixteen areas of critical infrastructure that I mentioned earlier. They are known as CyberStorm exercises. They run for three full days, and it is a comprehensive training on everything from recognizing the source of the attack to funneling resources to the area of infrastructure that has been hit."

Clark nodded again. "Yes, I recall reading about those last summer during the campaign. Are they scheduled again for this summer?"

"No, sir. They are biennial. We won't have them again until next year."

This caught Clark off guard. "Do you think that is sufficient?"

Leeds bobbed her head back and forth as if trying to decide between yes and no. "There is not a perfect answer to that, sir. Could we benefit from more frequent training events? Absolutely. Would training annually, or even semi-annually be guaranteed to prevent a digital attack? No." Her tone was firm.

"I understand," Clark said, nodding. "Same thing with a military operation. Let me ask you a better question. Are we trained and prepared if something happens?"

"Without a doubt, sir, with one caveat."

"What would that be," Clark replied.

"A cyber weapon that we haven't seen before. Richard mentioned that we have the ability to anticipate future technologies. That is a vital piece to our cyber defense. However, I never say never. The field we are discussing is on the cutting edge of what is deemed to be cutting edge. If there is one person, one group, one government out there somewhere with a weapon that we haven't seen before, all bets are off. We can't train for a weapon that we aren't sure exists."

CHAPTER 25

April 19
National Assembly Building
Beijing, China

A small group of Chinese officials had gathered "off the record" to meet with an unnamed and unknown woman regarding a topic described only as top secret and valuable to the republic's national security. Chinese men, particularly those at this level of power, did not care a great deal for the idea of a woman among them, but they made an exception this time based on her reputation.

The site of the meeting was the National Assembly Building. The building was more than 100 years old and had been used by many different agencies throughout the 20th century. It was currently used by the Xinhua News Agency as a location for events and banquets. Day-to-day, however, it was not open to the public.

The group met in a relatively small office. Nobody took notes, and nothing was recorded in any way. The number of people who knew about this meeting or what was to be discussed could not get any bigger than the six people in the room at the present time. Others would be brought into the loop later.

The visitor took the floor and spoke to them via a translator. "Their power grid is made up of three regional grids that are all large and quite complicated. The grids are known as the Eastern grid, the Western grid, and the Texas Interconnection grid. Together, there are nearly 500,000 miles of power lines crisscrossing the country. And here's the thing – they are not government owned. They are owned and operated by individual utility companies - more than 3,000 of them."

One of the Chinese officials asked, "Wouldn't the fact that there are so many different owners of the lines mean that if we got inside one of the systems, the damage would be limited to the lines controlled by that particular utility company?"

"That's why you hired me." The woman smiled in a manner that was somewhere between sly and deranged. "Because there are markets for the buying and selling of power, many times the company with the winning bid to supply power has to route that power long distances to fulfill their contract. Many times, that can cover more than one state. To make a long story short, these long routes and the interconnectedness of some of the major players assures us that a well-planned, coordinated attack on several of these companies' systems could cause a chain effect of cascading power outages across significant portions of the country."

The woman clearly had their undivided attention, so she continued. "On top of that, in order to avoid having to infiltrate their entire grid to maximize damage, we have identified nine of the prime substations. If we shut down those nine substations, 80-90% of the citizens of the United States would be in total darkness."

"How bad would the damage be?"

"It's hard to tell," she replied, "but my best estimate would be somewhere between catastrophic and apocalyptic. The damage would be extremely difficult to repair, and those affected would be in the dark for weeks, possibly months."

Heads turned in the room as a table filled with some of the most powerful people in China reacted in a way that was almost giddy at the thought of bringing America to her knees. But one voice spoke in caution.

"Let us not forget that the Japanese thought they had broken America's spirit at Pearl Harbor, but they soon realized that they had done no more than wake a sleeping giant. What are the chances that we would be doing the same thing?"

The visitor did not reply at first. She simply stared at her questioner as if insulted by the notion of a counter argument. "I know you have been waging war your way for thousands of years. It is fine to have a traditional army, and a traditional way of thinking. In fact, I recommend it. But don't fool yourselves. We are the new army. You may not like what our army does or how it does it, but you still want an army."

She continued. "This is not World War Two America," she said in a monotone fashion. "Americans today are soft. They are weak. Other than their country of origin, they have absolutely nothing in common with the people the Japanese attacked. How long do you think the average American will last without power? A week?"

The woman laughed heartily at her own question. Then she stopped, and her face was serious again. "Some of them won't last 48 hours before they curl up into the fetal position."

CHAPTER 26

May 24
Capitol Hill
Senate Intelligence Committee

"As far back as 1997, people were issuing warnings that the country's power grid looked like Swiss cheese from a security perspective, with thousands of holes that made it vulnerable to attack."

Senator Ben Wilson felt as if he was banging his head against the wall. He had been shouting from the rooftops about the weakness of the American power grid for nearly a decade. Everyone seemed to agree with his points; nobody ever argued with him. However, when it came time to vote on funding measures, the heads that routinely nodded in agreement in meetings like this turned in another direction.

"There are nearly 3,000 power plants in the United States and nearly half a million plants producing either oil or natural gas. Another 200,000 are pumping the water that we drink. Only 15% of these are government controlled. The rest are all run by private corporations. In other words, the government cannot force these companies to maximize the security systems for their infrastructure. We are relying on each one of them to do it independently. The only industry that the government regulates is nuclear power.

"Between 2012 and 2019, the Department of Homeland Security performed random evaluations on the systems at 100 sites across the country. The assessment included plants in multiple industries - everything from water to electric to oil and gas. They found more than 38,000 vulnerabilities in those systems.

"The number of ways to breach our systems is endless, whether it be utilities, government, national security, you name it. One of the most recent advancements that is easily able to be hacked is the "smart utilities" concept. Companies have been installing 'smart meters' in American homes by the tens of thousands over the past several years. Technology is rapidly outpacing security. The amount of money being spent on new technology dwarfs the amount being spent to protect that technology. The government has invested *billions* of dollars into the smart grid program without the first concern about whether or not they are putting all of us in harm's way by not securing the grid."

"Thank you, Mr. Wilson," replied Darren Hatfield, the committee chair. "We will take that into consideration as we move forward toward completion of our appropriation bill."

Wilson was tired of fighting. He had shouted and made scenes in meetings like this before, and it seemed as if the room was waiting for something dramatic from him. Instead, he leaned back in his chair and began planning his next foray into the abyss known as government bureaucracy.

CHAPTER 27

June 26
8:20 AM
The Oval Office

"God, the Father of mercies, through the death and resurrection of his Son has reconciled the world to himself and sent the Holy Spirit among us for the forgiveness of sins; through the ministry of the Church may God give you pardon and peace, and I absolve you from your sins in the name of the Father, and of the Son, and of the Holy Spirit." The priest made a cross in the air with his hands as he said the words of absolution.

"Amen," Sam said as he made the sign of the cross. Father Jerry smiled as he removed his stole and leaned back in the chair.

"I didn't realize my sins were so amusing," Sam said with a smile.

"Just the opposite," the priest replied. "I was just remembering back to your younger days. You thought you had some real dilemmas back then, as most people do in their day-to-day lives. I bet you would like to have some of those 'simple' problems now."

Sam got up and walked across the room to the window behind his desk. "No kidding."

Father Jerry realized the amount of value Sam placed in his counsel. He had already decided that his role as the confessor to Sam Clark, the President of the United States, should be no different than his role as confessor to Sam Clark, ordinary Joe. In fact, when Sam had tried to tell the priest that he did not need to call him Mr. President, Father Jerry laid out his personal guidelines on the matter. When the conversation was casual, he would call Sam Mr. President. When it was in the spiritual realm, and Father Jerry was speaking to him as shepherd to sheep, he would refer to him as Sam.

"Are you going to Mass, Sam?" The priest let the question hang in the air.

Sam turned around. "Occasionally," he replied. One of the things that Sam had learned during his fast rise in politics was the value of carefully crafted language. "Occasionally" was a word that was vague enough that it could mean a lot of different things, including "seldom" or "hardly ever." But during 41 years of service as a Catholic priest, Father Jerry had heard every angle.

"There is strength in numbers, Sam. Don't abandon your responsibility as a member of the Body of Christ. Nobody flies solo in the Catholic Church." He looked directly at Sam. "Nobody." He let that lone word settle in. In other words, not even the President. "I'm not going to pretend to understand your schedule and the limited amount of time you have available for things outside of your direct job description," Father Jerry said earnestly. "However, I am also not going to believe that 'occasionally' is the best that you can do. You need the nourishment of the Eucharist as much as anyone. It will strengthen you spiritually, which will in turn strengthen you in every other aspect of your life. Don't move Jesus down your priority list, Sam."

A wave of Catholic guilt swept over Sam, and it made him uncomfortable. However, deep down inside, Sam knew that was why he had called Father Jerry in the first place.

"Let me tell you a story." Father Jerry saw that his message had reached that place in Sam for which he was aiming, and there was no need to press him any further on the subject. He decided to close his visit with something less direct. Sam came back and sat in the chair across from the priest. Once Sam had settled into the chair, the priest began.

"A member of a certain parish, who had always attended Mass regularly, stopped going. After a few weeks, the parish priest decided to visit him. It was a chilly evening. The priest found the man at home, alone, sitting in front of a blazing fire. Guessing the reason for the priest's visit, the man welcomed him, led him to a big chair near the fireplace, and waited. The priest made himself comfortable but said nothing. For a while, the two men sat in silence, watching the flames dance around the burning logs.

"After a couple of minutes, the priest got up from his chair, took the fire tongs, carefully picked up a brightly burning ember and placed it on one side of the hearth all alone. Then he sat back in his chair, still having uttered not a single word. The host watched all of this quietly.

"As the one lone ember's flame diminished, there was a momentary glow and then its fire slowly faded away. Soon it was cold and dead. Even now, not a word had been spoken since the initial greeting. Just before the priest was ready to leave, he picked up the cold, dead ember and placed it back in the middle of the fire. Immediately, it began to glow once more with the light and warmth of the burning coals around it.

As the priest reached the door to leave, his host said, 'Thank you so much for the visit, Father. I'll see you Sunday.'"

Sam smiled, and then broke into a laugh. "Okay, I give. Mea culpa."

"Good, then." Father Jerry rose from his chair and headed toward the door. Sam walked with him, and the two men embraced.

"Thank you, Father Jerry," Sam said sincerely.

The priest pulled away from the embrace and looked Sam directly in the eyes. "You're welcome, Mr. President. I will keep you in my prayers."

CHAPTER 28

July 4
The Kremlin
Moscow, Russia

"Come in, Yuri."

George did not like face-to-face meetings with Nikolai Volkov. Although the Russian President was in a continuing state of failing health, he was still an intimidating figure. Aside from that, George knew that he would only be called into a meeting like this for one of two reasons - he was either going to be screamed at for a perceived misstep, or he was going to be asked to do something extremely dangerous. He wasn't sure which one to hope for.

"Yuri, we need you to do something for us."

Somehow, the thought of risking his life seemed like the less dangerous of the two options. George sighed in relief.

Volkov continued. "We need you to go to Canada. The work you are doing in Belgium has gotten the ball rolling. We need you to make one more trip there before we send you to Canada. Two of our contacts inside the Canadian government feel that the Prime Minister there could be persuaded to reduce the amount of oil exported to the United States by 10% in return for us paying a 12% premium on the oil they provide to Russia."

"And my job is to simply be the 'agent' for this deal?"

"That is correct, Yuri." Volkov leaned back in his chair. "If we close this deal, the United States will lose nearly 40% of its oil imports. They will lean on Saudi Arabia to replace some of that, but my Saudi friends are greedy savages, and they will immediately claim a shortage and make the Americans pay an even higher premium than we are paying. The combination of the sudden shortage and the steep price increase will send their financial sector into turmoil."

"How are we going to be able to pay such a premium? Will it not put our country's finances in peril?"

"Yuri, Yuri. How about you worry about your job, and I'll take care of the rest." Volkov did not want to mention his recent negotiations with the Chinese. Yuri would not understand anyway. But if all went as planned, they could destroy the capitalists without Mother Russia even having to use its military.

"When do I leave?" George asked.

"In an hour. We're putting our faith in you, Yuri."

"I won't let you down." George had never felt a stronger sense of national pride, even though he had not lived in Russia since he was a teenager.

"And do you want to know the best part, Yuri?"

"Absolutely," he replied.

"Here we are, putting this plan in motion on their Independence Day. It is poetic justice, Yuri, because by the end of this year, they will be anything but independent."

CHAPTER 29

July 23
Air Force One

Sam Clark was on the last leg of a seven-day foreign policy trip, and he finally had some down time. He grabbed a 44-page briefing memo on the current status of the American nuclear arsenal. Clark was aware of the nuclear triad, which was the ability for the United States to launch nuclear missiles from land, air, or sea. The goal of the triad was to avoid America's nuclear arsenal being destroyed by a pre-emptive attack. Clark had a pretty good understanding of both the land-based and air-based missile capabilities. Today he was reading about the Navy's Ohio-class submarines.

Clark had learned that the United States Navy had a total of eighteen Ohio-class submarines. Fourteen of them were ballistic missile (Trident) submarines, and the other four were cruise missile subs. The fourteen Trident submarines carried about half of the country's active nuclear warheads. The missiles did not have predestined targets, but they can be assigned targets quickly by US Strategic Command in Nebraska, using secure and constant radio communication links, including very low frequency systems.

Clark also learned that the Ohio-class submarines carried Trident C-4 missiles with up to eight 100 kiloton nuclear warheads each, with a range of 4,600 miles. The sub's top operating speed was 20 knots. Starting in 1990, the United States began transitioning from C-4 to D-5 missiles. The D-5 missiles had a range of nearly 7,500 miles. That allowed them the capability to strike any point in the former Soviet Union from the submarine base at King's Bay, Georgia.

The terms of the START II treaty at the end of the Cold War included provisions for the reduction in the number of Trident submarines from eighteen to fourteen. The 2010 New START treaty limited the number of D-5s deployed at any one time to 240 missiles. Regardless, both Russia and the United States maintained a strong enough arsenal to destroy each other several times over. After reading for a few more minutes about Russia's nuclear capabilities, Clark removed his glasses and squeezed the bridge of his nose between his eyes, trying to relieve the dull headache he frequently felt when trying to read while he was already tired.

He walked over to the couch and decided to take a cat nap before they landed. If he fell asleep quickly, he could get fifteen to twenty quality minutes of rest. Such were the sleeping habits, or lack thereof, of an American President.

CHAPTER 30

August 3
Las Vegas, Nevada

'Fred' pulled the arm on the slot machine one last time. Again, he was unsuccessful. Fred loved Las Vegas, where you could get off your plane and start gambling *immediately,* using the slot machines located in the airport. He especially loved flying in at night. He would purposely get a window seat, because even after coming to Vegas every year for more than a decade, he was still fascinated by looking out the window into pitch blackness until a tiny glow appeared in the distance. Then the glow became brighter, and soon he could see that one big patch of bright lights. It was Las Vegas, surrounded in all directions by darkness - there was something metaphoric about it. Vegas, baby.

Fred had been making the annual trip to Vegas for 11 years. He was here to take part in the annual CYCO Convention - one of the largest hacking conferences in the world. It dated all the way back to 1993, about the same time that the internet came on the scene for those outside the government. When the convention started in 1993, many people had become newly aware of hackers because of the movie *War Games,* where a teenager, played by Matthew Broderick, hacks into the government's most sensitive systems, and nearly starts a nuclear war.

It was a unique setting in that the conference had, as attendees, all kinds of people. On one hand, some of the most legitimate professionals in the world were there - employees of the top computer and security firms, along with attorneys, journalists, researchers, and federal employees. You could also find students in attendance, along with those who just had a general interest in software and hardware applications, and their cutting-edge functions. The future could be found here, along with those trying to learn about it in order to protect it. Many people came to watch the Wargames and other competitions among those in the hacking community.

The unspoken truth, however, was that CYCO was also the home of the underbelly of the hacking world. There were those among the crowd who were there to try to figure out how to do harm to the very systems being touted. The best of the best were usually not present at the conference, simply because most of them were on 'wanted' lists by governments around the world. But Fred relished the challenge and felt sure that nobody would recognize him, due to his well-planned disguise.

Fred was what the business world would call an independent contractor. He sold himself to the highest bidder for his elite status in the 'community of hackers,' and he demanded top dollar because, as he described himself to potential clients, he had absolutely no moral compass. At the ripe old age of 32, Fred had differentiated himself from the rest of the 'code warriors' (he *hated* that phrase) by adding excellent social skills to his knowledge base. He understood most of the people in his line of work may be excellent at the work, but they could not put two sentences together in a conversation, and they usually could not hold eye contact for more than two or three seconds. They did not have the people skills, nor the confidence, to do what he did, and that increased his value even more.

Fred considered himself nothing more than a disenfranchised citizen of the United States. He held no hatred toward his country, but he also held no loyalty. As the old saying went, love and hate are not opposites. Indifference is the opposite of love. That is where Fred stood. He could not possibly care less about the country. It was just a residence for him, although he did like the fact that the government seemed to get in its own way while trying to protect its operating systems, by allowing people such a strong right to privacy.

Fred became aware very early that there were people, organizations, and even governments, who would look for high school and/or college dropouts that were extremely sophisticated in their hacking skills. It also helped if they were anti-government. Again, Fred wasn't necessarily anti-government, but he liked the idea that his skills were marketable, particularly since he had been bored with the ignorance of the country's school curriculum since approximately the third grade.

By the time he was eleven, Fred was hacking into local utility companies, and by thirteen, he had worked his way into the state government's system. Fred laughed at the idea that a teenager could take advantage of weaknesses and vulnerabilities in these systems that were entirely unknown to both the creators of the system, as well as those who maintained it on a day-to-day basis. "Who pays these people?" he had frequently wondered.

He was here today as Fred Fleming, or as he referred to this particular alias, nerd #7. Fred realized early in the process that not only could he not use his real name, but that each alias needed to 'exist' in a manner that would never raise an eyebrow. He made sure of that on a regular basis with innocent day-to-day transactions in each name.

Meanwhile, he would also do business in many other names. Getting a new identity was not nearly as difficult as maintaining it, particularly if you had multiple identities. All it took was using information from an obituary to apply for a certified copy of the birth certificate that 'you' had lost. That information could then be used to obtain driver's licenses and other forms of identification needed to establish a residence.

Having multiple names meant multiple addresses, phone numbers, and many other aspects of day-to-day life. Maintaining those also meant consistently using credit cards and bank accounts. In addition, he had to use those accounts periodically at restaurants, malls, grocery stores, and the occasional hotel in order to establish and keep a paper trail, particularly from a financial perspective.

So now, here he was, king of the world in his early 30s, wandering the floor of CYCO to see if there was something new out there that might offer him a challenge. If no challenge presented itself, he would just 'people watch.' He had gotten quite good at determining who was from the business world, who was from the government, and who was representing the military industrial complex. He felt bad for the government folks. They were *so* late to the party. They had finally stopped with their 1950s version of recruiting and had come around to the idea that if they were going to hire people who had any chance of protecting government systems from hackers, they had to be willing to accept people with tattoos and body piercings. They had also learned to shrug off a hacker's past transgressions, sometimes even big ones, if they were good enough. Fred smiled. It did not matter. They were still not going to get anyone nearly as good as him. After all, how many people in his line of work could have walked into a room full of China's most powerful people and dominate the room like 'he' had done back in April?

CHAPTER 31

August 19
United Nations
New York City

President Sam Clark stepped to the podium. This would be his first address to the United Nations. Several painstaking meetings had taken place to prepare him for this speech. Those meetings included a considerable amount of disagreement over how to address the representatives of the member nations. Clark understood that a certain level of diplomacy was expected, and called for, but he also had no intention of dodging the elephant in the room, which was the disproportionate number of resources the United States provided to this organization for its equal membership.

Clark felt there was some middle ground between the most radical positions expressed by Vice-President Charles Sullivan – 'We should withdraw from this damn organization and see what it looks like then!' and Secretary of State Vance Harrison – 'Mr. President, I urge you not to rock the boat in your first address to the UN. Let's stay the course for now and seek reforms in the coming years.'

Clark looked out at the members and spoke. "Good morning. First, I would like to welcome all of you back to the United States, and I hope your arrival included safe travel from your home countries." Secretary of State Harrison had pleaded for Clark to exclude this opening line because it was too inflammatory. Clark replied that if welcoming the UN members to the country was inflammatory, then he knew even less about foreign diplomacy than he claimed to know, which wasn't much. Clark acknowledged to himself, even if he did not say it out loud, that he did indeed recognize the jab at the UN representatives – I am welcoming you to my country, which not only pays well more than its fair share of the cost to run this organization, but also provides its headquarters and all the costs that go with that.

Clark continued with his introductory remarks, including comments about being a new president and looking forward to continuing the long-standing leadership role the United States had played within the organization. He briefly touched on fundamental facts about the history and founding of the organization, including the United States serving as a charter member and its role as one of five permanent members of the UN Security Council. Clark could feel the eyes rolling in the room due to the elementary nature of his opening remarks, but in his mind, he knew he was laying the groundwork for what was still to come.

Clark paused as he prepared for his transition into the remarks that were sure to cause some uncomfortable shifting in seats. "Ladies and gentlemen, I know you are aware of the history of this organization. These facts are well known in most circles, even outside of the realm of the UN. Some of the numbers that I am about to review, however, are lesser known but equally important, at least to the people here in my country."

The squirming began even earlier than Clark had expected. They knew what was coming. "I just want to make sure you and the leadership of the countries that you represent are fully aware of the amount of sacrifice my country puts forth on behalf of this organization. We expect to lead, and we always have, but we also need to express the growing level of concern we have about the current system. Our country fought for its independence based partially on the protest regarding 'taxation without representation.' We now find ourselves, within the UN, in a situation of 'expectation without appreciation.'

Clark paused there and glanced around the room. He saw what he expected, which was a look of deep concern from many of the representatives whose countries paid practically nothing for their participation in this organization, nor for the benefits they received from it. He also saw some clinched jaws from those who represented the countries to whom this address was intended.

"These are the numbers that I have to justify to Congress, which is becoming increasingly difficult. Currently, there are 193 countries that are members of the United Nations. In recent years, the system used for calculating countries' 'fair share' payments has shifted dramatically. In order to fund the regular budget, the United States is now asked to pay 22% of the overall cost. That is more than the *combined* dollar amount contributed by 176 other member countries. The peacekeeping budget is even more lopsided. We pay 28% of that budget, which represents more than the combined dollar amount of 185 member countries." Clark paused before adding, "I remind you, there are only 193 countries in this entire organization."

Clark removed his reading glasses as a point of emphasis. "The combined amount of the regular budget and the peacekeeping budget for this organization is just over $13 billion. Thirty-five countries currently pay the minimum amount per the UN contribution guidelines. That amount is approximately $30,000 in US dollars. As I mentioned, my country contributes heavily to both the regular budget and the peacekeeping budget. Aside from that, we pay several billion annually as the host country. Our total annual contribution to this organization is approximately $8 billion. It's no secret that the United States is more than $20 *trillion* in debt. Based on that, I think we may need to revisit the concept of 'fair share.'"

Clark closed with an olive branch. "I don't want you to see this as an attack on this organization. Today's speech is part of my platform of attempting to control our spending across the board. The UN is just one piece of that very large puzzle, but it is a significant piece. In closing, I want to strongly recommend that we quickly begin working on a new model for the budget of this much-needed organization, with the understanding that we cannot continue to function the way things are presently structured."

CHAPTER 32

August 28
Hotel Campanile
Brussels, Belgium

Before George headed for Canada, he made a quick overnight trip to Brussels to see Elaine. Since they both had to catch early flights the next morning, George got them a room close to the airport so he could spend every possible minute with her before he headed to Canada. It would probably be months before their paths would cross again.

Elaine was dressed in her red silk pajamas that matched the color of the toes on her bare feet. George was preparing to shower. Of course, he had invited her to join him, but she said she preferred to wait for the room service they had ordered so she could have some wine. As soon as he closed the door, she grabbed his laptop and put it on the desk. She turned on the power, then went to the dresser and took the 128GB micro flash drive from her jeans pocket and inserted it.

It had taken Elaine only two short windows of time like this one to guess George's password. He seemed much too arrogant and lazy to use something difficult. George was predictable in nearly every way. Elaine had first tried all his family members' names with all the commonly used numeric combinations at the end. Then it hit her. He loved his cat more than anyone in his family. Elaine remained shocked at how many people used their pet's name followed by 123. In George's case, it was only slightly more sophisticated. Kitty1234. Really?

She smiled slightly as she remembered how easy it had been to hack George.

Elaine thought back to her training in this regard, and how easy most people made it to hack into their information. If people only realized that by adding a capital letter and an additional number to their password, the time to hack it goes up to two hours, although that is still relatively simple for a professional hacker. If they turned it into a phrase, it would be longer but still easy to remember. By simply adding 'MyDog' or 'MyCat' to the beginning, it would now take a hacker approximately three years to hack it. If they were to add a special character to the password, the time to hack it would be increased exponentially. If the password contained upper and lowercase letters, numbers, and a special character, it could hypothetically take up to 100 years to crack it. And, finally, if they were to simply double it (type it twice), it would make it as secure as possible.

Elaine quickly brought up the files she was trying to copy. The good news about George was that everything he owned was top of the line, so his computer was fast. 30 seconds, one minute, 90 seconds. In less than two minutes, the entire folder had been copied to the flash drive. Elaine removed the drive. She wanted to put it in the safe, but she knew George had put his handgun in there. She had decided to put the flash drive inside a false sleeve in her jacket. It wasn't the most secure place in the world, but it would have to do until she could get the drive to her source.

Elaine had time to spare before George emerged from the bathroom. He sat down and began to get dressed.

"What are you doing?" Elaine asked.

"The safe is too small for my laptop, and I don't want to leave it in here overnight. I know it's stupid, but I'm paranoid. I'm going to put it in my trunk. If anyone lays a single finger on my car, my alarm system will wake up the entire city."

George grabbed his keys and the laptop and told Elaine that he was also going to buy some antacids at the gas station across the street while he was out. Then he winked at her and told her to be ready when he got back.

Elaine smiled her best fake smile and agreed that she would indeed be ready.

George had been gone less than a minute when there was a knock on the door. Elaine warily approached the door and looked through the peephole. A woman was standing there. Elaine opened the door as far as the chain would allow.

"May I help you?" she asked.

"I am in the room next door and have locked myself out. I was wondering if I could use your phone to call the front desk. I don't want to go down there dressed like this."

Elaine was trained to observe her surroundings accurately and quickly. The woman was about 5′5″ with shoulder-length brown hair and little makeup. She looked much like Elaine with the pajamas and bare feet. Her look matched her story. But Elaine was an experienced field agent, and her guard was up. Something didn't seem right about this.

"Wait here. I'll call downstairs and have someone come up with a key."

As Elaine was closing the door, she was jolted back as the door hit her and the chain broke. As she was falling to the ground, she looked up to see that the woman in the hall had broken the chain when she burst through the door. Elaine was scrambling to get up when the woman tackled her back to the floor.

The two women struggled on the carpet momentarily until the intruder slipped behind Elaine and forced her onto her stomach. She twisted Elaine's left arm behind her back and applied upward pressure. With her other hand, she grabbed a handful of Elaine's hair and pulled her to her feet. She turned Elaine and slammed her face first into the wall.

"Where is the flash drive, bitch?"

The moment the door had knocked her down, Elaine realized this was about the flash drive, but now she knew for sure.

"Where is it?" The woman was screaming in Elaine's ear as she had her face pinned against the wall. She forced Elaine's arm up further and slammed her face against the wall again. Elaine screamed.

Elaine raised her left foot and slammed it down behind her. Fortunately, she hit the target, with her heel landing right on the intruder's toes. The woman released Elaine's arm from behind her back and Elaine elbowed her in the stomach. The intruder doubled over holding her stomach, and Elaine put a shoulder into her and ran her back into the hall and against the opposite wall. She heard the woman gasp for breath, and she turned and ran back into the room.

Again, she attempted to close the door, but the woman ran across the hall and stopped it before she could get it all the way closed. Both women were pushing the door with all they had, but Elaine felt her feet slipping. She finally realized she was not going to get the door closed, so she let it go and the woman lunged through and fell to the floor on her hands and knees.

Elaine saw the opportunity and came with a hard kick that she hoped to land under the woman's chin. She was not quick enough, however, and the woman grabbed her foot. She yanked hard and Elaine fell on her back, knocking the breath out of her.

The woman ran past Elaine and went straight to her jeans in the dresser. She began going through the pockets frantically. Finding nothing, she began pulling the drawers out and throwing clothes around the room. She was tackled to the ground by Elaine. The two women rolled around on the carpet, but the intruder was stronger and eventually got on top of Elaine, straddling her and punching her in the face three times before getting up and running for the door. She realized she had already been in there too long, and a lot of noise had been made. She had to get out.

Elaine was able to get a foot up and just barely trip the woman. She fell but got up quickly. She was at the door when Elaine jumped on her from behind and the two women slammed into the door together. They fell backward onto the floor, with the woman lying on her back on top of Elaine. She threw her head backward into Elaine's nose. Elaine screamed, but she held onto her as the intruder got to her feet. The woman pushed Elaine away and before Elaine could regain her balance, the intruder followed with a roundhouse kick. Elaine felt the woman's bare foot hit hard against the side of her face. She fell backward, and she flipped over the corner of the bed. Then the room went dark.

"Elaine! Elaine!" George was shaking her by the shoulders.

Elaine looked up groggily and tried to sift through the fog.

"What happened?" he asked desperately.

Elaine thought quickly about how much George really needed to know. She feigned incoherence, although she could feel the swelling on her face and realized she probably *looked* like someone who would be incoherent.

"I'm calling the police!" George walked toward the phone.

"No!" she shouted quickly. "Don't do that."

"Why not? You've been assaulted! Who did this?"

Elaine was ready to respond this time. "Some guy in a mask. He knocked me around and started rummaging through the drawers. Please, George, don't call the police." She was back on her game at this point. "The guy reeked of alcohol. He was probably high and just looking for some quick cash. If I file a police report, I'll have to miss my flight tomorrow, and I have to be back at work Monday morning."

"Are you sure?" He sounded as if he was relieved that he didn't have to go through the process.

"Yes, I'm positive. I'm just going to take some ibuprofen and try to get some sleep. I know the chain is broken but will you please make sure the door will still lock?"

George walked over and tested it. "The lock on the door itself still works fine. I'm going to put my gun on the nightstand just in case. I'm sure glad it was in the safe. And he didn't get my laptop either."

Elaine rolled her eyes as she took the ibuprofen, not at all bothered by the fact that George was much less concerned about her than he was about his belongings. That's okay, she thought to herself. The feeling is mutual.

Elaine felt grateful for one thing. If she looked anything like she felt, at least she had an excuse to spurn his heavy-handed advances. She was thinking about taking a hot bath. She needed one, and she could also use it as a stalling tactic. However, before she had a chance to mention it to George, she heard him snoring.

The next day, Elaine kissed George goodbye and promised to call when she was coming back to Brussels. She hailed a cab and George told the driver to take her to the airport. Once the driver pulled away from the curb, Elaine asked him to take her to Duden Park instead. Upon arrival, Elaine made her way to the designated location and sat down next to her contact, known to her by the alias Tommy, on the park bench.

"Holy shit!" Tommy said as he looked at Elaine's black eye and puffy lip. The sunglasses covered most of the shiner, but the damage was still noticeable. Her nose didn't look as bad but hurt worse. "What the hell happened? That fat son of a bitch didn't do this, did he?"

"Of course not," she replied. "I would kick his ass. I had an 'altercation' last night in my hotel room, but it wasn't with George. It was with a woman who caught me with my guard down and broke into the room. It's been a while since I've been in a scrape like that, and it's been *quite* a while since I lost one."

Elaine went on to tell him about the night's events. She described the woman to him.

"What was her nationality?" he asked.

"She was Caucasian," Elaine answered. "In fact, she had an American accent. After lunkhead fell asleep, I searched the room. She knew that I had pulled the flash drive out of my jeans before I copied the files because she ran straight to them looking for it. But she didn't see me put it in the sleeve of my jacket after I copied them. I started looking around, and sure enough, there was a tiny hole right beside the corner of the frame of a picture hanging on the wall. She could see most of the room, but not the closet by the bathroom, which is why she didn't know where I put the drive. Somehow, this woman knew we would be there, so she obviously knows considerably more about me than I do about her. But not for long."

"Why is that?" Tommy asked.

"Along with the flash drive, you'll also find inside there a small bag with a few of her hairs inside. She was clearly not wearing a wig. You can see the roots." Elaine smiled painfully. "I need you to run her DNA so I can track this bitch down and see who she is working for."

"How about you let me send someone else after her once we discover her identity?"

"No way." Elaine's response was determined. "This circle doesn't need to get any bigger than it is. Don't worry. I can handle her. She won't catch me off guard next time."

CHAPTER 33

September 2
Cabinet Room
1:35 PM

"As all of you know, this meeting was purposely set two weeks out from my speech to the UN, so that we could all have some time to absorb it from our own perspectives." Sam Clark looked around the room. "As I mentioned during the speech, and as you are all aware, it was indeed a primary goal of my platform to reduce spending in a real, but non-Draconian manner. The UN is not exempt from that pledge. Thoughts?"

The first person to speak was UN Ambassador Keith Keough. Keough was a rising star. He was a 42-year-old African American, who was also the first person in his family to graduate from college. That was followed with a degree from Harvard Law, where he was soon recognized for his stellar mind, excellent debate skills, and calm demeanor. His future was bright, and he was not afraid to speak his mind.

"Mr. President, as you know, the speech was not received well by the member nations. I also know that this was to be fully expected. That said, it was consistent with the groundwork I had laid in my first few months at the UN, so it should not have come as a surprise to anyone."

Secretary of State Vance Harrison was the next to speak. "I don't think the substance of the speech came as a surprise, but I think the tone and the condescension caught everyone off guard."

Clark turned toward Harrison. Condescension? He had purposely tried to avoid sounding condescending, but maybe he had failed. Clark was going to address that, but Charles Sullivan beat him to the draw.

"It's about damn time someone drew a line in the sand! For decades, we have been 'diplomatic,' (Sullivan said the word with sarcasm) and all that has gotten us is an increasing amount of financial obligation with nothing to show for it."

Clark interrupted. "Wait a minute. Let's go back to the idea of my tone being condescending. I know there are reports of that in the media, but in this room, just a quick show of hands, who thought I sounded condescending?"

Of the eight people in the room, four raised their hands.

Clark nodded. "Okay then," he said. "Let's chalk that up as a teaching moment. I will work on that."

Vance Harrison jumped back in. "But the horse is out of the barn, Mr. President. Nobody plays the 'How dare you' card better than the diplomatic core. It's a universal skill in my line of work. We have to find a way to make nice with these people."

Before Charles Sullivan had a chance to erupt, Ambassador Keough spoke. "Let me work on that, Vance. I plan to make the rounds and have one-on-ones with as many people as possible. While doing that, however, I am going to point out a few things. First and foremost, I will remind them about the PTF. For those of you who may not be familiar, the UN itself created the Procurement Task Force in response to the constant and legitimate claims that the UN was becoming corrupt. The PTF did indeed uncover corruption, as well as waste and even fraud. Not surprisingly, less than two years later, the PTF was eliminated as requested by the countries accused of those wrongdoings. There has not been an investigation of the UN since then.

"Second," Keogh continued, "I will point out that UN employees enjoy salaries that are approximately 1/3 higher than American civil servants doing similar work with an equivalent job title. Beyond that, I will speak to the fact that as long as the system is one country, one vote, we are going to demand better 'fair share' statistics than one country paying the share for approximately 40 countries. Those 40 countries are not going to vote against the current system. Why would they? We are going to have to find a different way to improve this system. That is my focus during my time at the UN."

Harrison, and a couple of others in the room, thought this was entirely too forceful of an approach for this matter. That was just not how the UN functioned. But they knew they were outnumbered, so they let the matter pass with the understanding that both Keough and Clark would make a concerted effort to work on their tone, if not on the substance.

CHAPTER 34

September 5
White House
Presidential Residence
10:35 PM

Labor Day was just another day for the President of the United States. Cookouts and trips to the lake were a thing of the past. During particularly long days, Sam relished the fact that they were also a thing of the future. They just were not a thing of the present. He looked forward to those days of leisure, when he could reunite with family and friends. But, back to reality, he reminded himself. This was still year one.

Sam had started the day with a morning speech to the AFL-CIO in a gesture to thank the labor movement for their long and proud history of representing the American worker. From there, it was lunch with some of the union chiefs, and then back to the White House for briefings the rest of the afternoon.

Sam really felt like he was up to speed on China, so tonight's foreign policy memos were Russia-based. What a history these two nations had in the last century! There were two World Wars that they won together before the sea change occurred. Sam found the history of the Cold War utterly fascinating. From the roles of Reagan to Gorbachev to Lech Walesa to Pope John Paul II, the cast of characters matched the story, if this had been meant to be a great novel. In this case, however, history was better than fiction.

After the fall of the Soviet Union, Russia fell on hard times. It reminded Sam of his meeting with Jim Graham and the discussion of China's century of humiliation. Although Russia had not struggled nearly that long, it had taken the government and its citizens a substantial amount of time to get back on its collective feet. But now that it had, Sam was seeing signs that made him wonder if some Russian leaders may have also had visions of retaliation in their minds. Many of the 'apparatchiks' from the Soviet days were still living, and although most were not in current elected positions, they still wielded plenty of influence. Another group that Sam was concerned about was former KGB agents, many of whom were young men when the Soviet Union fell, and they were now at the peak of their power.

Russia was not nearly as blatant with some of their aggressive actions as China. They were, however, extremely untrustworthy in Sam's opinion. He made sure plenty of eyes were always on the Russians.

CHAPTER 35

September 18
9:55 AM
Oval Office

Rain had been falling most of the day in Washington, D.C. Sam Clark had been planning to watch the Cubs and Nationals on TV later, as it was a relatively slow day. It appeared, however, that Mother Nature was going to wreak havoc with those intentions.

Tammy Leeds sat down across from Clark and Patrick Welch for their previously scheduled briefing and to review some items on the PDB. The meeting was relatively straightforward, but as the president removed his glasses, and he and his chief of staff closed their folders, Leeds held out her hand as if to stop them.

"One more thing, Mr. President."

"Sure, Tammy," Clark replied. "What is it?"

"We just got our hands on this earlier this morning, so we are still working out some of the details. However, I wanted to make sure this is on your radar."

Clark put his glasses back on. "Okay," he said inquisitively.

"We have an operative in Brussels who has been working a Russian businessman that we have had our eyes on for a couple of years. She has managed to get cozy with him, and during a recent encounter, she managed to copy some files from his laptop."

Clark leaned forward. Leeds continued.

"Among his files was some highly technical data regarding cracking sophisticated layers of encryption. This is not the type of thing a businessman would need. Frankly, there is no kind of businessman who would really have a clue as to what these files mean. Aside from that, we found some background information on NORAD. We are continuing to delve deeper into these files, Mr. President, but it appears that our Russian friends may be trying to get into our defense systems at NORAD. If that is the case, it is probably not the only system they are trying to hack into."

"You seem a bit flippant about this, Tammy. Is it not a major concern?"

"Not yet, sir. We come across information like this periodically. However, we do not usually find it on someone's laptop. It seems to lack sophistication. NORAD has been informed, and we have run through the standard protocols for when such information is discovered. All in all, Mr. President, it would typically be no more than a bullet point in your PDB, except for one detail."

"What is that?"

"The operative had little trouble accessing the files, but after she made the copy, she was confronted and attacked by someone who knew what she was doing and tried to get the flash drive from her. She had been watching from an adjoining room. She did not get any information, but the idea that someone was watching our person, who is one of our best, without her knowing…it is intriguing to say the least."

Welch interjected. "What is being done about that part?"

"We are looking into it, but we do not have anything solid yet. I will keep you posted."

"Excellent," Clark replied, removing his glasses again. "Anything else?"

"No, sir. Thank you, Mr. President."

Leeds left the room. Clark looked at Welch.

"What do you think about that? Something seems out of the ordinary there."

"Agreed," Welch replied. "I'll stay on top of it."

CHAPTER 36

October 13
Hamburg, Germany
Moenckebergstrasse shopping district

Elaine met Tommy at a coffee shop on the outskirts of the Moenckebergstrasse. She loved Germany, and this street was one of the few places in the world where she allowed herself to enjoy such creature comforts as shopping and drinking coffee at a table on the sidewalk. It was a beautiful autumn day. The air was warm, and the bright sunshine felt good on Elaine's shoulders.

As Tommy approached her table, she was brought back to the reality of the world in which she lived. One minute she could almost live like a typical woman, the next she would be discussing people and events that could endanger the world with a man that she knew very well but did not know his real name - nor did she want to know it.

"What have you got?" she asked as he sat down.

"Nice to see you, too," he replied with a smile.

Elaine couldn't help but think the same thought she did nearly every time she was with Tommy. If circumstances were different…

"We've got a hit on the woman who ruined your last night with George." George was the only one in this three-person inner circle who did not realize that when he and Elaine parted ways on the curb as she got into the cab in Brussels, he would never see her again. She had his files, which was *all* she had ever wanted from him.

He smiled again as he took a sip of coffee while Elaine laughed at the comment about her 'George duties,' as she had called them. What a woman will do for her country.

"This woman has more aliases than I have ties in my closet, but it appears that her real name is Amanda Curtis."

Elaine stopped as she was lifting the hot cup toward her lips. "That's a very American-sounding name."

"That's because she is indeed one of us. Whiz kid, scored a perfect 2400 on her SAT. Only one out of every 5,000 people who take the SAT gets a perfect score. She got a full scholarship to Georgia Tech, where she was kicked out after two years for repeatedly hacking into the school's computer systems."

"Why was she doing that? To change grades?"

"Nope," Tommy replied nonchalantly. "Her file says she was doing it 'just because she could.'"

"Her file?" Elaine replied. "We have a file on her?"

"Once she got kicked out of Georgia Tech, she began making a living on the black market, hacking into databases around the country. She even got into some sensitive government systems, which is why we hired her."

"She works for us?"

"She used to, but we were having the same problem with her. She kept going rogue - wouldn't follow orders. As the problem became bigger, she smelled blood in the water and simply disappeared. We believe she left the country immediately, and she is suspected of being a player in one of the world's most profitable 21st century enterprises - cyber warfare."

Elaine thought about that for a moment. "Do we know who she is working for?"

Tommy laughed. "The highest bidder. She is an 'independent contractor.' We know she has done work for Russia, Iran, and China, and we believe she has done work for some terrorist organizations as well. We aren't sure how she got on to George and his information, but it appears that she had been tracking the two of you for some time."

"What did she want with George's information?" Elaine asked. "I was getting it to make sure that the Russian government was not making sweetheart deals with international energy conglomerates, in an attempt to take over a large portion of the oil supply outside of the Middle East. What interest would she have in that?"

"It depends on who she was working for," he replied. It could be a government, it could be a corporation…hell, it could be that she was going to get the information and sell it to the highest bidder. This chick is bad news."

"Interesting lady," Elaine said. "Smartest of the smart, gorgeous, and she had a cushy government job that would have set her up for the rest of her life. Now she is using all of that against us, not to mention that somewhere along the way she also picked up some training in hand-to-hand combat." Elaine smiled, and Tommy could tell that she really hoped to run into this woman again at some point. Elaine was fearless.

"Speaking of that," Tommy said, "the guy at the lab says to tell you he had *plenty* of hair from which to get a good DNA sample. He wants to convey that you need to be looking for a woman with a slight bald spot."

CHAPTER 37

November 1
7:55 PM
The Oval Office

It had been another busy day of meetings and teleconferences for the President. Today was day number 283 of the Clark presidency. Sam was ready to call it a day, but first he wanted to knock out a few pages of the material he had ordered. The previous week, he had requested the minutes from every Senate Intelligence Committee meeting about cyber crime and potential cyber attacks to see what he could learn that might help guide him in the coming years.

The minutes he had on his desk were from February 18, 2018, and the speaker had been none other than Tammy Leeds.

"We've got hundreds, perhaps thousands, of major problems in the area of cyber security at the government level. You can multiply that exponentially in the consumer and industrial worlds, by the way. Among those at the government level is the burgeoning role of governments around the world, not only in the use of zero-day exploits, but in the buying and selling of them. Many of these issues have yet to be explored in any depth in Congress or through the courts.

"Meanwhile, we have allowed this buying and selling of digital weapons, something that used to be considered out of bounds, to become commonplace. The amount of government dollars flowing through this gray market on a global scale has created a booming underworld economy. What is worse is that even that market uses supply and demand to set price levels. These weapons are costing more and more by the month."

She continued. "Aside from the weapons themselves, another hot commodity is the number of mercenaries that can create a zero-day vulnerability. One of them posted a zero-day that he created on eBay, and that was all the way back in 2005. That finally raised some eyebrows. It was only then that people started to realize that the folks who were doing legitimate work in this field were both underpaid and underappreciated. Not that the government, or a corporation for that matter, could ever pay what these people can get by selling their skills to the highest bidder, regardless of their intentions, but it was at least a wake-up call that the work they were doing was extremely important. Most people want to do the right thing. Eventually, corporations like Microsoft created a bounty program where they paid researchers for the vulnerabilities they discovered in Microsoft's systems. They have paid up to $100,000 for exploits, along with an additional $50,000 for a solution to fix it."

"Is this still going on?" one of the committee members asked.

"Absolutely. No matter what the Microsofts, Apples, or Googles of the world do, they can never pay as much as what these people can get on the gray market, where business is booming. In that market, zero-day exploits are being sold to defense contractors and even private individuals, who in turn are selling them to governments for astronomical prices."

"How astronomical?"

"Well, it varies, of course, but the talented ones, who have created successful exploits in the past, are able to sell them for a quarter of a million or more, depending on their track record."

"If you know this, and now we know this, whose jurisdiction is it to prosecute them? NSA? FBI?"

"None of the above," Leeds replied. "Selling these exploits is 100% legal and not even regulated for the most part. Another burgeoning market is for exploit brokers. Just like any other broker, these people connect buyers and sellers. In this case, a broker has numerous hacker contacts who are nervous about closing deals face-to-face. He or she brokers the deals, typically with government contractors, for a 15% commission per transaction."

Sam dropped the papers on his desk and pinched the bridge of his nose. He had a headache, and this material was not helping. He was quickly realizing that this whole domain of cyberspace was a huge abyss. He decided to finish up her testimony and call it a night.

"Yet another example of the business side of this industry is a company like VIPER. They create extremely detailed reports on the most important exploits, including how to figure out their point of origin, their specific techniques, and their attack detections. The NSA pays millions of dollars per year to this company for their service, known as BAE – Binary Analysis and Exploits. But regardless of how much they prepare, no corporation or government can protect themselves entirely from a cyberattack. It's literally impossible."

One of the Senators asked Leeds, "You make this sound pretty ominous, Ms. Leeds."

Leeds replied assertively, "If we entered into a cyber war today, we would be defeated. We're the most vulnerable, and we have the most to lose."

The Senator followed up on that comment with a pointed question. "Give me a number - on a scale of one to ten, how well are we able to protect the most important systems regarding infrastructure, defense systems, and intelligence?"

"One being ill prepared and ten being guaranteed against an attack?" Leeds asked.

"Yes."

"Three," Leeds said.

Sam leaned back in his chair, turned it away from the desk, and looked out into the crisp autumn evening. He knew what he needed. He was tired but not sleepy. He walked to the door that led to the portico. One of his secret service agents was standing at the entrance. "Sir?"

"Will you get Patrick Henry, and bring him down here, please? I need to go for a walk."

Sam walked back to the desk and closed the binder, marking the spot where he had left off. He stretched and rubbed a hand over what was quickly becoming a weathered face. A smile crossed his face as he heard a bark in the distance. He walked toward the door, where he was met by the secret service agent and a seemingly unhappy Patrick Henry.

"I know, I know." Sam leaned over and rubbed the beagle behind the ears.

"He seems agitated tonight," the agent said.

"You might think I'm crazy, but today is November 1 and I swear on my soul I think he knows that it is opening day of rabbit season back home."

The agent's skepticism was evident, but Patrick Henry barked again as if to say, "You're damn right it is."

CHAPTER 38

November 21
3:20 PM
Ottawa, Ontario, Canada

"Piece of cake," George Leonard thought to himself as he walked out of the building formerly known as the Langevin Block. It was a rather ordinary office building that faced Parliament Hill in Ottawa. The building's name change matched its bland exterior. It was now known as the Office of the Prime Minister and Privy Council. George had landed in the Canadian capital three nights ago, and he had now met with Prime Minister Jacob Tremblay at his residence at 24 Sussex Drive as well as at his office. It took very little strong-arming from George to get exactly what was wanted from his boss - a 10% reduction of oil exported to the United States in return for Russia paying a 12% premium on the oil that Russia was importing from the Canadians. Tremblay asked even fewer questions than George had expected, and he was just as easy to persuade as Volkov had said he would be. George remembered the short conversation well. "He is soft, Yuri. Even softer than most of the Canadians that we deal with. Don't give an inch."

George was now walking away with a bounce in his step. He still had two nights to kill, and he planned to spend some time on the town (and hopefully in bed) with the woman he had met his first night in Ottawa, at the Babylon nightclub. They had agreed to meet there again tonight. George still had time to grab a bite to eat and go back to his hotel for a shower before heading to the club to meet Beth.

The music was thumping, and the lights were flashing inside the Babylon when George arrived at 8:30. He ordered a drink at the bar, and before it was placed in front of him, Beth snuck up behind him and whispered in his ear, "You look *really* good tonight."

"Not as good as you," George replied with a smile as he turned around to face her.

"What a moron," Beth thought, as she continued to flash the smile that had always been one of her best assets. "How was work today?"

"Good," George replied. "Real good. In fact, I am completely finished for the week, and I have two more full days and nights before I have to fly back to Russia Saturday morning."

"Excellent," Beth said as she leaned into him. "I don't know about you, but I'm not feeling this place tonight. Let's go somewhere quiet."

George was ecstatic. He hoped this meant one of their hotel rooms, but regardless, two nights in a row of this noise was more than he could handle. He knew there would be women here, and now that he had found one, there was absolutely no reason for him to stay. "What do you have in mind?"

"Let's go back to your hotel," Beth said, as she nuzzled up to him.

"Bingo!" George thought to himself. But he played it cool. "That sounds good. We'll order some champagne and relax."

10:55 PM
Fairmont Chateau Laurier Hotel
Ottawa

"Yes, a bottle of your finest champagne, and some strawberries. Just charge it to my room."

George hung up the phone and turned to Beth. She was sitting on the edge of the bed, and she took off her shoes. "I hope you don't mind if I get comfortable. That might have seemed like a short walk to you, but in heels, no walk is a short walk."

George laughed and took off his coat. "Get as comfortable as you like. I plan to do the same."

Beth began walking around the room, looking at everything with a sense of wonder. She walked over and looked out the window. "It must cost a fortune to stay here," she said.

"Well, I hope you like it. You can thank Mother Russia. The room and the champagne are on her." His tone made it quite evident that he was not shy about advertising his connections.

"What exactly do you do?" she asked, trying to be as nonchalant as possible.

"Just business stuff, oil primarily. But it's boring. I've got a few other things I would like to talk about."

As he approached Beth, the doorbell rang. "Wait right here," he said to her, "and don't be shy about making yourself even more comfortable."

George took the tray containing the ice bucket and champagne, as well as the strawberries, and wheeled it into the room. He poured two glasses and walked over toward the bed, where Beth had indeed made herself more comfortable and less clothed. He handed her one of the glasses and sat down next to her.

The sound of George's glass hitting the carpet was relatively quiet. His eyes bulged with a look of confusion as Beth pulled the knife out of his lung. George collapsed slowly to the floor, a pool of blood forming around him. The gurgling sound he was making told her that he would not be a problem. She quickly got dressed, washed her hands, and walked over to George's briefcase. She did a quick scan of the paper files inside and saw nothing relevant. She did take all three of the flash drives that she found in a side pocket. Everything she needed would be somewhere on one of those drives.

She had done quite a bit of research on this man, and she had grown tired of following him. She had almost gotten what she needed in Brussels, but now she had everything she needed to protect herself against any forms of retribution from the people with whom she was dealing. She put on her heels and looked in the mirror. No traces of blood on her. As she exited the room, Amanda Curtis smiled at the thought of just how good she was at her job.

CHAPTER 39

December 12
9:05 AM
NSA Headquarters
Fort Meade, Maryland

Abdul Nassar was on his fifth cup of coffee. He knew he needed to eat something, and sleep, and a change of clothes would be nice. He raised his arms over his head and stretched. He heard three pops in his back. He stood for a moment to get some blood flowing.

Abdul had not slept in 36 hours, so it was hard to tell if this was really his fifth cup of coffee *today*, since there was little way for him to differentiate between yesterday and today, other than the sun rising and setting. But the combination of too much coffee and not enough food was making him jittery. He would eat in an hour, he promised himself.

Abdul Nassar had been born in Syria. He was a teenager when civil war broke out in his home country. He was among tens of thousands of Syrian refugees that found a new home in America. Abdul had embraced his new country immediately, assimilating as quickly as possible, and had now been a citizen for nearly six years. He had zipped through college and soon found himself working in state government in Maryland before becoming recognized at a national convention as a whiz kid in cyberspace. That was when the federal government came calling.

Abdul had jumped at the opportunity to work for the government of the United States of America. He knew that his country of origin would cause him some consternation during the application process, and he felt sure that the amount of scrutiny he had gone through to get his top-secret clearance was beyond what a natural born citizen would have had to endure. None of it, however, had dampened his spirits as he began to excel in his new role as a front-line soldier in America's cyber war.

There were always threats to the government operations systems, but this one was different. Abdul had discovered what appeared to be a huge vulnerability, or hole, in the Pentagon's security system. It was what was known in his world as a zero-day exploit. Every system has security holes, and many times they are unknown to the vendor. If a hacker finds the hole before the vendor finds and fixes it, it can exploit that vulnerability and infect the system. The most dangerous form of such an attack is called a zero-day exploit.

As the lead analyst, Abdul felt a duty to beat this hacker and his creation. He had spent days working on it, nearly non-stop. He was, perhaps, the best reverse engineer in the country, and code analysis was his forte. He realized that his line of work was off the beaten path, but he loved it. He saw it as a dance competition. Each dance move executed by a hacker's exploit was broken down step-by-step and placed into reverse motion. He considered it a form of art. Anything you can do, I can do better.

The process involved taking binary language and converting all those ones and zeros into language that could be read by their computer programmers. He did this by using what was called a disassembler. This tool also allowed him to add notes, comments, or any other notations to the code in order to further assist the programmers.

But the work was painstaking. He had to work on and label small bits of code at a time. It required going back and forth between computers time after time after time. In a best-case scenario, it was a slow process. That process was taken to the level of excruciating due to the size and the multi-layered nature of this particular exploit.

The debugging program they were using was the best in the world, and it was every reverse engineer's dream. It allowed him to sort through each step of the code, separate it, and track its activity. Once they documented each section, they issued commands to decrypt the malware and find the keys. After that, each key was used to unlock a specific algorithm. Once they reached that point, they were able to begin the process of seeing how the virus operated during this initial infection process. And that was the easy part.

Just the thought of how much time and effort had gone into getting them through these very early stages made Abdul's head hurt. Aside from that, there was an unease that he felt about this. Something just wasn't right. With a deep breath and one more big stretch, he sat down and went back to work. He would eat in 52 minutes.

PART II

CHAPTER 40

Monday, December 19
The Truman Building
Washington, D.C.

Secretary of State Vance Harrison was in the middle of a mundane discussion with the ambassador of Chad about the effects of climate change on a specific species of lion in Northeastern Africa when his chief of staff Ron Barbour came into the room. From the look on Barbour's face, nobody else in the room would have been able to tell that anything was wrong. However, Harrison knew something serious was going on for two reasons - first, he knew that poker face better than anyone. Second, if it wasn't something urgent, Barbour would have sent someone else.

"Pardon me, Mr. Secretary," Barbour said. "I am so sorry to interrupt but there is a matter that I need to speak to you about that is quite time sensitive."

"Sure, Ron. My apologies, Mr. Ambassador. I will be back momentarily."

The two men walked out into the hall. "What is it, Ron?"

"Mr. Secretary, we have the Chinese ambassador on video feed from his embassy, and he is demanding to talk to you immediately."

"Video feed? Why can't he schedule an appointment or just come down here?"

"I have no idea, but I'm guessing that the answer to that question cannot be good."

"Come in with me Ron," Harrison said as they approached his office.

Harrison sat down in front of the video monitor, where the Chinese ambassador was indeed on the other end of the video feed. "Mr. Zhang, what can I do for you? I hope nothing is wrong."

The Chinese ambassador wasted no time. "Mr. Harrison. As we both know, we carry a great deal of your country's debt. I think we can agree that we have been there to purchase some of this debt during America's darkest times. However, it is now my country that is facing some economic challenges, and we are calling some of that debt. We will need payment on this within the next 72 hours."

Vance Harrison was a professional statesman. He negotiated for a living, and one of the primary requirements of his job was to be diplomatic. This, however, tested his skill in those areas. "What are you talking about? I am aware of the recent economic hardships in your country, but this is a highly unusual way to make such a request. Beyond all of that, I have never heard of a request like this. Or should I say a *demand* like this. It is a breach of protocol. There are proper channels through which such a request is supposed to travel. Although I admit that in such a case, I have no idea what those proper channels are, I feel pretty sure that a video feed from your embassy to the Secretary of State is *not* how this should be handled."

"I understand your position Mr. Secretary, and this is not our formal request. The formal request will be sent directly to President Clark in a matter of hours. But because I know it won't be easy to execute this transaction, I wanted to give you as much notice as possible."

Harrison's head was spinning, but he remained poised. "Let's say, just hypothetically, that this demand is not completely out of bounds from a protocol perspective. What kind of dollar figure are you talking about and when do you need it?" Harrison knew that using the word 'demand' instead of 'request' in his question would express his dissatisfaction in the most diplomatic way possible.

"One trillion dollars by the end of the week." The words themselves, as absurd as they seemed, were spoken as nonchalantly as could be imagined. Harrison would have used a similar tone and delivery at the drive-thru window of a fast-food restaurant.

Harrison laughed out loud. "You can't be serious."

"Unfortunately, I am quite serious. I assume you will be there for our country in our time of need, just as we have been there for you. Good day, Mr. Secretary."

Before Harrison could reply, the video feed was cut. He looked at Ron Barbour. "Let the President know that I'm on my way, and that he will need to get the team together ASAP."

By the time Harrison reached the Oval Office, the President had somehow already gathered several people together. In the room were the Vice-President, the Treasury Secretary, the National Security Advisor, and the President's chief of staff. The Defense Secretary and the Chairman of the Joint Chiefs of Staff were present via video.

"What in the hell did he say?" Clark asked before Harrison could even sit down.

"Well," Harrison said, "I'm not sure where to begin. He said the Chinese government has fallen on hard economic times and that they have to call one trillion dollars of our debt." Harrison chuckled in a tone that was more bewildered than comical. "And they want it by the end of the week."

The room fell silent for a few moments, then Clark spoke. "This is out of line in so many ways. Aside from the odd way they made such a huge request, the more fundamental problem is that the country's debt is on a structured repayment. Is the calling of these loans even legal?" He looked at Treasury Secretary Helen Donovan without asking her directly.

"Well, I'm not sure who the proper person is to answer that question," she replied. "Attorney General McMillan would be my starting point on that question, and he will need to be brought up to speed as soon as his plane lands. In the meantime, three things worry me. The first is that they absolutely know that they are breaking the terms of the debt issue by making such a ridiculous demand. So why do it? Second, they are *not* in the kind of financial bind where they would need a trillion dollars by the end of the week. And again, they know that we know that, so what are they doing? The third and most concerning thing to me is this. This demand must have been planned for some time. They know we don't just have trillions of dollars lying around in some bank account. What is their goal here? When we say no to their demand, what then? I feel sure that they have a response to that answer, and I feel like we are *not* going to like what it is."

Once again, the room momentarily fell silent. "Well," Clark said, "I guess we will find out soon enough. I am scheduled for a call with President

Ming in 10 minutes." Clark looked at the video monitor. "Harold and Tom, you guys need to be prepared for another video conference as soon as this call is over. You should also begin making plans to be back in Washington ASAP."

"Yes sir, Mr. President," came the answer, nearly in unison, from the Defense Secretary and the Chairman of the Joint Chiefs.

The rest of the room cleared out, except for Helen Donovan. "Helen, I need you here to answer questions about Treasury policy, if and when they come up. I'm not sure exactly how this discussion is going to go, but I damn sure want my Treasury Secretary in the room when people start asking us to gather up a trillion dollars by the end of the week."

"Yes, sir." Donovan smiled, unsure if the comment was a moment of levity or frustration.

Moments later, President Ming came on the video screen. "Good morning, President Clark," Ming said cordially.

Clark was in no mood for small talk. "My morning isn't so good to this point," he replied, "mostly because of your ambassador's conversation with my Secretary of State. I find myself quite curious as to which part or parts of this conversation got lost in translation. Or perhaps I simply misunderstood."

Ming replied with the same demands that his ambassador had made, almost verbatim. "...And we need the $1 trillion by the end of the week. We're not requesting the entire amount of the debt, just enough to get my country stabilized."

Clark stared at the screen long enough to make some of the people in the room uncomfortable. "I am going to assume that you already know that your demand cannot be met. I am also going to assume you know that your demand would not be met even if it was feasible for us to gather that amount of cash together that quickly. Third, you know that the terms of the debt you are carrying are set on a structured repayment and that the debt cannot be called all at once like this. On top of all of that, I love the fact that you're claiming not to be demanding the entire amount of the debt. We owe you 1.2 trillion dollars. Thanks for sparing us the 'point two.' What exactly is this *really* about, Mr. President?"

"My country finds itself in financial peril..." Ming did not get to finish his sentence.

"Mr. President. Please. My inner circle probably knows as much about your current economic situation as you do, and we know you are not in any kind of financial peril that would justify a demand like this, or anything close to it."

Now Ming stared at the screen. "Since we're being blunt, Mr. President, let me just cut to the chase. We will take cash payment. If that much cash is not available, we will accept a like amount in gold. A third option is some of your military technology. I feel sure we could agree to a fair market value on some of your advanced systems."

Clark's patience was wearing thin. "Under no circumstances will we even entertain these outrageous demands. I will be placing a call to the United Nations as soon as this conversation is over, and they can work out the details."

"I was hoping it would not come to this," Ming said. "But you will either meet our terms by the end of the week or we will consider you in default on your debt and we will have to find other ways to get our hands on the assets needed to stabilize our country."

"What do you mean by 'other ways?'" Clark asked. But the sentence had not quite been completed before the screen went dark. Ming had terminated the call.

CHAPTER 41

Tuesday, December 20
9:45 AM
The Oval Office

Sam Clark had his chair turned away from his desk, and he was glaring out the window as the snow began to get heavier. This was the third day of snow, and the totals were increasing gradually, with the worst yet to come. A major snowstorm was making its way up the east coast, and it was scheduled to hit Washington by the end of the week. He was lost in his thoughts when his chief of staff, Patrick Welch, came into the room.

"Everyone is gathered and ready, Mr. President."

"Send them in," Clark replied as he turned his chair back around.

The members of the National Security team were present, along with the Secretary of the Treasury. Clark began the discussion.

"Clearly, we are not going to give any legitimacy to this absurd request. However, I would like your thoughts on the possible motivation for this demand as well as whether we should expect repercussions when the deadline passes. Thoughts?"

Secretary of State Vance Harrison spoke first. "Does anyone besides me find it highly unusual that a circumstance such as this was initiated through my office? I am baffled by that. It's not as if there was any room for diplomacy, and even if there was, I still wouldn't be the first point of contact."

Vice President Charles Sullivan agreed. "I've wondered the same thing," he said. "Makes no sense at all. However, I have a strong feeling about our response to this. I think we tell them in the most diplomatic way possible to go straight to hell. This isn't how the world works. We know that and they know that."

Tammy Leeds spoke up. "Before we get too deep into the discussion, let me point out that there have been some issues with our cyber security. We have noticed an unusual amount of chatter in that regard, but nothing that really made sense. Cyberspace speaks its own language, but in this case, there is a significant amount of white noise, almost *too* obvious. It's as if it is meant to serve as a subtle distraction."

Cyberspace was not a point of interest for Clark, despite its obvious importance. He had no idea how that world operated, but he trusted his National Security Advisor as much as he trusted anyone in the room, with the possible exception of Charlie Sullivan. "What, exactly, are you trying to say, Tammy?"

"Here's my two cents. Based on what I've seen, I think someone, somewhere, is actively looking for weak spots in our cyber security system." Leeds paused for a moment, trying to find the right words. "We are watching this as closely as possible. You all know the political angle better than me, but I don't think the Chinese would make this random demand that they know we can't honor without planning some sort of consequence when we refuse or just quietly let the deadline come and go. Assuming China has made no visible movements militarily, I fear that they may be planning some sort of cyber attack."

Tom Stewart, the Chairman of the Joint Chiefs of Staff, spoke up. "Mr. President, I can speak to the National Security Advisor's statement. We have been monitoring China's military closely, and there has been no sign of significant movement in their navy, nor any active maneuvers by their army. We're watching their every move."

"Fucking internet," Clark mumbled under his breath. He looked around the room, then decided he had to get to the nuts and bolts of this conversation. His gaze settled on Defense Secretary Harold O'Bryan. "I want all branches of the military on high alert through the Friday deadline."

Vance Harrison spoke up. "Mr. President, I don't think we should make any aggressive moves between now and the deadline. This entire matter is highly sensitive, and anything we do that they might interpret as pre-emptive could cross a line."

Sullivan intervened. "Cross a line? Hell, Vance, hasn't the line already been crossed? They know damn well we're not going to hand over a trillion dollars based on an illegal request. They didn't just draw a line in the sand. They crossed it, walked right up to us, and spit on our boots!"

Harrison continued, unfazed. He was truly a skilled diplomat. "I understand that, Charlie. But if we confront brazenness with an equal amount of it, then we're basically at war. Can we not feel them out a little bit more before we put the lives of millions of people at risk?"

The atmosphere in the room was heavy. Harold O'Bryan spoke up. "We'll be ready at your command, Mr. President."

Clark took a deep breath. He felt comfortable with his next move. He spoke to his Treasury Secretary. "Helen, you're up to speed. This is where we are. I invited you into this meeting so you would be in the loop. The next time I speak to Ming, I want you present."

"Yes, sir," she replied.

"Before that, here is what we're going to do. Even though this job requires me to be much more diplomatic than I care for, we will try that route first. Vance, get back in touch with the Chinese ambassador this afternoon and let him know that we flatly refuse their demand. Feel him out and see if you can get some sort of rationale from him about their motivation. I'm willing to listen if they truly have some sort of economic need, but their language is going to have to change drastically before we even consider it. We will not speak with them about demands and deadlines."

"I will call him as soon as I get back, Mr. President."

"Thanks everybody. Let's proceed with eyes wide open." Everyone left the Oval Office except Patrick Welch. Clark looked at him. "What are your thoughts?"

"Well, Mr. President, without going into a lot of detail, I think we've got a big problem on our hands."

"I was afraid that's what you were going to say," Clark replied. "Unfortunately, I agree with you."

CHAPTER 42

Tuesday, December 20
11:35 AM
The Truman Building
Washington, D.C.

Vance Harrison was at his desk, waiting to be connected via video with the Chinese ambassador. He frequently had philosophical disagreements with President Clark. Harrison felt that Clark was a little too 'cowboy' for his liking. However, Harrison felt his handling of the current situation was right on target. "So far," he thought to himself.

Clark's stance was that since he could not handle the matter the way he really wanted, then he would show his spite by removing the conversation from the level of president to president and send it back to the diplomats. This 'downgrade' would send a clear signal that Clark did not take the Chinese demand seriously while also maintaining plausible deniability of the brush off by claiming that diplomacy was needed at this time.

Harrison's thoughts were interrupted by Ron Barbour. "The link has been established and the feed will be up momentarily, Mr. Secretary."

"Thanks, Ron." Harrison found himself curious as to how this conversation would play out.

The Chinese ambassador appeared on Harrison's monitor. "Mr. Secretary," he said. "It is always a pleasure to talk to you, but I am not sure why you and I need to carry on a conversation about a matter that has already gone…pardon my translation…over our heads?"

Harrison smiled his best diplomatic smile. "Mr. Ambassador, I assure you that President Clark's request that we speak again is with all due respect. However, as I told you yesterday, and as he told President Ming, we cannot and will not meet your $1 trillion demand (Harrison continued to use the word 'demand,' even though he knew it would be received as aggressive language in a diplomatic discussion). We have consulted legal counsel at the highest levels, and they have reached the conclusion that the terms of the debt agreement between the United States and all its debtors are set on a structured repayment that does not include a call feature. In essence, your demand is not legally binding, not to mention quite brash."

"I'm very sorry to hear that, Mr. Secretary."

Harrison waited for the ambassador to expand on that thought, but it soon became clear that he was not going to do so. "I do come with a message from President Clark to pass along to you that we are happy to offer financial support from the United States regarding your country's financial woes. That support, however, would have to come on much more reasonable terms."

"Our position is clear, Mr. Secretary. We have attorneys as well, and they feel that there is no specific language against the loans being called. We will still be ready to accept payment from you by the end of the week."

Harrison was undeterred, plus they really *had* reviewed the language in the debt agreements. There was no doubt that the loans did not have a call feature. "We are willing to take the agreement to the United Nations for review by their legal counsel to generate a neutral opinion on this issue."

"We are not interested in outside opinions." It was clear by his one-sentence answers that the ambassador had taken off his diplomatic hat.

Harrison's brow furrowed. Diplomacy is a two-way street, and he realized that he was not being met halfway, or even close. He had played all the cards that he was willing to play, and he was finished with the conversation. "On behalf of President Clark, please pass along our regret that we were unable to find a way to help your country during your time of need." Harrison's words were dripping with sarcasm, but he didn't care a great deal.

The screen went black.

CHAPTER 43

Wednesday, December 21
9:55 AM
Wall Street
New York Stock Exchange

Don Redding, host of 'Your Money in the Morning,' had just finished interviewing the CEO of UPS about the company's corporate earnings, as well as their final push to get packages delivered to homes in time for Christmas. The winter storm on the east coast had produced quite a challenge, the CEO said, but it was one that the company was handling, and they expected all deliveries to be made on time.

"Now let's go to Jim Brantley on the floor of the New York Stock Exchange for a market update. Jim, it is good to see some green numbers behind you for a change."

"Yes, Don, it appears that the market is off to a strong start today. The Dow is up 89 points; the S&P is up 12; the NASDAQ is up 27. The mood on the floor is upbeat following four consecutive days of losses. That is due in large part to the jobs report, which showed 460,000 new jobs…what?…"

Redding looked confused. "Jim? Are you still there?"

Brantley was indeed still on the air, but his voice changed instantly to one of extreme concern. "Don, it appears that we have had some sort of problem here. I almost called it a power outage, but the lights are still on. But the floor just fell silent. All the data has disappeared. The Big Board has gone dark."

CHAPTER 44

Wednesday, December 21
10:02 AM
The Oval Office

President Clark was reading a briefing memo on the latest measures to strengthen the country's cyber security when Patrick Welch burst through the door between his office and the Oval Office. He walked quickly to Clark's desk and grabbed the remote control. He pointed it at the TV and turned it on.

"We have a *big* problem," he said as he walked toward the TV screen.

Clark rose from his seat and slowly removed his reading glasses.

They watched together in silence for a few moments as the reporter on the screen described the sudden blackout of the entire New York Stock Exchange. It was only moments before Monica Jenkins, the President's secretary, entered the Oval Office.

"The Treasury Secretary on line one, Mr. President. She says it's urgent."

"Indeed," Clark mumbled as he walked briskly toward the phone. "What the hell is going on, Helen?"

"I hate to tell you this, Mr. President, but so far we don't know. I got a call from the head of the NYSE just about five minutes ago. They are trying to locate the source of the problem, but no luck yet."

"Stay on the line, Helen."

Clark paged his secretary. "Get the National Security Advisor on the line as quickly as possible."

"Yes, sir."

Less than a minute passed before Tammy Leeds came on the line. "Mr. President, we are already in touch with the NYSE and are currently analyzing their security system for signs of an intruder. We haven't found anything yet, but we are scanning their entire system. We should know more in about ten minutes."

Clark pounded the desk with his fist. "Is this the Chinese?"

"There is no way to know yet, sir. Once we find the source of the problem, we should be able to discern the identity of the intruder. There is a possibility that it is no more than a glitch in the system. However, that is unlikely in my opinion. As soon as we know more…"

"Mr. President," Helen Donovan interrupted. "They're back online. The Big Board is back up. Should we suspend trading until we figure out what is going on?"

"Absolutely," Clark replied. "Get with the powers that be over there and assess the damage and get an ETA when they feel they can safely re-open the markets. Tammy - you keep working on your end. I want to hear from both of you as soon as you know more."

"Yes, sir," came the reply from both lines.

Welch had gone to his office to take a separate call. He met Clark at the entrance between the two offices. "I just got off the phone with the FBI Director. He is going to work with Tammy to find out where the breach happened as well as where the attack originated. The market was down for 12 minutes, and trading has now officially been suspended until further notice. This is going to cause a shit storm in financial markets around the world. We may want to call the Fed Chair."

Clark grimaced at the suggestion, but he knew Welch was right. Richard Alexander had been appointed as the Chairman of the Federal Reserve by the previous administration, and he and Clark did not see eye-to-eye when it came to monetary policy. In this case, however, their disagreements would have to be set aside in order to attempt to avoid a global financial panic.

"Go ahead and call him," Clark replied. "In fact, call everyone in. We need all hands on deck."

CHAPTER 45

Wednesday, December 21
12:32 PM
Federal Aviation Administration Headquarters
Herndon, VA

Gene Williams was at his desk having the first of his two afternoon cups of coffee, to go along with the three cups he usually drank in the morning. As head of the FAA, early mornings and late nights were routine. Therefore, so was coffee in large quantities. He had spent most of the day keeping in touch with his regional contacts around the country regarding the snowstorm and the effects that delays on the eastern seaboard would have on air travel across the rest of the country. So far, the problems were minimal and there were fewer delays than expected. Williams was hoping to continue that good fortune through the holiday weekend, but he was not confident.

Christmas week was always crazy, Williams thought to himself. This year, however, was even more hectic than usual because Christmas was on a Sunday. This, of course, meant that many companies would be giving their employees Monday off since the paid holiday fell on a Sunday. People would be spending most of Christmas week trying to get to their destinations in time to enjoy a long holiday weekend. Combine that with a major snowstorm, and he would need a caffeine IV by the end of the weekend.

Williams turned his cup skyward as he finished the coffee. It was at that moment that one of his analysts burst into his office.

"We're down!" the analyst shouted.

"What do you mean, 'we're down'?" Williams replied with frustration.

"Our systems are all down. We have lost contact with all flights as well as all of the airports."

Williams stormed past him and into the operations center. All visual contact was down, and other employees confirmed that audio contact had been broken as well. Williams ran back to his office and called his closest colleague in Chicago.

"Gene," the man said frantically. "We've lost communication here. Are you guys okay?"

"No, we're down too," Williams replied. "I'll call you back. I have to make some more calls."

Williams proceeded to call contacts at airports in Atlanta, Houston, and Seattle. All the stories were the same. However, as he was speaking to them, each indicated that planes were landing safely and orderly on their runways. For those who were not in the room, it would appear entirely as if nothing was wrong.

Williams continued to make calls and continued to get the same story. No accidents, no collisions. No problems at all. He did learn, however, that no planes were taking off. Across the country, air traffic was being safely grounded, although nobody knew how or why.

Sam Clark was in the Oval Office with Vice President Sullivan. They had spoken with the administration's top financial advisors and made the decision to close the markets for the rest of the day while they assessed the situation. They all agreed that this would have a negative impact on the global markets, but most felt the impact would be limited to a few trading days if they could find the source of the problem and make sure it did not happen again.

Meanwhile, little progress had been made on discovering what had caused the outage. The initial scan showed nothing, so a more thorough and detailed scan was being run now that the markets were closed, and they didn't have a time constraint. Clark made it clear that he was to be informed immediately once they knew anything at all.

Patrick Welch burst into the Oval Office. "Jesus Christ, Pat! What now?"

"We've got another big problem, Mr. President." He went straight to Clark's phone and informed him that Gene Williams, head of the FAA, was on the line. He put Williams on speaker. "Go ahead, Mr. Williams. You are on speaker phone with President Clark and Vice President Sullivan."

The combination of the situation and being on the phone with the President of the United States had Williams sweating, but he tried to maintain his composure. "Mr. President, I don't know how to explain this, but we have lost all access to our controls. Audio and visual contact has been lost with all aircraft. The system is down nationwide. Somehow, though, planes are landing normally as if we are bringing them in. Someone is bringing them in, sir, but it's not us."

"This is unbelievable!" Clark was shouting at no one in particular. The other two men in the room were speechless. "Have there been any accidents?"

"None, sir. But no planes are taking off. All air traffic is in the process of being grounded. The general public did not even notice there was a problem until planes stopped leaving the airports. Frustration is building, and we are unsure exactly what to tell the airports as to how to handle this."

Welch stepped in. "Mr. Williams, I'm going to place you on hold for a moment."

The three men looked at each other. There was a meeting in the Situation Room in less than 30 minutes, but they didn't feel like they could wait that long to do something. Sullivan spoke up.

"How about if we have him tell the airports that weather delays are stacking up on the east coast, and all flights are on delay indefinitely because the weather is getting progressively worse."

Welch was nodding and Clark agreed as well. "In fact, have Donna announce it at the afternoon media briefing."

"I'll call Donna," Welch said, and left the room. Clark took Williams off hold. "Mr. Williams. Gene, is it?"

"Yes, sir," Williams replied.

"Listen, Gene. Here's what we're going to do…"

CHAPTER 46

Wednesday, December 21
1:20 PM
The White House Situation Room

Everyone was standing at their seats as Clark entered the Situation Room. He waved them into their seats and quickly sat down in his.

"Okay everyone, we are in an unprecedented situation in the history of our country. Through the years, there have always been unknowns when the United States has approached war-like situations. We seldom know all the facts right away, and many of the final decisions evolve over time. Few times in our history have we been in a situation where we knew less than we do as we speak, and few times have the ideas as to how to properly respond been so unclear.

"We have been hit today in two of our most prominent areas - finance and transportation. Interestingly, the adversary has purposely done this in a fashion that makes it perfectly clear to us that we are under attack, while going out of their way to keep it from being known to the public.

"Two things are important as a starting point. First, nobody has died. In fact, the attacks have purposefully been non-violent. Second, however, and I cannot stress this enough, this is an attack on our country. I am not ruling anyone out, but China is the primary suspect due to our conversations leading up to today's events. That is the point from which I am starting this meeting, and it will be my mindset moving forward. We need answers to questions, and we need solutions to problems. And ladies and gentlemen, we need them today. What do we have?"

Tom Stewart, the Chairman of the Joint Chiefs, spoke first. "Nothing internationally sir, as far as any troop movements. There is nothing out there to indicate that anyone is planning a military move of any kind."

Defense Secretary Harold O'Bryan followed. "All branches of the military remain on high alert, sir. Do you want to begin movements of any kind?"

"Hold that question, Harold." Clark looked around the room. "Do we have any information from anyone here that would give us an idea of who is behind these attacks? And, if so, what kind of evidence do we have to back it up?"

Tammy Leeds spoke up. "We have been closely following cyber threats for several years, Mr. President. Due to the circumstances, the most likely culprit is China, although Russia is equally capable of pulling off something like this. Under normal conditions, I would declare those two as unlikely candidates because we are so interconnected in many ways. Iran is the next most likely, and then North Korea. Neither of those countries share that interconnectedness I mentioned with Russia and China, so although they are less likely to be *able* to pull this off, they would certainly be more willing to do so.

"Then there are two other possibilities," Leeds said. "In today's world, we could always be talking about an individual hacker. There are literally dozens of people in the world who can get into just about any system worldwide. However, what do they have to gain from that? Nothing, really, *unless* they hire themselves out to rogue nations or terrorist organizations. That is the last, but in my opinion least likely, possibility.

"As far as what happened today, there is still nothing we can pinpoint, Mr. President. The FAA takeover is brand new, and the hit on the NYSE is still only a few hours old. Regarding the events on Wall Street," she continued, "we do know that Syria has a relatively low-tech cyber operation that regularly runs 'denial of service' attacks against the financial sector. There are quick fixes to these types of hacks. It is an inconvenience more than anything else. However, from Syria's side, I am quite confident that the attacks are sent as a signal that they could potentially do some damage if we were to pursue any sort of military action against them. I consider them a lesser threat, but their skill in the cyber arena is progressing quickly thanks to help from Iran. According to our sources on the ground, the Iranians have sent some of their best people to train the Syrians in cyber warfare. In summary, sir, we are working as quickly as possible, but nothing to update at this time."

The room fell silent. Clark shook his head. "In that case, let's hold off on any military movements. I am going to call President Ming within the hour. I am finished with diplomacy. We are going to stop dancing around the room with each other, and I am going to either confirm or eliminate the Chinese as the source of these attacks. Anyone else have anything?"

The room remained quiet. Clark spoke again. "Come on, people. We need you. You're the best and the brightest or you would *not* be in this room right now. We will meet again at eighteen hundred hours, and I have had enough of the silence in here."

CHAPTER 47

Wednesday, December 21
1:55 PM
The Oval Office

Sheldon Cavanaugh came into the Oval Office for a quickly called meeting with those most closely affiliated with the country's protections against cyber attacks. Cavanaugh had been the CIA Director for two years, and he had worked with cyber security in different forms for over a decade. His background in that area was one of the primary reasons Clark had nominated him to be the CIA Director. It was common knowledge that the United States was vulnerable to cyber attack, and Clark wanted an expert in that field on the front lines of his administration.

The small group took seats in a rough circle in the center of the room. Clark had informed Cavanaugh that he wanted a five-minute history of recent cyber attacks as well as his thoughts and opinions on the Chinese and what role they may or may not have played in any of the prior instances of cyber warfare. He also wanted Cavanaugh to speak as if he was giving a lecture on Cyber Warfare 101 so that Clark could grasp the concept. Clark simply nodded at Cavanaugh, giving him the green light to take the floor.

"Mr. President, all of us are too familiar with the problems that have been experienced in recent years in the cyber wars. Everyone has hackers, and many countries can get into the systems of many others. The public is vaguely aware of cyber attacks against a handful of major corporations in recent years, but as seems to frequently be the case in today's society, people see what happens, they become outraged for a few days, and then they move on to the next hot topic on social media.

"Those stories aren't the ones that keep me up at night. The ones that cause me to lose sleep are the stories that the public is *not* aware of. These are the attacks that have happened within the databases of different government agencies. As we all know, in 2015, there was a security breach in the database of the Office of Personnel Management. While this is not as glamorous as hacking into the systems for the Pentagon or the White House, the amount of vital information that was lost that day was simply unacceptable.

"First and foremost, the OPM handles employee records for all federal workers. It is also in charge of government security clearances. While the initial reports claimed that the breach affected more than two million federal employees and another two million federal retirees, we all know that the actual number was perhaps as high as twenty million.

"Now, Mr. President, here is where things get sticky. We feel quite confident that the OPM attack originated in China. The Chinese government, of course, denied any involvement. In back-channel conversations, they aggressively challenged us to provide evidence to back up the accusation. It was easy for them to be bold. They fully realized that if we did produce the evidence, we would be disclosing classified information as well as revealing the identities of highly valuable assets we have on the ground around the world. They knew that, and they knew we would not be able to provide the evidence. That practically verifies that they were the hackers while also protecting them from being exposed."

Clark let the information soak in for a moment before following up. "So, in your opinion, how many countries have the capability to shut down Wall Street *and* take over our air traffic control system?"

Cavanaugh continued. "There are plenty of 'independent contractors' who will sell their skills to the highest bidder. That makes the list of possibilities somewhat longer. However, in my opinion there are three primary suspects. China is one of them. The other two are Russia and Iran. They are all extremely sophisticated in cyberspace, and they are also skilled at disguising the point of origin of a given attack. Trying to track the source of the instruction usually ends up causing signals to bounce off numerous servers and sites around the world. In those situations, when the hacker is that sophisticated, it is nearly impossible to find where the attack originated."

Clark leaned back in his chair and ran his fingers through his graying hair. He interlocked his fingers and then released both of his index fingers, so they were pointing straight up like a church steeple. He closed his eyes and leaned forward, running the inside of his index fingers along the bridge of his nose. He then stood up and walked toward the window behind his desk. The people in the room had been around Clark long enough to know that this was what they jokingly called his 'processing process.' They knew another question was coming, and soon it did.

"At this point, I think we have to make some assumptions in order to plan for what may or may not happen Friday when the deadline passes." Clark came back to his seat. "I think we have to start with the assumption that the Chinese are behind this. If so, I find it hard to believe that something else is not in the hopper when we don't hand over $1 trillion Friday. Where are we exposed? We assume they have a significant amount of access to a lot of our systems. What are the most likely targets if we're thinking cyber attacks?"

Cavanaugh took a deep breath. "You're not going to like this answer, sir. We are vulnerable in many areas, but I will touch on the ones that we monitor most closely in fear that they could be compromised. Air traffic control was one, although Wall Street was not. We are also concerned with water sources, along with health care and telecommunications systems."

Cavanaugh paused there, and Clark realized there was something more. "What?" Clark asked.

"Easily our greatest exposure, when you combine the weakness of our security with the biggest potential impact, is the electric grid. In my opinion, we have big problems there."

"Why?" Clark realized he was asking simple, one-word questions, but he did not care.

Cavanaugh took a deep breath. "Well, Mr. President, I know you have been briefed on this, as have your three predecessors. The weaknesses in the security of our electric grid are numerous and they are easily accessed. All the electricity that flows throughout the country relies entirely on what must be a perfect balance between supply and demand. This happens through computerized systems that maintain that balance. There are three power grids that generate all the country's electricity. We happen to know that there are hackers out there that are entirely capable of gaining access to any of these systems. As I mentioned earlier, several countries already have the know-how. We are confident that

China and Russia have already penetrated the grid. Once they are in, they can look around and find ways to plant what we call cyber weapons that can be used some time in the future.

"Even worse, there are a handful of terrorist organizations who are actively seeking to pay an expert a *lot* of money to acquire that capability. Meanwhile, around the world there exists a rising number of young people who are highly educated but angry with the ways of the world and their role in it. They have trouble finding jobs that match their skill level, and the next thing you know they are unemployed or working at Starbucks. These people are ripe for recruitment by governments and/or terrorist organizations looking to play a larger role in cyberspace."

Cavanaugh didn't see anyone squirming in their seats, wondering if he was ever going to stop talking, so he continued. "As we all know, there is a growing sentiment in pockets of the world that is very much anti-American. In all honesty, sir, I am much less concerned with any army in the world than I am about all the young, educated radicals. I see it this way: uneducated radical equals suicide bomber; educated radical equals cyber warrior. The cyber warrior is my biggest fear, because one of them can do significant amounts of damage to large numbers of people.

"All they would have to do is throw the demand/supply balance out of kilter, even just a little bit, to throw millions of people into total darkness. As far as we can tell, Mr. President, there are countries out there, with whom we do not see eye-to-eye, that have either the capability or the resources to pay someone to throw us into darkness. All they need is a reason to do it."

Vice President Sullivan spoke up. "Holy hell, Cavanaugh. Don't feel like you need to sugar coat the situation."

Cavanaugh shrugged. "The only reason political pressure isn't applied about this is that it hasn't directly affected enough of the citizenry yet. They can tap into all the government agencies they want, and people simply don't care. Their attention spans are too short. Then they hacked into Target and people's credit cards got affected. Only then did it begin to become recognized as a serious problem."

Cavanaugh continued. "It's partially our fault that there isn't more of an uproar about cyber attacks. It is easy to understand why the attacker doesn't want the intrusion into our system to be publicized. Also, they know that we are not going to sound the clarion call either. It's not as if we're going to be shouting from the rooftops that someone somewhere keeps hacking into our highly secure systems and stealing classified information."

Clark asked another question that he felt would come with an answer he would not like. "Is there any way for us to prevent this? Can we pick up some traffic that would tip us off that a strike was imminent? If so, could we do anything to stop it?"

"Probably not, Mr. President." Clark agreed with Sullivan. Cavanaugh did not try to give evasive answers. "Our grid, in all honesty, is archaic by modern standards. The country is filled with equipment that is old and outdated, and most of it sits in wide open areas. We are vulnerable to physical attacks as well, although it is easier and quicker to hit in cyberspace. Plus, you can do more damage quickly. Unfortunately, the United States does not currently have a specific plan to combat cyber attacks."

Tammy Leeds spoke up at this point, and she added to the dark mood that was consuming the room. "The GRID act passed the house way back in 2010 but died in the Senate."

Sullivan jumped in. "I remember that. Refresh my memory, Tammy."

"The GRID act - the 'Grid Reliability & Infrastructure Defense' act. As some of you know, a confidential letter was sent to the chairman and ranking member of the House Committee on Energy & Commerce. It was written by ten former national security officials. These were Republicans and Democrats, from the Pentagon and the CIA…it was a diverse group. The letter was signed by all of them to stress the importance of the point they were trying to convey.

"Since I knew I was coming to this meeting, I brought a copy of it. Here's part of it:

'The consequences of a large-scale attack on the US grid would be catastrophic for our national security and economy. Under current conditions, timely reconstitution of the grid following a carefully targeted attack if particular equipment is destroyed would be impossible; and according to government experts, would result in widespread outages for at least months to two years or more, depending on the nature of the attack.'

Leeds looked up. "Again, that was in 2010. That's how long we have been talking about the problem, but little has been done because of the cost efficiency. There was a study that estimated the cost of protecting the electric grid at about $2 billion. To do that, both the government and the corporations would have to be on board to spend an astronomical amount of money to prevent a problem that hasn't occurred, and may never occur. It's a classic conundrum."

Clark sighed and spoke as he rose from his chair. This was the sign that the meeting was coming to an end. "Sheldon and I spoke before the meeting. We have some live intel on the ground internationally. Our contacts are embedded in some places that may be able to help us get some answers. But he was very clear that it is unlikely we will have those answers by Friday." He looked at Cavanaugh, who simply nodded his head in affirmation. Clark turned back to the group. "Everyone keep me posted on anything relevant."

CHAPTER 48

Wednesday, December 21
2:35 PM
The Oval Office

Clark had the members of the National Security Council in the Oval Office with him as he prepared to call Xao Ming. He was adamant that he would either get a denial from the Chinese President or he would be prepared to accuse him of cyber warfare and warn him to be prepared for retaliatory action.

As the connection was established, and Ming's face appeared on the screen, Clark thought he detected the slightest glimpse of a smug smile. The American President had to convince himself to stop gritting his teeth, and then he spoke.

"President Ming. I assume you have heard about our interesting day over here."

"Yes, Mr. President. I did hear about the American stock market. I hope the matter gets resolved quickly."

The group in the Oval Office had hoped to get Ming to say something about the air traffic situation, which would have given him away since the matter was not yet public knowledge. They realized the chance was slight, but Ming did not take the bait.

"I'm sure we will work everything out," Clark replied. "In fact, my team tells me we are close to detecting the source of the problem."

Ming's repressed smile surfaced again, and Clark took that as an assumption from the Chinese President that he thought the source of the cyber attack would never be discovered. Ming changed the subject and brought things full circle.

"So, Mr. President, have you given any more thought to our request?"

"No, I have not." Clark's reply was unequivocal. "You know our position. There is no binding language in our debt agreement that makes us obligated to repay a single dollar outside of the agreed terms. With all that is going on around here, I can assure you that it has not even crossed my mind."

Vance Harrison unfolded his arms and extended them in front of him, palms down. He moved them in an up and down motion in an attempt to get Clark to tone down his rhetoric. Clark gave him an acknowledging wave and nod, along with an eye roll.

"You still have approximately 48 hours to consider our request," Ming replied calmly.

"You don't seem to understand me. Are you having trouble with my English? If so, I will get a translator in here." Harrison stepped forward, but he stopped when the president gave him a stern look and extended his hand in a 'stop right there' motion. Then Clark continued. "Let me slow down and speak clearly. We will *not* pay you today. We will *not* pay you within 48 hours. We will *not* pay you in any way, shape or form outside of the terms of the debt agreement."

There was a momentary silence on the other end. Then Ming spoke. "Very well," he said. "That is very clear. I do not need a translator. And I hope my English is clear enough when I say that if we do not receive one trillion dollars cash, or a like amount in gold or military technology, then you are in default. If you default…"

Clark cut him off. "President Ming, I'm growing tired of the back and forth. We're both adults here.

Let's talk like adults. Was your country involved with the matter on Wall Street today?" Vance Harrison raised his arms in disgust and walked in a large circle. This was the side of Sam Clark that he did not like.

Ming stared into the screen. Clark stared back for a moment, and then simply said, "Well?"

Ming continued to stare, and then sharply uttered a single syllable in Chinese to someone that Clark assumed to be a member of his team that was outside of screen view. Clark wondered briefly if they were giving Ming the same advice that Vance Harrison was trying to give to him. If so, it didn't work on Ming either.

Ming looked back at the screen and smiled, this time in an unsuppressed fashion. "Yes, we were," he said. "And the air traffic situation."

Clark struggled not to show a facial reaction as he maintained his composure. The rest of the team in the Oval Office looked at each other in disbelief.

"And let me add, Mr. President," Ming said as he moved slightly closer to the monitor. "I show it being 2:43 PM in Washington. The clock starts right now. If we do not have payment in full within 48 hours of this moment, then all goes dark."

And Ming was gone.

CHAPTER 49

Wednesday, December 21
6:05 PM
The Situation Room

President Clark entered a room full of standing people that he quickly asked to sit down.

"Let's get straight to it," he said. "Tom, any movement from anyone that we need to be concerned about?"

Joint Chiefs Chairman Tom Stewart looked as if he almost felt bad that he had nothing to offer. "All is quiet, Mr. President."

Clark nodded, then looked at the Secretary of State. "Vance, was there any wiggle room at all to keep a dialogue going with the Chinese ambassador?"

"There were no signs that he was interested in finding a solution to this 'problem,' but I can always keep some sort of dialogue going if you would like."

"Let me think about that, Vance." He turned to Tammy Leeds. "Anything new on what happened with Wall Street and the FAA?"

Leeds became the first person to offer something to move the ball forward. "Since we have now narrowed our focus to China, we have been able to find some spots in our systems that appear to have their digital footprint."

Clark chuckled in a frustrating manner and looked at Patrick Welch. "Do I dare ask what a digital footprint is?"

Leeds answered for him. "Each hacker has certain ways or processes through which they get into a secure system. Many times, those points of entry can be covered up on their way back out, but sometimes just the how and where aspect of the breach can help us identify the source."

Clark really liked Leeds. She was clear and to the point. She had just turned what had been an entirely foreign concept into something that he now understood on a basic level. "Continue," he said.

"They are always in our system looking for weak spots, as are we in their system. However, traffic has increased substantially in the past three weeks, primarily in our defense database as well as in our telecommunications and electric grids. However, because of the common thread we share with them economically, we tried to find some information as to how badly it would hurt *them* if they executed an all-out cyber attack. We have a source on the ground that has informed us that the Chinese government has been hoarding large amounts of cash and liquidating holdings with other governments. This has been going on for nearly a year, Mr. President, and it has been done in small increments to avoid raising a red flag."

Leeds paused.

"What?" Clark asked. "If there's more, I want to know."

"This is no more than conjecture, sir, just my opinion. I think China has been secretly bracing itself for a cyber war against the United States, and I think that war starts as soon as the deadline passes on Friday."

Vance Harrison spoke up. "Wait a minute, let's calm down here. We can't allow ourselves to get carried away and make rash assumptions."

Vice President Sullivan spoke up. "Christ, Vance. You *do* know that we watched helplessly today as someone else, we have no fucking idea who, but someone else, landed thousands of our airplanes across the country. You remember that, right? What if they had decided to crash all of them instead?"

"But they didn't," Harrison retorted. "I think we can all agree that China plays to win in every aspect of what they do. If they wanted war with the United States, they would have caused those planes to crash all over the country. The fact that they didn't means that it was a bargaining tool."

"Bargaining tool?" Sullivan looked around the room. "This is a room full of serious people, Vance. Please don't insult us with your naivete."

Harrison chuckled. "So, what do you propose, Mr. Vice President? Are we ready to drop some nukes on 'em?" Harrison looked around the room, mocking what Sullivan had done. "Please, everyone, let's make a joint effort to take care of President Clark." He pointed at Sullivan. "Otherwise, this guy sitting across from me will actually be in charge if something happens to him!"

Clark interrupted the argument. He turned back to Leeds. "If your assumptions are correct, and they are planning an all-out attack on some part of our infrastructure, do we have a defense against it? Can we stop them?"

"All countries are better equipped to operate offensively in cyber space than they are defensively, Mr. President. If they come at us, we can retaliate in ways that could do an equal or greater amount of damage to them as they did to us."

Sullivan spoke again. "But their citizens are much less vulnerable to cyber warfare than ours."

"Agreed," Leeds said. "Technology is a luxury reserved for a select few in China. It is a way of life here. Although the amount of damage inflicted would be similar, the consequences of that damage would be exponentially greater here than in China. If we went without power for an extended period, it would throw our society back to something we would have seen at the dawn of the 20th century – no electricity, no mass travel, no creature comforts. Our citizens are not prepared to live that way."

Clark looked at Leeds. "You didn't answer my question, Tammy. Can we stop them from doing whatever it is they have planned?"

"No, sir."

CHAPTER 50

Thursday, December 22
United Nations Headquarters
New York City

UN Ambassador Keith Keough had been largely distracted from the day's agenda during the 45-minute flight from Washington to New York. He would be attending meetings today at the United Nations about the ongoing genocide in Darfur. However, he was more focused on the private meeting he was scheduled to have with the UN's Secretary General about the current situation with China.

Keough listened to the representatives speaking about Darfur, and he realized that as the representative of the United States, he needed to give his utmost attention to the situation. However, he could not help but wonder about the Chinese agenda. What did they *really* want? What was their true goal? They had to know that the United States was not going to pay them a trillion dollars under any circumstances, let alone in the manner they were demanding it. They had to be equally aware that they were not going to receive gold or any of the country's technology or intellectual property. The idea was simply ludicrous. So, what was it? What was their actual goal?

Keough labored through the day's meetings and entered the office of UN Secretary General Oleg Medinsky. Medinsky had been one of the leaders of the breakup of the Soviet Union and was a resident of Ukraine. He was acknowledged as an excellent diplomat and a much-needed positive influence for the United Nations, which had been losing credibility across the globe for the past two decades.

"Good afternoon, Secretary Medinsky," Keough said as he reached across the desk to shake hands with Medinsky.

"Good to see you, Mr. Ambassador," Medinsky replied. "I am sorry that it is under such unusual circumstances, but a pleasure, nonetheless. Please, have a seat."

Keough sat and moved directly to the point of the meeting. "As I explained on the phone, we have had an…'interesting' week with the Chinese. I gave you the background, but I wanted to give you the details in person."

"I hope you don't mind, Mr. Ambassador, but I spoke with a couple of members of the Chinese delegation yesterday, just so I could get a feel for where both sides stood on this matter. I must say, their version of the events of this week varies greatly from what you and I spoke about."

Keough was shocked but tried not to show it. "How so?" he asked.

"Well, they agree that there has been communication between your countries this week. However, they claim that they reached out to you for financial assistance and were summarily denied by both Secretary of State Harrison and President Clark."

"That is true to a point," Keough replied. "We did decline their demand to pay them one trillion dollars in cash, gold or military technology."

"That's where the disagreement lies," Medinsky said flatly. "They claim no dollar figure was discussed, and they also claim that they came to you…how do Americans say it...hat in hand? We both know it is hard for the Chinese to ever admit a weakness, and when they do, we would expect a country of your stature to respond in a much more mature fashion."

Keough could hardly believe what he was hearing. "Let me be sure I am clear. I have told you what they demanded from us. They have told you something entirely different from that. And from what I can gather, you seem to be taking the position that they are telling the truth and that we are lying and acting immature. Am I reading this accurately?"

"Mr. Ambassador, there is no need for such strong language. Nobody used the word lie or liar. And I didn't call you immature - it's just that I would expect the United States to be willing to help a country in need, especially considering the correlation in today's global economy. However, based on this short discussion and the one I had with Chinese leadership earlier, I am inclined to believe that perhaps your administration is misunderstanding the Chinese request. After all, the request, as you described it to me, seems ridiculous."

"Exactly!" Keough knew his tone was a bit out of line, but he simply could not believe what he was hearing. "It is absolutely ridiculous! Let's get together - you, me, and the Chinese ambassador. I want to see him say that with a straight face."

"I am afraid that is impossible at this point, Mr. Ambassador. They feel quite humiliated by your rebuke of their request, and it is not in their nature to take direct insults lightly. My guess is that diplomacy between your two countries will be quite cold for the foreseeable future. I think it would be best at this point to just move forward. Maybe we can find some ways for the two of you to work within a larger group of countries toward a common cause on a global issue or two to try to rebuild some good will."

Keough sat back in his chair. If *anyone* was being humiliated in this situation, it was the United States. Here this man sat, in his cushy office in a building that the United States built and continues to pay for, in an attempt to promote world peace, lecturing him about his country's dishonesty and immaturity. It was all he could do not to say exactly what he knew President Clark would say in this situation. Maybe his way wasn't as bad as the diplomats tried to contend. Instead, Keough stuck to his best level of diplomacy as he rose from his chair. "Good day, Mr. Secretary," he said as he casually walked out the door.

CHAPTER 51

Thursday, December 22
8:35 PM
Ritz Carlton Hotel
New York City

Keith Keough entered his room and set up his laptop. He followed the steps to set up a secure video feed, and soon he had President Clark and Patrick Welch with him from the Oval Office.

"So how did it go?" Clark asked.

"You are absolutely *not* going to believe this," Keough replied. "Medinsky basically accused us of abandoning the Chinese in their time of need and making up the story about the ultimatum for the $1 trillion."

"Has he not spoken with the Chinese?" Welch asked.

"They lied about damn near the entire story. They admitted to asking us to help them financially, but they told Medinsky that we refused, and they denied everything about the trillion dollars and the deadline."

"And Medinsky believes *them* instead of us?" Clark sounded incredulous.

"Yes," Keough said, "and they played it brilliantly. When you hear their version - their lie - and then you hear our version, ours is the one that sounds crazy. So, when they deny that it happened that way, we're the ones left looking ridiculous because the whole thing is so absurd."

"Why are they doing this? What is the end game?" Welch asked, somewhat rhetorically.

Keough rubbed his temples. "That is the question I spent all day pondering. What exactly is going to happen tomorrow afternoon?"

"I'm not sure, but I don't want you there if it's serious." Clark had been considering this, but now he was sure. He wanted all the members of his team in proximity when the deadline came. "Try to get some sleep, Keith. Then blow off tomorrow's meetings and head back to Washington. I want everyone here. We'll prepare for the worst and see what happens."

"Yes, sir, Mr. President."

Keough killed the link and looked out the window. He poured a drink from the bar and stared at the snow that continued to fall. The forecast sounded worse every time he heard it, but it wasn't stopping the New Yorkers. It was Christmas week, and this year was going to be a White Christmas for sure.

CHAPTER 52

December 23
11:40 AM
NSA Headquarters
Fort Meade, Maryland

After three weeks, Abdul Nassar and his team confirmed what he had begun to suspect during the past few days. At first, he assumed that the complexity of the attack was meant to steal sensitive and classified data of some kind - intelligence files, military operations, etc. The Pentagon had been briefed about the problem, and they were on high alert regarding sensitive materials and systems. But recently, the virus had infected other systems - the databases of the CIA, the White House, and the NSA itself. It was also quickly spreading to systems outside of the government, but he had no time to worry about private entities.

What Abdul had discovered was that the exploit was disabling alarms and working in a unique way to avoid detection as it spread from system to system. He had not seen anything like this before. It appeared that instead of being designed for espionage, it had been designed to physically damage or destroy its target. The hair stood up on Abdul's arms. He did not know exactly why, but something was wrong. This was different. It was big, and as the virus began to expand rapidly, then exponentially, he realized it was also imminent.

Abdul Nassar shot up from his chair and began shouting for Helene Albertsen, the head of the NSA's Cyber Command Division. They needed to call Tammy Leeds. Right now.

CHAPTER 53

December 23
12:45 PM
The Oval Office

Clark had called the US ambassador to China, Michael Caldwell, to the oval office for some background on China and their finances. He needed to know if they were indeed in trouble financially, or if that was nothing more than a ruse intended to distract them from something that was perhaps more devious. For the sake of any last-minute diplomatic efforts, he wanted to be as informed as possible. Patrick Welch was present, as were Charlie Sullivan and Vance Harrison. Caldwell's assistant, Tim Fournier, had accompanied him to the meeting.

Caldwell entered the oval office and sat down after greeting everyone.

"Give me the rundown please, Michael." Clark said.

"Yes, sir," Caldwell replied. "As a starting point, Mr. President, China has changed and is changing, and the world is noticing. Much of their 'sales pitch' is about leadership, and how their leaders earn their positions more so than the countries with elections. China, along with a few other countries, is trying to challenge our assertion that the democratic model is the most legitimate model by which to choose our leaders. And they are using technology to get their message out. Do you remember the cartoon video from back in 2013?"

"I do," Clark said, nodding.

Caldwell continued. "It got more than 10 million views in less than two weeks. It was released at the time of the government shutdown. It showed the meteoric rise of Barack Obama, who was the beneficiary of hundreds of millions of dollars in campaign funds, but lacked any real political experience. Then it depicted the route to the Chinese presidency taken by Xi Jinping. It was a steady rise through the ranks over the course of decades. His ascent included no less than a dozen promotions through each step of the Chinese bureaucracy, with each stage involving rigorous evaluations of his political and leadership skills as compared to his peers. The whole point, as the video expressed it, was to place negative connotations on our form of government, while stressing that their process of meritocracy was assured to provide better leaders. Then, of course, Donald Trump was elected. That only reinforced their position, specifically regarding the idea that American elections are no more than popularity contests.

"And you should read the comments section," he continued. "The number of people with American-sounding names praising the whole idea of a meritocracy was alarming, assuming the comments and the names were real. Either way, as propaganda tools go, it was an effective piece."

Vance Harrison chimed in. "And don't think the Chinese aren't politically skilled. Early in 2009, right in the heart of our financial crisis, while we were trying to find cash to pay for the stimulus plan to avoid catastrophe, China moved boldly. They rolled out a new program with a budget of 45 billion yuan, approximately seven *billion* dollars. This project was called, in their language, "waixuan gongzuo'. The English translation of that phrase is 'overseas propaganda.'

"In addition to that, their achievements of the last thirty years or so are astounding. They established a goal to reduce poverty as a key priority of their government. They knew to get to that point, economic growth would be the primary driver. Therefore, government officials were often promoted according to the level of economic growth in their district. Whether by coincidence or by the policies they implemented, China has witnessed what is perhaps the single most impressive poverty reduction statistics in human history: The World Bank estimated that the poverty rate fell from 85% to 15% between 1981 and 2005. That is the equivalent of approximately 600 million people being lifted out of poverty."

Caldwell then picked up the conversation again. "The fundamental idea of meritocracy as a form of governance is that everybody should have an equal opportunity to be educated and to contribute to politics, but some will simply be better and more skilled than others. So, the goal of this form of politics is to identify those with above-average ability and put them in leadership positions. If they perform well in those roles, the government leaders know that the citizenry will not put up an argument.

"What has happened is that the Chinese government has an extraordinary number of excellent scientists and world-class economists in political positions that they could never hold in a democracy because they don't have the personality to campaign effectively. The results are astonishing. During the past three decades, several hundred million Chinese citizens have been lifted out of poverty.

"Compare that with our current system. Our populace wants instant gratification. They want to be promised the world for their vote, and you better deliver. It does not matter at all to them whether the math adds up or if it seems to make any common sense whatsoever. And the idea of waiting for a few years for long-term structural reform or for politicians who impose fiscal discipline? Please. Do you remember what happened in Greece?"

Clark sat with his arms folded. He said nothing, and he didn't look as if he was about to say anything, so Sullivan leaned forward in his chair as if to speak. "Hang on a second, Charlie," Clark said calmly. "Let them finish."

Sullivan had been around Clark enough to know that the President was quietly seething. He leaned back in his chair, content that whatever he was about to say would be made very clear soon.

Harrison spoke again.

"So here we are. Entitlement spending and the national debt have exploded to unsustainable levels with no end in sight. But it has the potential to get much worse. The United States and Japan are the two most economically powerful democratically elected countries. Both desperately need to rein in their soaring national debts, but to do so would mean imposing serious cuts to popular programs. It would also mean that anyone who voted for such changes would not get re-elected."

Clark held out his hands in a 'stop' motion. "Enough!" The tone was unquestionably firm, but a level below shouting. Although some people, particularly in the diplomatic arena, saw Clark as a hot head, he seldom raised his voice. For Clark, this was out of character, and he had the room's undivided attention. Sullivan revealed a slight smile.

"Everyone in my administration knows that I am not a world-class politician. I never claimed to be, and I never wanted to be. If I ever notice myself becoming one, I will resign. I am also not the most intelligent person in this room. I recognize that as well. What I am, however, is a leader. By getting elected, I was allowed to pick world-class politicians. I got to pick the smartest people I knew, which includes everyone in this room. Oliver Wendell Holmes once said that FDR had a second-class intellect but a first-class temperament. However, FDR surrounded himself with the brightest minds, and he allowed them to state their views unequivocally, even when they disagreed with him, which was quite often. Then, together, they searched for the best ideas, and converted them into policies that the group felt would benefit this country.

"That was the model I followed when I got elected, and I feel like I did a pretty damn good job. However, I've heard quite enough about the Chinese model. Any political philosophy has some positives, and an argument can be made for any of them if the presenter is allowed to cherry pick the best parts. In the end, their people are not free to speak their minds; they are not allowed to worship freely; there is no free press; they are not free to own weapons. Does anyone know where I am getting these concepts?"

Clark did not allow time for anyone to answer. "From our Bill of Rights! And guess what? Out of all that rambling, I only touched on the first two of them. So, without basic freedoms, there is no liberty for those people, and no independence.

"We don't really have time for this, but I think it's important. When I was a young and green freshman at Loyola, I had a class in which we were given a list of ten values. Each of us was asked to rank those values one to ten based on how important they were in our lives. You could guess most of the choices – faith, family, friends, money, etc. Once we were finished, the professor asked for volunteers to reveal their personal rankings. Nearly everyone in the room had either faith, family, or friends as their top choice. *Nearly* everyone. In a room full of teenagers, there was one middle-aged Chinese woman who was working on her degree. She raised her hand to give her rankings. I cannot remember at all what she said numbers two through ten were for her, but I'll never forget what she ranked first. She simply said this: 'I rank freedom first, because where I grew up, I didn't have freedom. Without that, most of the other choices don't matter."

Clark paused and looked around the room at those who were present. "This is the last thing I am going to say on this topic. I am glad for the background on the Chinese model, and I understand that they are doing some things well there, especially politically. But I will never waver in my belief that a government that does not allow its people to speak or worship freely is not the model to follow. Ask yourself: how many Chinese Americans are there in this country? Now ask yourself this: how many American-Chinese are there in China?"

Clark stood and left the room. Sullivan left as well, content that for once he was able to just sit and watch.

Welch spoke to the three remaining men. "Vance knows this song and dance pretty well, but let me just say to you two that this is *exactly* what you were called in here for. He needs to hear the other side, even if it means we bring you in here in the role of sacrificial lamb. Thanks, guys. It really was very useful."

Welch and Harrison nodded to each other, and Harrison affirmed what Welch had said to the other two as he walked them out of the oval office.

CHAPTER 54

December 23
2:30 PM
The Oval Office

Sam Clark was sitting in the Oval Office with Charles Sullivan and Patrick Welch. They had just concluded a meeting with the Chairman of the Joint Chiefs and the Defense Secretary. The situation remained eerily unchanged. There was still no movement from the Chinese military. Harold O'Bryan continued to assure Clark that American forces from all branches of the military were on high alert. Unfortunately, there was also no progress in the effort to find a breach in any of the country's primary security systems. Without being the aggressor, there was nothing else that Clark and his team could do to prepare for what might happen in the next fifteen minutes, or at some other point in the near future.

Clark had decided not to communicate anymore with the Chinese leadership. It was clear that they had given up any attempt at diplomacy, and it was even more clear that the United States was not going to capitulate to their ridiculous demand. So here they were - watching the clock and trying to figure out what to do. Clark's agenda was set to pick up again at 3:00 if nothing happened, but he did not like the fact that they were sitting and waiting for some sort of punishment, like kids in the principal's office.

They continued discussing the situation as the clock moved to 2:35 and then to 2:40. The 24 hours ended at 2:43, and President Ming had been clear that he was talking about *exactly* 48 hours. Clark was getting frustrated. "If nothing has happened by 2:45, I'm on the phone with *somebody* and we're going back to work. This is ridiculous."

"Yes, sir, Mr. President." Patrick Welch knew Clark's moods well. He realized that Clark really didn't like the United States being in this submissive position, and he agreed that they weren't going to walk around on eggshells the rest of the day if nothing happened at 2:43.

Welch was thinking about the first phone call that he would arrange for Clark when it happened. The lights went out in the Oval Office. The back-up generators kicked in and brought the power back on, but although most of the clocks in the room were digital and were flashing 12:00, the battery powered clock on the wall told the story. It was 2:43.

"Damn it!" Clark rose from his chair and the plan went into effect. Welch went to his office to make calls to see how broad the outage was. It was hard to tell if power was out locally by looking out the window because it was the middle of the afternoon. A meeting had already been set for 3:00 in the Situation Room if the power went out as expected. Clark's curiosity was focused primarily on how widespread the outage would be. Did Ming mean the White House would go dark? Washington, D.C.? How broad was the outage?

He looked at Sullivan. "Let's go ahead. Patrick can meet us down there once he knows more. We've got to get to work."

"Yes, sir." Sullivan followed Clark out of the Oval Office.

CHAPTER 55

December 23
3:10 PM
White House Situation Room

Those present were already brainstorming possible scenarios and solutions when Clark and Sullivan reached the Situation Room. The room was lit by emergency generators, and the current discussion was regarding the unsubstantiated rumor that most of the eastern seaboard had gone dark.

"What do we have?" he asked as he sat in his seat at the head of the long table.

Andrew Byerly, the head of the Department of Homeland Security, spoke first. "We're not positive, sir, but our preliminary belief is that we have indeed suffered an attack on our power grid."

"A physical attack, or a cyber attack?" Clark replied, just for confirmation.

"Cyber," Byerly said with the tone that let everyone know that one of their worst-case scenarios from a planning perspective may be in play at this very moment.

"Shit," Clark replied under his breath. "Shit!" he shouted as he pounded the table with his fist. "Tom, any military movements now?"

"None yet, Mr. President," replied Tom Stewart, the Joint Chiefs chairman. "Without making any assumptions about who may have done this, we are looking in every direction. However, there is no movement yet from those we usually watch most closely - the Russians, the Chinese, and the North Koreans."

Clark sat quietly for a few seconds before looking at Tammy Leeds, his National Security Advisor. "Just for the sake of covering our bases, what are the chances that this is *not* a cyber attack?"

"Very small," Leeds replied, "especially with the events of the week."

Patrick Welch entered the room.

"Spill it," Clark said tersely.

"Sir, from what we can tell on a preliminary basis, it appears that the outage has affected the entire eastern seaboard, and a great deal of the west coast. It may be even broader than that, but those areas are confirmed."

Kelly McDonald, the Energy Secretary, spoke up. "Sir, I am trying to get updates, but it appears that telecommunication has been affected in much of the country as well. I am unable to reach many of the people who could provide more detailed information. If you agree, sir, I think I may be more useful outside trying to get some updates."

"Go," Clark replied, waving his hand toward the door. "Keep us updated."

Tammy Leeds spoke. "Mr. President, this event is occurring during one of the worst blizzards to hit the east coast in a decade. Hypothetically, if this is a planned attack, we would be getting hit at one of our most vulnerable times. It's apparent that this may very well be the scenario we have feared."

Clark turned to FEMA director Miguel Hernandez. "Best case, worst case."

"Well, best case is easy," Hernandez replied. "Nothing more than minor transportation problems - commuter trains being delayed, traffic lights out, airports unable to function. The source of the problem is found quickly, people's power is restored within 24 hours, and this becomes a holiday inconvenience that people joke about years from now." Hernandez paused. "Worst case is a situation we have discussed at length, but one that we are in no means prepared to handle."

"Give it to me," Clark replied tersely.

Hernandez looked around the room and then began. "Clearly, people have already lost their creature comforts - lights, TV, internet service, cell phone usage once their batteries die. In the first 24 hours, flashlight batteries will die. Refrigerators will not be able to keep perishable food cold.

"Grocery stores have generators that will keep their food cold, but most of those are gas powered, and gas stations will not be able to pump gas. Running water will cease in most places within a 2-to-3-day window. When this happens, not only do we lose access to drinking water, but toilets will no longer flush. Human waste will begin to back up, and that will quickly become a serious problem.

"There will be a rush on gas stations, pharmacies and grocery stores. Food, bottled water, and gasoline will disappear quickly, with no means to gain access to additional resources. With no way to communicate, and no way for people to understand how much longer this will go on, a sense of panic will begin to set in within 48-72 hours. By that time, the room temperature in most apartments and homes will be quickly dropping. Most people have no more than a few days' worth of food in their homes."

Hernandez paused. "Continue," Clark said grimly.

"First responders will be quickly overwhelmed with calls. Homebound people will be the first to die, many within the first week due to lack of access to their medicines and medical equipment. In cities with high rise buildings, there are hundreds of people in elevators at any given time. Those people will have been stuck there since the power went out.

"But it is the communication aspect that is most likely to cause a mass panic. People have become accustomed to instant access to information. The concept that they have no idea what has caused the outage, nor any knowledge about how long it will last, will cause their worst fears to build on themselves. Meanwhile, the police on the streets also lack information, as do local government officials.

"Let's take New York City as an example. We're talking millions upon millions of people in a very small geographic area who are suddenly competing for extremely limited amounts of the things they need to survive. Looting will begin within days, and the police will be quickly outnumbered. Even the most rational citizens will realize that the government is not prepared for a crisis like this, and even if they were, how long will it be before they get to my family? People will begin to fend for themselves, and the chaos begins to reach a new level that almost assuredly includes violence and death."

"What about the nuclear plants?" Clark asked.

"Regulations were put in place a few years back that stipulate that anytime a plant loses power, the switch to generator power triggers a gradual shutdown of the plant. It's automatic. We've already checked, and those shutdowns are in effect currently."

Clark nodded. At least one potential crisis had been handled proactively rather than reactively. He decided to follow that up with another proactive move. "None of us know how bad this is going to get, and it is my job to make sure this country is as prepared as possible to defend itself. That said, I want one of our priorities to be getting sufficient fuel to our weapons facilities in order to keep them functional in a scenario where we need the ability to launch."

The room fell silent, as nobody knew what to say, although everyone realized a nuclear strike was not out of the question, especially since there was no way to know if additional attacks against the country were imminent. Clark hated the silence and nodded at Hernandez to continue.

"Mr. President, everything I have mentioned to this point is all likely to happen in the first four or five days. People in the United States today are entirely unprepared for something like this, and worse yet, they are quite frankly *unable* to take care of themselves in most cases. If this matter extends into a second week...honestly...we will have an unprecedented level of hysteria in the streets of all our major cities on the east coast. The number of deaths will be unknown for an extended period for two reasons. First, our ability to communicate will have been greatly diminished. Second, most of those people may not be discovered for quite some time."

Hernandez concluded with an even grimmer outlook further into the future. "There was a congressional commission formed to look at this topic in 2008. The commission's report reached the conclusion that in the event of a blackout that lasted a year or more, only ten percent of the population would survive. Everyone else would either die of disease, starvation, or from consequences of the general breakdown of society at large."

Defense Secretary Harold O'Bryan spoke up. "Mr. President, based on the situation as it appears to be, especially the idea that we have no idea what is going to happen moving forward, I think we should consider looking at our Defense Readiness Condition."

Vance Harrison jumped in. "I think that is an overreaction, Mr. President. We don't have enough information yet."

O'Bryan was literally gritting his teeth. "Damn it, Vance! If a nuke was in the air on its way to this very building, you would be debating whether or not to go from five to four."

Clark, fully realizing at that moment the huge burden borne by the President of the United States, sat in his chair at the head of the table. He was surrounded by the people that he himself had chosen for situations such as this. The conversation was breaking down, so he began shaking his head and holding his hands out, his palms facing away from him.

"Wait," he said calmly. "How quickly can I get a briefing on the history of the DEFCON scale? I want to know when and why the status has changed through the years. I don't want to alarm the public with an unnecessary change, but I also need to know if any Congressional funding is tied to a change in the DEFCON status. Also, I want to know who is involved in the decision regarding a change in the DEFCON status. How quickly can I get something on this?"

Defense Secretary Harold O'Bryan and Tom Stewart, Chairman of the Joint Chiefs of Staff, glanced at each other. With a quick nod, Stewart spoke up. "We can give you the Cliff's notes version right now, Mr. President, and we can get you a more thorough right-up within an hour."

With a wave of his hand toward himself, the President silently acknowledged that he was ready.

Stewart began. "Let's start with the protocol. You are under no obligation to consult with Congress regarding a change in the defense condition. My experience has been that any change is made following consultation with the National Security Council. Statutory members include yourself, the Vice President, and the Secretaries of State, Defense, and Energy. Non-statutory members include the National Security Advisor and the Secretary of the Treasury. The Chairman of the Joint Chiefs serves as the primary military advisor to the Council. The Director of National Intelligence, the Attorney General, and the CIA Director are frequently involved, as are others if the situation pertains to their areas of expertise. If a change in status is believed to be appropriate, the participants narrow to the President, the Secretary of Defense, the Chairman of the Joint Chiefs, and any combat commanders deemed to be relevant to the conversation."

As the President weighed the information, the Defense Secretary spoke up. "Each DEFCON level defines specific security, activation, and response scenarios for the troops in question. Defense Condition five is peace time. The military is at normal readiness. DEFCON four entails a distinct increase in intelligence and security measures, and the military moves to above normal readiness. At DEFCON three, all branches of the military move to an increased state of force readiness, and the Air Force moves to a 15-minute mobilization window. DEFCON two is one step away from nuclear missile launches, and all armed forces are ready to deploy and/or engage within a six-hour window."

O'Bryan paused before continuing, as if he never thought he would have to say the words out loud.

"At DEFCON one, Mr. President, we are at maximum readiness to engage in all out nuclear war."

The weight of the words again caused an eerie silence to fall over the room. It was not as if they hadn't realized the gravity of the situation, but nobody is ever really prepared for the direst of circumstances until those circumstances are thrust upon them.

"Give me some examples of DEFCON levels four through two," he requested.

Stewart stepped in to answer this. "First, these classifications are not global. DEFCON status can be changed for a certain geographic area or a specific branch of the military. DEFCON four has been used fairly frequently." He continued. "Stateside, DEFCON three was declared on September 11, and we remained on standby for a potential increase to DEFCON two, which did not occur. DEFCON three was also declared during the Yom Kippur war in 1973 when it appeared that the Soviets might get involved. It was also initiated during the time of Operation Paul Bunyan in the DMZ in 1976.

"We've reached DEFCON two twice," Stewart said. "Once was during the opening phase of Desert Storm. That was primarily because we were concerned about Saddam Hussein unleashing chemical weapons, and we had to be ready to drop the hammer on him quickly. The other time, of course, was the Cuban Missile Crisis. Strategic Air Command was ordered to DEFCON two, although the rest of the forces remained at three. SAC remained at DEFCON two for about three weeks."

O'Bryan jumped in again. "Long story short, Mr. President, here's the situation in a nutshell." If the moment had not been so intense, Clark would have been admiring the efficiency of these two men. They were clearly used to working together, and they were giving him *exactly* what he had asked for. There was zero fluff or unnecessary information.

O'Bryan continued. "The only instances in which we reached DEFCON two were limited to a specific geographic area. We have never been beyond DEFCON three at a global level. The question, for now, is this. Do we feel like we are at a moment unprecedented in US history? That is the measuring stick. Leaders around the world are entirely familiar with our DEFCON status, and they are watching. It is not unusual to move more than one number at a time. I think this is too serious to only move to DEFCON four. A move to DEFCON three would be entirely reasonable under the circumstances. If we move to two, it will undoubtedly cause a global panic. It could potentially cause pre-emption."

The President looked around the room. "Vance, do you disagree with this thought process?"

Harrison looked around the table and realized he was a lone wolf. He also realized that this was an easier decision for the President if his advisors were in unanimous agreement. "No, sir."

Clark looked around the table. "Anyone else?" Nobody spoke. He looked at Stewart. "Mr. Chairman?" Stewart replied, "I agree 100%, Mr. President."

The President of the United States is also the Commander in Chief. In the end, this decision is his to make. Clark leaned forward and rested his elbows on the table. He rested his chin between his palms, with his hands and fingers running along his jawline on both sides. He sighed deeply, then leaned back and sat up straight in his chair. "Let's move to DEFCON three for now. Make all branches of the military aware that this could change at a moment's notice, and to be on high alert."

"Yes, sir," Stewart replied. "But I can assure you that the move to three will keep them on high alert without me having to tell them."

As the President stood to exit, everyone else rose as well. He looked around the room before speaking. "I'm prepared for this. My mind is clear." His voice was firm. "All of you are prepared for this too, or I never would have offered you the position you currently hold. We'll work our way through this together."

The President walked out of the room with his chief of staff by his side. Patrick Welch looked at him. "Operation Paul Bunyan?"

Welch had known this man for nearly twenty-five years. He knew when it was suitable to lighten the mood and when it was not. He also knew when the mood *needed* to be lightened. This was one of those moments.

The President smiled. "I had a feeling you might ask about that. It was truly bizarre and escalated quickly. Believe it or not, it is also known as the axe murder incident."

Welch stopped in his tracks momentarily before resuming his pace. "Give it to me," he said.

"From what I recall, there was a work party cutting down a poplar tree in the DMZ so the UN workers could have a better view. A group of North Koreans killed them with their tools, claiming that the tree had been planted by Kim Il-Sung. A couple of days later, we went in with an over-the-top show of force to cut the rest of the tree down. They were almost daring the North Koreans to confront them.

They didn't, of course. So, they cut the tree down. Mission accomplished. Operation Paul Bunyan."

"If only this one was that simple," Welch said.

"Amen to that," replied the President.

CHAPTER 56

December 23, 4:10 PM Eastern Standard Time
December 24, 4:10 AM China Standard Time
Beijing, China
Central Headquarters at Zhongnanhai

Chinese president Xao Ming walked into the communications room, where a secure video link had been set up. When he sat down, he saw a smiling man greeting him on the other end of the link. The smiling face belonged to Russian president Nikolai Volkov.

"Good morning, President Volkov," Ming said stoically, which was the way he said nearly everything.

Volkov laughed heartily while holding a celebratory glass of vodka in one hand. "Success!" he said boisterously, which was the way he said nearly everything. The two men were polar opposites in practically every way, other than their shared desire to destroy the United States.

"Phase one has indeed been successful," Ming replied. "We were able to achieve 100% success with the cyber weapon we purchased. Both it and the agent from whom we bought it did everything we were hoping for, which I would fully expect, considering the price we had to pay."

Ming paused, and Volkow knew exactly why. This was a cost that was to be split between the two countries, and Ming was waiting for an update from Volkov as to Russia's participation in the cost-sharing. The Russian contribution had to be a little more creative since they were cash strapped. The deal had been made based on the one consistent asset that Russia could always fall back on - oil.

"The price updates are in effect," Volkov said, his tone still celebratory. "Your first shipment at the discounted price is on its way to you as we speak, and that price will remain in effect until our half of the cost is paid, just as we discussed. Meanwhile, I have an envoy in Canada making sure their government clearly understands that they are to join us in reducing oil exports to the United States by 10%. They will not want to do this, but by paying a 12% premium on the oil we import from them, we will help ease their burden financially. Aside from that, we will be communicating very clearly to them the consequences of taking the wrong side in this matter. Once they see that America has been brought to her knees in such a short window of time, I feel sure they will do what we ask."

"And what about OPEC?" Ming replied.

"No problem at all. They have been in a holy war with the West for thousands of years. Trying to convince them to join us in crippling the 'infidels' was one of the easier sales pitches of my lifetime. Once all aspects of this phase are in place, we will have dramatically affected the flow of crude oil to the United States from its three largest suppliers. I still think we should have cut them off completely. I'm just not as diplomatic as you are, I guess."

Ming stared at the screen before speaking. "As we have discussed previously, we cannot execute this plan to the end if the rest of the world sees it as a direct attack. We have complete deniability on the power outage. They will eventually find the weapon we planted and fix the problem, but we have made sure they will never be able to tie it back to us. The outage will naturally cause significant harm to the global economy, thereby throwing supply and demand out of kilter. That will allow us to justify the supply reductions without cutting them off entirely. If the proper people keep their mouths shut, our role in causing these events will not be known until we are ready to unveil our plan to take over the United States."

"I do understand your position, *our* position," Volkov replied, withholding the tone and eye roll that he wanted to add. "I have already communicated with Medinsky at the United Nations. His first task will be to gather the world's UN representatives in the safe house we have put in place for them. It is stocked with enough food, fuel, and other resources for them to live there for months if necessary. Medinsky introduced this process months ago as part of the UN's long overdue update to its emergency plan. Everyone there realized the old plan was archaic, so nobody will think twice about it being tied to the outage. It had not been updated since the last major power outage in the northeast United States back in 2003. He modeled the 'emergency' after that, except with the contingency of an extended outage. Meanwhile, Medinsky is also going to work with your ambassador there to communicate to the other countries' ambassadors that Russia and China are willing to do everything they can to assist the United States in its time of need."

"Very well." Ming nodded in approval.

Volkov raised his glass and took another drink of the Russo-Baltique. The bottle was nearly empty, and even though the price had been heavily discounted for him, he had still vowed never to buy another one at such a ridiculous price. However, he knew when he bought it that he would be drinking it during the planning and execution of the downfall of America. He wanted the best vodka for this, and it was indeed the best. He would be sure to save enough for one last celebration when the United States of America collapsed for good, and Russia reappeared as the dominant force on the global landscape. He already had a plan to deal with the Chinese once the Americans were out of the way.

"On to phase two?" he said into the monitor.

"Phase two is already under way," Ming replied. "Good day, Mr. President."

As the two were disconnected, Volkov decided that the Russo-Baltique, as good as it was, would taste even better when combined with another one of Castro's Montecristos.

CHAPTER 57

December 23
4:55 PM
The Oval Office

Clark was in his seat, surrounded by Welch, his political advisors, and Press Secretary Donna Zimmerman. They had learned that significant portions of the country were without power, but they were not yet sure of the full extent of the outage. While it was clear that Clark would need to speak to the country, the current debate was when and how much information to divulge. On top of that, they had no idea how many people, if any, would be able to see the broadcast.

Anthony Jones, one of Clark's top advisors, spoke first. "If we tell the public that a cyber attack has knocked out power to a significant portion of the country, we will cause a panic unlike any ever seen in this country. It will make the market crash of 1929 seem like a sunny day in the park by comparison."

"I agree," Welch said. "Plus, we don't know exactly what is going on yet. We need a better grip on what has transpired, and we need more time to see if anything else happens before we put the President on TV. Donna, we need you to be purposely vague at the briefing – 'We aren't sure yet what caused the outage; we feel sure power will be restored relatively quickly; et cetera."

"Yes, sir," Zimmerman replied. It is set to start in just a couple of minutes, so I am going to head over to the briefing room."

She began to gather her things when the President's secretary knocked and opened the door. "Mr. President, I have Secretary O'Bryan on the line."

"O'Bryan? This can't be good," Clark said as he moved to the phone. "Harold," he said as he picked up the line. Clark listened and the entire room watched his facial expressions as he listened to the Defense Secretary. Clark's face took on a look of concern. "The Russians?" He listened for a few more seconds, then said, "Okay. Tell Tom to keep us updated."

Clark looked at Zimmerman. "Hang on, Donna. This whole thing just took an entirely different turn."

"What is going on with the Russians?" Welch asked.

"Chairman Stewart just informed Secretary O'Bryan that there are several large movements of Russian troops. The actions were coordinated, and they are not wasting any time. They are moving quickly to the southwest, in the direction of the Middle Eastern countries. Stewart said by his best estimate, the movement started at almost exactly the time that the power went out."

"What the hell is going on?" Patrick Welch was usually the calm voice in the room, but at this point the room was spinning for everyone.

"Get Leeds and Rockwell in here. And Cavanaugh," Clark said. Welch left the room to make the calls.

"What should I do about the briefing, sir?" Zimmerman asked.

"Same exact thing, Donna. We need to send a message that the government is up and running, but it is even more critical now that we not let any details get out until we have a better idea of what is going on. Tell them I plan to make a statement this evening if the power is not back on by then. That should buy us some time. If not, we will see if there is a way to get something out via print media."

"Yes, sir," Zimmerman replied, and she left the room.

CHAPTER 58

December 23
7:50 PM
New Paltz, New York

Within an hour of the power outage, UN Secretary general Oleg Medinsky had put the emergency plan into place. He explained to those who were implementing it that although this situation was not a true emergency, it would serve as a good trial run in case one came about at some point in the future. He assured the members that the location to which they were traveling had generators, plenty of food and fuel, and a fully stocked bar. He knew the third item would seal the deal if the first two didn't.

Travel was tricky. What was usually an hour and a half drive from Manhattan to New Paltz up Interstate 87 took twice that long due to the weather. Medinsky felt sure that the roads would not remain passable for much longer, so he was glad that everyone made it. Upon arrival, he again assured them that they would have plenty of creature comforts, and that an overwhelming amount of security was in place. He also assured them again that this was just sort of a drill for a true emergency, and that he had already been informed by leaders in New York City that the power should be restored relatively quickly. This, of course, was entirely untrue.

The group gathered in a large room for a quick, informal meeting and a roll call. Once the roll call was completed, Medinsky pointed out that the only person missing was Keith Keough. Medinsky said that while he had not heard from Keough, he felt sure that his absence was due to the outage, and that he was needed back in Washington more than he was needed here.

Medinsky made a brief introductory statement, during which he affirmed the previously scheduled meeting for the next day at 10:00. The agenda would not change from what was supposed to have taken place the following morning in Manhattan. He explained that other than logistical matters, it would be business as usual. As the two had previously planned, Liwei Zhang then asked for a moment to speak, and Medinsky gave him the floor.

In order to show that business as usual was the motto for their unplanned trip, several members of the United Nations Interpretation Service were present. The UNIS was part of the UN's Department for General Assembly and Conference Management. Since trying to translate to every language spoken by the members would be inefficient, the DGACM translated into six languages: Arabic, Chinese, English, French, Russian, and Spanish. As Zhang began to speak, everyone listened via their headphones, which were set to the language they preferred for the translation.

"I know some of you are aware that during the past few days, my country has had some difficult conversations with the United States. Even though we were disturbed by their lack of honest dialogue during our conversations, I am not here to point fingers or assign blame. I am just speaking to you to say that despite those recent differences, the People's Republic of China stands shoulder to shoulder with our American friends, and our government is ready to provide whatever assistance is necessary to ensure that America and its citizens get through this difficult time, although I feel sure the problem will be resolved in a timely manner."

CHAPTER 59

Saturday, December 24
5:30 AM
The Oval Office

Sam Clark had not yet slept, nor had any of the people in his inner circle. They had worked most of the night trying to gather information. They had learned that the grid was not compromised nationwide. However, the power was out everywhere east of the Mississippi River and along the entire west coast. The outage also extended through the outskirts of the mountain states. Phoenix and Las Vegas were out, as was Salt Lake City. The geographic center-third of the United States was still functional, except for Texas, which had been specifically targeted to be knocked out as well.

The portion of the country that still had power looked much more impressive on a map of the United States than it did from a population perspective. Much of the area in question was sparsely populated, and it had been estimated that only 10-12% of the citizens of the United States of America still had power.

There were two immediate problems as determined by the meetings that ran through the night, and there was a team assigned to each. One team was to work night and day trying to restore power. The second team's goal was to try to prevent mass chaos among those who had now been out of power for approximately 15 hours. A third team was going to make a best-effort attempt to communicate with the country. Media outlets were limited as well, but not nearly as limited as those trying to get access to news about what was going on and when power might be restored.

This meeting was the first of those, and it was about goal number one - getting the power restored. In the room were Clark, chief of staff Patrick Welch, Vice President Charlie Sullivan, FBI Director John Rockwell, Secretary of Energy Kelly McDonald, CIA Director Sheldon Cavanaugh, and Tammy Leeds, the one person that Clark was beginning to consider his go-to person. In his opinion, the National Security Advisor had been the most productive person in the room throughout the crisis as well as during the events leading up to it.

Clark spoke first. "Okay, people, I'm eagerly waiting for some good news."

McDonald, the energy secretary, spoke up. "Mr. President, if I may, I'm going to give you some background because it is vital to understanding our plan moving forward. I'll make it quick."

Clark gave him an affirmative nod.

"We have known for a long time where our weak spots are on the grid. Currently, there are three primary grids in the United States. The operation of these grids and the transport of power across the country includes the cooperation of thousands of power companies, all of which are interconnected. All of them use SCADA systems (Supervisory Control and Data Acquisition).

"The process of moving power across the country begins with the company generating the power. Once generated, it passes along a network that is overseen by regional organizations. At that point, the process is subject to federal regulation. After that, it is passed to local power companies, whose job it is to deliver electricity to its customers. State regulations take effect at that point. So instead of one entity overseeing the process, now there are fifty, and at the state level, the regulations are much more focused on the finances than on safety and security. Because this system of transmission is so complex and handled by so many different regulatory entities and power companies, the need for online control systems is more vital than ever.

"That would place the burden on each company along the transmission lines to provide top notch cyber security. Since some of the smaller companies have greater concern for cost, they tend to have the least security. Hackers do not have to get into the entire system to shut down a grid. They only need to hit a spot somewhere in the system. Hence, the entire grid was ripe for cyber attack. Unfortunately, the internet was not designed with the idea of keeping anyone out."

McDonald did not see anyone attempting to cut him off, so he moved forward.

"On the equipment side, the most critical piece of physical equipment in transmitting electricity across the country is the LPT - large power transformer. These things are big and bulky, but effective at what they do. They are located, in large numbers, all over the country, tens of thousands of them across our landscape. The problem with them is that many of them are ancient - thirty or forty years old. However, they are still highly functional because they don't have a lot of moving parts.

"The difficulty with the LPTs," McDonald continued, "is replacing them. They cost anywhere from $5 million to $10 million each, and because no two of them function in the same exact manner, which is because the local power companies all have different specs, they are not interchangeable. And because they are so reliable and durable, there is not much inventory.

"There are less than a dozen plants capable of building an LPT, and they would not be completed for a year or more, not to mention that transporting something that big could not be done over the road. It would have to be done on specialized rail lines, few of which still exist because they weren't used often enough. So realistically, even though there are some spare LPTs located here and there across the country, we are unable to get them from point A to point B."

"And that's the quick version?" Vice President Sullivan asked.

Clark ignored the sarcasm. "I've been aware of this threat, but I have to admit that I feel I have not been as informed about it as I should have been. Why haven't people been shouting from the rooftops about something with the potential to cause this much damage?"

"We tend to be a reactive society," McDonald answered. "The prominent cyber attacks of which the public is aware just did not raise the level of concern needed to get people to take more action. For example, it is a fact that bad traffic intersections simply will not get fixed until enough people get killed at those intersections to cause an uproar. On a much larger scale, how many times did terrorists attack vital US interests with limited public outcry? Then 9/11 happened."

Clark took a moment to soak in what McDonald was saying. He realized that the description of America as a reactive society was indeed accurate. He had one more question before moving forward. "The LPTs, why can't they be delivered over the road? We have a greatly reduced traffic burden and we can make all highways one way if we need the space."

"There are still numerous reasons, but primarily, it's the bridges," McDonald replied. "They can't bear the weight."

Clark nodded and began his 'processing process.' "I hope you didn't come in here to describe the problem to me without some sort of proposed solution."

"We really have limited options, sir, but here is the best temporary solution to at least restore a limited amount of power. There are places that store spare parts for the LPTs. These parts are small enough to transport by flatbed truck to the LPTs that supply electricity to the most people in a geographic area. We can, for lack of a better word, 'patch' some of them back into operation. We will try to get the cities back up first. That helps the largest number of people. Plus, those in the more sparsely populated areas are, quite frankly, better equipped to survive than those in the metropolitan areas."

Tammy Leeds joined in. "The other concern, Mr. President, is finding the source of the attack and cutting off the hackers' access to shutting the grid down again. The good news is that we think we have found the source of the attack. We are not sure yet exactly what or who we are dealing with. We have our best people trying to get inside of this thing and break it down to see how it works and where it may have originated, but so far it is unlike anything that any of us have seen before."

"That's a start." Clark sat back down. "How long?"

Leeds and McDonald looked at each other as if they didn't want to break the news. Leeds fell on the sword. "A month, possibly longer."

Clark was back up instantly. He walked over to the window and stared for thirty seconds, although it seemed like an hour to those in the room. Finally, he turned back to face them.

"You all know way more about this than I do. You are my team. I hired you because I trust you. Get to work."

The room quickly filled with chatter. They were already laying the groundwork as they left the room.

CHAPTER 60

December 24
9:15 AM
Central Kentucky

Johnny Sims was not "off the grid," as were some people who tried to eliminate any record of their existence. He was, however, adamant that the general public was woefully unprepared for any type of circumstance in which they lost access to their creature comforts for an extended period. He was thoroughly convinced that 15-20 percent of the people in the United States would be in a panic within 24 hours, and well over 50 percent would be certifiable in three days or less. Worse, he felt that in a situation where people lost power for a week or more, the death toll could be staggering. Few people had back-up sources of power or enough food and water on hand to last more than a couple of days. Now we were going to find out.

Aside from that, he was fascinated by the country's obsession with online transactions, despite the hacking that occurred every day across the country. The hacking was not limited to individual consumers. In recent years, hackers had caused major security breaches that were widely discussed on the news, from large corporate retailers to government agencies. Johnny was dumbfounded by the idea that people just continued with blind naivete that it would never happen to them.

Johnny was as prepared as a person could be for the current situation. He had read a great deal about the threat of a cyber attack on the United States, and while he did not consider himself a conspiracy theorist, he also felt there was no need to be unprepared. Through his hand cranked radio, Johnny had heard about the change to DEFCON 3. Granted, his source for that information was a conspiracy theorist that had a radio show where he frequently talked about aliens invading the planet. Johnny found himself slightly amused by the fact that the guy that everyone considered crazy seemed to be the only person in all forms of media that was prepared for the situation – his was the lone voice on the airwaves.

Johnny was gathered around the table with his wife Molly, his 17-year-old son Ben, and his twin 14-year-old daughters Emma and Jennifer. "What does that mean, Death con 3?" Jennifer asked.

Johnny chuckled. "DEFCON 3, D-E-F-C-O-N," he replied, "it means that the government doesn't think this is an accident. It also means that they don't think this is a short-term problem. Third, they must also think that this might be the first wave of an attack on our homeland."

Molly spoke to Johnny in a way he recognized – a tone that meant 'don't scare the kids.' She said, "Thanks for the uplifting information, Johnny, but I think she was actually asking what DEFCON means."

Johnny smiled, acknowledging the tone. "It stands for Defense Condition, or Defense Readiness Condition. It is an alert system for our military. The scale is numbered one to five, with five meaning we are at peace. The lower the number, the worse the situation."

"So how bad is it?" Emma asked.

Johnny shrugged his shoulders toward Molly, acknowledging that he needed to answer the question. Molly nodded her approval. "Well, it's bad, but it is seen more as a notice to be on high alert. It is a level of increased readiness and intelligence while also providing for higher security measures. My guess is they don't know yet exactly what happened, but they want everyone to be 100% ready just in case."

"I'm almost scared to ask," Ben chimed in, "but have we been at DEFCON 3 before?"

Johnny saw no need to sugar coat the situation. Plus, he had gotten the nod from Molly. "The last time we were at DEFCON 3 was a little event you might have heard of. We refer to it as 9/11."

CHAPTER 61

December 24
6:50 PM
Situation Room

As Clark entered, there was a debate in the situation room about the proper protocol regarding federal aid. In particular, the discussion was centered around which issues were state and local matters, and which ones were federal. It seemed to Clark that FEMA Director Miguel Hernandez had this issue under control. "With the breadth of the outage, there is no way this can be a federal issue. The states, in coordination with each of their local governments, will have to deal with the outage as best as possible for the first few days. If the power remains out beyond that time frame, then we must prioritize where to send federal assets once they are mobilized."

Attorney General Gabe McMillan spoke up. "Just so we're clear, there are very specific protocols in place for a situation like this. The first line of authority is with the governor of each state. They will work with local governments to make sure police and first responders have the assets they need to function. When or if it is needed, the governors will then mobilize their National Guard troops. This should at least temporarily stabilize the situation. At that point, it is at each governor's discretion to request federal assistance, and I think we should be prepared to receive such requests from all directions."

Defense Secretary Harold O'Bryan elaborated on the role of the military. "We have the ability to activate tens of thousands of troops relatively quickly. The National Guard takes the lead until we are activated. According to Title X, once activated, we would move into the primary role, supported by the National Guard and state and local police."

Clark intervened. "In this case, could we not consider this an act of war? I feel as if we have been directly attacked, albeit not in a traditional fashion. But I would most definitely consider this a hostile act against our nation."

McMillan pondered that. "That's interesting. I would have to do some research on that, but right now I would tend to lean toward maintaining standard protocols and waiting for the states to request assistance."

Charles Sullivan joined the fray. "I don't think we have time to wait around for a 50-page legal opinion. Our primary 'protocol' (Sullivan hated that word, and the tone with which he used it indicated that) should be to protect our people. We don't want another Hurricane Katrina on our hands."

McMillan countered. "I understand, Charlie, but the point is likely moot. We need time to organize anyway, and I feel sure that by the time we could get troops mobilized, we will have received numerous requests for assistance from the state governments."

"Fair enough," Clark said. "Let's move forward."

McMillan continued. "In a different type of emergency, it would also be up to the governor to order an evacuation. However, in this situation, it seems as if that would be the *worst* thing to do. I would think it would be in everyone's best interest to stay put where you have food and water and shelter."

"Agreed," Hernandez said. "This also gives the first responders easy access to get from point A to point B to better assist everyone."

Clark nodded. "That makes sense. We'll send that message to the state capitals. Everyone will be strongly urged to stay in their residences. Continue, Miguel."

"Once we arrive, we have to assess the situation and find the areas of greatest need. First and foremost, we need to make sure law and order remains intact. Police must be equipped with everything they need, up to and including additional firearms and ammunition. If we begin addressing problems without proper security in place, looters will destroy our progress.

"Once the area is secure, we have to find a way to keep the water on. We also need to maintain a functioning water treatment system. Sewage backup could become a public health crisis in a relatively short period of time. We will need all the generators we can get our hands on, and access to fuel to keep them running. The generators are the key to the whole thing. We *have* to keep the water pumping to the taps, and the wastewater pumping to the sewer plants."

"Miguel," Clark interrupted him.

"Yes, sir, Mr. President," Hernandez replied.

"I've been thinking about this. What about the hospitals? Aren't they near the front of the line? People will die quickly there without power."

"Most of the hospitals are well prepared for emergency outages, sir," Hernandez said. "Most power outages are extremely short - the average outage lasts less than two hours - but in a hospital, a patient without electricity for two hours is frequently not going to survive. Because of that, every hospital has the ability to keep the lights on and the medical equipment functional. Their main concern would be fuel, but that would only become an issue during a prolonged outage, and if we are dark that long, we will have time to get to them before it becomes urgent."

Clark was impressed with Hernandez. He had always assumed he was capable, but now that the chips were on the table, he was proving himself a cool customer.

Hernandez continued. "Once we have security and water, we have to get to the groceries. Most people's food supply won't last very long, and much of it is perishable. We will have to protect grocery stores, along with convenience stores and gas stations. Those are the first places looters will strike.

"Once we have done all of that, we need to get essential government departments online and functioning, so we can maintain appropriate levels of communication between us and the individual cities and states. We will also need to help media outlets get back online. Information will be the key to preventing a panic, and the ability to disseminate information is crucial to the recovery. We must properly prioritize, and it is vital that we do this in the right order, or these cities will fall into a state of utter chaos. These days, people don't know how to live without cell phones. How do you think they will react to not having food or water?"

Clark stood up and began walking around the large table. "OK, so once we have the logistics in place to stabilize the situation, we have to restock the cities. If I am understanding correctly, the three primary things we will need to get to them are food, water, and fuel. Correct?"

"Yes, sir," Hernandez replied.

"I know we have millions of MREs and large reserves of water. What about emergency fuel?"

"Collectively, the gas stations will have millions upon millions of gallons of fuel in their underground storage tanks. The key is to preserve that fuel and ration it accordingly. In a striking bit of irony, these stations will need fuel to access their fuel because their pumps are down. Unfortunately, because the kind of generators necessary to pump that fuel out of the tanks cost somewhere in the $50,000 range, many stations don't have one. They can't get the fuel from their tanks. Most states have emergency generators that are of this quality, but not enough of them. So, it is important that we oversee the delivery of these generators, so we can make sure they are going to the places where they are most needed."

"We handle the fuel, Mr. President," O'Bryan said. "We can deliver and allocate it as needed through the Defense Logistics Agency."

Clark nodded and continued his way around the table.

"We have a significant problem with the MREs, Mr. President." Clark stopped walking. He was directly across the table from Hernandez. Hernandez looked him in the eye. "Much like the generators, each state has a stockpile of MREs. We all know that 'Meals Ready to Eat' is a simple enough acronym, but the fact is that while military members can get by on those, the general public is not going to like what we consider a 'meal.'

"More importantly, we simply don't have enough of them. It's a bit of a Catch-22. We have tens of millions of MREs, to supplement those that the states have in storage. While that seems like enough, we need to do the math. During Hurricane Sandy, New York had 25 million MREs on hand. That seems like an abundant supply. However, New York City alone has eight million people. Let's say you limit them to one MRE per day per person, which is simply not enough food to survive for any length of time. Even at that severe stage of rationing, the food supply would only last three days.

"In this situation, we have hundreds of millions of people out of power. Because the shelf life of an MRE is only five years, we cannot simply stockpile them in order to keep enough on hand for a nationwide crisis, because chances are, they would go bad. On top of that, there are only a handful of companies that produce MREs, and they are all private companies that cannot possibly fill an order anywhere near the size that we will need."

"Even if we can't get enough MREs for everyone, we need these companies to be at full tilt, producing as many of these as quickly as possible," Clark replied. "Do you have any idea how many they can produce in a week under the current circumstances? We can get them generators or whatever they need to be functional."

Hernandez shook his head slowly.

"What?" Clark spit impatiently.

"It just won't work, Mr. President. Much like any other industry, there is a supply chain, and if all the links in the chain are not operational, the whole process falls apart. If a seat belt maker or a windshield supplier falls behind, the car makers fall behind. The capability to produce large quantities quickly is there, but the supplies are not. The amount of raw goods needed for such a mass quantity simply is not available from the suppliers. They would be buried by unfilled orders within days. This weakness was discovered when the tsunami hit Japan in 2011. Unfortunately, because disasters that would require a huge number of MREs are rare, there's not enough consistent demand for companies to stay afloat."

Vice-President Sullivan broke the silence. "Note to self - if we ever get out of this situation, find other alternatives..."

Hernandez, who butted heads with Sullivan frequently, could not let the comment go unanswered. "For future reference, Mr. Vice President, there are other options. The best one is probably freeze-dried food. They can last up to 25 years in some cases, so we would have the ability to store a much larger amount of them to be available as needed."

"Well why aren't we doing that now?" Sullivan demanded.

"The numbers have been crunched on this," Hernandez replied quickly. "The bare minimum amount of food it would take to keep a single person alive for a year would cost about $2,000. If we needed to provide that amount for, let's just say, 50 million people, you're talking $100 billion. It is an extremely pricey proposition. We have presented it numerous times. The failure to get that done is not a logistical problem. It is a political problem. No funding."

Sullivan saw the comment for what it was - a direct jab aimed straight at him. He opened his mouth to speak and his hand to point at Hernandez, but Clark beat him to it.

"We are all functioning on little or no sleep. And we're in the middle of a crisis of historic proportions that has no end in sight. We don't have time for this. Let's focus on possible solutions for the problem we have right now, not the next one."

Clark looked directly at Hernandez. "What are you not telling me?"

"Mr. President, in our disaster preparations, we have feared a situation like this. We are underprepared to assist our citizens for more than a few days. From a budgeting perspective, I understand that it is hard to justify spending hundreds of millions of dollars every year to prepare for something that may never happen.

"A lot of people in rural areas hunt, and many of them have their own freezers and generators. Because they are more sparsely populated, and frankly, more self-sufficient, I think they need to be secondary. We must focus on metropolitan areas, where we can help the most people in a relatively small geographic area. That said, the size of this outage will quickly deplete our reserves. We can help for two-to-three days at the most before we run out of MREs. At that point, Mr. President, we will run out of food."

CHAPTER 62

December 24
10:45 PM
Central Kentucky

Johnny and Molly Sims were sitting at the kitchen table, trying to get any kind of information about what was happening. Johnny's hand cranked radio was working fine, but most stations were still off the air because of the power outage. Other than the move to DEFCON 3, Johnny knew that nearly all the news he was picking up was being spoon fed by the government. One of the few actual news outlets he could pick up kept repeating that there was a massive power outage caused by the blizzard on the east coast, and that crews were working night and day to get the power restored.

"Total bullshit!" Johnny pounded the table with his fist.

Molly gave him a stern look. "If you wake the kids up…"

"Sorry," he said. "It just burns me up that they put that out there as if the weather caused it. I'm not sure what is going on, but I know we have never gone to DEFCON 3 because of a power outage."

"Do you realize how stupid you would look trying to explain to someone how you knew the country was at DEFCON 3? 'I heard the guy on the radio say it. You know, the one that the aliens abducted for testing a few years back.'"

As Molly finished proving her point, Johnny held up a finger requesting silence. He stared into the distance for a moment before getting up from the table. "Come with me," he said quietly to Molly.

Molly rose from her chair and followed Johnny outside. "What?"

"I hear a plane," Johnny replied. The two stood silently as Johnny stared toward the eastern sky. "There," he said as he pointed to lights in the distance.

"So, what's the big deal?" Molly asked.

"That's the first plane I've seen or heard since yesterday morning," Johnny said. "If the entire eastern seaboard is out of power and buried in a blizzard, what is this one plane doing in the air? And why is it flying so low?"

The two watched as the plane passed. "That's a pretty small plane." Molly observed.

"It's a private jet. What in the hell is it doing? It must be landing in Louisville." Johnny walked quickly back into the house.

"What exactly are you worried about?" Molly was concerned. Johnny was, by nature, a bit of a conspiracy theorist himself, but Molly had never once considered him irrational. After all, they had both been in war zones. They had been in the heat of combat, and Molly understood the hyper-awareness of people like Johnny. Although she had been able to turn that off somewhat, for the sake of her sanity, she recognized it in Johnny and knew that he sensed something out of kilter besides the weather.

Johnny turned to Molly. "Let's just say, hypothetically, that the power outage has nothing to do with the storm."

"Okay." Molly had known Johnny long enough to realize that she would have to play along to get her question answered.

"Let's say it's an attack of some kind - initiated by an outside source that has knocked the power out. What would happen next?"

"Are you talking about an invasion? On our homeland?" Molly's tone was one of dismissal, but Johnny could also hear a bit of concern there.

"Yes. What would happen next? You're a veteran. This is simple."

"Typically, an air assault of some kind that might try to take out strategic defense systems and/or drop large numbers of troops on the ground. Planes everywhere dropping equipment and soldiers. Invasion 101 stuff. But we saw one small jet, Johnny. Come on." Molly's tone was still dismissive, which she realized even though she was not trying to be condescending.

"Right, but we both know that those strategies are archaic, plus they would never work against a country like the United States. But let's say that a country wanted to invade the United States. What would they do to cripple us?"

Molly shrugged. "Tell me, Johnny. I'm tired of the games. It's Christmas Eve for crying out loud."

Johnny continued as if Molly was hanging on his every word. "First, I would knock out the power. Our country's day-to-day operations cease without access to modern technology. Then, knowing that a country the size of the United States with our military power could not be taken using standard tactics, I would hit individual targets that would hurt our country's vital interests - government operations, infrastructure, financial markets. To defeat America, it would have to be by a thousand pinpricks - micro, not macro."

Intrigued, Molly asked the obvious question. "Let's assume you're right. What are they going after here? I love my bourbon as much as anyone, but I wouldn't call it a vital interest. And I don't think the

Louisville Slugger plant qualifies. Attack by a million baseball bats probably wouldn't be the plan."

"I know," Johnny replied. "I'm probably overreacting." He didn't really feel like he was overreacting, but he could tell that Molly thought he was out in left field on this one. He turned to tell her he was going to bed.

"Oh my God," Molly said, and covered her mouth with her hand.

"What?" Johnny walked toward her quickly, hoping she had reached the same conclusion that he had.

Molly removed her hand and stared at Johnny momentarily before whispering, "Fort Knox."

PART III

CHAPTER 63

December 24
11:30 PM
Bowman Field, Louisville, KY

Tom Daniels had drawn the short stick – literally. The four men who ran the airport had drawn straws to see who got what they called the 'Santa Watch' - Christmas Eve to Christmas morning. Obviously, the airport was required to be staffed around the clock, and Christmas Eve was *never* busy. However, with the power outage, the short stick meant that the loser just had to make sure the building didn't catch on fire during his shift.

Bowman Field had a rich history. It was Kentucky's first commercial airport and still served as the oldest continually operating commercial airfield in North America. It opened in 1921, and served several airlines until 1947, when operations were transferred to Standiford Field, which was known later as the Louisville International Airport, and today as Louisville Muhammad Ali International Airport. During World War II, Bowman Field served as one of the nation's most important training bases, and at that time it was the busiest airport in the entire United States. It also had a place in pop culture lore, serving as the location of the Flying Circus in the 1963 James Bond film *Goldfinger*.

Fifty-one weeks out of the year, the four men in charge of the airport laughed at the idea that they were providing 'air traffic control' at Bowman. A mere 200 aircraft operations took place on an average day. Most of that activity came from the 175 private planes based at Bowman.

Most of the time, only two of the four men were in the building. At certain times of the year, three of them would be working together. However, the one week when all four were working was the week leading up to the first Saturday in May - the Kentucky Derby.

Derby week was chaotic, but they loved it. The entire city came alive every year during that time. Restaurants and tourist attractions were filled to capacity. There were activities all over the city for the entire two weeks of the Kentucky Derby Festival. The annual kick-off was Thunder Over Louisville, which was the largest fireworks show in North America. It was usually preceded by an air show. Half a million people flocked to Louisville's waterfront on the Ohio River for a day of festivities. Combine all of that with the beauty of springtime in Kentucky, and it was always a great time to live in the Bluegrass State.

Typically, there were at least two of them at the airport. However, since it was Christmas Eve and the power was out, they had received permission from the Louisville Regional Airport Authority to leave only one of them there until further notice, with another on call around-the-clock. Tom Daniels was mulling over his bad luck when he heard a vehicle pull into the parking lot. He moved out of the air traffic control room and into the lobby, where he looked out the window into the parking lot. Two identical white passenger vans pulled into the parking spots closest to the entrance.

Tom considered this strange circumstance. Surely the drivers knew that no flights were inbound due to the weather and the power outage. All flights had been grounded until further notice. He didn't care to trudge out into the snow, but clearly someone had misinformed these poor guys. If he let them know that no planes were coming in tonight, maybe they could get home in time to get in bed and get some decent sleep so they wouldn't be zombies all day on Christmas.

Daniels walked out the door and across the parking lot. His footprints from walking into the building were the only ones on the entire property. As he approached the first van, the driver's side window came down. Daniels was preparing to ask how he could help the man when he saw the muzzle and attached silencer extending through the open window. The bullet had penetrated Daniels' brain before he even had a chance to offer his help. As the puddle of red began to expand through the pristine white snow, the vans pulled around to the tarmac and waited for the plane, which was scheduled to arrive in twenty minutes.

CHAPTER 64

December 25
12:20 AM
Fort Knox, KY

The white vans exited the Gene Snyder Expressway at the Dixie Highway exit and headed west. Inside each van were the driver and six Chinese paramilitary troops. Each man was equipped with AK-47s and hand grenades, along with a sidearm. One man in each group carried a rocket launcher with three RPG charges. The men inside knew the plan down to the finest points as well as all available contingency options. They rode in silence. The vans were thirty minutes away from the front gate of Fort Knox.

"Merry Christmas. I love you, too." Corporal Jamie Mattingly hung up and stared at his cell phone. Although the base had enough juice to charge his cell phone, they were not running at full capacity. He knew that was the last conversation he would have with his wife until he got home when his shift ended at 5:00 PM. She did not have power and her cell phone was about to die. They had gotten rid of their land line several years ago, so Jamie would have to wait and hear about the kids and their Christmas presents until then. They were loving the power outage and felt like they were living like pioneers. However, both Jamie and his wife knew that feeling would wear off quickly once they were without access to all their gadgets for more than a few hours.

Mattingly walked over to Steve Duncan, who was looking directly at Mattingly and shaking his head.

"Here we are, guarding over 4,000 metric tons of gold, and we are almost as vulnerable to a power outage as some guy living in a $500-per-month apartment five miles up the road."

"That's because there's not any gold in there anymore. I've been telling you that for years. This proves it. Do you think we would be operating off generators if all that gold was really in there?" Mattingly pointed his thumb in the direction of the fortress that housed the vault.

Duncan chuckled. He had heard this concept many times, especially from the locals and the conspiracy theorists of the world. "Well, do you think they would hire the commando squad to protect this place if there wasn't gold in there?"

The two men laughed at that thought. Their mocking was directed at the officers of the United States Mint Police, a government agency tasked with protecting Fort Knox. They also guarded the United States Treasury and the United States Mint facilities in Washington, D.C., Philadelphia, Denver, and San Francisco. Beyond that, they guarded historic documents such as the Constitution and the Gettysburg Address. Locally, they also provided much of the security detail for the Kentucky Derby. In short, the men laughed at them because they had all the high profile, cushy jobs and had never worked a tough shift in their lives.

"True," Mattingly said. "Plus, once the invaders get past us military chumps out front, little do they know what's waiting for them inside where it's nice and warm. If they make the Mint guys get up out of their recliners, there's gonna be hell to pay."

"What on God's green Earth are these guys doing?" Duncan was looking toward the entry road to the property and saw headlights. "Are we expecting anyone?"

"Not that I'm aware of," Mattingly replied. "Those look like government vans. Maybe something to get us back to full power?"

The two men stepped outside of the guard station to meet the vans. The vans slowed to a stop. Mattingly and Duncan approached the first van from each side. Much like the man lying in the snow at Bowman Field, Jamie Mattingly was dead before he hit the ground on the driver's side. One moment before that, Steve Duncan had noticed that there were additional men in the back of the van. Something wasn't right. He had gotten a hand on his weapon before the bullet dropped him to the ground.

It was a two-mile drive from the front gate to the entrance to the fortress that was the actual gold depository building. The two vans killed their headlights and stopped about halfway there. Everyone except the driver got out of the first van and into the second one. The second van held its position while the first van proceeded with only the driver. The building was surrounded by another gate and tall fence with barbed wire around the top. As the van approached, one man emerged from the building by the gate. He stood in front of the gate and signaled for the driver to stop.

The driver killed his lights and waved to the man through the windshield. The guard came around to the driver's side door and said in a questioning voice: "Dave?"

Dave Ross smiled. "Hey Chuck! Front gate tonight, huh? Tough gig on a night like this."

Chuck Richardson laughed and answered, "You got that right! Are you here to try to rescue us from our semi-darkness?"

"I'm here to give it my best shot," Ross said. "It feels weird with it being this dark around here. Usually, it's lit up brighter than a sunny day."

"For sure," Richardson replied. "I didn't hear anything from the guys out front. You saw them, didn't you?"

"Yeah. One of them was talking into a hand-held as I drove away. I assumed he was talking to you."

"No. I didn't hear anything from him." Richardson checked the volume on his hand-held.

"Let me take a look at that," Ross said. "Sometimes a power outage can mess with the frequencies."

Ross put the van in park and got out. Richardson removed the radio from his belt and handed it to Ross. Ross looked at it and asked Richardson if he had any tools that he could use to get the screws out so he could look at the inside.

"Sure," Richardson replied and turned to walk into the guard station.

Ross removed the knife from his vest and quickly moved behind Richardson, slashing his throat from behind and supporting him as he slowly collapsed to the ground. To avoid getting blood on his clothes, Ross dragged him by his feet back into the room. Then he propped him in his chair with his back to the entrance so it would appear he was still watching the gate.

Ross went back to the van and turned it around, so the front of the van was facing the entrance. He flashed his lights quickly one time and waited for the second van. Once it arrived, he opened the gate and closed it behind them once both vans were through. They were inside the gates.

CHAPTER 65

December 25
12:50 AM
Fort Knox Gold Depository

Johnny and Molly Sims knew every back road, paved and unpaved, within an hour radius of their home. They were using some of them tonight. They knew a way, via a dirt road on a farm owned by one of their few close friends, to drive right up to the security fence along the southeast border of Fort Knox's property. They had parked their truck about 500 yards back and walked to the fence. From this location, they could see the main entrance where vehicles went in and out.

They had been sitting there for nearly 45 minutes. They were just about to admit that their imaginations had gotten the better of them when they saw headlights in the distance. They watched in stunned horror as the two guards were shot and killed at the perimeter gate. Molly had to cover her mouth in order to remain silent. They considered retreating to their truck at that point, but Johnny whispered to her to stay so they could see what happened next, and if they could get a glimpse of the people doing this.

They saw only one man drive to the next gate. "Holy shit!" Johnny whispered as he watched the man in the van, who clearly knew the guard by the body language of their conversation, grab the guard from behind and run the knife across his throat. They continued to watch as the other van drove up. They both gasped as they saw the Chinese soldiers filter out of the van. "We have to get out of here, but extremely slowly and quietly," Johnny whispered.

Molly simply nodded as they backed away from the fence line and began a quiet walk back to their truck. It took them about twenty minutes to get back, but they knew it was more important that their retreat be undetected than it was for it to be fast. Johnny was glad he had parked so far away. He felt comfortable that he could start the truck from this distance without being heard. He did so, and he circled around without turning on the headlights. He was nearly a mile down the road on the way back toward their house before he turned on the headlights. He looked at Molly. "Call the kids. Tell them it's time to implement our plan."

Molly grabbed the Motorola Talkabout that was sitting in the seat. The two-way radios were marketed as having a range of 35 miles, but Johnny and Molly had tested them due to their rural surroundings. The range of the radios in their neck of the woods was more in the 20-to-25-mile range. They were on the outer edge of that range right now as Molly tried to reach their children.

"Ben? Ben? Can you hear me?" Ben had been told to keep the radio close as Johnny and Molly were running out the door.

"Yeah, Mom. I'm here." Ben was brave beyond his years, but a little too gung-ho about it for Molly's taste. The Sims family, including the children, was more prepared for what appeared to be happening than anyone they knew, Molly realized, but Ben almost seemed to *crave* becoming a survivalist. Molly had told him over and over about the horrors of war, which she had seen up close. Ben pretended to be appropriately concerned about it, but she could always tell that he was just like his father. In the end, Molly realized two things – first, that's just how 17-

year-old boys are. Second, being just like his father was not a bad thing.

"Ben, when we get home, we're going to have to start implementing our protection plan. Don't say anything to the girls. We're not sure what exactly is going on, but we need to be prepared for the worst."

"They're asleep. I'll be quiet. Do you want me to start bringing things in from the garage?"

"Yes, dear." Molly tried to sound calm while telling her son to begin implementing their family's emergency protection plan.

"Got it, Mom. Anything else?"

"No, Ben, that's all for now. We'll be home in a few minutes." She said it in a tone that could have easily been the same tone she would have used if she and Johnny were on their way back from the movies.

Molly had been totally on board with Johnny's plans since day one. However, she hated his terminology. As they had put the plan together, Johnny had wanted to give it a code name. Molly absolutely refused. He also wanted to use the word 'fortress' to describe what they were going to do to secure their home if the plan had to be put into effect. Molly nixed that one also. She loved Johnny and respected him beyond what words could describe, but she also tried to give the kids a sense of normalcy in their teenage lives while also being adequately prepared. Code names and words like 'fortress' were not used in typical, day-to-day life. However, as they drove down the windy country roads toward their home, Molly was indeed ready to turn her home into a fortress.

Johnny and Molly Sims lived in a house on 48 acres. The land was sloping and mostly tree covered. Their house sat on a flat spot at the highest point on the property, and one of the highest points in the general vicinity. As they pulled into their driveway and reached the top of the hill, their headlights shone on their son, who was walking from the garage to the house with two boxes stacked in his arms. He paused as they pulled the truck into the garage and got out.

"I wasn't sure what all we needed, so I was just grabbing everything I could carry," Ben said.

"Great job, son. Take those two inside, then let's go back into the garage and assess where we are."

Ben nodded and walked through the back door of the house while Johnny held it open. He held it open for Molly as well. As she walked through the entrance, she looked directly at him with a 'take it easy, cowboy' look. Then she smiled at him.

Molly had convinced Johnny not to mention seeing Chinese soldiers less than 30 miles from their home. Instead, they had decided to stick with the story they had told Ben before they left - that they were going to drive around for a while and try to determine the extent of the power outage. They informed Ben (truthfully, Molly reminded herself), that the power was out everywhere they went, and that they needed to expect a prolonged outage under the circumstances.

Johnny began opening boxes. He had stockpiled large amounts of typical supplies needed during a short power outage - basically the things needed to provide light, food, and water. This included things like candles, flashlights, batteries of all types, lighters, matches, bottled water, canned goods, and dry ice.

They decided to wait before opening what would be considered intermediate term supplies - the ones that would not be needed for a few more days. This included things like emergency tinder kits, which could be used to start fires without matches. It also included packs of hand warmers and extra blankets they had in storage. They had several boxes of ammunition they could get out of the safe, for use with shotguns and rifles, as well as their handguns.

Johnny had three large freezers in his basement that held meat of all kinds. This supply could last for several weeks. He owned four generators and had a significant amount of gasoline stockpiled, so they could keep the meat frozen for at least a month. He also took great care in keeping large amounts of canned goods of all kinds, but since they were perishable, he routinely rotated newly purchased items into his storage space while removing previously stored cans for current eating. They also had about 110 gallons of water.

As Molly kept Ben occupied, Johnny began to gather some items together. Eventually, Molly made her way over to him to see what he was doing, although she knew him well enough to know he was going to try to find a way to inform someone about what had happened at Ft. Knox.

"What's your plan," she said as she approached.

Johnny didn't even look up from stocking his travel bag. "I'm driving to Louisville. I guess I will go to city hall. They need to know what is happening, and maybe they will have a way of contacting the powers-that-be in Washington."

Molly kissed his cheek. Johnny looked up and told her, "Nobody comes in this house except me. No friends, no neighbors. Nobody."

"Don't worry about that," Molly replied. Then she smiled. "Just make damn sure you identify yourself clearly when you get back."

CHAPTER 66

December 25
1:10 AM
The Oval Office

President Clark was in the Oval Office, taking a 30-minute nap on a cot he had requested to be kept there. Patrick Welch was going to let him sleep an hour despite Clark's 30-minute maximum stipulation. It had only been fifteen minutes, but the nap was over.

"Secretary O'Bryan on the line, sir. It is urgent."

Clark stared at Welch briefly, with a look of frustration that indicated that *everything* was urgent at this point, although he knew the Defense Secretary would not be calling if this wasn't particularly urgent. Welch recognized the look from Clark but ignored it. The man that he was looking at was under unbearable pressure, and Welch knew it was about to get worse.

Clark picked up the phone. "Yes, Harold."

Welch saw the look register on Clark's face. "Fort Knox? Do you mean to tell me that we lost power at a military base? The location of the gold depository? Please, *PLEASE* tell me I am misunderstanding something!"

Clark put the call on speaker phone, although Welch already knew the details. "Unfortunately, sir, that is correct. They have a back-up system, but it is limited. They have some basic lighting, but other than that they are operating at about 20% capacity."

Clark was rubbing his eyes. "Is this just at Fort Knox or at all of our military bases?"

"All of them, sir," O'Bryan replied.

"Are they all connected to the grid in their surrounding areas? They are not self-sufficient?"

O'Bryan explained, with the understanding that this would not go over well. "In the 1980s, all of our bases produced their own power. From a security perspective, it was the best way to guarantee against a situation like the one we find ourselves in as we speak. However, it was extremely expensive to operate a power plant on every military base. In the 1990s, we started transitioning the bases from self-sustaining sources of power to a situation where each base worked out an arrangement with the company that supplied the power locally. Basically, we plugged into their grids to reduce cost at the bases."

Welch left the room, as he heard his phone ringing again.

Clark leaned back in his chair. "I am baffled by the number of profound weaknesses and vulnerabilities we have," he said. "And I'm scared to ask how many more there are that I don't even know about."

"I will keep you updated, Mr. President."

"Thanks, Harold." Clark had barely disconnected the call when the light started blinking again, and Welch re-entered the room. "Tammy Leeds," he said.

Clark punched the button. "Tammy, you're on speaker with Patrick and me. What have you got?"

"We've got a big problem at Fort Knox, Mr. President."

"I know. I just got off the phone with Harold about the military bases being at 20% capacity."

"No sir, this is something different. There has been a security breach at Fort Knox. At first, we thought it was a false reading because our systems are sending all kinds of alarms due to the outage, but our analysts were convinced that this was an actual breach."

While Leeds was speaking, Welch left the room again. He came back with a sense of urgency. "The Defense Secretary again, Mr. President."

Clark brought O'Bryan in on the call. "Harold, I have Tammy on the line with you. She says we've got a security breach at Fort Knox."

O'Bryan responded. "I wish that was the extent of it, sir. Although phone lines are down, we can still communicate with the military bases using sat phones. We have been continuously trying to reach the base." O'Bryan paused. "Sir, I have just been informed that nobody is answering us from Fort Knox, and that just doesn't happen."

Clark shot up from his chair and stared at the phone. He ran his hand from his forehead all the way over the top of his head to the back of his neck, where he squeezed, attempting to release just a little bit of the tension back there. "Who can we get there and how fast?"

"The National Guard is closest," O'Bryan replied. "But we are not waiting for them to report to us. We are preparing an assault team as quickly as possible, but even if everything goes smoothly, we're looking at two to three hours before they are on the ground there."

Clark was slowly shaking his head. He was in utter disbelief. "Tammy, are there any indications of security breaches at the other bases?"

"We don't think so, sir. One of the reasons that we were slow in confirming the breach at Fort Knox was that we were getting false alarms from secure locations all over the country. The one at Fort Knox was much more subtle, and we think that was done purposely to keep the attention on all of the other distractions."

O'Bryan interjected. "Tammy, what exactly is the extent of the breach? Is it the gates? The depository itself? Surely not the vault?"

Clark realized that was an obvious, but great question. Leeds, for the first time since the lights went out, was less than confident with her answer. "There are numerous layers of security there, and more firewalls than you could ever imagine. Fort Knox is a fortress physically, as well as from a security perspective. But my honest answer, at this point, is that we just cannot tell how bad the breach is."

Clark sat back down in his chair. Patrick Welch, who was known as the man with the ultimate poker face, was staring blankly at the phone. There was a pause of five seconds, ten seconds.

"Mr. President?" O'Bryan inquired.

Clark was nodding, although only Welch could see it. Finally, he spoke. "All warfare is based on deception."

Now the pause came from the other ends of the line. Then O'Bryan spoke.

"Sun Tzu," he said.

"Exactly," Clark replied. "From *The Art of War*. This was never about them being in economic turmoil. They have found our country in a state of weakness. Our reliance on technology for everything we do is a huge vulnerability. They knew they could never invade our country in a traditional version of warfare, but what if this is their invasion? An extended power outage that literally paralyzes our citizens and our institutions, combined with the potential theft of our most valuable tangible asset? We could be brought to our knees simply because of our reliance on technology, and the fact that they are using it against us.

"Get boots on the ground at Fort Knox as quickly as possible; find out what is happening. I want an update as soon as you know something. Tammy, put a team on the matter at Fort Knox. However, I still want your primary focus to be on making sure that if we find a way to get the lights back on, they stay on. Get whatever this is out of our system."

"Yes, sir," came the reply from both lines.

CHAPTER 67

December 25
1:45 AM
NSA Cyber Command Headquarters
Fort Meade, Maryland

Helene Albertsen was a 37-year-old woman who had moved to the United States with her parents when she was twelve years old. The move had been difficult for her. She had loved her home country of Norway, and she was in the middle of an ideal childhood when everything she knew was yanked from under her. She was an angry American all through her teenage years, and she regularly let her parents know how unhappy she was.

The best thing about life in Minnesota was that when she decided to go to Cal Poly Tech for college, she was nearly 1,500 miles away from her parents. Helene had spent a great deal of time by herself in Minnesota, because her parents were working constantly to provide the kind of life that they thought she wanted. She became a self-described computer geek, and, being rebellious by nature, she was fascinated by hackers. However, Helene was not interested in a life of crime. She was a good person who had been uprooted from a life that she loved very much. She decided that she wanted to devote her life to what she realized at a young age was the wave of the future - cyber security.

Helene flew through undergrad studies in three years and went to work for a small cyber security firm. That lasted a mere 18 months before she decided that she could do this better than anyone in the company for which she was working. So, at the ripe old age of 23, she started SafeNet, a security company aimed directly at protecting corporations and their computer security systems.

Within two years, SafeNet was the talk of the cyber security world, and Helene's company had gone from two employees to ten, to twenty-five, to nearly one hundred. She had landed contracts with six Fortune 500 companies, and then one day she received an unexpected visitor - the Deputy Director of the National Security Agency.

Following two visits to Washington to discuss her opportunity, Helene had a life-altering decision to make. She was at a crossroads. She was currently making more money in the private sector than she could have ever imagined. She had mended fences with her parents, and they spent time together when it was possible. Her life was better than she could have ever imagined when she came to the United States as an extremely unhappy young girl. The question was simple - was she willing to give up the money in exchange for making a difference? She was enticed by the fact that at the government level, she would be fighting cyber crime on an international playing field.

Helene gave the decision a considerable amount of thought, but she realized early on that she was going to take the job with the NSA. Deep down, she wanted to make the world a better place, and she realized she could leave a much bigger mark on the world from Washington. And, although she would have never believed it when she was younger, she had grown to love the United States and everything it stood for. She felt honored to be asked to help what she now considered to be her country. She took the job.

Helene had moved swiftly through the ranks of the NSA, and she was now the head of the NSA's Cyber Command division. This unit had been formed in 2010 from the combination of the offensive and defensive operations of the Pentagon's Joint Task Force Computer Network Operations. Less than six months after the US Cyber Command was formed, the Pentagon formally recognized cyberspace as the 'fifth domain' of warfare after land, air, sea, and space. While still part of US Strategic Command, the division was under the command of NSA director Tammy Leeds. This gave Leeds and future NSA directors authority over cyber operations as well as intelligence operations.

Helene Albertsen was seen by many important people as one of the brightest minds in the cyber world. It was in this role that she found herself working approximately 20 hours a day trying to figure out how to get power restored to her fellow Americans. Everyone's worst nightmare, the one that everyone in her line of work knew was likely, if not inevitable, had finally arrived. The power grid had been struck, and so far, nobody had been able to figure out the source of the problem, nor its solution.

Helene leaned back in her chair and rubbed her eyes. How long had it been since she slept? She couldn't remember if this was her third or fourth day with nothing more than a handful of 30-minute cat naps. She had not yet even realized that it was Christmas morning. She had consumed entirely too much coffee and refused to drink anymore because, at this point, it was doing nothing but making her jittery. She probably needed some rest to be as sharp as possible, but she prided herself in her ability to focus. Helene also had an ego. She truly believed that even if she was operating at only 85 or 90 percent of her best, she would still be better than anyone else in the room. She stood up, stretched as tall as possible all the way up on her tiptoes (she had abandoned her shoes hours ago), and sat back down.

Helene had never been happier that she had taken the job with the NSA than she was presently. She was confident enough to believe that she was the right person in the right place at the right time. She would find the source of the problem, no matter how long it took, although time was of the essence. Plus, if her confidence ever did get shaken, all she needed was a pep talk from Josh to get her back on track.

Josh Reed would not stand out in any room. He was 5'7", 145 pounds, and extremely ordinary looking. His intelligence matched his looks. However, Josh had one well-placed relative who was able to get him a job at the NSA because of Josh's squeaky-clean background (there was not much trouble to be found in his mother's basement). Now, he was Helene's assistant, and he was good for Helene to have around. If she was stressed out, he told her a funny joke; if she was exhausted, he would bring a cup of coffee without her having to ask; if she said run through that brick wall, Josh would try his hardest.

Because Helene was under a lot of pressure and needed a break, Josh got her to take ten minutes to eat something at her desk. He knew that Helene was easily distracted if someone started a conversation about anything tech related. He thought the time was right for a diversion, if only for five minutes. He had already gotten her started.

"I'm not sure how much you know about this," Helene said. "Sometimes computer geeks get lost in our own little world. In 2004, the NSA began a project whose aim was to produce the world's most powerful supercomputer. It took nearly a decade, but once it was completed, it was a marvel beyond comprehension. This thing can execute a quadrillion operations per *second,* which created a new term - petaflop."

Josh cut her off. "Slow down…just how big is a quadrillion? I've never even heard that word before."

Helene smiled at the two different worlds in which they lived. "A quadrillion is 1,000 to the 5th power, or 10 to the 15th power, or a thousand trillion, whichever you prefer. Either way, it's a one followed by fifteen zeros." This advanced the fastest computer speed previously known to exist by a factor of one thousand."

"Where is this thing," Josh replied, "and is it secure?"

"It is located at an extremely secure site in Oak Ridge, Tennessee. You know, the place where they worked on a little experiment called the Manhattan Project. It is linked to another one of our facilities in Nowhere, Utah. We are talking about what is easily the largest data mining center on the planet. Nothing else globally is anywhere near this level of sophistication."

Josh had reached the point where he did not know anything else to ask to avoid sounding ridiculous, so he simply uttered the word "fascinating." Without a second thought, Helene took one more bite of what was now a half-eaten sandwich and turned back to her monitor. Josh took the cue and went back to his desk.

CHAPTER 68

December 25
2:05 AM
Fort Knox Gold Depository

Dave Ross had been recruited four years ago. He didn't turn immediately, but as the payments continued to funnel into his checking account, he was able to provide for his ailing wife, and that had generated more loyalty than the government paycheck he received as the head of the IT department at Fort Knox. He had initially tried to convince himself that he wasn't a spy, but eventually he had just made his peace with it.

Jeannie Ross had been diagnosed with Parkinson's Disease seven years earlier. Her slow decline was painful for Dave to watch, particularly since the demands of his job did not allow him to spend as much time with her as he wanted to…as he *needed* to. They did not have any children, and Jeannie's parents had died a decade earlier. He was the only one who could take care of her. His request for a leave of absence had been denied, as had his request to be moved to a less time-consuming position. That had led to a deep bitterness within Dave Ross, and eventually he had agreed to turn against his country in return for enough money to allow he and his wife to be flown out of the United States. He was also assured of enough money to pay for the newest stem cell therapy that had shown promising results against the dreaded disease. Jeannie had no idea what Dave was doing, but he had an extremely sophisticated and well thought out story ready for her once they got on the plane.

Ross had planned extensively for this night. He had worked with several unknown people to prepare the base for tonight. He had integrated the virus in an undetectable manner into the system at the base. It was set to trigger a release of the vault's security features in the short period of time between the power outage and the establishment of limited power through the generators located on the base. He had also installed a program that would disable all forms of telecommunication, including the sat phones on the base. Now it was time to see if his work was going to produce the desired result.

Five additional vans full of soldiers had arrived just as planned, giving the Chinese a total of 38 highly trained special forces soldiers. The security force inside the depository was surprisingly small considering what they were guarding. Ross had always been fascinated by that. A larger force was guarding the primary entrance to the base, but most of the soldiers on the base had been sent either to Louisville or Lexington to assist with any civil unrest in the state's two largest cities.

The number of active-duty soldiers on the base was already down significantly from earlier years. In 2010, the Armor Center, which was the training school for tank soldiers, had ceased its 70-year connection with Fort Knox and was moved to Fort Benning, Georgia. Although some of the armor had returned in 2018, most of the soldiers who used to train at Fort Knox had been replaced by more white-collar types that included those involved with recruiting, human resources, and engineering. None of those people were going to stop what was taking place tonight.

Once Ross had disabled the alarms and released the locks, the Chinese soldiers had launched four

RPGs into the depository. They followed that with a frontal assault that killed the handful of remaining soldiers who had survived the RPG blasts. Only five members of the Chinese assault team had been killed getting inside the gates of Fort Knox and into the gold depository. Four other Chinese soldiers had been wounded, so that left a total of thirty people, including Ross, to load the gold.

Three M939 trucks had been commandeered for the task of hauling the gold back to the airport, where two cargo planes were scheduled to land precisely four hours and thirty minutes after the planes that had brought the first wave of soldiers. The M939 was the primary vehicle for hauling heavy loads. Each truck could hold 10,000 pounds, and it could carry the load over any kind of terrain in any kind of weather, which was handy tonight. Aside from that, this would be one of the few times that three M939s on a passenger highway in the middle of the night would not look suspicious.

Ross led the soldiers to the vault. He began to enter codes, slowly working his way through the numerous layers of security. The process took nearly twenty minutes. He had told the officer in command that it would take thirty minutes, just to play it safe. Once ready, Ross dramatically hit the 'enter' button on the last layer of code, and the huge vault door beeped several times, green lights shone, and the big locks released.

"Bingo!" Ross shouted, as he looked around at the soldiers. They said nothing, but they quickly began moving forklifts and skid steers into the vault.

CHAPTER 69

December 25
2:55 AM
Louisville, KY

Colonel Robert Thompson was fifty-three years old and was twenty-nine years into a military career that had been one of distinction. He had served honorably in both Iraq and Afghanistan, where he had received the Distinguished Service Medal. It was an entirely foreign concept for Thompson to see an American city the size of Louisville paralyzed like this. By the time his unit had reached the city, it looked like Kabul, other than the architecture of the buildings. Looters were everywhere, and shots could be heard from several directions. Although the power had been out less than 48 hours, the drastic drop in temperature in the last ten hours had caused a sense of desperation. There appeared to be two distinct groups of people – those who had barricaded themselves inside their homes, and those who were taking matters into their own hands on the street.

Thompson's unit was just beginning to implement its plan to clear the streets and regain control of downtown when Major Ben Hammond approached with a sat phone. "Colonel, it's General Wesley from the Pentagon."

Thompson stopped in his tracks. "Are you sure?"

"Yes, sir," Hammond replied. "He says it's urgent."

Thompson took the phone. "General Wesley, how can I help you?"

As Thompson listened, Hammond became even more concerned by the look on the colonel's face. He asked the general if it was possible that there was some mistake, because he had been at Fort Knox less than four hours ago. However, as Thompson again listened to the general, the realization set in that something was indeed terribly wrong.

"Yes, sir. We will organize and get back to the base as quickly as possible."

Realizing that he could not just leave the citizens of Louisville to fend for themselves, Thompson left approximately half of his unit there, and took the other half with him back to Fort Knox.

As the convoy made its way down US Highway 60, Colonel Thompson discovered firsthand that the information he had received was correct. Although he had been in communication with the base less than thirty minutes ago, he was now receiving no form of return communication. He turned and looked around at the men in the vehicle. "Combat ready," he said, then peered out the windshield at the rapidly accumulating snow.

The thirty-three remaining Chinese soldiers, along with Dave Ross, were inside the three M939 trucks. Even though Ross had spent months developing tonight's plan, including poring over every possible contingency, he was still surprised at how smoothly it had gone. They had not experienced a single glitch. It seemed so easy that it made him apprehensive. He tried to assure himself that it had gone so smoothly *because* of the extensive planning, but he knew the wrath that the American military could reign down on its enemies, and he got chills imagining what would happen to him if he were to be captured by the people he had just betrayed.

The route back to Bowman Field had also been thoroughly planned. Because of the potential of meeting troops coming from Louisville on US 60, the plan called for taking state highways back toward Bowman Field. They had left the gold depository eight minutes ago, which put them twelve minutes ahead of schedule.

Johnny Sims had no idea where to go to report what he had seen. He had given it substantial thought as he headed toward Louisville. He had decided to go to the police and let them get the word to whomever they felt needed to know. After all, he was just one man, and even Johnny recognized that his bushy beard and long ponytail might make him look more like someone who caused these events rather than someone trying to stop them.

Headlights shone in Johnny's windshield for the first time since he left his house. As they approached, he realized it was a military vehicle. It was followed by two others. Johnny attempted to flag them down, but they did not stop. Realizing that finding military members right in front of him was a better option than driving another thirty-five minutes to talk to the police, Johnny turned his truck around and pursued the military vehicles. He passed the convoy, honking his horn and flashing his lights.

It took a moment for Johnny to realize what was happening as his passenger side window shattered. Additional rapid fire caused Johnny to duck down in his seat as more glass shattered around him. He felt the back end of his truck sliding, and as he crashed hard into the ditch on the side of the rural highway, Johnny realized that he had just encountered the getaway vehicles.

Thompson's unit was less than five miles from the base when he tried radioing someone, anyone. It was then that he realized that his sat phone was malfunctioning. He reached for the other one, but it was having the same issue. Thompson had served in communications when he first entered the military, and he remained up to speed on the latest technology. He had a hunch about what was happening. "Someone has scrambled the signal within a certain radius of the base," he said to the group, although nobody knew what to say. Nor did they know how to reply when he said, "How did they do this right under our noses?"

Thompson told his driver to increase speed to the limits of where he still felt in control of the vehicle. "Already there, sir," the driver replied. Thompson nodded his approval and smiled at the young soldier.

Six minutes later, they entered the front gate of the gold depository. They drove all the way to the entrance and saw the guards lying dead on the side of the road, nearly covered with the snow that had fallen since their deaths. "We've got a big problem here, gentlemen. Be prepared for anything."

The men spread out into flanking positions as they jumped out of the vehicle. They approached the depository and entered through the wide-open door. They wound their way through the destruction caused by the RPGs, and they came across several deceased fellow soldiers along the corridor that led to the vault. There was no sign of anyone present. Thompson waved the guns down and advanced toward the vault, which was also open. He walked to the entrance and looked inside. "Mother of God…it's gone, all of it. The vault is empty!"

CHAPTER 70

December 25
3:10 AM

Johnny Sims knew what he had to do, and he was developing a plan while walking around his truck. First, he had to find a way to get the truck out of this ditch. No tires had been blown, and the ditch was not deep. The ground was frozen, which meant that in four-wheel drive, Johnny might be able to get his truck back on the road. Johnny was always prepared, so he pulled a couple of two-by-fours out of his back seat and placed them underneath his back tires. He already had chains on his tires and concrete blocks in the bed of his truck. In the end, he had gotten out of the ditch relatively easily, considering the conditions.

There was only one reason they would have taken this road. They were moving toward Bowman Field, and they were trying to do so while being seen by as few people as possible. Johnny was unsure if anyone else even knew what had happened yet, so he decided to take matters into his own hands. He had brought with him a hunting rifle, a handgun, and an AR-15. He had plenty of ammunition. He was getting into the driver's seat when he heard a familiar sound. He looked up and saw two cargo planes making their way across the sky at a relatively low altitude. The planes had no identifiable markings, but he could not imagine a reason for there to be American cargo planes airborne in this situation. These were the planes that were going to take all the gold from Fort Knox out of the United States. Johnny stepped on the accelerator as he tried to make up ground with the military vehicles that had driven him off the road.

3:8 AM

"How much longer to the airport?" Dave Ross was impressed with the command of the English language exhibited by the unit's translator. They had been on the road for twenty minutes, barreling along in the lead vehicle of the convoy at 30-35 miles per hour on the narrow state road.

"Using this route, it would take an hour in good weather. At this pace, probably closer to an hour and a half. I would guess we are still at least an hour away. That is consistent with the amount of time I told my contact it would take." Ross felt uneasy. At this point, he was entirely expendable.

It was then that they heard the cargo planes overhead. The Chinese man looked at him with cold eyes. "The planes are going to be there well before we arrive." He looked at the driver. "Faster." Ross felt the vehicle accelerate as the driver pushed on the gas pedal without a word.

CHAPTER 71

December 25
4:05 AM
Situation Room

Clark entered the situation room with Patrick Welch, and everyone rose to their feet. Clark waved them back into their seats. Aside from Clark and Welch, others in the room were National Security Advisor Tammy Leeds, FEMA Director Miguel Hernandez, Secretary of Homeland Security Andrew Byerly, Secretary of State Vance Harrison, Chairman of the Joint Chiefs of Staff Tom Stewart, Attorney General Gabe McMillan, and Defense Secretary Harold O'Bryan.

Clark took a deep breath. "At this point, ladies and gentlemen, as out of the ordinary as the recent events have been, there can be no doubt that we are in a state of war. The problem is that Congress is out of session for the Christmas holiday, and due to the circumstances, we cannot get them back here quickly enough to take any action. Since I cannot appeal to them to declare war on China, we will have to move forward in an unprecedented manner. I have spoken with the attorney general about proper protocols to follow in such a situation, if there are any. Gabe - do you think we have the legal justification to proceed? Is there any precedent for such a move without Congressional approval?"

McMillan responded. "I have been looking into it, Mr. President, and there simply is no time in our past that provides guidance on how such a situation has been handled before. My opinion, sir, is that as Commander-in-Chief, under the circumstances, you would be justified in unilaterally declaring war. However, I would strongly urge you to make this look as legitimate as possible, and I have prepared a document to be signed by any Cabinet members who are willing, showing their support for your decision, just so it doesn't *look* unilateral."

Clark looked around at those present. "I would strongly urge everyone to sign this document. I think it is vital that we make this move in a united fashion. Does anyone have any objections, or any questions?"

Vice President Sullivan spoke up. "Mr. President, for what it's worth, I agree with Gabe. We need to sign this and get the formalities out of the way so we can move forward. Any messes, legal or otherwise, that need to be cleaned up can be dealt with after the fact."

"I agree, Charles," Clark replied, "but I want this document in place to show that we were being as prudent as possible, with the understanding that we didn't really have time to be prudent."

Clark looked around the room. "Anything else?" He realized that he had one hundred percent support from those present. "No questions?" Again, he surveyed the room. No questions were offered, and there were no looks of indecision from around the table.

Clark nodded, and McMillan passed the document around the room. He watched each person sign, and he could not help but wonder if this was what it was like when the Declaration of Independence was signed. Clark thought about the irony. That group had signed a document declaring the country's independence. This group was signing a document trying to preserve it.

When the document reached Clark, he signed and handed it back to McMillan. He paused and collected his thoughts. "I know everyone in here is aware of the facts I am getting ready to state, but I want to be clear where we are at this moment. We have suffered an attack on our power grid by a foreign entity, specifically timed to occur during a devastating weather event. The attack was obviously planned well in advance. Following that, there was an invasion of our homeland. Foreign troops entered our country. There are shenanigans at several military bases, including and especially Fort Knox. Much like the events of 9/11, we have no way of knowing if the attacks are over, or if more are coming. Are foreign troops on the ground somewhere within our borders? We don't know. We have no imminent time frame on getting power restored, and while we are working on it, Americans are dying across our country. In some cases, it is at the hands of other Americans, because of a sense of desperation."

Clark paused briefly, then continued. "When we get the power restored, we will also have to restore order across the country. Meanwhile, if we were to lose control of our gold, we would be a country in financial ruin. In my eyes, that leaves us with the following options. We *must* get the power restored. We *must* find out if there has been a military assault on the gold depository at Fort Knox. If so, we *must* make sure our gold remains secure. Even if all those goals are successful, our stature on the global stage will be nothing like it was less than two weeks ago. We will suddenly be seen to be vulnerable and weak, a paper tiger."

Again, Clark paused. He looked around the table. "Does anyone disagree with any of the points that I have made so far?"

"No, sir," came replies from every direction.

"Good, because I don't want anyone to think I am making this decision in a rash manner or due to not having given this an appropriate amount of thought. We have one remaining tangible asset that separates us from every other country in the world, and that is the substantial ability to make war on a foreign entity, combined with the best people in the world to use those tools. We absolutely, positively need to punish those who brought this harm to our country. Ladies and gentlemen, it is time to move to DEFCON 2."

CHAPTER 72

December 25
3:25 AM
Fort Knox

Once he had discovered the empty vault at Fort Knox and gotten over the initial shock, Colonel Thompson realized the magnitude of the moment. His first thought was the obvious conclusion that this event was a career killer. Quickly, however, his thoughts had shifted to the bigger problem. If the gold left the country, this could be a nation killer. He gathered his men around him, and they held a quick brainstorming session trying to construct a hypothetical exit route.

The first thing the group realized was that this had to be an inside job. Someone, somewhere, had divulged information that had allowed all security measures to be compromised, up to and including the ability for someone or a group of people to get into the vault. Now came the next question in this progression: where would they take the gold? It was safe to assume that the goal was to get it out of the country, but all air traffic had been grounded.

They were in the middle of discussing the fact that military vehicles had to have been commandeered to haul all the gold when Captain Bob Henderson held up a hand and shouted, "Quiet!" The group stopped talking, and in the few seconds of silence that followed, they all heard it. Then they saw it. Two cargo planes were flying overhead, and collectively, the group instantly realized what was happening. Thompson spoke as he began jogging back toward their vehicles. "Bowman Field! Let's go!"

Once inside the vehicles, Thompson mentioned that on their way back from Louisville, they had not seen any vehicles of the kind it would take to transport that much weight. It was quickly deduced that they must have taken back roads to avoid being seen. "I'm not sure how far behind them we are, but I think it will be quicker for us to take the primary roads. It is longer from a mileage perspective, but in this weather, it has to be faster to be on wider, straighter roads." Everyone else agreed, and the group headed back in the direction from which they had come.

4:35 AM

Thompson ordered the driver to kill the headlights as they got within a half-mile of the airport. The moon was not full, but it provided enough light, combined with the group's familiarity of the area, to get them closer without using the headlights. When the truck was about 300 yards out, Thompson ordered the driver to stop and kill the engine. The cargo planes were side-by-side on the small airport's primary runway, but no military vehicles nor people could be seen.

The group had already discussed their plan of approach. They exited the vehicle silently and spread out to their points of approach. Silence. It did not appear that anyone was present, which made no sense. Had they made good enough time to arrive before the group that had stolen the gold? Thompson could not imagine that to be the case, so he continued using extreme caution as he drew within 150 yards of the nearest plane. At about 100 yards, he saw what appeared to be a body lying in the snow. It quickly became obvious that people and vehicles had been present here. Tracks and footprints were prevalent around that plane, which now had enough snow on it to give the impression that it had been sitting in that spot for at least thirty minutes.

As Thompson continued to approach, he looked at the front of the plane. He raised his hand for everyone to stop. He inched forward several more steps. He initially thought his eyes had been deceiving him, but now he realized they had not. The glass windshield was shattered, and he saw what appeared to be two dead pilots in the cockpit.

"Don't shoot!" Every gun on the property turned toward the sound of the voice. Emerging from a wooded area was a lone figure with his hands raised high over his head.

"Stop right there!" Thompson commanded.

Johnny did as he was told. "I shot the pilots. They are dead. So are the ones in the second plane. I need to tell you what happened, and I need to tell you quickly."

"Proceed slowly and keep your hands above your head."

Johnny walked quickly toward them, and while still moving he shouted, "Chinese paramilitary! About two dozen of them. They killed this guy, the American. I assume he was their 'in.'"

"That's close enough," Thompson replied. Johnny was still about 25 yards away. He did not wave down the guns that were pointed at Johnny. "Tell me what you know, and make it quick," Thompson shouted.

Johnny explained what he had seen, as well as the confrontation that had driven him into the ditch. He then described how he took shortcuts to arrive at Bowman before the military vehicles. He parked a few hundred yards away and found a good spot. Then he took out his rifle and killed the pilots from across the runway before they knew what happened. When the military vehicles arrived, he saw the two dozen or more Chinese soldiers and one American. He had decided to find cover and observe. They found the pilots dead and then three of them spoke in a small huddle. Clearly, none of them knew how to fly the plane. They emerged from the meeting, then they shot and killed the American. After that, they all got back in the vehicles and drove south. Johnny had then decided to wait at the airport. He knew the Americans would figure it out and get there eventually.

"How long ago did they leave?" Thompson asked.

Johnny looked at his watch. "Twenty-three minutes ago."

"Where would they be going that is south of here?" Thompson wasn't speaking specifically to Johnny, but Johnny had had time to give this some thought.

"The only thing I could think of was that they wanted to get away from the city, unless the southward movement is part of a contingency plan."

At that point, Thompson waved the guns down. He approached Johnny and extended his hand. "You have bought us some valuable time, sir. Thank you."

Johnny shook his hand. "Thank you, sir."

CHAPTER 73

December 25
6:49 AM
NSA Cyber Command Headquarters

It had become clear to Helene and her team that this was a zero-day exploit. Exploits are codes that hackers use to install worms and viruses on computers, usually by either going through applications on the computer or the software on the browser. Once the exploit is planted, all it takes to activate the virus is for a user to do something as simple as click on a link or open an email attachment.

Once that happens, the victim is forced to try to fix the problem by using what are known as 'patches'. Then they add signatures to their scanners in order to detect any future exploits that might enter the system. The zero-day exploits, however, are extremely advanced. Helene was familiar with them through her research, but she had only come across two of them in her entire career. Zero-day exploits attacked openings that neither the software maker nor the antivirus companies had discovered. Therefore, there was not yet a signature to detect the exploit and no patches created to fix the problem.

Because of the time involved to find and attack holes in a system, most hackers used standard exploits to attack it. They are aware that most computers are not up to date with the highest level of antivirus protection, and they also lag in providing patches to their system. This explains the fact that only one in a million exploits are zero-day exploits.

Helene knew all these facts. However, she also knew that in the case of the United States government, the standard exploits were insufficient. It was during the hours and hours, day after day since the attack had taken place, that she had gone back through everything she knew about zero-day exploits. And she was at a total loss. It was then that she went back and looked once again at the most sophisticated cyber attack the world had known to that point - Stuxnet. The United States had used Stuxnet to disrupt the centrifuges in an Iranian nuclear facility, derailing their program and setting it back years.

She was reading back through the Stuxnet process when it hit her. She needed to look for a rootkit within that exploit. A rootkit is a set of software tools that are designed to enable unauthorized access to a computer system or its software, all the while masking its existence within the system.

Much like Stuxnet, this rootkit had found a way to disguise itself from the antivirus engines, and it was now using the exploit to move from one computer to the next via the Windows operating system. Every time they scrubbed a system, and even when they had installed entirely new operating systems, they were immediately re-infected.

Helene began examining each module, which was a mundane and painstaking task. Hour after hour she searched, finding nothing and wondering if she was even on the right track. Then she saw it - one of the modules was not actually a module, but a kernel level rootkit. She jumped out of her seat and screamed, "I've got you!"

Helene knew that there were numerous kinds of rootkits, but none was more difficult to detect than the kernel level variety. Most rootkits function in the outer layers of a computer's system, where most of the applications are located. However, those are usually detected by the antivirus scanners. Kernel level rootkits dig into the inner workings of a computer, into the core, right next to the location where antivirus scanners do their work. It blocks the scanners while the malware destroys the inner sanctum of the computer.

Helene felt sure that a flash drive had been the cause of this. Everyone, even entry level people in the government, knew that flash drives were a no-no for this very reason. They were the easiest way to spread a virus, both accidentally and purposely. As she continued to probe, she discovered what appeared to be a .LNK file. They are responsible for the transfer of information from a flash drive onto a computer. When a drive is inserted, the operating system scans it for .LNK files that will display all the recognizable icons – things such as word documents or programs. In this case, when the operating system scanned the file, it triggered the exploit into action, and the virus spread through the government systems like lava smothering everything in sight as it came down the sides of a volcano.

Helene was torn. She was ecstatic about finding what she was sure was the cause of the outage. On the other hand, she felt sick to her stomach. She knew from the moment that she sat down that something did not seem right about the idea that she could not find the source of the hack. Now that she had found the kernel level rootkit, her worst fears were confirmed. This level of depth into their system had to have been executed from someone on the inside. They had a mole.

CHAPTER 74

December 25
7:10 AM
Bowman Field

Once Johnny had spoken to Colonel Thompson about his military background and his extensive knowledge of central Kentucky, Thompson agreed to let him join them as they followed the heavy tracks laid by the M939. The snow was not deep, but due to there being no other traffic, there was no way for the Chinese troops to hide their escape route. Thompson radioed Major Ben Hammond, who was back in Louisville with the remaining troops, to brief him on the events. Understandably, Hammond was floored by the report. Thompson told him to continue to provide support in Louisville, but to be ready to gather the unit and move at a moment's notice.

"Where could they possibly be going?" That was all Johnny could think about as they drove southeast out of Louisville. Clearly, they had a contingency plan, and probably a contingency plan for that plan. He tried to put himself in their shoes. Thompson realized what Johnny was doing and spoke up.

"Talk it out. Maybe we can help."

Johnny looked around the vehicle and realized he had everyone's attention. He paused, unsure of where to begin.

"They have to get the gold out of the country. Otherwise, the mission is a failure. I assume they didn't use the primary airport because there is a police presence in the city. If they didn't land there originally, they won't go there now. That leaves Lexington, which has a regional airport."

"We are on the same page so far," Thompson replied. "But they have a big problem."

"Right," Johnny agreed. "No plane. Unless additional planes are landing in Lexington as part of the contingency plan. But there is still a snag with that possibility."

Thompson was not following him on this one. "What's that?"

"Even if they are trying to dodge the interstates, they are going ridiculously out of their way if they are going to Lexington. I'm trying to think of another destination that they could be driving toward."

"What towns will we pass if we stay on this course?"

"Depending on which way they go, we could pass through Mount Washington, Taylorsville, Bloomfield, Bardstown…"

Johnny paused, and the look on his face worried Thompson. "What? What else is this way."

"Pine Bluff. The President's hometown. They are going after his father."

7:33 AM

Following the logic that the Chinese troops were heading to Pine Bluff to kidnap John Clark, and realizing that they could not get there in time to stop them, Colonel Thompson decided to stop chasing them across Kentucky. With the understanding that they still had to find a way to get the gold out of the country, Thompson made the decision to get on I-64 and head directly to Lexington. If that was the new destination for the Chinese, perhaps they could beat them there, or at least make up a lot of ground. If the airport in Lexington was not the destination, then they would have to reevaluate. In the meantime, they proceeded to Lexington, because they could not think of another way for the Chinese to get the gold out of the country. At this point, it was a risk they were willing to take.

CHAPTER 75

December 25
8:25 AM
The Oval Office

Despite all that was going on around him, in the back of his mind, Sam Clark had a persistent thought. He was concerned about Father Jerry. After being assured yesterday that his family back in Kentucky was safe, Clark had coordinated with Patrick Welch to bring Father Jerry to the White House to stay until they had the power back on. Welch excused himself in order to find a couple of aides to locate the priest and bring him to the White House.

He realized he had to turn his attention to matters in the room. Everyone else was already present. Clark spoke as he sat down. "I understand we have identified the source of the problem. Obviously, I feel like if we had a solution, the mood in here would be a little more vibrant. What have we got?"

Tammy Leeds introduced Helene Albertsen. It was clear that she was nervous. Clark had seen the look many times when people made their first trip to the Oval Office.

"Ms. Albertsen, I understand the situation you find yourself in. I would like to offer you a cordial greeting, but your first visit here is unlike any others. Are you ready to brief me, in layman's terms as best as possible, on the current situation?"

Helene composed herself and said with resolve, "Yes, sir."

Clark nodded, and she continued. "We have indeed found the source of the problem, Mr. President. There is no way for us to indicate yet that the Chinese are the guilty parties, but I think that is assumed at this point. Our grid was compromised by a unique malware. It was a combination of a worm and a virus. Once a worm is in the system, no action is needed by a person for it to spread. Then it began infecting files everywhere it went, like a virus. This part, as is the case with most dangerous viruses, was caused by human action."

"How?" Clark's frustration was evident. "Who could make such a stupid mistake? Aren't these people trained better than that? Even I know not to insert a personal thumb drive into a work computer!"

Albertsen looked at Leeds. Leeds spoke up. "She didn't say it was a mistake, Mr. President. Best we can tell, sir, this was done intentionally. Unfortunately, we have not yet been able to trace this back to the computer in question, but we are still working on it."

Clark thought he understood what Leeds was saying, but his shock was evident. "You mean they had someone on the inside?"

"It appears so, Mr. President." Leeds said.

"Even with help on the inside, which I am still trying to wrap my mind around, how did it cause *this* much damage, and how were we entirely unaware? I get threat assessments daily on potential cyber warfare."

Albertsen spoke up again. "I know you want layman's language, sir. I'll do my best."

Clark nodded.

"Like traditional weapons, most digital weapons have two parts. The first is the delivery system, which is responsible for getting the malware onto the machines. This is the equivalent of a missile. The bomb, for the sake of comparison, is the virus that performs the actual attack. It may be placed there to steal data, or to infect the machines in order to make them inoperable. In this case, the payload was the malicious code that targeted our software.

"The initial file had several layers of encryption. The first layer was a relatively simple packer." She paused before continuing, trying to keep from getting too 'techy.' "A packer is a digital tool used to distort code. This makes it harder for antivirus engines and our people to figure out what the code is doing. That part was not tough to figure out once we found it. They used a relatively simple packer in order to reduce the worm's digital footprint. It also tracked everything it used on a computer, and it made sure to move out of each part of the system once it was finished in order to reduce the amount of processing power used. If it used too much power, the malware could cause the processing speed to slow down, and that would raise a red flag in the system."

Leeds stepped in. "That's where the thumb drive comes in. Most of the time, hackers will try to get malware onto a system by using e-mail or malicious websites to spread a virus to numerous systems at once. However, in this case, none of these exploits used the internet. Instead, they relied on someone physically planting the infection on computers either through use of a flash drive or, once in a system, by using local network connections. Typically, a flash drive would be blocked from use in any secure device. We are still not sure how they worked their way around that.

"Based on what we have uncovered so far, it appears that the hackers were targeting systems they knew were not connected to the internet, and, given the unprecedented size of the file as well as the number of zero-day exploits they used to do it, they were clearly looking not only to take down the electric grid, but also aiming for other high-value, high-security targets."

"Like Fort Knox," Sullivan said, expressing the disbelief felt by everyone in the room.

"Correct, Mr. Vice President," Leeds replied before continuing. "The virus itself is stuffed inside the file like a jack-in-the-box. Once it was unpacked and released into the system, it expanded into a larger file that was more than a megabyte in size – it is the largest file known to have been released in this age of cyber warfare. Our Stuxnet file that we used against Iran's nuclear centrifuges was the biggest to date. It was 500 kilobytes. This one is more than twice that size."

Clark was wearing a path in the carpet of the Oval Office. He had to move the ball forward. "Any idea how long it will take to get rid of this thing and get the power back on? And yes, I realize that is a simplistic question, but try to give me a practical answer."

Leeds deferred to her cohort on this one. That was why she had brought her to the meeting. "Helene?"

Albertsen shook her head, not in defeat, but like a person who is giving a very rough estimate. "Here's the problem. We're still not sure exactly what we're dealing with. The core of this thing is an extremely large .DLL file with dozens of smaller .DLLs. They are all wrapped up in a bundle with layers of encryption. We are taking it apart piece by piece, but in all honesty, this is beyond anything we have ever dealt with. We have only peeled back about 10-12% of a very large onion. We have everyone working on this, in several groups. The next step is to reverse-engineer this thing so we can decipher it."

"With all due respect, Ms. Albertsen," Clark said patiently, "you're the pro here. That's why you are in this room right now. I don't want to know *what* you are going to do or *how* you are going to do it. I need to know *when* we can begin to restore power, even if it is only to certain areas. We need a win, here. I don't care if it's in a town of 5,000 people in Vermont. I need to be able to announce that we are restoring power."

Albertsen knew they were in her realm. She was speaking to the President of the United States, but this topic was her turf. Besides, it did no good to exaggerate or sugar coat the situation. She decided to be blunt.

"To be honest, sir, we are in the very early stages of figuring this whole thing out. The ETA on any success with the grid is probably 3-4 weeks at the earliest."

There was an audible gasp in the room. Clark looked her right in the eye. "Ms. Albertsen, you are the modern-day George Washington. You are the general in this battle for the very existence of our country. I need the power on in some way, shape, or form in ONE week. I'm not asking you if this is possible. I'm telling you this *has* to be done."

With that, Clark turned and walked back to his desk, where he sat and turned his chair toward the window. Patrick Welch knew that meant the meeting was over, and he escorted everyone out of the room with instructions to be ready to provide updates as needed on a moment's notice.

Tammy Leeds walked out with Helene Albertsen. "Well done," Leeds said.

"He doesn't realize what he's asking," Albertsen replied in a somewhat defiant tone.

"I know," Leeds said as they continued walking. "But here's the thing..."

"Tammy!" Patrick Welch came trotting up behind her. "The President wants you to hang around for a moment."

Welch walked Leeds back to the Oval Office. Clark was back in the chair where he had been sitting during the meeting, during the limited amount of time that he was sitting.

"Have a seat, Tammy."

Leeds sat across from him.

"You realize this is the irony of ironies," Clark began. "They hacked into what we considered to be an impenetrable system and used that to break into what we considered an impenetrable fortress and an impenetrable vault. Sister Martha would be very disappointed with me. You see, she taught me English in grade school. And she was the one who made me copy pages from the dictionary as punishment for misbehavior. So, with all the vocabulary I learned from copying every damn page of that dictionary, I clearly still don't understand the meaning of the word impenetrable."

Leeds realized that she had become the President's sounding board. He might want advice, he might want her expertise, he might seek her counsel. Or, as was the case presently, he might just need a person to whom he could express his frustrations. She had always told Clark exactly what she thought, good or bad. She felt like that was what he wanted from all of his advisors. She did not see a need to go soft now.

"Here's the long and short of it, Mr. President. There are people out there working all day, every day, trying to get into one little nook of our security system. Meanwhile, we must establish a system that is foolproof 100% of the time without the privilege of knowing which part of the intricate system a hacker is trying to get into. It is, quite frankly, an impossible goal. On top of that, there is considerably more money to be made on their side of the equation. And you know what they say about money and bullshit? One talks, and one walks."

Clark chuckled a bit. Of all the people to drop the word "bullshit" in the Oval Office, Leeds would have been his last guess. Sullivan, of course, would have been his first. He leaned back in his chair and relaxed for a moment.

"She's really good, isn't she?" Clark asked.

"Helene? The very best we have," Leeds replied without hesitation.

"Do you really think the country will be without power for another three or four weeks?"

"I do, if that's what Helene says. However, I will give you one glimmer of hope."

"Please do," Clark said.

"She is the most competitive person I have ever been around, and I work with highly successful and motivated people. She will take your…pardon me for saying this, sir…unrealistic one-week demand and use it as motivation. Most people would have left this room with sagging shoulders. She left with fire in her eyes."

CHAPTER 76

December 25
10:35 AM
Lexington, KY

Once they had assumed the Chinese were heading to Pine Bluff and then to Lexington, Thompson again radioed Major Hammond in Louisville and told him to gather the rest of the unit and head to the Bluegrass Airport in Lexington. Now, just over two hours later, the entire unit was back together. However, so far there had been no sign of the Chinese.

Johnny had been introduced to Hammond and the rest of the unit. Thompson made it clear right away that without Johnny, the gold from Fort Knox would already be on its way back to China, so Johnny was going to be involved in every decision as if he was part of the unit. Inside, Johnny could not help but find a little bit of humor thinking about the impression that a guy with his current lack of grooming must be having on these clean-shaven soldiers.

He looked around at them. "Are any of you familiar with Kentucky?"

Thompson spoke up. "Other than the immediate area around Fort Knox and Louisville, these guys don't see much. Personally, I'm from South Carolina, so I'm no help." He looked at the others. "Anybody?"

None of the members of the unit had any knowledge about this area of the state. Johnny decided to speak his mind.

"In that case, you all may very well think I'm crazy, but I have an off-the-wall idea about where they may have gone."

"The rest of us have nothing to offer," Thompson admitted. "Let's hear it."

"Well, if we are still under the assumption that they are going to fly out of Lexington, then they would have to be hiding somewhere. Now that daybreak has come, they will have to find a place to hide those military vehicles. Otherwise, people will seek them out for help."

"I'm with you so far," Thompson said, with a tone that implied he was ready for Johnny to get to the point.

There are not many places to hide those vehicles. My first thought was a barn on a farm, but farmers are probably on edge right now. They may shoot first and ask questions later. Plus, the last thing the Chinese want is to be seen."

"Johnny..." Thompson was growing impatient.

"Okay, Colonel, here goes. Do any of you know what tourist attraction is close by?"

"No." That was all Thompson said.

"Well, believe it or not, there's a castle a couple of miles down the road."

A couple of the guys chuckled. Thompson just stared.

"I'm serious," Johnny said. "It's a long story about a rich guy trying to impress a woman, but there is a castle down the road. It would not be unreasonable, if this is indeed a contingency plan, for the Chinese to be hiding the military vehicles inside the doors. It would be a five-minute drive to the airport if they heard planes coming."

Thompson's face did not hide his skepticism, but they were getting absolutely nothing done at the airport. He looked around. "Major, you stay here with your unit in case they show up. The rest of you, load up. Let's go see if there are any tracks leading up to this…castle."

"Holy shit!" Colonel Thompson spotted the spires of the castle from a good distance away. It was not hard. Sitting atop a slope on a 50-acre roadside tract approximately 200 yards off US Highway 60 stood a huge castle. Thompson turned to Johnny. "If we get through this alive, I want to hear this story." A slight smile from Thompson exuded the type of confidence that a person needed to get through a situation like this.

Johnny pointed to the road that led to the only entrance. As they approached the road, Thompson shouted again. "There they are! Tracks! Pull over!"

The driver followed Thompson's instruction to pull off the side of the road. He looked at Johnny. "How many ways are there into this place?"

Johnny raised an eyebrow. "Look at me. Do you really think I've ever been in there?"

"Fair point," Thompson replied. He was just beginning to think of a plan to approach when gunfire erupted and began to pelt the side of the truck. The men hit the floor of the truck as the gunfire continued. Glass was shattering all around them.

Thompson got on the radio. "Hammond! We're under fire! Shattered windows and pinned down. Get over here ASAP!"

"On our way, Colonel," came the nearly immediate reply.

"Approach with caution. They're shooting from the spires."

As Thompson was saying this, the two monstrous wooden doors at the front of the castle swung open and two men walked to the entrance. In the back was a Chinese soldier. In the front, with a gun against the base of his skull, was John Clark, the father of the President of the United States.

"Shit..." was all that Thompson could say.

Clark held up what appeared to be a piece of paper. He walked about 20 yards in front of the castle and laid it on the ground in front of him. Once he did that, he was forced to backpedal into the castle. The gun never left his head. As the doors were closing, the soldier waved his hand toward himself and pointed to the paper on the ground.

"That must be a list of their demands," Thompson said. "Do they expect us to walk up there and get it? That's a suicide mission."

"I'll do it," Johnny replied quickly.

"No way," Thompson dismissed the idea immediately. "We're not sending a civilian up there."

"Their only goal is to get that gold out of the country," Johnny replied. "Whatever is written on that paper is the best possibility, in their eyes, of accomplishing their mission. They *want* us to have it."

"Agreed." Thompson thought for a moment. "But you're not going up there. I will go."

His men protested that idea, but Thompson held up a hand to silence them. "Johnny is right. They have a hostage, and a valuable one. They gain nothing from harming me. In fact, if they do, they know we will storm the castle. Aside from that, I want to get close enough to communicate with them. I feel sure they have someone among them who speaks English. We need to stall them as long as possible, and hope that Washington can give us some guidance on how to handle this particular hostage situation."

Colonel Robert Thompson exited the vehicle and approached the front entrance to the castle. For some reason, he did not feel nervous. He was not even apprehensive. However, he was perplexed as to what the note might say and how to respond. He was trying to anticipate the demands. Surely, they were requesting cargo planes like the ones that arrived at Bowman Field. His main source of concern was what role John Clark played in this, and how they could safely secure him. What would they have to give up in order to keep him safe? Could they possibly give the Chinese what they wanted? If not, was he willing to be the one to declare that John Clark was disposable? Could he consider the thought of the father of the president as collateral damage?

Thompson came upon the note. It was a simple list with a statement at the end. There were three demands.

1. More Chinese planes were in route. They were to be allowed to land at the airport in Lexington unharmed.
2. All of Thompson's troops were to clear out. They were to be out of the area entirely. If the Chinese saw any of them on their way to the airport, the president's father would be killed.
3. The Chinese were to be allowed to load the gold onto the cargo planes and fly away unhindered.

The note ended with this statement: "If the planes leave American airspace safely, Aurum Regina, we will land in a country to be determined and release John Clark."

Thompson had been ready to dismiss the note and declare the terms unacceptable, except for the phrase "Aurum Regina." Based on the grammar alone, it was clear that John Clark had written the note. It was also evident that he had slipped the phrase into a random place in the note so it would go undetected. Evidently, none of the soldiers were fluent enough in English to understand the full context.

Thompson backed away from the castle, then eventually turned and began to jog back to the vehicles. He was going to need help with this one. John Clark was trying to send them a message. What was it?

CHAPTER 77

December 25
11:40 AM
Lexington, KY

Colonel Thompson got back to the truck and looked around. "Do any of you know any Latin words?" The looks of confusion said it all. Thompson continued. "This note was clearly written by John Clark. They killed Dave Ross at the airport, and nobody has seen another American in their presence. Assuming Clark wrote it, he snuck a phrase in here that I don't know. It appears to be a tip of some kind. It is two words – Aurum Regina."

One of the soldiers instinctively pulled out his phone to look it up before snapping back to the reality that not only was his phone dead, but there was also no way to charge it and no way to look anything up if it still held a charge. The whole thing was still hard to fathom.

Jason Mackin, the driver, turned quickly toward Thompson. "Regina means 'queen.'"

"Are you sure?"

"Yes, sir. The Salve Regina prayer is Hail Holy Queen."

Thompson looked at Mackin for a moment, then decided the explanation sounded legitimate. He nodded.

"Okay. Good. Anyone know what 'Aurum' means?"

Johnny spoke up. "I'm still trying to figure out what kind of clue would have a Latin word for 'queen' in it. What could that *possibly* mean?"

"One thing at a time, Johnny," Thompson replied. "Maybe it will make more sense once we know what 'Aurum' means. Anyone?" Thompson waited a moment, saw the blank stares, and realized they were wasting time. "The rest of the note says more Chinese planes are on their way to this airport, we are to leave the area, and that they are to be allowed to load the gold and fly away. If that happens, they will land in another country and release John Clark. However, if they even see us present while they are moving toward the airport or while they are there, Clark will be killed."

One of the men asked the obvious question. "We can't just let them take him, can we, Colonel?"

"Of course not," Thompson replied. "But we have to clear the area for now and try to figure out what to do next. We will get the other truck and regroup somewhere down the road, out of sight of the castle and the airport."

Thompson waved to the other truck to follow them as they exited the castle property and got back on US 60. They drove nearly a mile down the road before stopping in the parking lot of a restaurant. The other truck pulled up next to them, and the driver rolled down his window. Thompson's passenger side window had been shattered by the gunfire.

Thompson quickly relayed the details of the note, including what was perceived to be a secret message from John Clark. He told them that they knew Regina meant queen, but they did not know what Aurum meant. They also had not figured out what queen was supposed to mean. Major Hammond listened to the explanation, then looked behind him to see if anyone knew what Aurum meant.

Thompson could not hear the words, but he did hear a voice. Somebody back there was saying something to Hammond. Thompson was trying to read Hammond's face. Hammond continued to listen for a moment, then he said, "Are you sure?"

Hammond turned to Thompson with a smile. "It's always good to have a science nerd in your crew, Colonel."

"What have you got?" Thompson did not have time for small talk.

"Aurum means 'gold'", Hammond replied. "As Bill Nye the Science Guy back here informed me, on the periodic chart, the symbol for gold is Au. Au is short for the Latin word Aurum, which means gold."

"Gold! Well, hell, that makes sense!" Thompson exclaimed. He thought for a moment. "But gold queen? What in the hell could that mean?" There were no answers from either truck, so Thompson spoke up. "Here's what we will do. Both trucks will have separate impromptu brainstorming sessions to try to figure this out. Talk among yourselves, and we will do the same. Make it clear to everyone in there that if they have an idea of what it might mean, any idea, spit it out. There are no stupid ideas. In ten minutes, we will get back together and see what we have come up with."

Thompson turned to the men in his truck. "Guys, we have to figure this out, and we don't have much time. Does anybody have *anything*?"

Private Adam Brickley was a quiet young man. He was from a rural area of Tennessee, and before entering the military, all he had ever known was farming, hunting, and fishing. He was the lowest ranking soldier in either truck, and he was the last one that anybody expected to hear from. When he spoke first, he caught the entire truck by surprise.

"Colonel," he said sheepishly.

Thompson tried to hide his surprise, but he did not do it very well. "Yes, Brickley. Do you have something?"

"Maybe," Brickley replied. He looked at Johnny. "Mr. Sims said there were three trucks, right?"

When Brickley said this, Johnny realized that he was the only one who had seen the soldiers, the trucks, or anything that had happened. Everybody else in the truck was simply going by what he had told them. None of them had seen the trucks enter the castle, and they had not seen them while they were there. He looked at Brickley. "Yes, that's right. Three of the M939s."

Brickley looked back at Thompson. He looked unsure.

Thompson used a calm voice. "Go ahead, son. Remember, the goal here is to throw out ideas. If you have one, let's hear it."

"It was hard to tell for sure," Brickley began. He looked at the others, most of whom nodded their heads at him to continue. "There are no vehicles on the road, and there haven't been since we have been here. When we got to the castle, the only tracks I saw at the entrance would have been made by the Chinese. Sir, I only saw one set of tracks."

The truck fell silent. Thompson and Johnny Sims seemed to have reached the same conclusion simultaneously. Johnny deferred to the colonel. "They separated after they kidnapped John Clark." He paused, then looked at Johnny, who simply nodded. "John Clark is trying to tell us that the gold is on the other trucks."

CHAPTER 78

December 25
12:25 PM
NSA Headquarters

Helene Albertsen had just finished a briefing with Tammy Leeds. When she returned to her office, she found Josh Reed waiting for her.

"What's up, Josh?" Albertsen tried to sound cheerful, but she assumed that he was either coming to see her to complain about the long hours or one of the other employees. Albertsen was prepared to tell him, as she always did, that everyone was working long hours under the circumstances. She was also prepared to tell him, as she always did, that in the type of setting in which they worked, everyone had to be willing to overlook things about the personality traits of their co-workers. Reed was a good young analyst with some potential, but he was also extremely high maintenance. The word 'diva' came to mind, although Albertsen tried to bury that opinion as deeply as possible.

Reed closed the door behind her. This was unusual. Maybe this was different. She motioned with her hand for him to take a seat as she sat down behind her desk.

"I'm concerned about Abdul," Reed began.

Now it was a conspiracy theory, Albertsen thought to herself. Nobody in the building other than herself and Tammy Leeds was aware that they had a mole. Aside from that, if Abdul Nassar's work was being questioned by Reed in a suspicious manner, this was going to be a big problem. Albertsen hated inter-office gossip, and she really hated finger-pointing. She continued to play it casually. "Why?"

"He has been acting really strange." Reed looked over his shoulder and out the window of Albertsen's office, then he slid his chair closer to her desk and leaned in. "I went into the restroom yesterday, and when I walked through the door, I heard a low voice in one of the stalls. It was speaking a Middle Eastern language, but I am not sure which one. I used the urinal, washed my hands, and then positioned myself in an office so I could see who came out of the restroom. About ten minutes later, Abdul walked out, looked suspiciously in both directions, and then went back to his desk."

Albertsen leaned back in her chair. "Josh…"

"I know, I know," Reed interrupted. "It could be anything. He could have been speaking to a friend or relative that doesn't speak English. He was doing it while he was using the restroom to be more efficient. I know how you think, Helene."

Albertsen smiled. "Okay," she replied. "I admit, you are exactly right. Now, if you know my thought process that well, you must also realize how upset I would be if you came in here and told me of this suspicion without anything more than what you just told me. Am I correct?"

"You bet your buns you are." Reed looked like a kid on Christmas morning. "I continued to watch him after that."

Albertsen tried to hide her disdain for Reed 'investigating' a co-worker. She hoped she had not changed her facial expression.

He continued. "I managed to position myself where I could see into his cubicle from the extreme corner of an empty cubicle a couple of aisles behind him. As he was working, he kept looking around, as if he did not want anyone to see what was on his screen." He paused.

Albertsen was growing irritated. "Come on, Josh. Get to the substance."

Reed did not care for the dismissive tone, but he decided to let it slide this time. "Eventually, I saw him reach in his pocket and pull something out. Then he looked around more thoroughly to make sure nobody was watching. Helene, he put a flash drive into his computer!"

Albertsen's facial expression changed this time. This was most definitely not what she was expecting to hear. "Our system will not accept a flash drive. Abdul knows that. Are you sure that is what it was?"

"Absolutely!' Reed replied. "And listen, Helene, I don't know how he did it, but usually, as you said, the system will reject a flash drive. But he inserted it, then was working furiously for the next ten or fifteen minutes, all the while looking over his shoulder periodically. I have never seen Abdul act anything like this."

The situation as Reed described it was indeed troubling. Josh was an attention seeker, extremely high maintenance, and a difficult person to manage. He was not, however, one to make up a story like this.

"Helene, let me make this significantly easier for you. When I was growing up, I was a curious child. School was boring to me, so I was constantly trying to build things, or fix things, or create things. One of the things I learned as a kid, and have continued to hone as an adult, is that I can pick 85-90% of the standard locks in the world. Clearly, I have never used this in a criminal manner, or I would have never received my security clearance. That said, when

Abdul finished whatever he was doing, he locked the flash drive in one of his desk drawers."

"No," Albertsen began. "We're not going to break into his desk without more information than what you have provided me."

"Too late," Reed replied. He pulled the flash drive out of his pocket. "Something is going on here, and we need to know what it is."

Albertsen was getting ready to protest, but Reed cut her off. "Listen, Helene. I have thought this through. Abdul will have no way of knowing what happened to the flash drive or who did it. On top of that, what is he going to do? It's not as if he can come to you and say, 'Someone stole my flash drive.' Having one in the building is a fire-able offense. But, if there is something nefarious on this drive, he would not want anyone to know it, and his actions will show it."

"Damn it, Josh!" Albertsen stared at him as she tried to weigh Nassar's admittedly suspicious actions against the actions that Reed had taken. "You can't do these things unilaterally. There is a chain of command in this building. If this is some sort of misunderstanding, you will have placed me in an extremely difficult situation."

Reed's shoulders sagged. Albertsen had seen this before, but she didn't care. "Let me figure out what I need to do with this, *and who I need to involve in my immediate chain of command*." She said those final few words with added emphasis. But then, as it always did, her human side intervened. There was something about Josh that made him seem like a small child that needed protection. "I do appreciate you looking out for the agency, but there is protocol in place for a reason."

"I understand, and I am sorry."

"Get back to work, and do not mention this to anyone."

"Will do," Reed replied.

"I mean anyone, Josh. I'm serious."

"My lips are sealed," Reed said as he rose from his chair and left the room. Albertsen leaned back in her chair, looked at the flash drive, and picked up the phone to call Tammy Leeds.

CHAPTER 79

December 25
1:15 PM
The Oval Office

Everyone in the room was physically and mentally exhausted. Nobody had slept more than 10 hours since the blackout, and Clark had slept less than six. Even those six hours were forced upon him with the understanding that if anything happened that could be considered *possibly* important by *anyone* while he was asleep, he was to be awakened immediately. Clark knew people were dying by the hour, and the thought of sleeping through it was unfathomable. In the end, however, he knew he had to get enough rest to be fully functional. He felt as if he was teetering right on the edge of that need.

Clark was agitated. He had just been informed that Father Jerry could not be convinced to come to the White House. As the aides had reported, his actual answer was, "Absolutely not! Not under any circumstances whatsoever!" Clark was disappointed, but not surprised. Father Jerry was the shepherd watching over his sheep.

Clark spoke to Andrew Byerly, his Homeland Security Secretary. "Andrew, what is the latest? Is there a way to relocate people to areas of the country that have power? If so, is it feasible?"

"First, let me say that Miguel and I are coordinating these efforts. Some of this is more FEMA related than Homeland Security, but frankly, we are in uncharted territory regarding such a broad crisis within our borders. So, here's the latest."

Byerly's tone was confident. "We have good news and bad news. The good news is that there are parts of the US that are fully functional. Primarily, they are the areas east of Phoenix and Las Vegas, and west of the Mississippi. The exception is Texas. Most of Texas is out. From a geographical standpoint, that's a lot of land that has electricity. As we know, however, most of that area is sparsely populated. The other piece of good news is that many areas within the outage are populated by people that can provide for themselves for a reasonable amount of time - people who can hunt and fish. Many of those types of people also have generators…while their fuel supply holds out.

Byerly continued. "The bad news is that the population centers along the east and west coasts are not at all prepared for this. The ability to even *survive* for more than another two to three weeks is in question for those in the northern areas of the blackout, primarily because of the weather conditions. The further south you are, the longer you can stay warm. Those who were in the path of this storm have to be our priority because they will be the quickest to die from hypothermia."

Byerly paused to let the people in the room process what he knew was a description of their country that was hard to comprehend. Clark was the first to speak.

"Let's use New York as an example. Is it possible to get people out of the city? If so, how do we get them, logistically speaking, to places with electricity? Buses? Trains? Airplanes?"

Byerly nodded as if expecting the question. "Logistics are indeed the problem, on both ends. How do we begin moving groups of people without causing an uncontrollable wave of panicked citizens from overrunning whatever mode of transportation shows up first, whether that be city buses or military vehicles? Keep in mind how desperate these people must feel. They don't know if there will *be* another bus. If there is another one, how long before it arrives? Will their family still be alive? Because communication is down, they have no way to know anything other than what they are told. We will need significant numbers of National Guard and law enforcement personnel on the ground, and they will have to communicate with the populace in the best fashion possible." Byerly paused. "And, quite frankly sir, as bad as this sounds, the worst thing we can do right now is tell them the truth."

Byerly looked around the room. "In summary, Mr. President, every day that passes with large numbers of people growing more and more hungry, cold, and confused will increase the potential for desperate acts. We have to assume that will mean looting and violence beyond what we can control."

"Christ!" Vice-President Sullivan rose from his chair and ran his hand over his face.

Byerly continued, his tone as even keel as if he was giving a lecture at an insurance seminar. "There is more potential for successful relocation on the west coast. While there is not room for everyone, we can find accommodations for large amounts of people without having to transport them nearly as far. Presently, we have located approximately 130,000 hotel rooms within one day's travel by bus or train from anywhere on the west coast. If we can get eight people in each room, that's over one million people relocated to acceptable living conditions, in the short term."

Sullivan countered. "Eight people per room? I'm not sure I would consider that 'acceptable living conditions.'"

"We have considered that," Byerly replied. "We need to maximize our space. We plan to let people know what their living conditions will be if they decide to relocate. When they compare that to what they currently have, we feel like 90% or more will get on that bus."

Byerly was fully in charge of the room. Clark nodded in affirmation for him to proceed.

"Beyond that, there are also numerous convention centers, basketball arenas, schools, and other facilities that can accommodate people on a short-term basis. The situation in the western part of the country is not good, but it is easily the more reasonable crisis to manage. May I touch on one more piece, Mr. President?"

"Absolutely," Clark said without a moment's hesitation.

"This is going to be extremely taxing on our first responders, particularly on the east coast where the storm hit. We must get these people where we need them to be. They don't have fuel or any creature comforts either, but we need them desperately. Here's my point. These people are human beings. They're just as concerned about the well-being of their own families as they are about everyone else's. We are asking them to prevent mass chaos while also protecting the points of distribution once we are able to get supplies to the designated areas. But all of that assumes that these people show up. What if they all decide that their families are more important to them than their jobs as public servants? What if they decide against protecting other people's families when their own kids need Mom or Dad more than they ever have in their lives? This is a very real problem that we have to consider."

Clark stood and began to pace. "Okay," he said as he gathered his thoughts. "First, thank you Andrew. That was excellent information. Now, help me out, people. In my opinion, finding a way to communicate is priority number one. It helps us inform people, and it helps us organize. Based on what Andrew presented, my thought is that the first thing we must do is figure out a way to establish a line of communication between Washington and those first responders. They need to hear from us that we need them, and that we will do everything we can to support them and keep their families safe. Then we try to get radio communications up. Television is out for now. We will have to communicate in an old school fashion at first.

"Meanwhile, we develop a plan to implement Andrew's idea on the west coast. We face fewer obstacles there. If we can begin to have some victories, we can boost morale across the country. Unfortunately, many of our citizens have never faced real adversity. They will need to be encouraged and given pep talks. Whatever it takes to keep them fighting. Thoughts?"

There were some nods around the room, but everyone was beyond exhausted. Clark had been in situations before where he had to focus on an important task and fight through fatigue. It would not be easy, but they had no choice. He did recognize, however, that nobody else in the room had been trained to handle such situations. "Hey," he said just to regain their attention. "This goes for all of you. Find a time in the next three hours to catch a 15-minute nap. It will refresh you. Don't try to fight through without it. That's an order."

Clark had barely finished speaking when Patrick Welch quickly came through the door, with a smile.

"What?" It was all Clark could manage through the fog of his fatigue.

"We have reestablished limited communication. We still don't have cell service yet, but our sat phones and radios should be back to 100%!"

"Get me in touch with Fort Knox!" Clark had always been fascinated by the power of adrenaline. Thirty seconds ago, he felt as if he may fall asleep while standing; now he felt entirely refreshed.

CHAPTER 80

December 25
1:20 PM
Lexington, KY

Thompson jumped from his seat to the ground and smacked the door of the second vehicle. Instead of standing in the snow, he climbed back into his truck, although it was not much warmer in there, due to the shattered window. As soon as the other window rolled down, he explained what Private Brickley had said. But that was only part of the solution. "We need to know what 'Queen' means. Does anybody in there have any ideas?" Thompson turned around. "Or anybody in here?"

Thompson interlocked his fingers on top of his head and closed his eyes. This whole thing was moving so fast. He needed to slow down and work through this.

"Colonel? Colonel Thompson?"

The voice was not crystal clear and came through a bit of static. It took a split second for Thompson to realize that it was coming through the sat phone. "Shit!" Thompson reached for the phone and replied. "Yes! This is Colonel Thompson! Who is this?"

"Colonel! Thank God! This is Major Klein from the Pentagon. Please hold. I'm patching you through to the White House."

Thompson appeared calm to the others in the truck, but they could only imagine how he felt inside. The truck was totally quiet. The White House! Although the wait was only fifteen seconds or so, it seemed like an hour. Finally, a voice came across the radio.

"Colonel Thompson, are you there?"

"Yes, sir," Thompson replied. Johnny thought he recognized the voice, but could it really be?

"Colonel, this is President Clark. We are making some progress here in Washington. I really hope you are doing the same in Kentucky. I need an update, and I need the quick version."

Thompson could not believe he was talking to the President of the United States, but he had to overcome that feeling and do his job. He began to prioritize the facts in his mind to give a clear but concise summary. Unfortunately, part of that summary included informing the President that his father had been kidnapped by Chinese paramilitary troops.

"There is a lot to report, Mr. President. How much do you know?"

"Really, all I know is that the gold is gone, and I am hoping you have some idea of where it is."

Thompson gathered his thoughts. "Well, Mr. President, I guess I should start by saying that we have a civilian with us who has been instrumental in the progress we have made."

"A civilian?" Clark was obviously surprised.

"Yes, sir. I'll get to that. Before we lost communication, we were told that there was a breach at Fort Knox. When we got there, the gold was gone, soldiers were dead, and the place had been decimated by RPGs and other explosives. Turns out, Mr. President, their ability to get into the vault included assistance from one of the IT employees at the base. I don't know what his incentive was, but they have since killed him."

Thompson continued with the pursuit to Bowman Field and Johnny's role in keeping the gold on the ground. He also explained that Johnny knew this area of Kentucky better than any of them, which was why he was still with them. It was then that Thompson had to get to the uncomfortable part. "I'm sorry to tell you this, sir, but once they left the airport, we discovered that they had a contingency plan that included driving to your hometown. Mr. President, they kidnapped your father."

Thompson was preparing to continue, but before he could do so, he heard a single word shouted from the other end. "What?"

"We know where he is, sir, and he is unharmed, but I could sure use some guidance on how to proceed. May I continue?"

"Colonel, this is Admiral Stewart. President Clark is still here, but obviously shocked by that news. Please continue."

If Thompson wasn't nervous enough speaking to the President, now he had the Chairman of the Joint Chiefs on the line. He trudged ahead, describing the decision to go straight to Lexington in order to beat them there. He went through the rest of the details up to the point where he had to say out loud that the President's father was being held hostage inside a castle in central Kentucky. The words could not have possibly sounded more preposterous, and even though it was true, Thompson still felt ridiculous.

"The castle?" It was President Clark again." You've got to be kidding me."

Thompson knew that the statement was just a sign of frustration and not something he needed to answer, so he proceeded to the demand note and Aurum Regina. He explained the parts they had figured out, especially that the gold may be somewhere else, and ended the summary with two questions that he needed help with – what did 'gold queen' mean, and how were they supposed to handle the hostage situation?

"Colonel, this is Vice President Sullivan. Excellent work to this point. Let us talk this through and we will get back with you in just a few minutes. For the moment, just sit tight."

As soon as the call was disconnected, Sam Clark looked directly at his Vice- President. "I'm fine, Charlie. I can work through this." Everyone else had left the room except Patrick Welch.

Sullivan nodded. "We have several things going on. Let's talk through them. First, if the gold isn't with the group at the castle, we must make finding it before it leaves the country priority number one. We still need to get the power back on and make sure it stays on. Then, of course, we have to find a way to make sure your father is secured and unharmed." Sullivan paused before continuing. "Let's try to figure out your father's message."

Sam Clark knew that he needed to push the reset button. He was dealing with a crisis the likes of which America had never seen. There was no way to know if the country as they knew it would exist a week from now. He couldn't remember the last time he had slept more than two hours at one time. His burst of energy from the news of restored communication was short-lived. He was back to feeling exhausted physically, mentally, emotionally, and spiritually. He closed his eyes and took a deep breath.

"We can do this," he said while nodding. He looked up and focused on the topic at hand. "Gold Queen…the reference to gold, of course, is that it is not in their truck but in the other one. But I am drawing a blank on 'queen.'"

Welch chimed in. "There's not a Gold Queen boat? Something on the Ohio River?"

Clark shook his head. "No, the river boat is the Belle of Louisville. Plus, a boat doesn't do them any good. The only way to get the gold out of the country is by air. They need a plane."

The phone rang. Welch answered it. Clark and Sullivan were still trying to figure out the queen reference. "Damn it!" Clark walked toward the window. "Dad left that message for me. I know he did. Why am I not figuring it out?"

Welch spoke up. "Mr. President, it appears that the Chinese unit is moving toward the airport. We assume your father is with them. But there is no evidence that any planes are approaching. Colonel Thompson is waiting for instructions."

"Tell him to hold his position. Tell him to watch and listen for planes. If he sees or hears anything, we will reevaluate."

"Yes, sir." Welch relayed the message and hung up the phone.

Clark was still staring out the window. Suddenly, he turned to face the other two. "Queen…queen city. They need an airport. Cincinnati is the closest city with an airport big enough to land cargo planes. It is straight up I-75 from Lexington." Clark paused. "Of course! Cincinnati is known as the queen city! Aurum Regina - They are taking the gold to the Cincinnati airport!"

CHAPTER 81

December 25
1:40 PM
NSA Headquarters

Tammy Leeds had worked with Helene Albertsen long enough to know that when Helene called and said she needed to see her ASAP and that it was urgent, she needed to drop everything. She did just that and agreed to meet Helene in an unused secure office. When Tammy arrived, Helene was already there. Tammy unlocked the office and the two women entered.

"Tammy, I may have an update on the mole. I need access to a system where we can insert a flash drive."

"A flash drive?" Leeds' tone indicated how unusual it was to even mention a flash drive in this building.

"Yes. It was discovered in the desk drawer of an employee." Albertsen pre-empted the reaction that Leeds' face showed she was getting ready to give. "I know, I know. That is why I think this might help us discover what is going on. However, this could potentially do damage to the computer that we use, so I want to make sure it is not connected to any of our networks."

"Of course," Leeds replied as she led her to a stand-alone workstation. "This one will work."

The two women pulled up chairs. Albertsen inserted the flash drive, and they were greeted by several file names in Arabic. "What in the hell is this?" Leeds was totally bewildered.

"As much as it pains me to tell you this, this drive was found in a locked drawer in Abdul's desk."

"Abdul Nassar?" Leeds asked the question as if they had numerous co-workers named Abdul.

"Yes. I'll give you the details later. Do you speak Arabic?"

"As a modern-day director of the NSA, I probably speak better Arabic than most people in the Middle East."

Leeds began reading the file names. "These file names are gibberish." She opened the first one. Both women's jaws dropped as they stared at a detailed map, aerial photos, and diagrams of seven different military bases. A second file contained detailed coding and encryption information. Each of the remaining files contained similar coding.

Leeds looked at Albertsen. "Who found this?"

"Josh," Albertsen replied.

Leeds shook her head. "I'm having a hard time wrapping my mind around this. Abdul had to clear so many hurdles to even make it into this building because of his country of origin. Something doesn't smell right about this, but if this is true, and we have a spy inside the NSA that is named Abdul Nassar, the amount of criticism we will receive will be unprecedented."

Leeds paused, then continued. "Bring Josh in. I want to hear this directly from him, every single detail."

"You got it," Albertsen replied. "I'll be back in fifteen minutes."

CHAPTER 82

December 25
2:05 PM
NSA Headquarters

Josh Reed entered Tammy Leeds' office with Helene Albertsen following behind him. Albertsen closed the door. Leeds motioned to a chair across the desk from her, and Reed sat down. He looked around at Helene, almost as if for moral support. She said simply, "Tell her what you told me."

Reed looked at Tammy Leeds, and the look did not inspire much confidence in her. He looked indecisive at best. "I don't have time for your silence," she said. "I need to hear what you told Helene. Every word."

He began to tell her what he had told Albertsen. The story was consistent, even under the probing questions from Leeds. When she had finished questioning him, Leeds said, "You broke numerous security protocols. If Abdul turns out not to be guilty of what you are accusing him of, you are in serious trouble, and not just from a career perspective."

"I understand," Reed replied. "But I was afraid if I told someone who told someone else, he would get spooked and delete everything."

Leeds nodded, conflicted by the idea that if Reed's accusations were true, he could possibly become a hero despite breaking numerous agency regulations and protocols. She didn't like his method at all, but she realized that she needed to pursue it because of the gravity of the situation.

After fifteen minutes of Reed telling his story and answering pointed questions, Albertsen saw that

Leeds was finished with him and spoke up. "Let's go, Josh. Until we decide what to do next, we are going to move you into an isolated workstation, so you do not have any form of contact with Abdul."

Reed rose from his seat and exited the room. Albertsen made eye contact with Leeds before she turned to leave, and both understood the non-verbal communication. They were going to have to treat one of their own like a criminal until they could determine whether he was betraying their country.

CHAPTER 83

December 25
2:35 PM
NSA Headquarters

Abdul Nassar was being led down the hall by two security guards. He was demanding to know what this was about, although he knew that he wouldn't get any information from them. He was led into what he recognized as an interrogation room. Once inside, he saw two men that he had never seen before. They were dressed identically. Both wore white, short sleeve dress shirts with dark ties. One had a crew cut, and the other had ordinary brown hair parted on the side. They could not have looked more stereotypical if they had tried. A lone chair was unoccupied across the table from them, and Nassar knew it was for him. But he was not going into this like a lamb being led to slaughter.

"I want a lawyer," he said without offering a step toward the chair.

"Sit down," one of the men replied in a monotone voice.

"Not until I talk to a lawyer."

Nassar had barely finished the sentence when the two security guards grabbed him by both arms and began forcing him to the chair. Nassar fought back, digging in and pulling against them. One of them punched him in the stomach. He had not expected this, and it knocked the breath out of him. He was gasping for air as they forced him into the chair.

Now the other man spoke, but in the same monotone voice. "Are we going to need to restrain you?"

The two security guards released him and let him recover. Nassar took the opportunity to evaluate his options. He realized he was not going to get a lawyer, and he also felt sure that they would resort to further efforts to 'convince' him to cooperate if necessary. He decided to comply and sort out the details later.

"No," he said defiantly. He gathered himself and sat up in the chair.

One of the men held up the thumb drive but did not speak.

"What?" Nassar said.

"Why was this in your desk drawer?"

"It wasn't," Nassar replied.

The two men just stared at him.

"We aren't allowed to have those in the building. Aside from that, no system in the building will accept one. What is this about?"

One of the men pulled a laptop out from underneath the desk. He inserted the thumb drive and turned it toward Nassar. As soon as he saw the files in Arabic, he realized something was wrong. "You did *not* find that at my workstation! I have no idea what that is!"

"Is that how you plan to play this?"

"How else would I play it? I have never seen that drive, and I have never seen those files." Nassar was no longer shouting. He was now copying the monotone voice of his questioners. He would say nothing more, as they had already made up their minds that he was guilty of something.

One of the men looked at the security guards. "Close the door behind you."

As the door closed, Abdul Nassar felt a cold chill go all the way down his spine. For the first time, he noticed what one of these rooms looked like. The steel door made a clear sound as it closed that indicated nobody was coming in or out of that door unless they were being escorted. There were, of course, no windows. The twelve-foot ceilings held fluorescent lights. The walls were bare. The table and chairs were metal. It was cold and bland and lifeless, and he knew it was that way on purpose. The thought occurred to him that he may never see the outside of this building again. His fight or flight instincts were kicking in, but he realized that neither fight nor flight were legitimate options under the circumstances. He closed his eyes and took a deep breath, then he decided to use what appeared to be the two most practical strategies available to him: honesty and reason.

The one with the crew cut appeared to be in command. He simply nodded.

"I fully realize that very few spies come out and admit they are spies. In fact, nearly all criminals lie about their role in a crime. But please listen. I am from Syria. I am BROWN! Do you realize how hard it was for me to get hired into this position? Do you realize how frequently I am scrutinized by co-workers? I'm not just clean; I am squeaky clean. My lifestyle would put you to sleep. Research me; look at my habits; talk to Helene Albertsen. If all of that is insufficient, let me add this. I am not trying to brag, but I am the best at what I do. I can dance intellectual circles around everyone else in this building. If I *was* a spy, do you really think I would use a flash drive and then simply lock it in a desk drawer? That is such a terrible version of a set-up, it would be entirely comical if I wasn't scared shitless."

Helene Albertsen and Tammy Leeds were watching the interrogation via a live feed, although so far it was a filibuster. Nassar was still talking as

Leeds looked at Albertsen. "What do you think," she asked.

"Something's going on. He's not our guy. The points he is making are the same ones I thought about - why such a low-level tool? Why would he leave it in his drawer? It doesn't add up. Aside from that, look at him. He's physically trembling."

Leeds nodded and spoke into a small microphone. "Shut it down."

The lead interrogator held his hand up and Nassar stopped talking. "We'll be back," was all he said as he and his cohort rose from their chairs and exited the room.

Considering this was an unprecedented time in American history and considering her role in trying to save lives and perhaps the life of her government, Helene Albertsen really did not have time to be scanning archived video footage of Abdul Nassar's workstation. Under the circumstances, however, she did not feel there was anyone she could delegate this duty to because fundamentally, if there was a mole, there was no ability to trust anyone. Albertsen felt like she could trust Tammy Leeds wholeheartedly, but Tammy had even more pressure on her than Helene did.

As she fast-forwarded through the footage, looking for a flash drive and/or any suspicious behavior out of Abdul Nassar, Albertsen had to pause the video for a moment to rub her eyes. She then proceeded to stand and stretch. She needed some blood flow, and she could no longer look at coffee due to the enormous amount she had consumed in recent days. She sat back down, and as soon as she proceeded with the fast forwarding of the video, there was a glitch. It was momentary, almost like an old home movie that had been spliced. She hit rewind and looked at the time stamp, then hit play.

Nassar was working at his desk, nothing looking out of the ordinary. It was 3:12 PM on December 19. Then came the glitch, and Albertsen stood again in amazement. Nassar was still working diligently at his desk just like before, but the timestamp now read 3:24 PM. Someone had manipulated the surveillance footage. Now Albertsen had an entirely different problem. Who had done this, and how in the world would she be able to find out?

CHAPTER 84

December 25
United Nations Meeting
New Paltz, New York
3:05 PM

Oleg Medinsky waited for the world's representatives to gather in the room that was specifically built for such emergency meetings of the United Nations. Medinsky recognized in himself that he was not the most punctual person in the world, but it drove him crazy that no meeting started less than thirty minutes after it was scheduled to begin. In this case, Medinsky needed the meeting to start by 3:00, so he scheduled it for 2:30. As the last few stragglers took their seats, Medinsky was unexpectedly a little bit nervous about what was getting ready to transpire. He looked at the empty seat designated for American representative Keith Keough.

Medinsky called the meeting to order. He waited for everyone to get their translation headphones in place. He had considered wishing a Merry Christmas to those who celebrated the ridiculous holiday, but he thought better of it due to the gravity of the situation. The Chinese ambassador, as planned, left his seat and came to the front of the room, where he sat next to Medinsky. Medinsky nodded to him and then began speaking. He decided not to beat around the bush.

"As all of you know, many of the countries represented here today have had financial, cultural, or philosophical differences with the United States over the course of this body's existence." He paused momentarily in order to look around the room. He clearly had everyone's attention.

"Many of your countries have also had military confrontations with the US. In each case, America has emerged stronger and more financially secure than before, while those confrontations have thrown many of your countries into political and economic despair. In some cases, thousands upon thousands of your people have been killed by the American military."

As Medinsky paused again, the room was entirely silent. "The leaders of my country, along with those of China, have decided that America has no intention to do anything but continue to make itself stronger at the expense of every other country on the planet. Therefore, we have taken action against the United States of America."

Medinisky explained that the cyber attack that had caused the power outage had been coordinated between China and Russia. He also described the involvement of his country in manipulating future oil prices offered to the United States by countries in the Middle East as well as Canada, as well as the seizing of the gold at Fort Knox. He then proceeded to list nearly two dozen countries that had verbally agreed to side with China and Russia in this action against the United States.

"We have crippled America. We have seized their most valuable tangible asset, and we have made it impossible for them to function on several critical levels. America, as you knew it less than a week ago, no longer exists. As we speak, the leadership of our two countries is reaching out to all of your leaders with the same proposition we are offering to you today. All of you are invited to join our coalition in bringing an end to the United States of America.

Framework is in place for Russia and China to share with all of you the riches we will seize in America, in order to make all of your countries more stable and financially secure than ever before. This will create a new world order based on peace and mutual understanding. Those of you who decide to accept our proposal will dramatically improve your position in the global community. Anyone who refuses our offer will be deemed to have sided with the United States and will be treated as a hostile enemy. I hope you make the right decision."

CHAPTER 85

December 25
3:30 PM
The Oval Office

As had been predicted by the meteorologists before the power went out, the entire eastern seaboard had gone into a deep freeze. This was the third consecutive day with temperatures below zero, and wind chills between 20 and 30 degrees below zero. With no power, the number of deaths from exposure would accumulate quickly. Sam Clark knew he had the best and brightest people in the world working on getting the power restored, while others who were the best at their jobs tried to maintain law and order during a societal breakdown. The X-factor in the whole thing was that regardless of everything else, there was absolutely nothing Clark could do about the weather, and he did not like being powerless.

He spent the next thirty minutes reading the latest briefing memo, which had some substance now that they had regained the ability to communicate, albeit on a limited basis. The memo included nothing but updates on the multiple layers inside of which the current crisis was wrapped. The information seemed to get worse by the hour - more riots, more violence, more looting. America's cities were filled with people who were neighbors a week ago, but who now considered each other combatants. Everyone suddenly found themselves trying to bring home to their families a share of the finite and rapidly dwindling amount of the resources needed to live.

The word from outlying areas was no better. People who had access and the ability to get out of the city looking for food and shelter were being met by those who were considerably more capable of providing for themselves, but entirely unable to provide for the growing number of people beginning to encroach on their property. There were descriptions of fortified homes with threatening signs warning those who approached that they needed to move on to another place to seek what they were looking for. After passing three or four such locations, the weary, cold, and hungry travelers had reached a point of desperation, which was beginning to result in attempted sieges that usually ended with the deaths of those trying to break into a home or property. The countryside was slowly becoming littered with bodies across areas east of the Mississippi River.

Information from the western half of the country continued to be less dramatic, as the weather wasn't as unbearable, and there were bigger land areas available for fewer people. That was the lone positive in the current situation. Half of the country was not experiencing survival of the fittest…yet.

Clark was relieved to hear Patrick Welch tap lightly on the door as he entered the room. He had read enough about desolation and despair. As Clark looked up, however, it was immediately evident that he was about to hear more of the same.

"What?" Clark's one-word response indicated his frustration with the ceaseless barrage of bad news.

"I'm very sorry to tell you this, Mr. President." Welch paused and collected himself.

Clark stood and turned away, looking out the window. He had an eerie feeling that he knew what was coming.

"Father Jerry is dead."

Clark did not respond, and he remained as he was, staring out the window into the frigid landscape that he felt sure was the cause of the demise of his dear friend.

"Churches are where people go when times are hard," Welch continued. "Because of that, there has been some looting. People know that churches routinely serve food to the homeless. Once the primary food locations had been emptied out, people figured out they could raid the churches."

Still nothing from Clark. Welch knew him well enough to understand that he would stop him if he did not want to hear any more, so Welch continued.

"It appears that all of the food had been taken from his church. It also appears that he put up a fight. He had been wounded, but it does not appear that he died from his injuries. He was found in front of the altar, among a group of 10-12 people gathered under a pile of coats and blankets. They died due to the cold."

Welch paused momentarily, then walked over and placed his hand on Sam's shoulder. "He was a shepherd to the end, Mr. President. Every one of those people died with a rosary in their hands. It appears that he was leading them in prayer when they passed."

Welch turned and walked back toward his office. As he got to the door, he stopped, and he winced visibly as he said, "I'm sorry, Mr. President, but we have a meeting in the situation room in ten minutes."

Clark nodded, and Welch turned to leave.

"Patrick," Clark said.

"Yes, sir."

"Send someone to get his body. I don't want him lying there forgotten. When this is over, I want to be able to properly honor him."

"I will send someone right away, sir."

Sam Clark turned and walked back to his desk. He sat down in his chair. He was tired. He was carrying unbelievable amounts of stress. His emotions were on the brink. He could feel them welling up inside of him. But he could not, *would* not, let them take over. He took a deep breath, then another. He took a third breath, as deep as he could get his lungs to expand, and he let it out slowly. Then he gathered himself, got up, and headed for the situation room.

CHAPTER 86

December 25
3:55 PM
Situation Room

Clark entered the room for a brief meeting to discuss the latest on the ground, which included news that food and water supplies were running extremely thin.

Homeland Security Director Andrew Byerly spoke first. "Sir, we have reports of groups of people gathering in significant numbers, and it appears that they are pooling weapons."

Clark thought for a moment. "Like a militia?"

"Well, sir, in some cases that might be an accurate description. But others would be better described as mobs. Some are gathering in groups for protection, but others are gathering for looting and confiscation. It is quickly becoming every person or group for themselves. We have a rapidly deteriorating situation here, Mr. President."

Clark thought about that for a moment and realized the populace had forgotten all about their smartphones, their petty political arguments on social media, and all of their other mundane activities. They were converting to survival mode. The bad news, he realized, was that not all Americans were interested in fending for themselves. Aside from that, only a small percentage of them were *capable* of doing it.

FEMA Director Miguel Hernandez interjected at this point. "One of my people on the ground just told me of a strategy session she attended in New Hampshire, most of which was unaffected by the outage. They are developing a plan as to how they would handle mass evacuations from surrounding areas. They are gathering state and local police, the National Guard, and civilian volunteers wearing official paraphernalia. Those people would be stationed in key locations, and they would be offering small amounts of food and water, as well as directions to the next gas station. However, the message they are planning to give these people is direct. They will tell them that New Hampshire is simply not able to handle significant numbers of evacuees, and this food and water is all we have to offer you. Please move along."

Vice President Sullivan looked around the room. "I assume we all know where this is leading. When desperate people, many of whom are now arming themselves, reach what they consider to be safety for them and their families, only to be told they cannot stay..."

Hernandez finished the thought. "Anarchy."

"Exactly!" Sullivan replied.

Byerly spoke again. "Here's the current problem. Americans are not accustomed to being inconvenienced. They are used to doing whatever they want to do, whenever they want to do it. Those who live in the northeast and have experienced a couple of short-term but significant power outages are currently implementing a very shallow 'survival plan' that is based on getting in their cars or taking a taxi to the closest place in which the power is still on. Here's the problem with that strategy. As Miguel said, in a prolonged outage such as this, where thousands of people have that same idea, they are not going to be welcome in most of those places.

"Think about the dynamic of people interacting with each other. Historically, there is an inherent trust among most people. If you find yourself among a large group of people - at the beach, at an amusement park, in Times Square - you assume a certain level of humanity, the following of social norms. You don't think the people around you are going to do you harm. Think about driving down the highway. You are placing a level of trust in the driver of each car that you pass. You trust that they are going to follow the rules of the road. Any one of them could cross the center line and kill you, but generally, they don't.

"But what if the people in a large group setting found themselves competing for a limited amount of goods that would allow their families to survive? What if there was one restaurant selling the last 50 meals to be found in the state, and there were 2,000 families staying at a beach resort? Do you think the same common courtesies would be extended toward each other? Now, think about the last 50 cases of bottled water in Manhattan. These kinds of situations don't lead to impoliteness; they lead to chaos, and eventually to total anarchy and the breakdown of society as we know it."

The heads in the room turned toward the man at the head of the table. Clark was in deep thought. He looked at Byerly. "We're going to have to implement martial law. The only people who will be allowed to travel out of their communities are those that we will be moving as part of our coordinated effort. Anyone, or any group of people, found moving on their own is to be detained."

Clark thought for a moment, then continued. "I realize this is a drastic measure, and these are words that I never imagined would enter my mind, much less actually be spoken out loud. Does anyone think this is a step too far? If so, please offer an alternative."

Sullivan spoke up. "This is the right call, Mr. President. Drastic times call for drastic measures."

"I agree completely, Mr. President," said Byerly. "This will save lives."

As he looked around the room, heads nodded in unanimous agreement.

"All right then," Clark concluded. "Martial law is to be implemented for all of the affected areas, effective immediately. I need all of you to coordinate with city and state officials to get this in place as quickly as possible. For the rest of you, if this does not fall under your purview, let's get back to work."

CHAPTER 87

December 25
5:10 PM
Situation Room

Clark and Patrick Welch rushed through the door to the situation room and saw a flurry of activity. Joint Chiefs Chairman Tom Stewart was on a sat phone with General Smith at US Strategic Command. "You're positive?" Stewart said, seemingly in disbelief. He paused briefly. "Very well."

He turned to Clark. "Mr. President, it appears that three of our Ohio-class submarines have been destroyed, and we have lost radio contact with six others. We are currently trying to get status updates from the remaining five."

"Destroyed?" Clark replied. "By whom?"

"It appears that there was a surprise attack from several Typhoon class submarines, sir."

"Typhoons? The Russians?"

"Yes, sir," Stewart replied.

"Ohio class, those are the Trident subs, right? The nuclear subs?"

"Yes, sir," Stewart confirmed.

"The limited communication we have has only been back up for a few hours. Is there any chance this information is incorrect, or that the hackers are simply leading us to believe this is what happened?" Clark realized he was grasping for straws.

"No, sir."

One of Stewart's aides picked up a call. He sat stone-faced, then turned to look at Stewart. "Four of the six with whom we had lost radio contact have now been confirmed as destroyed, sir. Strategic

Command is assuming the other two are gone as well and are focusing on trying to reach the five that are presently unaccounted for."

"How many sailors are on these subs?" Welch asked.

Stewart turned to Welch. "Fifteen officers and 140 enlisted on each submarine, sir."

"More than one thousand souls," Welch said to nobody in particular.

"So far," Clark muttered as he sat down. "Mr. Chairman, is it possible that the reason we haven't been able to reach the others is because they have gone dark?"

"Absolutely, Mr. President," Stewart replied. "In fact, at this point, no news is good news. There is no reason for those subs to be communicating with us and exposing their position. If we get any more calls, it won't be because they contacted us. It will be to confirm that we have lost more of them."

"Call the Pentagon and get the Defense Secretary on the line," Clark said.

"We already reached out to him, sir," Stewart replied. "He should be on the line any moment."

"We have him, Mr. President," one of the aides said.

"Harold, are you up to speed about the subs?"

"Yes, sir."

"What is our present military capability, and what is the level of contact we have with each branch?"

O'Bryan started with the Air Force. "Our jets are still grounded, sir. We have not been able to fix the issues presented when they hacked into our flight system technology. The land missiles are sketchy at best. The systems are semi-operational, but I would be hesitant to use them in that condition unless it was a last resort."

"Damn, Harold," Clark replied. "It may well be that we are near our last resort. Are you speaking only of our nuclear weapons, or conventional also?"

"Both, Mr. President." There was a pause and then O'Bryan continued. "If we have a few subs that have gone dark and have not yet been destroyed, they may be our best chance at retaliation unless we have a breakthrough with the cyber team."

"So, you're saying those few subs may be our only chance, and we have no way of knowing whether or not they have been destroyed?"

"I'm afraid that is correct, sir."

"And we cannot communicate with them, even if we want them to launch nuclear missiles."

Stewart stepped in to answer that question. "That's not entirely accurate, Mr. President. We have five Trident subs that are on 'hard alert' at all times, and they are capable of responding to a surprise nuclear attack. Two of them are among the subs that we cannot locate or confirm as destroyed. There is a chance that we have two down there that are still capable of retaliating."

"But if we give that order, we give away their position." Clark fully understood where this was going.

"Yes, sir, Mr. President."

"If there are two down there and I give that order, they will be an easy target and that will be 300 more lives lost."

"These sailors understand that, Mr. President. If you had them in this room, all 300 of them would tell you to give that order."

Patrick Welch chimed in. They knew everything there was to know for now, and he realized that Clark needed some time to think about this. "Is there anything else we need to know at this time, Mr. Chairman."

Stewart understood perfectly what Welch was doing and nodded his approval. "No, sir. We will update immediately as needed."

CHAPTER 88

December 25
6:20 PM
The Cabinet Room

Sam Clark had his entire cabinet gathered around him per his request. Although the matter was as sensitive and confidential as possible, there was not enough space for everyone in the situation room. Now that everyone was present, Sam decided to dive right in, as there was really no time for formalities nor for tiptoeing around the topic of this meeting.

"Some of you know why we are here, and most of the rest of you have probably figured it out. That said, I am going to get right to it. Our country is on the precipice. If we survive this as an independent nation, and that is a big if at this point, the United States may never be the same. We will have an unfathomable rebuilding project on our hands. We will also have a power grid that remains vulnerable, along with so many other areas of infrastructure and functionality. Aside from that, we will be in or near financial ruin, which means that we will be fully reliant on global allies to help us get back on our feet.

"All of this is assuming we are still the United States of America at the end of this. Right now, as I see it, we only have one option short of surrender, and surrender really isn't an option while I am sitting in this chair. That option is nuclear warfare. Before any of you protest, let me finish. As I see it, we are in an unprecedented situation. This is worse than Pearl Harbor; it is worse than 9/11; it is worse than the Bay of Pigs and the Cuban Missile Crisis. Because of that, I am recommending that we move to DEFCON 1."

The room immediately filled with voices attempting to shout over each other. This had been fully expected, and Patrick Welch stood and extended his hands for calm. Once the room became quiet, he spoke. "President Clark and I planned this meeting meticulously. Everyone here will get an opportunity to speak his or her mind about this, but first let me cover some matters that I know everyone will want to know."

Welch paused, and the room seemed agreeable. He continued. "First, just like when we moved to DEFCON 2 and formally declared war on China, we realize that Congress is not in session, and we realize there is no way to get them back here from all parts of the country in order for us to consult with them about this decision. We have spoken again with the attorney general about this, and he reiterated that there does not appear to be any precedent on the specific protocol regarding a Congressional role in DEFCON status changes. In summary, we have already moved down to DEFCON 2 without Congressional approval, so in our eyes, a move to DEFCON 1 is no different than our previous moves."

Again, several members began to speak simultaneously. Welch stood again, but this time the voices continued. Clark stood beside his chief of staff. "Stop," he said sternly but without a raised voice. "Let Patrick finish, and then we will get your input. We need to discuss this as thoroughly as possible without these interruptions."

The room calmed again, and Welch continued. "Here is what we ask of you. We will work our way around the room, and any of you that have input will be welcome to share it. However, just to be clear, the president has made his decision regarding the move to DEFCON 1. We ask that you not waste your time trying to convince him to change his mind. Instead, we would like for the focus of your comments to be on the process. If you think what we are doing is unconstitutional, we are extremely open to ideas that would make this process as clean as possible, so that we will be able to make our case to those who will protest our decision once we get through this and get back to a reasonable sense of normalcy."

Welch sat. "Thank you, Patrick," Clark said. He looked around the table in silence, and then he began nodding his head. He looked supremely confident in a situation that did not seem to inspire confidence. "First, let me be clear on what DEFCON 1 represents. It does not mean we launch nuclear missiles before the ink is dry. In fact, we currently are not even *capable* of launching. That is why it is of the utmost importance that we are prepared once our systems are back up and running. Even then, DEFCON 1 just means that we are at maximum readiness for nuclear war. Under the current circumstances, I think that verbiage represents exactly where we should be."

Clark continued. "We are part of the current governing body of the greatest country in the history of civilization." Clark looked around the table again. "Each and every one of us is about to play a vital role in the story of this republic. We are about to write what is either the most exciting chapter to this point, or the final chapter. As I look around this table, I refuse to believe that this is the final chapter. I will not be convinced that we cannot overcome this situation." He paused again. "I know each of you has heard me talk ad nauseum about Teddy Roosevelt's 'Man in the Arena' speech. It is a perfect fit for this moment. Here we are. It is our faces that are marred with dust and sweat and blood. Now is our time. Let us begin."

Forty-five minutes later, the cabinet room had fallen silent. Patrick Welch spoke. "Does anyone have anything else to add?"

The silence continued for another ten seconds. Clark looked at Tom Stewart, the Chairman of the Joint Chiefs of Staff. "Are we ready, Mr. Chairman?"

"Yes, sir," Stewart replied in an unwavering fashion.

"Okay," Clark replied confidently. "Let's proceed to the situation room."

Clark stood, as did everyone else in the room. It was then that Sam Clark, President of the United States, Commander-in-Chief, said the words that nobody in the room ever imagined hearing. "Ladies and gentlemen, we are moving to DEFCON 1."

CHAPTER 89

December 25
7:08 PM
NSA Headquarters

Helene Albertsen finally got the email she had been waiting for. As if trying to restore power to the country by an unrealistic deadline set by the President of the United States was not enough of a burden to carry, she also had to handle the investigation of Abdul Nassar. She and Tammy Leeds had agreed that only the two of them should be involved in looking into the matter. They had no way to know for sure whether Nassar was the mole or whether he was being set up. Tammy had just received a call from the president's chief of staff, so for the time being, Albertsen would have to investigate this matter by herself.

The email was a time log of Nassar's security badge. It showed when and where his badge was scanned. Basically, the badge served as a tracking device, and Albertsen hoped to learn enough information from his movements to either prove or disprove his denials. From her notes, Albertsen recalled that on the day in question, Nassar had been working at his desk at 3:12 PM. That is when the glitch occurred, and the time stamp moved immediately to 3:24 PM, with Nassar still at his desk.

Albertsen scanned through the long list of badge numbers until she reached the one belonging to Nassar. She scrolled to the date in question and followed his movement. Nearly every room required the scanning of a badge for entry, including the restrooms. "Big Brother *is* always watching,"

Albertsen thought to herself as she tracked Nassar's day. He scanned himself into the room in which his cubicle was located at 1:51 PM. The next scan was at 3:16. Albertsen looked back at her notes. That scan took place during the time of the missing footage. She looked at the directory for the entry number scanned at 3:16. It was for the break room on that floor. The next scan was at 3:21, and it was Nassar coming back to his desk. Albertsen went back to the video footage. THERE IT WAS! When the footage resumed at 3:24, there was a soda on his desk that was not there at 3:12.

Nassar had left his desk for less than ten minutes. At no point before that time, nor after it, had he placed anything in the desk drawer in question. That could mean only one thing - someone else had planted the flash drive during the time that Nassar was away from his desk. Whoever that someone was, they had also altered the video footage. Abdul Nassar was not their mole.

Albertsen was trying to figure out how to proceed when her phone rang. Tammy Leeds' name popped up on the caller ID screen.

Albertsen picked up the phone. "Hey, Tammy."

"Sorry about that. Patrick Welch had a few follow up questions for me. What can I do to help?"

"Well, I'm not sure," Albertsen replied. "This would have been considerably easier logistically if I had seen Abdul put a flash drive in his desk drawer, but that isn't what happened."

She went on to explain what she had discovered using the video footage and the time stamps from Nassar's badge. "He's not our guy, Tammy. In one way, that makes me extremely happy. But in another way, it makes me sick to my stomach."

Leeds knew right away what Albertsen meant by that comment. "That means Josh's story falls apart."

"Has all of this happened right under my nose without me having a clue?" The distress in Albertsen's voice was palpable.

"Most of the time, the closer we are to someone, the harder it is to believe they could be involved in something this nefarious." Leeds hoped she could alleviate some of Albertsen's apprehension, but at this point, that concern was a distant second to getting Josh Reed back in front of them. "We're going to have to talk to Josh again. Do you want to be here, or would you prefer I handle it myself?"

Albertsen's emotions had changed quickly from surprise and disappointment to anger. She had been betrayed. "Oh, I want to be there. I'm on my way. Please don't start without me."

Leeds wanted Albertsen present for this meeting, in case they needed to squeeze Reed for information. She smiled as she hung up the phone. Now she might have to control just how hard Helene squeezed.

CHAPTER 90

December 25
8:10 PM
NSA Headquarters

Josh Reed knocked on Tammy Leeds' door and was signaled into the office. It was clear that he did not have a clue what was about to happen. He was preparing to sit down in the chair across from Leeds' desk when he saw Helene Albertsen standing in the corner behind the door. Josh paused before sitting. "Hey, Helene. Is everything okay?"

Albertsen walked toward him very slowly. "I don't know, Josh. *Is* everything okay?"

Reed's reaction was somewhere between confused and scared.

Before he could speak, Albertsen pointed to the chair. "Sit down."

Reed sat without saying a word. He looked to Leeds, who had yet to speak. She just stared at him.

"What?" Reed was nearing a state of panic.

"We need to go over your version of events again, Josh," Leeds said calmly. "It appears there are some discrepancies."

"I don't know what kind of discrepancies there could be," Reed replied. "I told you what I saw. You saw the files. What else is there?"

"Well, there is the truth." Albertsen was beginning to encroach on Reed's personal space. He leaned away from her.

"What is wrong with you?" Reed could almost be described as shrieking. He looked at Albertsen, then to Tammy Leeds, then back to Albertsen.

"We're not stupid, Josh. You should know that. You work with us every day." She paused before continuing. "Abdul was not at his desk when the flash drive was put in the drawer...but you were."

"No, I wasn't!" Reed's eyes were bulging. "What are you talking about?"

Albertsen placed a laptop on the desk in front of Reed. As she explained her process, including the missing time, the tracking of Nassar's badge, and the video evidence going back three days, it was clear that Abdul Nassar had not placed the flash drive in the drawer. She went on to explain that the only time it could have been put there was during the time of the missing video footage. Abdul Nassar was somewhere else during that time. She closed the laptop and looked at Reed.

"So, you told us you saw something that did not happen. You lied. Since we know Abdul isn't our mole, who do you think we are looking at now?"

"Helene...wait. I didn't do this."

"Save it! I am tired of looking at you, and I am tired of hearing your voice."

Tammy Leeds picked up her phone and dialed an extension. After a brief pause, she said, "Send them in."

Before he could say anything else, two security guards entered the room and planted Reed face down on the floor. They applied handcuffs and took him away. Helene Albertsen turned her back to him as he was taken away.

Tammy Leeds and Helene Albertsen were experiencing mixed emotions as they walked down the hallway to where Abdul Nassar was being detained. They were happy to be telling him he was free to get back to work...if he didn't tell them to go to hell. They realized that their relationship with him was damaged, perhaps irreparably. As they discussed the process, however, neither could think of anything they could have or should have done differently.

The guard unlocked the door and let them in. Nassar looked up to see who it was. Upon seeing the two, he looked back down at the table – no outrage, no pleading. Both women found themselves wishing he would just curse them out and get it out of his system.

Tammy Leeds spoke. "Abdul, we wanted to tell you in person that someone else has been detained and is currently being questioned. At this point, you are free to go. I know I speak for Helene when I offer our sincere apologies. I hope you realize that we had to follow protocol."

Nassar stood and held his hands up. He was still handcuffed.

"Oh my gosh," Albertsen was already heading for the door. "Let me find someone to get those off of you."

Leeds looked at him. The two held eye contact. Nassar would not look away. Finally, Leeds spoke. "I sincerely hope that you will return to your desk. We need you. I know you know that."

Albertsen returned with one of the interrogators, who unlocked the handcuffs. Nassar walked toward the door. She walked toward him. "Abdul…"

Nassar stopped in his tracks, looked at her sternly and raised his hand in a 'stop' motion. Then he turned to Leeds. "I need my badge."

"Someone is waiting to let you back in. Everything you need is on your desk. Thank you, Abdul."

Abdul Nassar left the room. Albertsen closed the door behind him and looked at Leeds. "Ugh…that was terrible."

Leeds stared at the door. "He's a better American than nearly anyone I know. He is not going back to his desk because he needs us. He could make three times the money he makes here if he decided to work in the private sector. He is going back to his desk because this country needs him…*his* country. Did you notice that he did not even bother to ask who we had detained? He is just getting back to work." Leeds paused, then looked at Albertsen. "We should do the same."

CHAPTER 91

December 25
9:25 PM
NSA Headquarters

It did not take long for CIA operative Don Markle to realize that although Josh Reed was extremely deceptive, he was not tough - not at all. Reed had spilled the beans relatively quickly. He gave accurate responses to questions for which Markle already knew the answers, but he had also given them the answer to the burning question that they were leading him to – namely, the identity of the person on the other end of a number that he had called more than a dozen times in the days leading up to the attack on the grid.

The name he gave was Amy Reed. Josh described her as his sister, and assured Markle that the calls had nothing to do with his work. His repeated use of the phrase 'lone wolf' to describe himself made it hard for Markle not to roll his eyes. He was preparing to suggest to Josh that perhaps his repeated use of the phrase was an attempt to inflate his own ego, or perhaps an unconscious overcompensation for his physical shortcomings. But before he had the chance to make those suggestions, there was a knock on the window of the interrogation room.

Markle could not resist. "I'll be right back, Mr. Wolf."

As Markle closed the door behind him, fellow CIA agent Margaret Williams handed him a sheet of paper. "Amy Reed's aliases," she said with a smile.

"Wow," Markle said as he examined the sheet, which had fourteen different names on it.

Williams watched him scan the names until he got to number thirteen. His eyes bulged. "No way!"

Williams took the sheet back and held it in the air. "Amanda Curtis! Josh just made himself a pawn in a game of chess we are getting ready to play."

Markle walked back into the interrogation room chuckling. Josh Reed sat quietly. He wasn't sure what to make of the laughter. Markle looked at him. "Damn, Mr. Wolf. I need to give you credit. You are the most honest crook I've ever come across."

"What do you mean?" Aside from his other shortcomings, Reed also had a terrible poker face.

"You actually gave us an honest answer on the question about the phone number. And you were even truthful about her being your sister."

Josh knew they had access to his file, so he felt a little surge of confidence. They had verified his information. That's all. "I told you. I have nothing to hide. I'm…"

"…A lone wolf. Yeah, I know," Markle actually did roll his eyes this time. "Do you really think we are that limited with our information?"

Reed's poker face cracked again. "What do you mean?"

"Let's talk about Amanda Curtis," Markle said with a smile, as he watched Reed's shoulders sag.

CHAPTER 92

Steigenberger Hotel El Tahrir
Cairo, Egypt

Over dinner and a drink in the hotel lounge, Elaine got Tommy up to speed on Josh Reed and Amanda Curtis, along with their potential roles with the Chinese government in relation to the attack on the power grid. At this point, they were finished for the night, and both felt like Tommy was prepared for the 10:00 AM call with Curtis the next morning. If she had played an integral role in causing the outage, there was a strong possibility that she could play a similar role in restoring the power. People like her had no loyalty to a country, nor to a client. Each agreement was a stand-alone transaction, and they hoped to strike a deal with her. "This gives a whole new level of authenticity to the adage about making a deal with the devil," Elaine muttered, only halfway kidding.

Tommy laughed, and the two made eye contact. It wasn't as if he had never looked at Elaine before, but this time the eye contact lingered. It would ordinarily have been awkward, but neither of them felt that way at this moment. Elaine smiled at Tommy. She was a pro, but right now she felt a warm sense of affection for this man. That feeling was combined with one that was more urgent than affectionate. The latter feeling must have been the one that was showing on her face, because Tommy asked her if she would like to come up to his room for a night cap. Every logical, professional, and common-sense defense mechanism that she had mastered through the years sounded alarms that shouted at her, 'No! Absolutely not! Under no circumstances! You know better!'

"Sure," she replied.

Once they reached Tommy's room, he poured each of them a drink and sat down beside Elaine. He smiled.

"What?" She could not help but smile back at him.

"Wanna play a game?"

"Absolutely," she replied without hesitation, and scooted a bit closer.

"One question," he said. "We get to ask each other a single question about our lives outside of work."

"No. No way..." Elaine stood and walked across the room. She placed her drink on the table and stood with her back to him.

Tommy rose and walked over to her. "You're right; bad idea. I'm sorry. I just want so badly to know more about you." He stood behind her and put his hands on her arms.

"I feel the same way," she said, still facing away from him. "But not when our lives have to be lived like this." Now she turned to face him. "Would you ever consider walking away from this line of work?"

Tommy looked at her intently. "Is that an invitation to walk off into the sunset with you?"

"Maybe," Elaine replied. Her smile had returned. "But for now, let's play a different game."

"I'm up for that," Tommy replied. "What game do you want to play?"

"Zero questions," she said. She kissed him, tenderly at first, but it soon became passionate. They began to undress each other as both became more comfortable with the idea of continued anonymity, at least for now.

CHAPTER 93

Next Morning

Elaine woke to the sound of the shower turning on. She looked at the clock. It was 8:15. She could not remember the last time she had slept this late, but she also could not remember the last time she had felt the way she felt last night. She acknowledged in her mind that it had not been a good idea, but she also realized without a doubt that if she was presented with the same situation again tonight, the outcome would be the same.

By the time Tommy had finished showering, Elaine had all the equipment set up and ready for testing. There was a sense of apprehension as Tommy came out of the bathroom. Would he regret last night? Would he act like nothing had happened? Her stomach was churning as she sat on the edge of the bed and waited for her turn to shower.

"Good morning," he said with a smile as he walked across the room. He kissed her on the forehead and tousled her hair with his hand. "Nice hair."

Elaine loved it. He was not dismissing what happened, but he also wasn't making it awkward. He had struck the perfect balance. She was trying to match his playful nature, while also hoping that what she was about to say wasn't over the top. "Looks like you missed a few spots. I'll be glad to get them for you if you want to come back into the shower." She rose from the bed and walked into the bathroom, confident that he would follow. She was correct.

Elaine checked the recording devices as Tommy prepared to call Amanda Curtis. Once Don Markle had told them Reed's story, they had quickly developed a plan to call Curtis from Reed's phone and see how much they could leverage the brother/sister relationship. At this point, there was a high probability that she was indeed the agent who had sold the digital weapon to the Chinese, and they felt sure she was savvy enough to have a counter measure in place to restore the grid - if the price was right. That was the eternal problem when dealing with crooks. They have no loyalty to anyone, including their customers. Elaine and Tommy knew this, and they were relying on it. They had been given the green light to throw in a hefty wire transfer of up to $100 million for verifiable information regarding the restoration of the grid.

Tommy dialed the number. It rang twice, and then a female voice simply said "What."

Elaine shook her head while listening through her earpiece. "This woman has no soul," she thought to herself.

Tommy spoke. "Hello, Amanda, or should I say Amy? Or Beth? Or Carla? I really don't know how you keep them all straight."

Curtis did not miss a beat. "It's not that hard actually, if you have living brain cells. I'm sure you have a cheat sheet in front of you. May I ask who this is, and more importantly, what you want? I am a busy woman."

"Do you have any interest at all in what happened to your brother?" Tommy asked.

"Well, I know he is alive, because Americans are too weak and have too many tidy laws to follow to have done him any significant harm. So, you're calling for a reason. Let's not beat around the bush. What is your offer?"

Elaine and Tommy looked at each other. Amanda Curtis was either insane, a total narcissist, an evil genius, or a combination of all three.

"We know you sold the Chinese the technology to attack our grid, and we assume you have the technology to restore it."

"Good Lord, are you serious? Of *course,* I do! I said, what is your offer?"

Tommy played along, and he began with what they both knew would be a low-ball offer. "I am authorized to offer you ten million dollars."

Curtis laughed hysterically into the phone, for five full seconds. Elaine thought to herself, "Insanity is clearly the dominant trait of the three."

She stopped laughing instantly. "You're going to need to add a zero to that," she said with an even-keel voice that was eerie.

"$100 million?" Tommy replied. "Never mind. I'll tell your brother you said hello."

"Wait, dear," she replied, now with a sophisticated, light-hearted laugh. "I was only joking. That is the price I charged those lunatics in China. One third up front, another third when the lights went out, and the rest once they remained out for 48 hours. So, your call comes at a perfect time. I am paid in full and ready to deal. Because I am an American and feel such a sense of patriotic duty, I will cut my American brothers and sisters the deal of a lifetime. Twenty percent off. $80 million. I will need half wired to me immediately, and the other half wired once your so-called experts receive my file and get the lights back on."

Tommy had been authorized for $100 million, and since he was more interested in sealing the deal than haggling, he agreed to the terms. Curtis proceeded to give him the routing and account numbers to her Swiss bank account, and she agreed to send the file once she saw the $40 million hit her account.

Tommy was prepared to end the call when she said, "Wait."

"What?" Tommy replied, in the same tone she had used to answer her phone. He did not like having to deal with people like Amanda Curtis.

"I will deliver the file to you, in person."

"Why?" Tommy asked, although he already knew the answer.

"Call me sentimental, but I do care about the little twerp. Bring my brother with you, and we will do the deal in person. And don't bring your little girlfriend with you. I would hate to have to kick her ass again."

Tommy saw Elaine's jaw set. She was biting her tongue…literally.

"Place and time," Tommy said.

CHAPTER 94

Cairo, Egypt

The United States had always been at the forefront of technology in all aspects, but nowhere was that more evident than in the CIA. Today was no different. The tiny wireless microphone and camera were state of the art. The microphone was barely visible in Tommy's ear, even when Elaine was specifically looking for it. Meanwhile, the camera was shaped like a button, and it perfectly matched the rest of the buttons on Tommy's shirt. When they had tested them in the hotel room, the sound was perfect, and the picture was crystal clear.

Tommy was already inside the industrial warehouse, where the meeting was going to take place. Josh Reed was with him. Elaine was always fully alert during a mission, but this time she was experiencing a new feeling - concern. She would be watching the live feed from one of the vans that had the warehouse surrounded at a safe enough distance to be undetected.

As the group inside the van followed the camera view through the warehouse, Tommy and Josh entered a large open area.

"Stop right there." The voice had come from somewhere out of view. There was a brief pause, and then Amanda Curtis came into view. Elaine felt a visceral reaction. She had to fight to control herself.

"Well hello, dear brother," Curtis said with dripping sarcasm. "And hello to you, as well," she said to Tommy. "I assume you came alone."

"I did, and I assume you did the same."

"I always work alone," Curtis replied. "And I trust absolutely no one. I'm sure you can see why," as she looked at Reed, who had not yet spoken although she had now referenced him twice. Tommy got the impression that he was scared to death of this woman.

"And you are unarmed, as I asked?"

"Yes," Tommy replied curtly.

"Josh, step away from him."

"Wait," Tommy said, grabbing Reed's arm. "Where is the information?"

Curtis smiled and walked over to a nearby table. She pulled out a laptop and inserted a flash drive. "I am prepared to show you what I have, although I don't imagine you are capable of understanding it. You can take the drive with you."

Tommy moved toward the table with Reed.

"Wait. I need to search you first. Josh, stand behind him. If he makes a move, kick him or bite him - whatever you are best at." Tommy could not imagine why Reed was part of the deal. She seemed to have nothing but disdain for him.

Amanda Curtis moved toward Tommy. She indicated for him to raise his hands. She began to frisk him, although it was immediately apparent that she wasn't really looking for a weapon. She lingered too long in places where she knew there wasn't a weapon, and she smiled at him the entire time. Her face was extremely close to the camera button on Tommy's chest, and Elaine wanted to punch the screen.

She squatted and legitimately checked Tommy's ankle areas to make sure he didn't have a gun in an ankle holster. As she stood, she slipped the knife from her boot without detection and rammed it into Tommy's stomach, right at the belly button. Tommy grabbed her wrists, but Curtis knew how to kill, and Tommy realized right away that he was in trouble. She stepped away and he tried to follow, but he fell to his knees, and then to his face. Reed stood a few feet away, with both of his hands covering his mouth.

"No!" Elaine shouted from inside the van. "No!" The agents had to restrain her, as she was attempting to get out of the van and run to the warehouse.

The microphone on Tommy's ear made some noise and everyone turned to the monitor. Curtis was rolling Tommy over onto his back. Her face came back into view. She motioned toward Reed. "Come over here. I want to show you something."

Reed walked hesitantly, a look of horror on his face as he looked down at Tommy. Curtis spoke to him. "Covert intelligence 101, my beloved brother. The spy *always* has a camera and microphone on him for the people outside." She bent over toward the button. "This is the most elementary operation I have ever seen in all of my years. You are pathetic. Now, come on in. You and I have some unfinished business. Leave your friends in the van. See if you can save your country $80 million. You've got five minutes. Oh, and by the way..."

Everyone in the van watched as Reed, who was still frozen in horror, failed to notice his sister walking behind him. She reached around him and slit his throat. Reed's eyes bulged as he grabbed his throat. Blood was already oozing through his fingers. As he fell to the ground, literally on top of Tommy, he covered the camera. Curtis rolled him over and wiped off the button so they could see her again. "You'll get no more secrets from baby brother," she said coldly. "Now, I won't count that time against you. Your five minutes starts now."

Elaine was feeling several different intense emotions that she knew she had to get under control. They all looked at her. "Stay here, no matter what!" she said. "I'll be back with the drive, and then we will need to get it back to D.C. as quickly as possible."

CHAPTER 95

Elaine entered the warehouse. She wasn't sure where to find Curtis, but she soon heard her voice in the distance, counting backward from five minutes. She was currently at 2:28. Elaine walked into an open area where she saw Curtis facing her, continuing to count even though Elaine was in clear sight. Elaine saw the two bodies behind Curtis, but she quickly realized that if she was going to walk out of this building alive, she had to forget about that for the moment. She could grieve later.

Curtis turned away and threw the knife across the open room behind her. Then she spoke, as Elaine tried to bring her thoughts back into focus. "I'll give you ten seconds to tuck your tail and run, so you don't have another experience like you did in Brussels."

Elaine stepped forward, her hands in fighting position. She didn't speak.

"Good. I will enjoy this," Curtis said with a devious smile.

The two women faced each other. Elaine struck first with a quick jab. Curtis attempted to counter, but Elaine ducked the punch and slipped behind her. She twisted Curtis' arm behind her back and slammed her face first into the wall.

"Looks a little different this time, doesn't it?" Elaine said into her ear.

Before Curtis had a chance to make a move, Elaine stepped back and drove a knee into her lower back. Curtis dropped to a knee, and Elaine followed with a kick to the back of her head, causing her face to hit the wall again. Curtis moaned as she slid to the floor.

Elaine grabbed her by the hair and was pulling her to her feet, but from her knees, Curtis landed a punch to Elaine's stomach, then a second one. Elaine doubled over. Curtis got to her feet, grabbed two hands full of Elaine's hair, and drove her knee into Elaine's face.

Elaine fell back to the floor holding her face. Curtis kicked her in the stomach. She grabbed Elaine's hair with her left hand and punched her in the face with the other. Elaine saw the room becoming fuzzy, like a movie image of someone dreaming. Curtis grabbed Elaine's hair and picked her up. Elaine was unsteady on her feet. Curtis laughed. "I loved how this movie ended last time, so let's have a sequel."

She swung her leg up high to finish Elaine with another roundhouse kick. Elaine, through the fog, realized this was coming. She managed to tilt her head back just enough for Curtis' boot to miss her face. While Curtis was still on one foot, Elaine threw a straight kick into her knee on the leg that was planted on the ground. The sound of ligaments snapping as Curtis' knee bent in an unnatural direction caused her to scream and collapse to the ground.

The screaming continued as Curtis held her knee while rolling back and forth on the floor. Elaine gathered herself and wiped the blood from her mouth. She looked down at her. "Generally, at this point I would just call a couple of friends in the business to detain you for 'questioning.' However, this time is different. Aside from the fact that I don't like you, you are a traitor to my country."

"Just stop talking and kill me," Curtis said through gritted teeth.

Elaine laughed. "No chance. You're not getting off that easy. Friends of mine have a lot of questions for you, and I plan to be there for every one of them. But, before that, I have one little gift for you. This one is for Tommy." Elaine planted a kick right under Curtis' chin, and she was out cold.

Elaine sat on the ground beside Curtis. She couldn't help but wonder what causes someone to be this evil. Aside from her being a threat to the civilized world, she had taken a good friend from Elaine. The hardest part was that now Elaine would never know whether Tommy could have become more than just a friend and colleague. Worse yet, Elaine realized that she would never even know who he was. She knew that Tommy was not his real name, just like Elaine wasn't hers. In their line of work, knowing too much about your colleagues could be hazardous.

Elaine felt emotion bubbling up inside of her, but she would not cry in front of this woman, even if she was unconscious. Elaine gathered herself, got to her feet, and looked down at the defeated woman. "That's what happens when you don't catch me by surprise," she said.

CHAPTER 96

The Oval Office
9:35 PM

"Any luck?"

Patrick Welch had barely taken a step into the Oval Office when Clark asked the question.

"Nope," Welch replied. "Worse yet, According to Tammy, the whole thing went south, but we do have her in custody."

Clark took off his glasses and pinched the bridge of his nose. He needed substantially more ibuprofen right now than would be recommended. "So, where are we with her?"

Welch shook his head. "This woman is a raving lunatic...absolutely crazy. The whole meeting was set up as a trade - her brother for the information. As she is frisking our guy, she shanks him. The brother...*our* mole...is mortified. As our team watched from the vans, she stood up and slit his throat ear-to-ear. Her *BROTHER*!"

"So how did we take her into custody?"

Welch chuckled and shook his head. "She challenged our female asset to a fight - and said she would destroy all of the evidence if anyone else came in with her."

"Why?" Clark's face clearly showed his confusion.

"Because she is a raving lunatic," Welch replied. "Evidently, she bit off more than she could chew and ended up getting knocked out cold. Unfortunately, the drive that she claimed had the information to reverse the outage was a fake. We have a full court press on her as we speak, but have you ever tried to negotiate with a raving lunatic?"

Clark sighed deeply. They were running out of time and options. "They have one hour to get her to talk. Meanwhile, call the joint chiefs together along with the Secretary of Defense. I want all of them present. If we don't have some sort of progress within an hour, we may have to contact the subs that have gone dark."

CHAPTER 97

10:25 PM

Amanda Curtis sat calmly on the edge of the cot in her cell. She smiled at the men who had come to question her.

"Hello, boys. Did you bring cards? How about some poker?" She looked specifically at one of the men. "Hey, Skippy, you look like the peon in this crew. Go grab the cards, and while you're at it, fetch some brandy and cigars."

None of the men reacted. They walked to the cell door and looked in at her. Finally, one of the men spoke. "Today is your lucky day."

Curtis laughed. "Nothing I do is luck. It is all planned in more detail than you could ever imagine. That includes three or four levels of contingency plans." She looked at the men individually before continuing. "Here's how I know this isn't luck. I know why you are here. You are here to offer me immunity in exchange for the technology to turn China's cyber war back on them and destroy their systems in much the same way they did yours. And yes, I know *exactly* how to do it."

The men stood there stone-faced. She was exactly right.

"Oh! I almost forgot," she said, feigning surprise. "I will get the immunity, of course, but I also forgot about the pay."

The same man spoke again. "We have already wired you $40 million for nothing. You lied about the information you had. You are greatly overestimating the amount of leverage you hold here."

"Then why are you here, darling?" Curtis got up and walked to the front of the cell. She placed her face within an inch of the bars and smiled. "If you think this is going to be a conjugal visit, you have another thing coming."

She turned and walked back to her cot. "I do have the ability to reverse this. I think you know that. Now take your mute goons out of here, and don't waste any more of my time until you are ready to deal."

It was evident at this point that she held all the cards. "We are ready to deal. You will be granted full immunity and paid the remaining $40 million that was owed to you from the original deal, but only *after* we are assured that we hold the ability to take over control of all of China and Russia's technology and weapons systems."

Amanda Curtis shook her head and waved her index finger back and forth. "No, no, no. $80 million was for restoration of the grid, which I will still handle for you. It will be another $50 million to turn the tables on the Chinese, and $50 million more to do the same to Russia. And please, stop wasting my time. I know your situation. Time is of the essence. Once I see that in writing, we will talk further. Until then, I am finished with you." She waved the back of her hand at them. "Off with you, now. Chop, chop."

They were a step ahead of her this time. The spokesman looked at the others. Now he was the one feigning shock. "What? She doesn't know?"

For the first time, there was a crack in her façade. Her facial expression changed, but only momentarily before the poker face came back. "Okay, I'll play along. What don't I know?"

"We're about to get the power back on." He smiled.

"You're bluffing, and you're doing a very poor job at it."

The man pulled out his phone and showed her a news clip of people celebrating in the streets. The headline read, "Some communication restored, but much left to do."

"We will pay you the remaining $40 million for the ability to cripple China and Russia immediately. Our people are confident they will be able to do this without you within 48 hours, but President Clark is willing to pay you and grant immunity to do it within the next three hours. You have five minutes to make the decision."

"You know, of course, that I am going to need to see that in writing. No deal until I see it and read it. And no bullshit, boys, I know what an immunity agreement is supposed to look like."

"We can get that done."

Amanda Curtis stood and snapped to attention at the foot of her cot. She placed her hand over her heart and recited the pledge of allegiance. When she finished, she said, "Let's do this. After all, I am an American above all else."

As the cell was opened and cuffs were placed on her, everyone in the group realized they were in the presence of a truly evil person who did not have any semblance of a moral compass. But she had what they needed, and they were going to have to deal with her.

CHAPTER 98

Situation Room
10:40 PM

Sam Clark was surrounded by the people he trusted as much as anyone if he had to make this call. The procedures to announce the nuclear attack across the country via the Emergency Alert System were discussed. The problem with that was that even though they now had the capability to send the EAS, most of the people in the country would not be able to receive the notification.

Also present were the Gold Codes – the authentication codes that would be used to launch the nuclear missiles that were aboard the Trident submarines. The President, with the help of those in the room, had chosen numerous targets in both China and Russia to strike. Because of the gravity of the situation, both the Zhongnanahi and the Kremlin were included on those lists. Every nuclear weapon that was available aboard the submarines would be fired until they either ran out of targets or ran out of missiles. The goal was to destroy both country's centers of government along with as many of their nuclear weapons as possible.

Clark pulled out "the biscuit," a plastic card that contained the codes. The card itself was about the size of a credit card, and Clark carried it with him at all times. The codes were also held at the NSA, the Pentagon, and United States Strategic Command. Although he had been through the drills, Clark could not believe he was physically pulling out the card. He broke and removed the plastic cover so the codes could be seen. The protocol was going to have to be slightly altered due to the lack of ability to communicate with some parties, including possibly the submarines themselves. Clark would verify the codes with the Secretary of Defense, and then read them to the Chairman of the Joint Chiefs. In this case, they were all present in the room. They were not currently able to reach Strategic Command, who would usually repeat the order to those launching the missiles. Once the codes were verified, they would attempt to contact the submarines directly and prepare them to launch.

"How many people's deaths am I getting ready to cause?" Sam Clark had been in war zones in two countries, had nearly been killed, and had lost a leg. He had killed men - many of them. War had hardened him, but he always felt grounded in his faith...until now. He could not justify this decision in his mind from a moral perspective, but he also could not justify inaction.

The tension in the room could not possibly have been any heavier. Sam Clark had made his decision as Commander-in-Chief of the United States of America, and he could not afford to waste any more time looking back or second guessing himself. He pulled his rosary out of his pocket and held it in his right hand. He held the launch codes in his left. "Father, forgive me," was all he could say as he prepared to read the codes.

"WAIT!" Clark, along with everyone else in the room, collectively jumped. Patrick Welch was gasping for air as he burst in. "Amanda Curtis is willing to deal."

"Are you sure?" Clark replied, admittedly with a sense of desperation.

"We had to give her the farm, but she can get this turned around, and is willing to do it. Of course, she wants to see the immunity agreement and review it before complying fully. Something tells me this isn't her first rodeo."

"Let's move forward with that," Clark replied. "She really can't hurt us any more than we are already hurt, and if she can do something that allows me to put this damn card back in my pocket, I won't care what we gave her."

CHAPTER 99

11:35 PM

Chinese president Xao Ming was seated in his office, reading the latest memos on the American situation. An aide burst into the room without knocking. Ming looked at the man sternly but said nothing. "Sir, the telepresence channel is notifying us that the Americans are attempting to make contact."

Ming had heard nothing about the Americans restoring power. This was not good. He looked at the aide. "Gather the team together and establish the link."

"Yes, sir."

Amanda Curtis was standing outside the White House Situation Room. Nobody who was present could believe it, but they understood the desperate circumstances. Curtis stood stoically. She had already signed the immunity documents and agreed to assist first before being wired the additional $40 million.

Clark and the others were inside, waiting for the link to be established with the Chinese. They would deal with the Russians later. Aside from that, Clark felt the Russians were no more than puppets in most of what had transpired.

The connection was established and there was Xao Ming. "Well hello, President Ming! Let me say, we are very happy to see and talk to you. I have some big news!"

Ming said nothing, and Clark waved a hand toward the door. He looked back at the screen. "Look who we found!"

Amanda Curtis walked into the room and smiled at the monitor. She had been informed not to speak a single word, and for once she was following orders. She had been on the screen less than five seconds before Clark had her ushered out. Her presence in this room made him nauseous.

He looked back at the monitor. "She's a tricky one, but it turns out we are willing to pay her more than you did. Well, that and our agreement to release her once she assists us in reversing everything that was done here and turning it directly back on you and your friends in Moscow."

Ming opened his mouth to speak, but Clark cut him off. "Hold on. You will get your turn. But first I want to tell you how this is going to work. You have deliberately killed thousands of Americans, and you led our country to the precipice. We were clinging by our fingertips, but now we have managed to pull ourselves back up to the cliff's edge. Now, Mr. President, as I see people whispering in your ear, I am sure you are getting notice that some of your systems have begun acting strangely. That would include your military systems, including your nuclear capability. Yes, we disabled that before anything else. The same goes for your Russian friends.

"We expect the immediate resignations of both you and President Volkov, along with your entire administrations. There will be extreme sanctions placed on your countries in order for you to avoid nuclear devastation; how extreme those sanctions will be has not yet been determined. You probably would not want me to make that decision at the present time. Many of our traditional allies reached out to us following the ultimatum at the UN. You misread the tea leaves on how many countries would side with you.

"Now, first things first. You will immediately call back the cargo planes that are on their way to my country. We have boots on the ground at both locations, and they will get word to your soldiers as to what has transpired. I assume they will not believe us, so you will be ready, willing, and able to confirm the facts. If they surrender peacefully and the hostage is released unharmed, the soldiers will be allowed to come back to China unharmed."

As the call ended, for the first time since December 21, Sam Clark finally felt like he had regained command of an airplane that had been spiraling out of control. The tension in the room was still prevalent, but he could tell that there was at least a minor sense of relief. Clark involuntarily got chills as he thought about it - they had been mere moments from all-out nuclear war.

That thought brought him back to the moment. "Ladies and gentlemen," he said with a hint of a smile, "let's move to DEFCON 2." Spontaneous applause broke out in the room and congratulatory handshakes were passed around, but only momentarily. This was just the beginning.

CHAPTER 100

NSA Headquarters

Helene Albertsen's pace was about as fast as possible for someone walking without it being called a jog. She finally decided to go ahead and run down the remaining length of the hall to Abdul Nassar's office. He was wide-eyed and working his keyboard like a man possessed as she entered the room.

"Please tell me what I just heard is true," Albertsen said as she tried to catch her breath. "Have you cracked the encryption code?"

Nassar did not even acknowledge her presence. He continued to type furiously, and she let him. His actions were answering her question. She took a moment to assess the situation. Nobody in the building had worked as tirelessly throughout this crisis as the man sitting in front of her. That thought caused her to feel yet another pang of guilt about questioning him.

Suddenly, Nassar stopped typing and momentarily stared at the monitor. He stood, still staring. Then he cautiously reached down and hit *enter* on the keyboard. Another pause - five seconds, ten. Albertsen nearly jumped out of her shoes as Abdul Nassar raised both fists over his head.

"Yes! Yes! Yes!" He began pumping his fist in the air in celebration. Albertsen was pretty sure that he still didn't realize she was in the room with him.

"Abdul, tell me, specifically. What?"

He turned toward her. "Call the White House," he said. The smile on his face was literally ear-to-ear.

"Are you sure?" Again, Albertsen knew the answer, but the very last thing she needed was to give President Clark false hope.

"Positive," he said. "Let's turn the lights back on!"

"Abdul…" Albertsen was at a loss for words.

He looked at her and smiled a comforting smile. "It's okay. I understand, I really do. But *man,* do you owe me one!"

Albertsen smiled and pointed at him as she turned and began running down the hall. "You bet I do!"

Patrick Welch rushed into the Oval Office. "Pick up line three," he said to Clark. "It's Tammy, and you're going to want to hear this."

The look on Welch's face had Clark excited, but he maintained his composure as he picked up the phone. "Hey, Tammy, what have you got?"

"Mr. President, Helene Albertsen just informed me that her team has cracked the last layer of encryption on this monster, and they are ready to coordinate restoration of power."

"Tammy, listen to me…are you sure?"

"Yes, sir," Leeds replied without hesitation.

"How much of it?" Clark was hoping for a good answer.

He got a great answer. "All of it," she replied. "They are going to try one particular line as a test run. If that is successful, we should begin to see power restored throughout the country."

Clark could not contain his excitement. "Thank you, Tammy, and pass along my sincere thanks to all of those who were working on this. I know they have been working as hard as anyone since this happened, and I am grateful to them."

"I will be glad to pass along the message, Mr. President."

As Clark hung up the phone, he stood and rubbed his hand over his face. "Let's get Donna in here, and we will coordinate a press briefing once power begins to get restored and people can actually turn on an electronic device to be able to see what we are saying."

"Yes, sir." Welch sensed a lack of joy under the circumstances. "Is something wrong, Mr. President?"

"Has Amanda Curtis already signed the immunity agreement?"

"Yes, sir," Welch replied.

"Damn it," Clark mumbled the words through gritted teeth. He thought back to his conversations with Attorney General Gabe McMillan about the immunity agreement. "Gabe is so 'by the book' - he even told me before we presented it to her that if circumstances changed after she signed, we could not renege. I tend to agree. That's not who we are, but the timing…we were so close."

Welch tried to provide some comfort. "We will still be able to watch every single move she makes for the rest of her life."

"True," Clark replied as he stared into the distance. He quickly refocused. "Nonetheless, this is the best news I have heard in quite some time, but it is only the beginning. Once we have the power restored, then we also need to restore order, repair our cities…" Clark paused.

Welch knew where he was going with that line of thought and finished his sentence. "And then we have to start collecting bodies while trying to contact next of kin for what could be tens of thousands of our citizens."

Clark turned and looked at his chief of staff.

"Exactly."

CHAPTER 101

Colonel Robert Thompson picked up the sat phone and called the White House via a direct line to which he had been given access (he could not wait to explain this to his family). He was patched through to the Oval Office, where Patrick Welch spoke. "Go ahead Colonel, President Clark is here."

Thompson quickly collected his thoughts. "Mr. President, I have good news. First, we have secured your father. He is safe and unharmed."

"Thank God!" Thompson was not sure whether to proceed or if the president had more to say.

"Please continue, Colonel," Welch said.

"The meeting and the call to President Ming could not have gone better. The translator we had on the three-way call made the president sound…conciliatory to say the least. The word from our unit in Cincinnati is similar. They have secured the gold and are awaiting instructions on how to proceed."

Clark spoke. "First of all, Colonel, thank you for a job well done. There is no way to understand or appreciate yet the role you just played in the history of our republic. Second, I also want to thank you from a personal perspective. They had my father. As if that was not bad enough, all I could think about were the decisions I may have had to make regarding him. So, thank you for saving me from a potential lifetime of second guessing and guilt."

"Thank you, Mr. President. I cannot express how much I appreciate those sentiments, but there is one more piece of business I need to discuss with you."

"Of course," Clark replied. "I should have asked you that first. What else?"

"There is one Chinese soldier here in Lexington that speaks some English. None of those in Cincinnati do. The one here is claiming asylum, and he says he is speaking for all of them. He says none of them want to go back."

Clark and Welch looked at each other, then Welch spoke. "We will get to work on that, Colonel, and we will get the proper people to the two locations ASAP with translators to take statements from them individually."

"Yes, sir," Thompson replied.

Clark spoke again. "And tell the unit in Cincinnati to bring the trucks back to Fort Knox. There still isn't much information available yet to the general public, so nobody will know that all the gold from Fort Knox is driving down the interstate. Once they get back, we will find a way to secure it temporarily until we can work out a longer-term solution. And thanks again, Colonel."

"My pleasure, Mr. President."

As Welch disconnected the call, Clark began to chuckle. "What?" Welch smiled as he wondered what this could be about.

"Once we get some semblance of normalcy back in place, I want to call a meeting to rehash our conversations with the folks that were singing China's praises. It appears those soldiers don't understand the benefits of their meritocracy. Maybe we can have our folks explain to them how grand their system is."

For the first time in more than a week, the two men laughed heartily.

CHAPTER 102

Manteigas, Portugal

Amanda Curtis loved the mountains. She was a loner by nature, and she was also an avid hiker. She enjoyed the peace and solitude that could be found in mountain ranges like the Serra da Estrela, which she was currently looking at from the back deck of a mountain chalet. She had a cup of coffee in her hands, and she was contemplating what was next for her. The life she led was extremely dangerous, but she was not sure that she could ever walk away from the adrenaline rush associated with her line of work. It would also be difficult to walk away from the money, of course.

The money…she smiled and shook her head as she thought about the amount of money she had made in the last year. It was almost beyond her comprehension. She knew it would be continuously harder to remain incognito. Few people knew her name, but she had heard through the grapevine that "the woman hacker" that was dominating so many conversations in her world was becoming internationally known. Jobs would be harder to come by, but more lucrative. That was the way she liked it.

The echo of the cracking sound from the sniper rifle had not even reached Curtis' ears before the bullet pierced her skull. She was dead before the hot coffee spilled across her lap.

CIA Director Sheldon Cavanaugh was reading the latest updates from security agencies across the globe. Everyone in his line of work was doubling down on the amount of time, effort, and money they were investing to protect their countries from what had happened to the United States. Cavanaugh shook his head as he finished the report. "Good luck," he said to the empty room.

His phone rang and he picked up the receiver. He did not recognize the number. "This is Sheldon Cavanaugh."

"It is done." That was all that was said before the line went dead. Cavanaugh hung up the phone, picked it up again, and called Patrick Welch to relay the news.

Seven minutes later, Patrick Welch shared the same message with the President of the United States.

CHAPTER 103

Patrick Welch poked his head in through the door of the Oval Office. "He's here, Mr. President."

"Great," Clark replied as he rose from behind his desk. "Send him in."

Welch brought the guest in and introduced the two before excusing himself.

"It's a pleasure to meet you, Mr. President," the man said.

"The pleasure is mine," Clark replied.

The two men sat opposite of each other and talked in detail for about ten minutes. Finally, the visitor asked, "Shall we proceed?"

"Yes, please." Clark's reply was quick.

The priest pulled a purple stole from his pocket, kissed it, and placed it over his shoulders. Sam Clark knelt on the floor of the Oval Office and bowed his head as he spoke. "Bless me, Father, for I have sinned..."

CHAPTER 104

December 27
12:20 PM
Office of the Vice President

Charles Sullivan was meeting with Larry Case, deputy to Tammy Leeds, and Rob Sanderson, deputy to Sheldon Cavanaugh. As nearly everyone else in the government was focused on the transition to rescuing as many Americans as possible, President Clark's team had reached the conclusion that recovering from the effects of this catastrophe was only as good as their ability to keep the situation from happening again in the future.

Sullivan realized that government work was full of nuance and gray areas. As a black and white thinker, he had little patience for this. He felt there was a considerable difference between learning the details about a topic and listening to hours of fluff around the edges. However, in this case, he realized that he was going to have to tolerate some of that fluff in order to get his arms around the material and the background.

Sullivan looked at the two men and said, "As I mentioned when I called this meeting, I want to learn how we got to this point. Give me the background, but please give me the short version. I'll ask questions if I need you to fill in some gaps."

Case began. "Most people think cyber warfare is something that has developed in the last three or four years. That notion could not be further from the truth. I brought a handful of documents with me to illustrate that point. Here's an NSA report from 1997 listing the advantages of cyber warfare versus traditional warfare - 'low cost of entry to conduct campaigns; flexible base of deployment - don't have to be in range of target; diverse and ever-expanding set of targets.'

"And here's the cover of Time magazine from August of 1995. 'Cyber War…The US rushes to turn computers into tomorrow's weapons of destruction. But how vulnerable is the home front?' But here's my favorite. It's a RAND article that says, 'we anticipate that cyber war may be to the 21st century what *blitzkrieg* was to the 20th century.'"

"Yeah, we've heard that quote more than once this week," Sullivan replied.

Case continued. "At this point, I don't think anyone is doubting the reality of that statement. But here's the amazing part - this RAND article is from 1993! That's how long we have been fighting this battle, a fact unknown to an overwhelming majority of our citizens. The Air Force has cyber divisions, and I have always loved the motto of the 1st Cyber Division, 609th Information Warfare Squadron. In three words it summarizes the seriousness of the work we are undertaking every day: 'Anticipate or perish.'"

Sullivan leaned back in his chair. Case knew that he had just dropped a significant amount of information in the lap of the Vice President, a man that Case knew did not understand this world very well. He sat quietly and let Sullivan mull this over.

After a few moments, Sullivan leaned forward again, ready for more. Case restrained a smile as he considered the concept that the speed at which Sullivan would be able to process this technical information would be akin to dial-up internet access.

"Am I safe to assume that there is only so much protection the government can provide? I mean, aren't people going to have to shoulder some of this burden themselves? It strikes me that we have an unbelievably large amount of education that we need to provide to the general public."

"You are absolutely correct, Mr. Vice President," Case replied. "The government team's primary job is to keep the government systems safe and secure. The citizens are going to have to either fend for themselves or rely on services provided by the private sector to protect their personal information. It is unreasonable to assume that we can protect the government's security 100 percent of the time. It is simply impossible to imagine we can do that while also protecting 330 million people."

Sullivan considered this for a moment, then he replied. "How do we go about such a task? Is it even possible?"

Case considered whether to give his opinion that it would be impossible to protect people from cyber attacks because of the ever-increasing dependent nature of the citizenry. He decided to stick to the facts. "It is an odd thing in our society, and it is quite generational. Generally speaking, the people we would label as Baby Boomers have a deep distrust for things that they can't see on paper right in front of them. Most don't like online transactions, they don't use e-commerce, many don't participate in social media. Hell, a lot of them have never owned a computer, much less a smart phone. They are highly skeptical of all technology and the real and perceived pitfalls that come along with it.

"The group referred to as Generation X, those who grew up in the 70s and 80s, are very much in the middle. A strong majority of them use online capabilities extensively. Online banking and shopping got off the ground through this group. The

Gen X crowd and cyberspace have basically grown up together. This group, however, has also grown up with the side effects of new technology - many of them have had bank accounts hacked, or had their identities stolen. However, they are very reluctant to go back to paper. They prefer to try to fix the problem. It is their peers in the tech world that came up with the earliest forms of cyber security - the Life Locks of the world.

"And then, there are the youngsters. Those thirty and under are the most vulnerable, and they care the least. The digital landscape is their world - not only have they never used a rotary phone, most of them have never used a landline. They have the world at their fingertips, with immediate access to any kind of information they want. But they don't see any risk in it. Perhaps it is their immaturity; perhaps it is because most of them do not yet have assets that can be stolen from them. Regardless of the reason, they do very little to protect themselves from the dangers of cyberspace.

"This group, this youngest crowd, is our long-term problem moving forward. As the threat is increasing, our collective consciousness about the problem is decreasing. Unless they become less reckless with their trust of every site they visit and every link they click, we will continue to have substantial problems. As the population gets older, there will be fewer and fewer of the people who take the most precautions, while there will be more and more who will find themselves susceptible to hackers and other cyber threats. And, of course, rather than put forth the effort to protect themselves, many will rely on the government to fix it. Government has fostered this 'We will take care of you' mentality for decades, and those promises are now coming back to bite us. They don't hope we will do something to help them, they fully expect us to fix their problem." Case hoped that letting his opinion slip in at the end would not cause trouble for him.

At this point, Sanderson joined the conversation. "I agree wholeheartedly with Larry's points," he said. "However, let me add that aside from the lack of awareness from most of the public about the threats that are out there, I think there is a little bit more to it. The development of the internet came to fruition to the general public in the early 1990s with the concept of the worldwide web. It was less than two decades between that and the first iPhone. The technology developed so quickly that a huge bureaucracy like the federal government could not possibly keep up with its pace, particularly when it came to security.

"Second, think about it this way for the sake of comparison. During the arms race, we knew who the players were. We knew the groups who were regional threats, and we knew those who were global threats. Everyone was spying on everyone to try to gain access to information, but you had to have assets on the ground to get that intelligence. Now, some 18-year-old can hack into the Pentagon's system and learn the same things overnight that a spy network would have spent years trying to accomplish. Aside from that, we don't even know who to concern ourselves with. Cyber warfare is so different because it is now a global playing field. Any government with the capability of paying the bounty can get a sophisticated hacker to level the playing field for them.

He continued. "Another factor is that historically, the cost of war in both lives and dollars has encouraged countries to use as much diplomacy as possible. However, cyber warfare can eliminate both of those concerns, not to mention the origin of the attack has every ability to remain unknown. These factors cause many countries, especially rogue countries, to be much more likely to launch a digital attack than to use traditional means of diplomacy and warfare."

Sanderson could see that the vice president was beginning to look impatient. "Let me finish with this," he said. "We are as good as anyone with our ability to get into the systems of other governments and foreign entities. The problem, again, is that it's not a level playing field. If North Korea finds a way into our system, and they have the resources to do so, they can hurt us a lot more than we can hurt them in a cyber war. Their people have practically zero access to information, and even less access to creature comforts. Have you ever seen satellite photos of Earth at night? The Western world, and the United States in particular, is lit up like a rock concert. North Korea is dark. As of 2014, there were barely one *thousand* IP addresses in the entire country. There are city blocks in Manhattan that have twice that amount."

Sullivan's head was swimming. He counted himself among those who placed *zero* trust in the internet and everything it stood for, especially now. But as the vice president, he realized he had to set his personal feelings aside and try to find a solution to this current problem that seemed destined to be the problem of the future.

"Okay. Thank you for the background information. In your opinions, what do we need to do to begin setting up a system of protecting ourselves against this shit moving forward?"

Case took this one. "That's a tough question, sir. Our problem is not offense; it's defense. In the end, it's a First Amendment question, and it's a Fourth Amendment question. Because we are a free society, we must walk a very fine line between providing security and protecting people's privacy. We have been through similar conversations about listening to people's phone calls. People want us to protect them from terrorists, but they don't want us to use the tools that will help us do it. It's the same thing with cyber warfare. I call it the Apple problem."

Sullivan rolled his eyes as he recalled the showdown between the government and Apple over access to the iPhone belonging to the terrorists in the San Bernadino shootings.

Case continued. "Another example was when the North Koreans hacked into Sony Pictures. We immediately saw that as an extreme escalation in cyber warfare. By taking Sony offline, the North Koreans humiliated them in retaliation for the goofy film Sony made about Kim Jung Un. North Korea was offline for *months,* but the only story that made news was the hot gossip about who sent inappropriate texts and emails to whom, and which actors were making the most money. The people at Sony were more worried about their private information being exposed than they were about the fact that cyber warfare had just accelerated exponentially, and permanently."

"I would assume that a global company like Sony would have a strong security system. Am I wrong about that?" Sullivan asked.

"Not at all," Case said. "*The Wall Street Journal* and *The New York Times* both did investigative pieces about the hack. They learned that Sony's system was protected by *forty-two* firewalls."

"Then how in the hell…" Sullivan didn't finish the sentence because he realized from Case's nodding of his head that he knew the answer.

"Human error," Case replied. "Sophisticated digital techniques were used to compromise a systems administrator's password. This person had top level access to Sony's systems. His credentials were stolen as well. Here is the question. Are we prepared as a society to surrender some of our personal privacy in order to be better protected against enemies, both foreign and domestic, that wish to do us harm? Until we answer that question, Mr. Vice President, there cannot be a solution. The answer to a problem cannot be given before the question is asked. In the end, it is a debate about personal privacy versus the common good. That's where we are."

"So, is every government in the world sitting around on their thumbs, just accepting the fact that we are all going to continue to hack into each other's systems? This sounds suspiciously like the MAD doctrine of the 21st century. Is anyone out there taking proactive measures, or are they all defensive?"

Sanderson smirked.

"Is something funny?" Sullivan asked.

"Well, sir," Sanderson paused briefly. "I don't know of any new offensive measures that are in place, but I am aware of a unique defensive idea. You might not believe this, but after Edward Snowden released the information about the NSA's operations in different parts of the world, a handful of countries are seriously considering a return to typewriters and the use of paper files."

"Well, I'll be damned," Sullivan replied as he leaned forward in his chair. "Now we're speaking my language."

CHAPTER 105

It had been a long and painful beginning to a recovery from what the media had dubbed "The Christmas Catastrophe." The death toll was estimated to be somewhere between 18,000 and 20,000 Americans. Once the plan had been discovered, the allies of the United States had stood together to follow through on the retaliation that the Americans had started with the reversal of the cyber attack. They also helped to relieve the international tensions that had been caused by the event. Markets had taken a beating all over the world, and a global recession was imminent. Intermediate range economic forecasts showed signs of a few potential hints of silver linings, but people in all corners of the globe would suffer from the attempted takeover.

Most of the members of the leadership of the Chinese and Russian governments were facing hearings in front of a war crimes tribunal. Nikolai Volkov was not one of them. The Russian president had finished his bottle of Russo-Baltique vodka and one more of Castro's fine Cuban cigars before putting a revolver in his mouth and pulling the trigger. Chinese president Xao Ming had yet to speak a single word since being taken into custody. He ate minimally and spoke to no one.

The seemingly endless sadness and tragedy of the situation was bringing everyone in the administration down. It was determined that for one night, now that the weeks of rescue and recovery efforts had been completed, there should be a celebration, albeit a muted one. The next phase of the recovery would transition from human concerns to those of infrastructure. That would be a long and trying process, so tonight was a time to slow down and breathe.

Invitations had been sent to individuals across the country who had acted bravely, even heroically in many cases. Johnny Sims was present with his family, as was Colonel Robert Thompson and his entire unit. John Clark was present. The room was full, and the night's festivities were serving as a pep rally as much as anything else. There was still a lot of work to do and anguish to bear, but for one night they would celebrate the fact that there was still a United States of America.

Clark's favorite moment so far of the post-DEFCON 1 period was a meeting he had in the Oval Office with Tammy Leeds, Helene Albertsen, and Abdul Nassar. Patrick Welch had also been present. The Syrian-born American citizen had to wipe away tears as he came into the Oval Office. "My parents...would be..." It was all he could get out. "Extremely proud, I'm sure," Clark said to take the focus off Nassar, who nodded as he gathered himself.

Clark listened as the two ladies, Nassar's superiors, sang his praises and condemned themselves for their treatment of him. When given a chance to speak, Nassar said that if the tables had been turned, he would not have done one single thing differently than they had done.

It was at that point that Clark nodded to Welch, who left momentarily and returned with a box. Clark opened the box and showed the guests a beautiful medal. Clark spoke as he removed the medal from the box. "This is the Presidential Citizens Medal. Other than the Presidential Medal of Freedom, this is the highest medal awarded to a civilian."

He approached Nassar and asked him to turn around. Nassar, who clearly thought the medal was being given to someone else, stood in shock momentarily before turning his back to the president. Photographers entered the room on cue and snapped dozens of pictures as President Clark said, while securing the medal around Nassar's neck, "Abdul Nassar, I do hereby award you the Presidential Citizens Medal for exemplary deeds or services performed on behalf of your country and your fellow citizens."

More pictures were taken, and handshakes were passed around the room. Nassar was walked out by Welch, and Clark asked Leeds and Albertsen to stay. He looked back and forth at them before saying, "I have no idea what you do or how you do it, but I know we owe you a debt of gratitude that can never be properly repaid."

"It was a team effort, Mr. President," Leeds replied. "And let me say, sir, you sure do know how to choose a team."

They all laughed, and as Clark shook their hands, Helene Albertsen spoke. "Mr. President, do you remember the last time I was in this room?"

"Vaguely," Clark replied, laughing. "Things were moving pretty quickly around here."

"I am sure." Albertsen wanted to say something, but she could not pull the trigger. Leeds gave her a reassuring nod. Helene looked at Sam Clark. "I just want to make sure you realize that I made your deadline."

Clark laughed out loud, with his head back. "Yes, yes you did. And don't worry, Tammy went out of her way before, during, and after to tell me what a ridiculous deadline it was."

Leeds nodded and looked at Albertsen. "I did." Her gaze turned to Clark. "And it *was*."

Clark reveled in the laughter that filled the Oval Office. It felt good to enjoy such simple pleasures again.

CHAPTER 106

Paul Flaherty was walking around the grounds of St. John cemetery, picking up the artificial arrangements and other debris that had been blown all over the cemetery during the blizzard. The sun was finally out, and a welcome sight it was, even though the high temperature for the day was still expected to fall short of 25 degrees.

Flashing lights caught Flaherty's eye, and he turned to see two black SUVs, unmarked, parking on either side of the cemetery entrance. A car pulled between them and made its way up the hill toward Paul. It stopped as it pulled next to him, and two men in suits and sunglasses exited the car. They opened the back door, and Sam Clark stepped out.

Flaherty laughed as he looked at his childhood friend. "You sure know how to make an entrance, Mr. President."

Clark shook Flaherty's hand and smiled. "Knock it off, Paul."

Flaherty laughed again. "I wasn't going to call you 'Sam' without permission, with these guys staring a hole through me."

"Fair enough," Clark replied as he patted Paul's arm.

Flaherty looked at his friend. "I thought I might see you here the first chance you got."

Clark nodded. "I wasn't there when he died, and I couldn't make it to the funeral, so I need to pay my respects."

Flaherty pointed to the stone that Clark had purchased for Fr. Jerry. "He's right over there."

"Thanks, Paul. It's good to see you. Tell Ellie hello."

"Will do," Flaherty replied, as he continued cleaning up the grounds.

Clark walked through the snow to the plot where Fr. Jerry had been laid to rest. Clark learned that Fr. Jerry had not made funeral arrangements for himself, nor had he purchased a plot or designated where he wanted to be buried. Clark approached the priest's family, as well as the archbishop, and with their permission, he had arranged for Fr. Jerry to be buried in the Clark family section of the cemetery.

The president unfolded his hunting chair and sat down next to the tombstone. Then he pulled his rosary from his pocket. Since it was Monday, he prayed the Joyful Mysteries, which he felt were appropriate to the situation. Once he was finished, he looked at the tombstone and smiled. "I know you would *hate* that this stone is so nice, but I don't apologize." He continued. "I used to enjoy our conversations about who was more stubborn. I knew I was right, but it turns out that you were even more hard-headed than I realized."

Clark laughed to himself as he stared at the stone. Then the smile dissipated. "I've been to a lot of places and done a lot of things, including being involved in many decisions that few human beings have ever had to make. I have never prayed harder or more frequently than I have in the last year, and most especially in the last thirty days. Without that prayer life, without that moral foundation, I would not have known where to turn."

Clark paused, then continued. "History will record this, because the memoirs I will write someday will include it, but I just want you to know that you have played a vital role in my life since the time I was a teenager. I know I have told you this before, but it is something that cannot be said frequently enough. I could not have possibly done this without you."

Clark stood. He took a deep breath as he looked down at the tombstone. Sam Clark was a deeply religious man, a man of rock-solid faith. He was not, however, one who could quote dozens upon dozens of Bible verses. But he did know a few that were near and dear to him. His favorite was Psalm 46:10 - "Be still, and know that I am God." At that moment, a different one was coming to mind. It was one that was perfect for Fr. Jerry. It was Matthew 25:23. "Well done, my good and faithful servant…come, share your Master's joy."

Sam Clark packed up his chair and walked back to the car. With one last wave to Paul Flaherty, he got in the car and refocused. It was time to be the president again.

CHAPTER 107

Hamburg, Germany
Tschebull Restaurant

Elaine sat in a corner booth of Tschebull. This was one of her favorite restaurants in the world, but she could not eat. She could do no more than drink a cup of coffee and wonder about what might have been. She had come back to Hamburg on purpose. It was less than three months ago that she and Tommy had sat outside together on a beautiful fall day. She could see the exact spot from the window she was looking through. It was less than three weeks ago that she and Tommy had made love in the hotel room, and in the shower, and in the hotel room again. That was during their whirlwind love affair that had lasted less than 17 hours before his death at the hands of *her*. Elaine would never mention her name, and she would never again allow the name to be mentioned in her presence.

The night of passion with Tommy went against every professional instinct Elaine had developed over sixteen years in this line of work, as well as everything she had been taught. Now, she could not help but think about whether the breaching of this unwritten rule had caused Tommy to lose his focus, and then to lose his life. There was a side of her that forced the thought from her mind, but it still lingered back there in the dark recesses. She could not escape it. Would anything have come from the sparks that flew during their brief time together? She would never know, but since she broke the most important rule, she now wished she had played Tommy's game of 'One question.' At least that way she would have learned *something* about him.

Elaine was lost in her thoughts, and she jumped when her phone buzzed on the table. She looked at the screen and saw that she had a text message. The sender was "unknown." She smiled at the irony. "The story of my life," she said to no one in particular.

Over more than a decade and a half in a job that burned most people out within five years, Elaine had earned an unmatched level of respect from those who knew her at all levels of the CIA. She also had professional relationships with many people in the agency who would do things for her that would not be done for anyone else under any circumstances. This was one of those times. She opened the message, where she saw the words, "It is done." Elaine put the phone down and took another sip of coffee, as she looked back to the spot where she and Tommy had talked and laughed so naturally and easily. It seemed like yesterday.

EPILOGUE

One Year Later
State Dining Room
White House

Sam Clark was walking down the hall with Charles Sullivan. They were on their way to the big celebration marking the one-year anniversary of the power being restored. It had been planned with a great amount of detail as a celebration of the American spirit, which was going to be described using examples of individual and team heroism during the crisis of a year earlier.

Clark looked at Sullivan. "I am really looking forward to this." Sullivan nodded, and Clark continued. "Can you believe it has been less than two years since we took our oaths of office? I'm sure this is exactly what you thought the vice presidency would look like."

Both men laughed. Sullivan put his arm around Clark's shoulder and leaned in. "Thank God we won. We would already be speaking Chinese if those other morons had been elected."

More laughing. Sam realized how good it felt. Although great amounts of progress had been made in the past year, there still was not a great deal of time for sincere, light-hearted laughter. He stopped and turned toward Sullivan. "All kidding aside, Charlie. I couldn't have done this without you."

Sullivan's smile disappeared. He looked at Sam and nodded. "You're damn right you couldn't have." He laughed again, slapped Sam on the arm, and headed into the dining room.

Much had changed since the power had been restored. Things got worse before they got better. Nearly 20,000 Americans had lost their lives in the coordinated attack on the United States. The united front that formed across the country in the aftermath had been amazing. People across the country helped each other. It did not matter if people lived in rural America or populated cities, whether they were Republican or Democrat, whether they were rich or poor. People supported each other, helped each other, and raised money for those in dire need. The events had given renewed meaning to the name 'the *United* States of America.'

Once the immediate concerns had been addressed and the first stages of normalcy began to creep back into American life, however, old divisions and new debates began to chip away at the unity. The media began searching for scapegoats and passed judgment in wide swaths. Old social media arguments picked up where they had left off. Some Americans credited Sam Clark with saving the country, placing him on a pedestal with George Washington and Abraham Lincoln, while others considered him an imminent threat to the country because of his decision to move to DEFCON 1 without Congressional approval. Many on that side were still demanding his resignation.

Clark had taken it all in stride. He was glad to see Americans able to communicate and state their opinions again. He kept trying to remind the people around him, who wanted to defend him more vigorously, that these very differences were the foundation of the country they had been fighting for throughout the crisis.

Sam Clark waited outside the door. He loved the pomp and circumstance surrounding the office of the President, but he did not care for it at all when it was directed specifically at him. This was one of those moments. He waited for his cue, and then he heard it. "Ladies and gentlemen, the President of the United States."

Clark entered the room and waved to those in attendance. As soon as the applause died down, the first person he saw was a smiling Tammy Leeds. "You look like a kid who is up to something no good," Clark said warily.

"That would be an accurate representation, Mr. President, except for the kid part."

Clark saw his National Security Advisor look past him over his shoulder and he turned to see what she was looking at. He saw her right away, even though she was in a crowd of people on the other side of the room. He knew exactly who she was, and he could not have been more surprised, as Clark Griswold told Cousin Eddie in *Christmas Vacation*, if he woke up with his head sewn to the carpet.

He turned back to Leeds. He was bewildered to the point that he could use only single-word utterances. "How? When?"

Leeds laughed heartily - not too heartily, she hoped. She composed herself and explained. "I plan to touch on all six of your single-word questions," she began. "But first I need to ask, although I think I know the answer. You know 'who,' right?"

"Absolutely," he replied, and only then did he realize that he was still staring at her. He turned back to Leeds. "Well, I kind of know 'who.' She was my nurse after I got wounded. She was always jovial, and I was rude to her sometimes. But she never let me get to her. That woman doesn't know it, but she helped me through some very, very dark times. I tried to find her at one point, but she was no longer working there. I don't even know her name."

He turned back to look at her again. She was talking to Patrick Welch, and Clark was seeing her profile. She had not yet turned in his direction, but Clark felt a lump in his throat as she gave Welch the smile that he remembered so well. It was the only positive thing that he recalled from the first few days in the hospital, when nothing seemed positive. Even when he was at his worst, her smile that lit up the room shed a tiny bit of light into his dark recesses.

Leeds realized that she needed to reel him back in for the details. "Well then, let's start with 'who.' Her name is Monica Satterly. She was a first year RN working in her hometown when 9/11 happened. She was young and single, no kids, and she volunteered to serve overseas treating wounded American troops. So that also covers 'what'. As far as 'when,' we became aware that you had searched for her a few years ago. Patrick decided to try to track her down for you, but then we were distracted by the near global disaster."

Clark turned back to Leeds. "How did you know I had looked for her?"

She smiled. "Hello? I'm the head of the NSA, Mr. President! Plus, you might not believe this, but before anyone gets to sit in that comfy chair behind the desk in the Oval Office, we know a thing or two about that person."

Clark laughed, realizing what a stupid question that had been. "Touché," he said.

"Back to my list," she said with a smile. "The 'when' part was just last week. Once things got back to their 'most normal version of normal' (this phrase was a running joke in the administration), we found her pretty quickly, which leads us to 'where.' Believe it or not, Mr. President, she's one of you. She's from Kentucky. She still lives there."

For some reason, this made Clarks' pulse quicken. "Where in Kentucky?" He realized he was replying much too quickly and enthusiastically - very undignified - but he did not care at this point.

"Springfield," she replied.

Clark could not contain himself. "Springfield? That's less than 30 minutes from where I grew up! How do I not know her?"

"We were wondering that ourselves, sir," Leeds replied. "You grew up close together geographically, but you were in different school districts. I guess you never crossed county lines to visit other people. Plus, she's a few years younger than you, so it's not all that surprising that your paths didn't cross."

Clark thought about that, and realized it was logical. He was nodding his head. Then a thought hit him. He looked at Leeds. He had respected her work from day one. She was smart, bold, and a true professional. Growing to like someone is dangerous in government work, but Clark could not help himself. He had to admit that he truly liked Tammy Leeds. He needed to know the answer to the next question. He looked her in the eye. "Why?"

She looked directly back at him without blinking an eye. "Because your staff really wanted to do this for you, Mr. President. Without pouring too much syrup on this conversation, you have given more to this country than most people could ever imagine." Clark knew she was talking about his leg and the emotional journey he had taken to get to where he stood today, but she did not imply anything specific. She continued. "They felt like you were due something…a favor of some kind. They knew you wouldn't want anything that involved fanfare and adulation, but they knew you were looking for this woman, and they wanted to make this happen for you. When they approached me with the idea, we got to work on it."

"I don't know what to say," Clark began.

"Don't thank me too much. I'm used to tracking criminals and terrorists. It only took me about 15 seconds to locate her."

They both laughed and Clark gave her a hug. Leeds pulled away, smiled, and said, "You still haven't heard how."

"Uh-oh," he replied. "You have that look on your face again."

"Yes, I do," she said proudly. "We sent for her because she is receiving special recognition for her work in nursing. So, the 'how' part was easy. When the White House calls wanting to honor your work, you go. No questions asked. But here's the kicker. She knows she is going to meet you, but she doesn't know that you were ever looking for her."

Clark nodded his head. That made sense. How would she know?

"Oh, and one more thing," Leeds added. "She doesn't even know there is a story between you two. She doesn't remember you in the hospital. I'm sorry, Mr. President, but you didn't leave much of an impression on her."

Her work done, Leeds walked away smiling, leaving Clark to ponder that thought. At that moment, Patrick Welch looked over and made eye contact with Clark, and led Monica Satterly across the floor to him. It was clear at this point that the timing between his National Security Advisor and his Chief of Staff was not coincidental. They seemed to be having quite a bit of fun with this. Welch looked at Clark knowingly. "Mr. President, this is Monica Satterly. She is one of our honorees tonight."

Clark did not become President of the United States by wilting under pressure. He collected himself and extended his hand in full presidential mode. "It is indeed a pleasure to meet you, Mrs. Satterly. I have read our report on your work. It is truly inspiring."

Clark could not figure out what impressed him more, her elegance or her grace. She extended a gloved hand and replied, "Thank you, Mr. President. I feel entirely inadequate knowing that there are probably more deserving people out there, but it's not as if I was going to turn it down."

Welch laughed at the comment, and Satterly smiled. Clark smiled as well, a genuine smile. Her eyes had his full attention. He was enamored with this woman on several levels, but he had to find a way not to show it at this very moment. As every chief of staff does, Patrick Welch knew when to step in and bail him out. "Come, Ms. Satterly. Let me escort you to your seat. I believe we are about to begin."

Was it Clark's imagination, or had Welch enunciated a little too hard on Ms.? Was he indicating she was single? Clark had referred to her as Mrs. Satterly and she had not corrected him, but she also did not have a husband in attendance with her. Welch came back to the table and said, "That's right. I said 'Ms.' No husband." He then proceeded to walk away and sit down in his seat.

Throughout the evening, Clark felt like a kid in high school trying to figure out how to approach the prom queen. Should he tell her the story from the first time he saw her, or just carry on conversation as if they had never met before? He watched her accept her award, impressed again with her poise. She was captivating. He decided to speak to her casually and see what happened. If it led to something, he would prefer it to be natural, not having to do with any pity she might feel for him or embarrassment at not remembering him.

Once the awards ceremony was completed, Clark headed to the mural room where he was to meet and congratulate each recipient individually. He felt sure it was no coincidence that Monica Satterly was last. He had finally regained his wits and was going to try to remember how to have a casual, non-professional conversation with a member of the opposite sex. He realized it had been decades since he had done it. He had a plan if their conversation went well.

When she entered the room, Welch excused himself as planned and left the room with the photographer. Now it was just the two of them. Clark was ready. "We have basically had the discussion that I would typically have with you during this meeting and photo-op, so if you don't mind, I would just like to talk to you a little bit more about your work."

Satterly looked surprised. "Sure," she said.

The two talked for a while longer, and Clark sensed that she was comfortable talking to him as a man, not as the President of the United States. He was glad. The music that had been playing in the background changed to a song Clark had planned. It was *When I Fall in Love* by Nat King Cole - a song that he loved, and one that he knew she loved also. She had mentioned it to him one time while he was lying in the hospital bed. It came over the sound system just like it was doing at this moment. She went on and on about how she liked the duet version his daughter had created, but she greatly preferred the original. He remembered it well. The only difference was that when she mentioned liking the song at that time, it only deepened Sam's depression. He thought he would never love anyone again. He did not want to love, nor be loved. Now, all these years later, he could not have felt more differently.

"Oh my, I *love* this song. Are you familiar with it? It's Nat King Cole."

"Yes, I am," he replied. "It is a perfect song sung by a perfect voice." The two looked at each other intently. Sam lived every day with the feeling that he had wasted many years of his life feeling sorry for himself. He woke every day with a prayer of thanks for the coming day, and a promise to himself that he would live the rest of them to their fullest. It was with that in mind that he said, "I hope you don't find this inappropriate, but may I have this dance?"

Not only did Sam not catch her off guard, she seemed to be hoping for the question. "Yes, you may, Mr. President."

"Please, in casual moments like this, call me Sam," he said as they came together.

"Well, okay Sam," Monica said, and gave him that smile that could not be more beautiful. The two danced for a few moments. She did not seem intimidated at all about dancing with the president, and Sam was happy about that. He was trying to figure out if he should converse with her or just dance silently. Then she spoke. "I like the version with his daughter, but I like this one so much better."

"I know," Sam replied with a smile.

"You know?" Monica gave him a confused look. "How could you know?"

Sam looked at her wistfully. "Let me tell you a story..."

Made in the USA
Monee, IL
30 April 2022

95665488R00233